THE *Missionary* AND THE MARINE

A Novel by

Michael Joens

Also by Michael Joens

The Crimson Tapestry (Book 1 Twilight of the Gods)

The Shadows of Eden (Book 2 Twilight of the Gods)

The Son of Caelryck (Book 3 Twilight of the Gods)

The Dawn of Mercy

Triumph of the Soul

An Animated Death in Burbank

Blood Reins

Angels Descending

Last Ride to Stillwater

Dedication

To Jessie and Nettie Miller and Family, who shone a great Light in a dark place

Acknowledgements

KINDEST REGARDS TO Carol Craig for her insightful editing and never ending encouragement. As always, thank you, Rick Harding, for your much needed encouragement. Many thanks to my longtime friend Dennis Venizelos for the beautiful watercolor of the Bay of Naples. Many thanks to Shahbaza358 for the great interior design. Thank you to Moxibelledfreed for the painting of the girl on the cover

Photo of author as a US Marine in Roccaraso, Italy,
December 1971

Chapter One

Naples, Italy, 1971

THE FLEET WAS in. The running lights of the ships shone yellow moons on the black water of the bay, showing bottles and debris bobbing in the iridescent slick made by the liberty boat from the *USS Columbus*, flagship of the 6th Fleet. It was night.

The engines of the liberty boat bubbled low and throatily with exhaust pluming low over the surface as she hauled a load of sailors and Marines to the Fleet landing. The flotsam and jetsam of countless nights of liberties rose and fell with the wave pulse, catching in the breakwater of the Molo San Vincenzo, where a dozen varieties of small Mediterranean fish hunted the rocks with mindless appetite.

A cold December wind from the bay blew dead leaves and litter over the sidewalks. Crowds of military from every NATO nation, some off the Fleet, others from land bases, moved in and out of piazzas and trattorias and cat houses and bars, or prowled the bonfire-lit roads in Fiats, Alfa Romeos and Lamborghinis. Like mechanical wolves, their headlights burning yellow in prurient mists, the men's engines growled hungrily as they slowed at each bonfire; the girls turning their heads and looking with dark wary eyes as the men hunted. Always hunting to fill an ache, a belly, fill a dream born at sea, or on land, and nourished on duty until nothing could fill it.

Maddie Gallagher edged through the throng jostling in and out of bars around the Piazza del Municipio—or the Square as it was known. Men were laughing, pushing, eyes roving, wolf whistling, the street teeming with every kind of pickpocket, pimp and prostitute practicing their trade on servicemen who, flushed with cash and hormones, were easy marks.

She extended a religious tract to a fresh-faced sailor going into the Swiss bar. "May I give you something?" she asked with a smile.

The sailor stopped and looked at her, his leering eyes making a quick sweep. "Anything, beautiful."

"Jesus loves you."

The sailor blinked, stepped sideways. "Uh-uh…not tonight He don't," he said, brushing past her into the bar.

Maddie said a quick prayer for the sailor, offered the tract to a passing airman. "May I give you something?"

And so it went as she moved around the Square: "Jesus loves you," to a scoff, "Jesus loves you," to a hostile eye, "Jesus loves you," to eyes fixed with desperate hunger, the men racing against the last call of the liberty boats. A few took her tracts, shoved them into pockets as they hurried away, others tossed them to the ground, others still, hunting for the evanescent prize, waved her off like a bad smell.

Maddie came to the San Pedro bar, stood at the entrance and prayed, "Give me one soul tonight, Lord. Just one."

THE SAN PEDRO bar was located in the downtown hub, across the Square from the Castel Nuovo, overlooking the port. Inside the bar was crowded with military. At the far left corner of the bar, Private Michael "Mick" Donovan lifted his glass to the two Marines celebrating his return from Rota, Spain, where he had been serving temporary additional duty in the Navy brig for the past three months.

Lance Corporal James Cooper, a man of medium height and build with light brown hair cut short, back and sides, was standing on Donovan's left; Private Lundgren on his right. The former clapped a hand on Donovan's beefy shoulder, raised his glass, and with the sonorous tone of an undertaker, said, "To Private—formerly Corporal—Mick Donovan…finest Marine ever to belt a noncom in the mouth."

"To Mick," Private Lundgren echoed with equal solemnity. The Marines raised their glasses, bottomed up, then pounded their glasses on the bar with shouts of "ooh-rah!"

Mick Donovan held up a deprecating hand. "I sincerely thank you for that, boys," he said with feeling. "But honestly, I thought he was a second louie."

The Marines roared.

Donovan slapped his hand on the bar. "Another round for the leathernecks, Enrico!"

The bartender, a plump, balding man in his early forties, refilled everyone's glass from a bottle of Jack Daniels that, Donovan noted, had probably come from the PX at NSA, via Marine or sailor, and sold to Enrico at black market prices. "It is good you are back, Meek."

"You know it, *amico*." Donovan looked over the long, narrow and dimly lit, low-ceilinged room of the bar at the dozen or so round tables crowding the floor. Men from every branch of service were drinking at the tables, Americans mostly, each wearing a variation of a counterculture theme—bellbottoms, long-sleeved, wide collared shirts, bead necklaces or chains with peace symbols or wooden crosses dangling to their navels—as if to help them blend into the scenery.

Crisscrossing the floor were high-heeled, mini-skirted, dark-eyed Neapolitan girls, hauling drinks, or working their trade in the shadowy booths that edged the walls. An old Wurlitzer stood against the right wall of the bar, Joan Baez crooning "The Night They Drove Old Dixie Down."

A pink-cheeked sailor leaned against the glass, crying into folded arms.

Donovan took a deep breath of the man-smelling, booze and cigarette-smelling, and the too sweet air of perfume-smelling bar that reminded him of a dive in Chicago. "Almost brings a tear to your eyes, don't it, boys?" He lit a cigarette. "I missed this old burg. I surely did."

Enrico smiled slyly. "She is *Bella Napoli*, no?"

"*Bella*."

"Armpit of the Mediterranean," Cooper added.

"Hit me again, *amico*," Donovan said. "Leave the bottle. This is going too slow."

"I cannot do that, Meek. You know I must sell drinks by the glass."

"Fine." Donovan pointed to the half-empty container. "Calculate the number of drinks left in the bottle, *amico*, add your percentage, and hand it over. There's too much drinking time wasted on chin music."

"As you wish." Enrico took a pencil from his ear, licked the tip, and made calculations on a slip of paper.

Donovan took the bottle and drank off several ounces, then wiped his mouth with the back of his hand. He filled Cooper's glass, and held onto the bottle. "I hear things've been lively in my absence, Coop," he said. "Six, six and a kick, huh?" Donovan topped off Lundgren's glass, filled his own and raised it.

"Straight to Leavenworth."

"Corporal Lister," Cooper and Lundgren intoned.

Donovan shook his head admiringly, sighted his glass at the bad nude over the mirror. "To Corporal Lister…an inspiration to us all…." He started to drink but looked quickly at Cooper. "He emptied a magazine into the Disbursing building?"

"They loused up his pay three weeks in a row."

Donovan threw back his drink in a gulp. "For that I'd've emptied two magazines."

Lundgren must have thought that was funny because he started laughing. Private Henry "Gorilla" Lundgren was a big man, well over six feet, with thick sloping shoulders, and long, powerful arms that ended in meaty slabs with fingers thick as thumbs that curled rearward, simian-like, so that the men called him Gorilla. "Tell us about them *senoritas*, Mick," he said, chuckling through his words. He thumped Donovan on the arm with his knuckles, spilling Mick's drink. "I hear they got some pretty *senoritas* at Rota, Mick."

"Wouldn't know about that, Gorilla," Donovan said, shaking the spilled drink from his right hand. He refilled his glass and changed drinking hands. "I mostly saw their mothers when I got PX liberty."

"Don't they give you base liberty if you keep your nose clean? I thought they gave it to you after a month, Mick."

"Blew that the first weekend. Did you know they got beer machines at the golf course?"

Gorilla thumped his arm. "You ain't foolin', Mick? Sometimes I don't know when you're foolin'."

"Ain't lyin' to you, son. Beer machines. Schlitz...Bud...Pabst. A regular cornucopia of beers."

"I seen 'em," Cooper said. "Right outside the clubhouse."

"When was you in the brig, Coop?" Lundgren asked.

"Wasn't. Came through Rota on my way here."

"But don't you worry, Gorilla," Donovan said. "You stick around here long enough, you'll do some brig time. Guaranteed."

"I wouldn't mind it if they had beer machines. You ain't foolin' about that, are you, Mick?"

Donovan blew a cloud of smoke at the bar, dropped his cigarette on the floor and stepped on it. "Got so blitzed that first liberty, I put the moves on a foursome of officers' wives." He filled his glass. "They were good moves, let me tell you. Don't know why they got so uppity. I gotta tell you, Gorilla, them PX mothers looked pretty good after a month in the hole. Here's to the mothers." He raised his glass and emptied it.

"Uh-huh, uh-huh-huh," Gorilla laughed, a slow, lumbering, up-from-the-belly laugh that sounded like a cold engine turning over. "Guards, too, I bet, huh, Mick? They look pretty good, I bet."

"Joke's over, Gorilla," Donovan said, rubbing his shoulder where Gorilla had thumped him again. He picked up the bottle, examined its contents against the neon bar light, and drained it. He banged it down on the bar. "Nuther dead soldier here, Enrico buddy. *Subito.*"

"Take it easy, Mick, okay?" Cooper said. "We got all night."

"Take it easy yourself. I'm just startin' to get a personality. Hurry up, amico. *Subito. Una bottiglia d'hootch, per favore.*"

Enrico pushed a bottle in front of Donovan, wrote something on the slip of paper.

"Here we go," Donovan said, filling Cooper's glass. "Put that where the sun don't shine."

Donovan lit another cigarette, put out his arm to stop a girl walking past him. "*Ciáo, bella.* Buy you a drink?"

The girl smiled, nuzzled under his arm. Her dark brown hair was teased in the back. "Marine good friend."

"You bet Marine good friend," Donovan grinned. He signaled Enrico. "Bring me a clean glass for the lady, *amico.* She ain't drinkin' no sugar water, not with me she ain't."

He poured the girl a drink. "You like whiskey? Good American black market whiskey?"

She smiled at him with eyes heavy with eyeshadow and liner as she took a sip of her drink. "Marine good friend."

"You don't understand a word I'm saying, do you, baby?" Donovan glanced over the girl on his arm. "That's all right, we'll connect the dots later."

The girl nuzzled him some more, looked over at Enrico who nodded at her. "You want good time, Meek?"

"I'm your man." He blew smoke over their heads. "*Con molto amore,* baby."

"I make good time, Meek. Twenty dollar."

Donovan frowned. "A tad inflated, don't you think?"

"Twenty dollar." She spoke Italian in his ear.

"You don't say?" Donovan let out a howl. "We're gonna have ourselves a time, ain't we, buckaroos?" He took a solid pull from the bottle, shuddered. "That one had the payload." He handed the bottle to Cooper, signaled Enrico. "Say *amico*, we're gonna need more juice here, *subito*."

Enrico slid the strip of paper across the bar, upon which he'd been making calculations. "There is a question of the tab, Mick."

"Let it run, *amico*. We're just gettin' the wind up."

"The bill is fifty-one thousand lire."

"You make it sound like a lot of money."

Enrico held the index finger and thumb of his right hand about a half-inch apart, and smiled. "Eighty-three dollars is a small amount for rich Marines. If we could settle accounts first, and then run a second tab." He put out his beefy paw. "Fifty-one thousand lire."

Donovan dug into his pockets. "It's gettin' so's nobody trusts nobody. I got about ten bucks," he said, sorting through a wad of crumpled bills. "You boys got any money? I've been sorta dry the last three months."

"I got about twenty bucks," Cooper said. "How 'bout you, Gorilla?"

"I thought Mick was buying."

"You no got twenty dollar, Meek?" the girl asked.

"Sure I do, baby. You wait and see if I don't."

The girl left.

"You pay tab now," Enrico demanded. A large Italian with bushy eyebrows and a knife scar from his left eye to the corner of his thick lips stood next to Enrico.

Donovan snapped his fingers. "Wait a minute, fellahs…where's the newbie? I forgot about the newbie." He looked over the crowd. "Don't tell me we lost him already."

"Over there," Cooper said, pointing at a shadowy booth in the far right corner of the bar.

Donovan grinned, lifted a finger at Enrico. "Don't you worry about a thing, *amico*. Follow me, boys."

They headed for the booth, cutting a circuitous path through the tables, stepping over a passed out sailor, then on past the Wurlitzer where Dixie had gone down in flames and Rod Stewart was now trying to wake up Maggie.

Occupying the booth was the lank, boneless, nearly comatose body of Lance Corporal Nathan Kessler. He was listing about forty-five degrees to port, the side of his face flattened against the ample bosom of Rosa, his Italian escort. He was snoring peacefully.

Donovan raised his eyebrows at the pyramid of empties started on the table. "Four beers?"

Cooper lifted the top beer can off the stack, gave it a shake. "Three and a half."

"The spirit is willing, but the liver is weak." Donovan leaned over the table, grabbed a hank of Kessler's fair hair, lifted his head a few inches off its heaving pillow, and frowned. "What's that on his upper lip? I hope it's not contagious."

Cooper said, "I think it's a mustache."

"It could use some fertilizer." Donovan shook Kessler's head a little. "Hey, Marine, wake up! It's a barracks tradition that the newbie picks up the tab at the first watering hole."

A low gurgle, followed by a glob of spittle, bubbled out of Kessler's mouth. *"Ti amo...bella."*

"I'll take that as an affirmative."

Rosa the escort, looking sideways at the gape-mouthed Kessler, asked with a note of incredulity, "He is Marine like you?"

"He has faltered under fire, I'll admit," Donovan said, lowering Kessler's head down onto its former pillow. "But the night is young." He patted Kessler's trousers for a wallet, grabbed hold of his right leg, planted it on the table and found it stuffed in his sock. He blew a whistle. "Boy's got a wad fat enough to choke Moby Dick's aunt Gertie." He counted out a number of bills to Cooper. "That'll do 'er. Run this over to Enrico, Coop. Looks like he's ready to pass a stone."

Lundgren frowned down at Kessler's ruined corpse. "Can you believe he's Lister's replacement?"

Donovan waved a hand. "Cut some slack, Gorilla. He'll shape up with training. Give us a hand." He unplanted Kessler's right leg, took hold of his left wrist and dragged him, long-armed, out of the booth. Kessler's loose body hit the deck without missing a snore.

Lundgren took his legs.

"Grab his other arm there, Coop," Donovan said. "Enrico happy?"

"Ecstatic. What say we head over to the Flamingo and lose the rest of Kessler's money at the tables?

"Now you're talkin'."

"I come too?" Rosa asked, scooting sideways out of the booth. She pulled down what there was of her miniskirt over thighs that resisted her efforts.

Donovan shuddered. "If you must," he said, shaking it off. "Hold this, will you, darlin'," he said, handing her an arm. He glanced over the crowd. "Say, where's Luigi? We lose him too?"

"Last I saw, he was blowing clam sauce in the head," Cooper said.

"Well, you better go tell him we're taking his cab if he don't show up pronto."

The Marines and Rosa the escort hefted Kessler's limp body, and navigated through the crowd.

"We're runnin' hot, straight and normal," Donovan boomed. "Keep 'er goin'. Full steam ahead to the Flamingo."

MADDIE GALLAGHER STEPPED back from the entrance of the bar as three American servicemen and a rather large Italian woman carried a fourth passed out serviceman out of the bar by his arms and legs. She guessed they were Marines by their close-cropped haircuts, and by an intangible something that set them apart from other servicemen.

Staggering behind them came a short, round-bellied Italian with glassy eyes, singing "*O Sole Mio*" at the top of his lungs, making dramatic sweeps with his arms. His unbuttoned shirt was pulled out of his trousers, revealing a soiled sleeveless undershirt, his fly was unzipped and he was wearing only one shoe. *"Che bella cosa é na jurnata 'e sole…"*

The Marine holding the passed out Nathan Kessler by an arm shouted over the din, "Hey, *amico*—Luigi. Cut the comic opera."

"N'aria serena doppo na tempesta!"

"Can it, Luigi!" The Marine grabbed him by the shirt, and said, "We'll wait for you here while you fire up the chariot. Okay? *Subito.*"

Luigi saluted sloppily, "Ho-kay, Meek…Marine good friend," and hobbled one-shoedly down the sidewalk toward a line of cabs, singing at full voice. *"O sole mio…sta nfronte a te! O sole, 'o sole mio…"*

Then the Marine noticed Maddie, looked her over carnally and grinned. "Hey, sweet lips."

"Jesus loves you," she said, offering him a tract.

"I wish *you* would, darlin'."

"May I give you this?" she asked.

He took the tract, frowned at the cover, handed it back as if it was crawling with ants. "I'm beyond savin', sugar. Why don't you give it to Teddy Roosevelt here? He just got baptized. I think the shock killed him."

The huge Marine holding a leg started laughing. "Uh-huh, uh-huh-huh, that's funny, Mick."

Maddie looked at the drunken Marine they were carrying, slipped a tract into his shirt pocket, a shiver racing through her as she recognized him. *Nathan!* She'd heard his name while on base. "Jesus loves you," she said, taking his hand in hers for one brief moment and giving it a gentle squeeze. It was the Marine she'd seen helping the little boy and his mother at the main gate of the NSA compound the day before. The boy had been crying, but Nathan had knelt down and given him a piece of paper with something drawn on it, something that had helped to dry his tears and bring a smile to his face. She felt a warmth for the Marine stir in her breast.

Nathan, reviving momentarily, opened his eyes and gazed drunkenly at her. "*Ti amo, bella,*" he said through bubbles of spittle. He reached for her hand as though it were a lifeline and held it for several seconds before allowing it to fall. "*Tu sei molto bella.*"

"He speaks pretty good wop lingo for a newbie, don't he?" Mick said.

"I think he's got some Italian in him," the Marine holding the other leg added.

Maddie looked at Mick, clearly the leader of the group. "There's a Way Station in the Galleria Umberto," she said. "We've got Ping-Pong tables and home-cooking."

"You don't say…Ping-Pong?" Mick shivered.

Just then a beat-up, faded red Fiat sedan, missing a front fender and left headlight, driven by the drunken Italian with operatic leanings, bumped up over the curb and shuddered to a halt on the sidewalk, the driver singing, "*Ma n'atu sole, cchiu' bello, oi ne'…*"

"Our limo's arrived, boys," Mick said, hefting the passed-out Marine past Maddie. "'Scuse us, sister, we got us a binge to catch."

The Marines stuffed Nathan into the back seat of the cab, pushed the large Italian woman in behind him, indelicately—the woman emitting a squeal of laughter. They climbed into the cab around her, laughing.

Maddie stood on the curb and watched as the cab lurched off the sidewalk into speeding traffic, the sound of squealing tires and horns and angry protestations following them around the Square. She didn't know why, but seeing Nathan in that condition had touched her deeply. "God, please help him find his way to you," she prayed.

THREE HOURS LATER the cab rolled up to the main gate of the Naval Support Activity compound in Bolanaro, the entrance washed in a yellow glow from an overhead incandescent light. The Marine guard, wearing a long-sleeved beige shirt, dress blues trousers, and white barracks cover, stepped out of the lighted brick and glass booth, stepped to the edge of the cement curb of the island and held up a hand.

Mick Donovan leaned his elbow out the driver side window. "Hey, Skip, what's shakin'? Convert anyone lately?"

Lance Corporal Donald "Skip" McPherson, a tall, blue-eyed, dark blond ballplayer from Texas, with cheeks made pink by the cold, chuckled. "Very funny, Mick. Why are you driving Luigi's cab?"

"This ain't a cab, it's a hearse. Don't you see dead people in the back seat?"

McPherson looked in the back window, glared. "Who's that?"

"That's Rosa and the corpse—Kessler. Great guy, Kessler. Won two hundred bucks at the Flamingo Club then blew it all on a roll. Took it like a champ. Him and Rosa knocked back a fifth of hootch and danced a jig on the blackjack table. It was a vision to behold, but I think we contained it in a military manner. You might check his pulse."

McPherson looked past Donovan at Cooper, whose face was plastered against the passenger side window. He was staring, dead-eyed, straight ahead, his mouth opened like a bottom feeder. "Where's Luigi?"

Donovan jerked a thumb toward the rear of the cab. "In the trunk."

"The *trunk*?" McPherson looked, stepped over and rapped on the trunk. "You in there, Luigi?"

He heard a muffled groan that only an Italian cabbie stuffed in his own trunk can make.

"You gonna let him out of there, Mick?"

"Can't. He crawled in there himself with the keys in his pocket. We had to hotwire this baby."

McPherson stepped back to Donovan's window. "Well, I can't let you into the compound with a prostitute, Mick, you know that."

Donovan shook his head. "That's no way to talk about Admiral Zumwalt's daughter. She's a sensitive girl."

"She's pie-eyed."

"There's no denying it. But she's got *esprit de corps.* They'll be singing songs about her at the Marine Corps Ball."

McPherson frowned, wearily. "I still can't let you in with her, Mick. The SOG's on the roll. He just left AFSOUTH and is headed back to the barracks. He sees me letting you in with a prostitute, I lose my stripes."

"Don't your Bible say somethin' about Jesus lovin' the prostitutes? I'm surprised at you, Skip."

McPherson's frown crumbled. He peered down at Rosa, then looked across the parking lot at the lighted quarterdeck of the barracks, about a hundred and fifty yards from the main gate. He glanced over at the adjoining post, where the Disbursing building was a dark silhouette in the moonlight. He couldn't see the Marine guard on roving patrol. Across the street from the main gate, a single cab was parked in front of the Hideaway Hotel, the driver's head back on the seat, as if asleep. McPherson narrowed an eye at Donovan, who wore one of his alligator grins. Then he peered back at Nathan, the corpse, and shook his head.

"Well, hurry up about it," McPherson said. "She stays in the cab."

"I don't care if the other guys think you're light in the loafers, Skip. You're okay by me."

Chapter Two

MADDIE FELT THE hot water giving up the
ghost earlier than its usual five-minute life-span, so she
hurriedly rinsed the soap from her body and turned off
the taps. Immediately she felt the damp cold in the tiny
bathroom slipping over the curtain rod into the three-by-
three tiled shower stall that was cracked along the floor.

She reached behind the plastic curtain, grabbed a
towel off the towel rack, and quickly pulled it back into
the shower, trying to keep what was left of the warm
steam from escaping. Then she quickly toweled herself
dry.

That done, she wrapped the towel around herself,
slid back the curtain, felt a rush of cold air, and stepped
out of the stall onto the terry cloth floor mat. She dried
the soles of her feet, padded over to the radiator and
touched it. Freezing. A shiver goosed up the length of

her body. Radiator on the fritz, hot water heater on the fritz. *Bella Napoli* in December.

Stepping over to the sink in a watery fog, she felt a pang of conscience. "Buck up, Maddie," she chided herself.

She rubbed a circle in the mirror with a fist and looked at her face. Next she took off her shower cap, freeing a tangled mass of wavy red hair that fell past her shoulders. She made a face at her reflection. "I look like Raggedy Ann."

There was a knock at the door; her ten-year old brother by the impudent sound of it. "You in there?" he hollered.

"I'm in here," she yelled back.

"Hurry up, I gotta go," he whined.

"I'll be out in a minute."

"I gotta go bad. Hurry."

"Cross your legs."

"Maddie!"

Maddie collected her toiletries, opened the bathroom door and, with a sweeping gesture of her arm, bowed. What she would give for a bathtub full of hot water with bubbles and steam and an hour in which to luxuriate without interruptions.

She smiled at the top of Sean's blond buzzed head as he brushed past her without ceremony. He turned with a scowl and slammed the door.

She shook her head, padded down the hall to her bedroom at the end of the hall and closed the door behind her.

It was a small room, affording space only for a single bed against the right hand wall, a child's dresser against the wall opposite, and between them, a tiny window that rattled in the winter and was swollen shut in the summer. It overlooked the glass and steel dome of the Galleria Umberto, and beneath it was a small writing desk where she did her correspondence. But it was hers. Her sanctuary.

She heard the rain against the window and walked over to it. The window faced south where the rain fell outside in long slanting sheets against the columns and arches of the San Carlo Opera House. The streets and sidewalks were teeming with pedestrians, moving beneath a jostling canopy of umbrellas, and a crush of Monday morning commuter traffic rushing along the Via Vittorio Emanuele 111—Vittoriano as the locals called it. Buses, cars, motor scooters and bicycles lurched back and forth recklessly through the ancient narrow streets, blasting horns in the rain.

Rain always made her feel a little melancholy, and excited too, for she knew that things grow in the rain, flowers and trees and she imagined people grew as well.

She felt a shiver in her arms, touched the radiator beside the desk. It was cold like the one in the bathroom. She walked two steps to her dresser, doffed the towel, donned underwear, followed these with a pair of embroidered bell bottom jeans, a cotton flower print shirt and wool sweater. Then she sat on the edge of her bed, wiggled her toes to air them, and then pulled on socks and boots.

She went back to the mirror and did the best she could with brush and comb, but with so much moisture in the air her hair would not behave. She tied it back with a macramé ribbon, but instead of a ponytail it looked more like the wild red spray of a wicker broom.

She brushed her eyelashes with mascara, added eyeliner and then a touch of blush to give her cheeks a little color and to hide the light spray of freckles. She stopped what she was doing as she saw something else in the mirror—the smile on his face as he gave a drawing to the little boy. An act of kindness. The image that had been turning in her mind like a carousel since the morning she first saw him had come round again, making her feel a little breathless.

The Marine.

She knew now that he was lost like so many others of the young men and women in uniform. God had prompted her to pray for him, which she did when she first saw him at the main gate, and then again last night in front of the San Pedro bar. "Draw him to you by your Spirit, Father," she prayed.

She left her room and walked down the hall, past her brother's and parents' bedrooms, her boot heels thudding softly on the linoleum tiles. When she opened the door leading into the kitchen and great room, she smelled breakfast.

Kitty Gallagher, wearing a sky blue sweater and navy slacks, was standing beside the griddle, beating pancake batter with a wooden spoon and frying sausages while singing, "He Touched Me."

"Morning, Mom."

"Good morning, honey," Kitty said, beating the batter without looking up. "Breakfast will just be a minute."

Maddie leaned her elbows on the Formica-topped counter that separated the kitchen from the dining room. "Need any help?"

"I'm fine."

Maddie watched her mother ladle three large batter coins onto the griddle. The batter spread outward into saucer-sized puddles. "Radiator's busted again," she said.

"Your father spoke to the landlord yesterday."

"So we might have it fixed by summer?"

Kitty gave her a playful look, turned the sausages with a pair of metal tongs.

"I think the hot water heater's about to kick the bucket too," Maddie said.

Kitty made a face. "Not again."

"Again."

Her mother shook her head plaintively. Her straight, silky blonde hair, streaked now with gray and cut in a shoulder length pageboy, moved in a shimmering sheet.

"You look great, Mom."

"Thank you, honey." Kitty had the long, lithe limbs of a dancer, had in fact been one of the dancers in the

1946 film "Ziegfeld Follies," was well on her way to a dancing career, but gave it up the night she came to Christ at the 1947 Billy Graham crusade in Los Angeles.

"Do you ever miss dancing, Mom?"

"What makes you ask that?"

"Just wondering. Do you?"

"Sometimes. It was fun. But I wouldn't trade a thousand stages with Fred Astaire or Gene Kelly for a minute here with your father."

"Were they fun to dance with?"

Kitty edged the spatula around the pancakes. "I didn't dance *with* them. I was stage decoration, along with a couple dozen others. They never looked twice at me."

"You could have been another Cyd Charisse."

"That isn't what God had in mind when He made me. I love my life with your father. To see a serviceman come to Christ." She flipped the pancakes, smiled reflectively. "Besides, every now and then your father will twirl me around the room."

Maddie covered her mouth in mock horror. "Scandalous."

"He's a fine dancer, you know."

"You love him, don't you, Mom?"

"Yes, I do." Kitty looked at her, her hazel eyes sparkling. "Sleep well? You look tired."

"I had a hard time going to sleep."

"Oh?"

"It's nothing. I was just thinking. Once a thought gets a toehold—you know…"

"Good thought?"

"I don't know yet."

"I'm a good listener." Kitty shoveled the pancakes onto a plate. "Why don't you have a seat, honey? There's a pitcher of orange juice on the table."

MADDIE STEPPED OVER to the dining table at the kitchen end of the wide, long, high-ceilinged great room, a room large enough to accommodate fifty seated guests, or a crowd much larger if the ping-pong and shuffleboard and foosball tables were moved to one side.

She took the seat at the head of the table nearest the kitchen entrance, where she had a view of the harbor and the bay beyond the Municipal Square. She poured a glass of orange juice, took a sip and glanced over at the bank of windows going along the left wall of the great room, and saw it was still raining. "I hope it lets up soon."

"We need the rain," Kitty said. "It cleans the bad smell from the air, don't you think?"

"It does that," Maddie admitted.

Kitty came into the dining room holding a plate of pancakes and sausages. "Here you go."

"Thank you, Mom." Maddie leaned forward and breathed in the vapors of the pancakes and sausages. "Mmmmmm."

Kitty took the chair beside her daughter. "Is my dancing career what you were thinking about last night?"

"No, Mom." Maddie lifted the pancakes one at a time and slathered butter over them, then reached for the Aunt Jemima maple syrup.

"Are you sure?"

"I'm sure."

Maddie drowned her pancakes with syrup, shoved a dripping steaming wedge into her mouth and chewed. She could feel her mother's deep hazel eyes burning a hole in the side of her head. "I was thinking about that Marine at the main gate when you and I went to the commissary."

"The Marine with the little boy and his mother? He told the boy his name as I recall."

"Nathan."

"I thought that was sweet of him, a Marine giving something to the little boy that stopped his crying. What about him?"

"You asked…that's what I was thinking about."

"He smiled at you."

Maddie raised an eyebrow. "He smiled at you, Mom—you were driving. He couldn't see me."

"He smiled at *you*." Kitty reached over and stroked Maddie's head. "And why shouldn't he? You're a beautiful young woman."

"I look like Ronald McDonald. Why couldn't I have inherited your hair instead of dad's?"

"Your hair is gorgeous, silly—so thick with natural wave. And you've got your father's beautiful blue eyes."

"And freckles. And Irish temper."

"You have a lovely figure—a dancer's figure. I've seen the way men look at you."

Maddie shook her head incredulously. "Are you talking about the hormone cases that have been cooped up on a ship for six months? They'd look at a female gorilla, if she batted her eyes at them."

"You're being silly." Kitty stood and walked back into the kitchen. "So the Marine had a toehold on your thoughts last night?"

"I saw him in front of the San Pedro bar. He was drunk. I prayed for him. Sorry, no palace intrigue." Maddie poured more syrup over her pancakes, glanced into the great room at the chairs going around the walls. "Think we're gonna be busy tonight?"

"We ought to be, now with the Fleet."

"I hope so." Maddie saw that someone had opened the bookstore door, at the far end of the room. "Dad in the bookstore?"

"No, he left about twenty minutes ago. He had a meeting with Chaplain Simms."

"What's Dad meeting him for?"

"He wants to talk to him about Lance Corporal McPherson."

"Skip? What about him? He's not in trouble, is he?"

"The Marines at the Barracks give him a hard time. Your father hopes the chaplain will encourage him."

Maddie cut another wedge of pancakes. "Skip never said anything to me about trouble at the Barracks," she said, chewing. "I'll ask him about it. By the way, did those new tracts come in yet? I ran out last night. The Square was hopping."

"They came in the morning post. You be careful down there, Maddie, it's dangerous."

"I'll wear combat boots."

"He had a great smile, by the way."

"Who?"

"The Marine. The one you were thinking about last night."

Sean came into the room lifting his sweatshirt with one hand, digging something out of his bellybutton with the other. "Hey, Mom, when's Maddie leaving for college?"

"She's sitting at the table, honey, why don't you ask her."

Sean slid his eyes sideways at Maddie, grunted. "Can I have her room when she leaves, Mom? She's got a window."

"I'll miss you too, Sean," Maddie said. "Pull your shirt down, please. I'm eating breakfast."

"I got an itch."

After breakfast Maddie went into the bookstore where they sold Bibles, commentaries and religious books to the servicemen. Sitting on the counter was a box from Campus Crusade for Christ. She opened the box, removed the bundles of tracts, got out the stamp pad from beneath the counter, and began stamping each of the tracts on the back with the address and phone number of the Station.

Chapter Three

NATHAN KESSLER SMELLED the sulfur even before he woke up. It had fingered through the webbing of his subconscious mind with a vision of hell, of devils prodding him onto a raised platform where faces rose out of murky darkness, laughing faces that encircled him. An enormous woman with black eyes and ruby red lips, and hips that moved to a lurid conga came at him with clicking nails. The faces leered at the woman then melted into a blur that whirled about his head.

When he opened his eyes he didn't know where he was. The ceiling was spinning obliquely, making him nauseous. He thought for a moment that he was at home in Morro Bay, but the bed across from him wasn't right, and the smell of sulfur was like nothing he had known. And then, blinking open his eyes, he recognized where he was located. He was in hell.

His head hurt something fierce, as though it had been poleaxed. He closed his eyes, felt his eyes throbbing, and lay very still. Then he remembered last night—bits and pieces of it; all the drinking he had done, and some of the wildness he had done, and with whom. He wondered what happened to the woman they had picked up at the San Pedro bar.

He sat up, carefully, swung his legs over and, planting his feet on the floor, sat on the edge of his bed that he saw he had not slept in. His mouth tasted of foul paste, with an edge of bile gurgling in his throat. He was still in his civvies. A stain dripped down the front of his shirt. His shirt reeked of vomit. He looked between his feet at the polished terrazzo floor of the room, holding himself very still for fear that his head might whirl off his neck. It seemed as though he were looking at the world through cracked glass.

"You sure got plastered, didn't you, Nate?"

"I sure did, Frankie."

"I never seen you that drunk before."

"There was a time, Frankie, but you don't know about it."

He glanced at the framed photograph of his family on the side table. Then he looked across the room at the white gear and holster laid out on the bed that was tightly made, the black leather holster spit-shined in the white cotton holster sleeve, the brass gleaming in the sun coming through the wide horizontal window to his right. A pair of shoes were placed beneath the bed, the toes and heels like mirrors.

At the foot of his bed was a desk facing the wall, and abutting the desk, standing six and a half feet tall, were three navy gray wall lockers, their backs facing him, so that coming into the room you would see the front of the lockers. Three more just like them stood against the opposite wall, belonging to his roommate, the locker nearest the center of the room open. Two sitting chairs and a table and lamp stood between these and the foot of his roommate's bed. Hanging on the vented door on a hanger was a uniform, showing lance corporal stripes on the sleeve, behind which hung a pair of dress blue trousers.

Jim Cooper came into the room, wearing a white towel around his waist and flip-flops on his feet, and was carrying a leather toiletry bag that he put into his wall locker. "He's alive," he grinned around the door at Nathan.

"I don't think so."

"Better get a move on. It's six forty. You've got twenty minutes until inspection."

"Right." Nathan smelled the sulfur. "I don't think I'll ever get used to the smell here."

"We're situated in a volcano."

"It smells like hell."

"The Romans thought this place was the mouth of hell. The CO is the devil, didn't you know?" Cooper was dusting athlete's foot powder between his toes. "He's gonna flame your rear-end, if you don't get rolling."

"I'm rolling." Nathan stood, felt a stab of pain between his ears, and sat back down very slowly. He waited a moment, fighting a twinge of nausea. "What time'd we get in last night?"

"Three-thirty."

"It's a blur."

"You were asking everybody if they'd seen a chaplain," Cooper said. "You wanted to marry Rosa."

"Rosa?"

"The sweet thing we picked up at the San Pedro. You don't remember her?"

"Was she big?"

"Like three kinds of water buffalo." Cooper laughed. "Mick tried to sneak her past the Corporal of the Guard––said she was a trained nurse that specializes in bringing people back from the dead. You. Carlos sent her and Luigi packing…gave McPherson the business for letting her into the compound."

"That Mick is a character."

"I give him a month before he's back in the hoosegow."

Cooper dropped his towel, stepped on it and wiped up the powder off the floor, picked up the towel and chucked it into a laundry bag on the bottom of his wall locker.

Nathan unbuttoned his shirt, felt something in the breast pocket. A small pamphlet. "What's this?" He read the stamped printing on the back. "Don't tell me we went to this place?"

"Some American chick gave it to you in front of the San Pedro. Jesus freak."

"She have red hair?"

"Like a house on fire. What's it say?"

"God loves me and has a wonderful plan for my life."

Cooper laughed. "His plan better include gettin' you to inspection on time, or the devil's gonna eat you for breakfast." He put on clean skivvies then brushed his hair in the mirror. "I'm sure looking forward to Roccaraso. You still want to come?"

"Where?"

"Roccaraso. The ski resort."

"Right. I dunno."

Cooper padded around his locker buttoning his shirt. "You got something better to do?"

"Nope." Nathan stared at the space between his feet. "Sure, why not? Be fun."

"You bet fun." Cooper reached for something. "Soon as we finish this lousy guard cycle it'll be five days of glorious shushing down the slopes. Wait till you see the place. Lousy with rich Italian snow bunnies. This your family?"

Nathan looked up, saw that Cooper was staring at the photo on his side table and grabbed it out of his hand. "Don't touch my stuff, okay?"

"Sorry. Didn't mean anything." Cooper nodded at the photo. "Nice looking family."

Nathan said nothing. He set the photo back on the table, angled it to face his bed.

Cooper shrugged, headed back to his locker. "Shake a leg, Kessler."

Nathan felt a wave of nausea, a prickling in his stomach. "I gotta go to the head."

THE BARRACKS WAS a U-shaped building of red brick and glass, with the main part of the building—the apex of the U—rising five stories, with two wings, each four stories high. The Marine detachment occupied the left wing of the building, Navy permanent personnel occupying the right. The sun was just rising over the Navy, a couple of whom were peering out their windows at the formation below them, snickering like hyenas.

The Marines stood in three ranks of twenty-five men, the men standing at attention according to height. The Marine wing of the barracks was behind them, and beyond were the hills of Bolanaro covered with grapevines cut back for the winter. The mustard smell of sulfur seemed less noticeable outside, especially now with a southeasterly wind bringing a smell of vegetation and the sea, and with it the dark, red-bellied clouds of a storm over the Bay of Naples.

Nathan Kessler was standing in the first rank, at the opposite end of the inspection entourage. Private Lundgren, the tallest man in the barracks, stood on his left; Private Donovan, an inch shorter, was on his right. Corporal Cooper stood to the right of Donovan, everyone wearing the dress blues trousers, beige shirt and white barracks hat of a Marine assigned to barracks duty.

Standing with left thumb along the seam of his trousers, right thumb behind the polished black leather holster that was empty, Nathan Kessler was downwind from Donovan. Nathan could smell Donovan's rank breath, but the pungent odor of sulfur replaced it when the offshore wind shifted, now curling over and down the hills onto the tarmac. He couldn't decide which was worse. His stomach was prickling dangerously.

Captain Brickner, Commanding Officer of the barracks, was a tall, square shouldered no-nonsense Marine with square hips and an arrogant crag of jawbone overhanging a beefy chest. He was working his way toward Nathan from the shorter end of the formation, pointing at various uniform discrepancies on the men with a brass-tipped swagger stick. Dressed in barracks blue and beige with a white, gold-banded dress hat, and a chest full of meritorious ribbons, he was a Marine's Marine by all appearances.

Behind him were the Executive Officer, Sergeant Major and 1st Platoon sergeant, Sergeant Rockman; the latter, a meaty-shouldered, heavy-muscled man from Georgia with a face like a pit bull, who wrote the CO's comments on a clipboard.

Captain Brickner drew alongside Cooper, quarter turned so that they were face to face and snapped his heels. He looked him over. "You look sharp, Marine."

"Thank you, sir."

And then Brickner was standing in front of Mick Donovan. "Good to see you back, Donovan."

"It's good to be back, sir."

"Are you going to keep your nose clean this time?"

"You can bet on it, sir."

"I don't bet, Donovan. No more brawling?"

"No sir."

"You don't look well, Donovan."

"I feel outstanding, sir."

"What were you drinking last night?"

"Just some mixed drinks, sir. Nothing heavy. I'm up and at 'em, sir."

"Your breath smells like kerosene."

"I haven't had chow yet, sir."

"I believe it. I got a call this morning from the manager of the Flamingo Club. He told me that some Marines had caused a stir last night. You wouldn't know anything about that?"

Nathan could feel Donovan tensing. "Sir? No sir. Are you sure he said Marines, sir?"

"Marines, Donovan."

"Must've been Fleet Marines, sir. There was a mess of 'em in town last night."

"You don't know anything about a Marine dancing with a rather large Italian woman on a blackjack table."

"Sounds like them fleet Marines, sir. They get pretty riled, bein' cooped up all those months at sea. They gotta blow sometime. Yes sir, I'd bet—er—that is, I'd bank on it being them fleet Marines."

At which point Nathan, feeling it coming up in a rush, leaned forward from his waist and, without breaking formation, blew the contents of his stomach onto the tarmac. He straightened back at attention, glassy-eyed, his thumbs still planted on trouser seams, a plaintive groan in his bowels.

Captain Brickner looked over at him, peered down at his feet, stepped a little to one side, then glanced back at Donovan. "Brass needs shining, Donovan," he said for the benefit of the Platoon Sergeant. "Get some chow."

"Will do, sir."

Brickner stepped over the mess and came around to the opposite side of Nathan, so that he was staring at his left temple. "Rough night, Marine?"

"No sir. Just getting used to the air quality, sir." He groaned inwardly.

"It doesn't seem to agree with you."

"I'll get used to it, sir."

Brickner looked over Nathan's uniform, starting from his shoes then on up to his face, his eyes, mouth, upper lip. "I understand you drew a comic strip when you were at Camp Lejeune. *Ol' Prive*, was it?"

"Yes, sir. *Ol' Prive*, sir."

Brickner grunted. "I've seen it. Better not catch you drawing on post, Kessler. You'll receive no preferential treatment from me. I'm a fair man. But step out of line and not even God can save you."

"Yes, sir."

Brickner glanced at his feet. "I expect this mess to be policed after formation."

"Yes, sir."

Brickner started away but stopped, glancing back at Kessler's upper lip. "Lose the cookie duster until you can grow one that Chesty would be proud of."

"Aye aye, sir." Kessler could feel Lundgren tensing as Brickner snapped his heels in front of him.

"Suck in your gut, Marine. You shine your shoes with a wood rasp?"

"Huh?" Lundgren looked down. "Uh . . . no, sir."

"You're at attention, Marine."

"Yes, sir."

NATHAN SAT AT the desk in his room, inking a cartoon of a raw recruit fresh off the bus, standing at the gates of a subterranean cave with fiery stalactites and stalagmites. Plumes of sulfurous smoke rose from the stalagmites. A burly devil with sergeant stripes and campaign hat, with a globe and anchor in the crown, sat at the gates with a log book. Behind him were more devils in campaign hats forking Marine recruits into fiery coals. The devil at the gates grinned evilly at the raw recruit.

Nathan penciled the caption beneath it.

Ol' Prive: *Excuse me, Sergeant, is this hell?*

Devil: *No, Private, it's Parris Island.*

"You draw funny, Nate. Think I'll ever be able to draw like you?"

"You have to work at it, Frankie. Don't give up."

"I'm gonna start drawing right now."

"Thatta boy."

Nathan erased the pencil lines from the drawing on Bristol board with a kneaded eraser, signed his name to the drawing, then slipped it into a ten-by-fourteen manilla envelope with other cartoons he'd recently finished. He stood, went over to his locker and locked the envelope inside.

Chapter Four

Maddie WAS HEADING southwest along the road to the American school in Bolanaro, about seven miles from the center of town. She was driving the family's Fiat 500—the "*cinque cento,*" as the natives affectionately called it. They were everywhere in the city. Slightly larger than a roller skate, four adults could just squeeze into it, if the passengers in the back seat didn't mind the taste of their kneecaps.

Sean was sitting in the passenger seat, staring glumly out the window, his schoolbook satchel on his lap. He was holding a small wrapped present for the Christmas gift exchange. The traffic was heavy, bumper to bumper, yet moving fast and dangerous in the early morning recklessness that typified Neapolitan commuters.

"Looking forward to the Christmas party?" Maddie asked.

"No."

"No? Why not?"

"I got Marsha Merkel. She's weird. She probably got me a book or something. "

"Heaven forbid."

The harbor and Fleet Landing were on her left now with the ships side-by-side and shrouded in fog, so that they looked like a ghost fleet. To her right the Castel Nuovo stood a sad and lonely sentinel sullen in the fog. Heading west out of the downtown square, she was driving against traffic and moving at a fair pace.

Soon she was on a road that was lined on both sides with car tires, bonfires in each of them. Girls huddled in groups of six or more, holding their hands over the fires. Cars rolled along the curb, slowing at each grouping, the girls only glancing over when a car came to a stop. Maddie watched a driver lean over and talk to a girl looking in through the passenger window. It was a scene she had witnessed many times—different girls, different cars, different parts of the city—but it was the same scene.

"Don't they get cold?" Sean asked.

"That's why they build the fires," Maddie said, wishing there was a route to the school that was free of open prostitution, but all of the roads into town had them. Every town with a military presence had them. The Italian police looked the other way, so did the *carabinieri*, since the economy of the city would likely collapse without them. "So, maybe Marsha will give you something you might actually like."

"You don't have to distract me," Sean groused. "I know all about the campfire girls. They talk about them at school." He looked out the window as a girl, no older than fourteen, blew a kiss at him. "They don't bother me."

"You're ten."

"So?"

Maddie turned west along a road where the bay opened on her left, with Vesuvius now dominating the skyline in her rearview mirror. On her right the gray, red-tiled roofline of the buildings of Naples slid by in a watery vagueness, like the footage in a black and white newsreel that she neither saw nor heard. Once again she was thinking about the Marine. Once more she was prompted to pray for him, which she did last night in town, and again this morning at the Station, and now as she made her way along the road that showed the bay shining where the morning sun had broken through the clouds.

She turned north and followed the road past the broken volcano crater rising on her left. Then she turned onto the Bolanaro road and drove about a mile, passing the NSA base on her right, and on past the Naval hospital. She took another right into the parking lot of the American school, where she dropped off Sean. She wished him a good day, received a grunt in return, and then she drove back to the base to do some last minute shopping for the men.

She filed into a queue of cars waiting to enter the compound through the main gate. Most of the cars belonged to Italian workers, but there were military as well, officers and noncoms who lived off base.

The Marine at the gate, a huge man, well over six feet, with a white barracks hat that seemed too small for his head, was standing in front of the booth on the cement island separating incoming and outgoing traffic.

He glanced at the sticker in the window of her car and saluted perfunctorily. It was one of the Marines she'd seen in front of the San Pedro bar the night before. She wished him a Merry Christmas as she went through the gate, but the Marine was already looking at the car behind her.

Maddie parked in front of the administration building, a long, several-storied rectangular block of brick and glass at the upper end of the compound. The sun was shining with just a hint of warmth in the air. She walked up the wide flight of stairs and into the building, walked through the lobby over large polished terrazzo squares, past a couple of offices that were decorated with holly wreaths and aluminum trees, and then into the cafeteria to the left of the wide granite stairs that led to upper floors.

There were mostly military sitting at tables, eating, talking, reading papers, and smoking. There were a few civilians as well with Italian workers behind the counter or bussing tables. A Christmasy feeling permeated the air, an air of jubilation, despite the Crosby, Stills and Nash song piping through the jukebox speakers. The Fleet was in, spouses and families reunited, holiday leaves anticipated.

Maddie picked up a Danish from under the counter with a pair of tongs, poured a cup of coffee, paid the cashier, and went over to a table by the windows that was just vacated by a couple of Navy JAG officers.

A busboy came over and wiped the table with a damp towel while Maddie held her cup and Danish. "*Grazie*," she said.

"*Prego.*"

She sat drinking coffee and eating the Danish, feeling the clean damp coolness of the Formica tabletop with the palm of her hand, as she listened to the song that reminded her of her home in Santa Cruz. But then most of the songs reminded her of home.

She glanced out the window at the high cinderblock wall, about fifty feet from the Admin building, that wrapped around the compound. Just then a platoon of Marines in bloused utility trousers, sweatshirts and boots, ran below the window in formation, singing cadence. It was the platoon coming off the last guard cycle, she guessed. She saw Skip McPherson in the middle. She said a silent prayer for him as she watched the Marines run around the corner of the building, the drumming of their boots fading.

At the table across from her three Waves were bent over the extended hand of a fourth woman, also a Wave, the three taking turns holding the fourth one's hand and admiring a chunk of stone that seemed to draw every bit of light from the room.

Maddie smiled. She had seen the women before. One worked in Disbursing; the other three were nurses at the Naval hospital. The song changed to a Carol King number.

Maddie exhaled a melancholy sigh. She took her wallet out of her purse, removed a photograph from one of the plastic windows, and looked at it. It was a photo of her and her friends on the beach at Carmel, taken two summers ago when the family had gone home to Santa Cruz on furlough. She remembered the fun they'd had that day, looking through the galleries and shops, then eating lunch in the shade of a Monterey pine, *al fresco*, while watching boys with long sun-bleached hair walking by with their surfboards. Then on a whim the three of them drove down to Big Sur to watch the sun sink into the Pacific. Later, after eating a late supper on the Monterey pier, they drove back to Santa Cruz, exhausted, ready for bed, until someone suggested they go to the Boardwalk and ride the Ferris wheel.

It was like that the entire summer, each day a different itinerary. Now one of her friends was studying English Literature at Oxford, the other newly engaged to a man she'd met at the Bible College in Scotts Valley, and Maddie was in Naples with her parents. Maddie wondered if there would ever be a time when the three of them would get back together and enjoy such carefree times. Probably not. Or if they did, there would likely be husbands and children, and riding the Ferris wheel at the Boardwalk would be a topic to laugh about at someone's dinner table.

She slid the photo back into her wallet, glanced across the cafeteria as two Marines in barracks' blues entered the room; one medium height and brown-haired, the other tall and straw blond. She felt something move deep inside her, an excitement. It was the Marine. Nathan.

The Marines went over to the counter, took metal trays and utensils from the bins, and ordered breakfast from the cook behind the counter. The tall Marine removed a glass from a plastic tray stacked with glasses, poured orange juice into it, and then set the glass on his tray. He surveyed the room—for an empty table, Maddie presumed. When their eyes met, he held her gaze momentarily before looking away.

Maddie glanced over at the Waves, who were still making a fuss over the chip of diamond. When she turned back to the Marine he was staring at her, and she felt her pulse quicken.

The Marine with him motioned to a table clearing near the jukebox. The tall one said something to him, looked back at Maddie and walked over to her table.

"Mornin'," Nathan said.

"Good morning. Merry Christmas."

"That's right, it's Christmas, isn't it?"

"In three days. You're not a Grinch I hope."

"I gotta work. You weren't by any chance passing out religious tracts in town last night, were you?"

She smiled. "I'm surprised you remember me."

"Your hair."

Maddie made a face. "It stands out in a crowd, doesn't it?"

"I had dreams about it." He stood holding his tray with both hands, his white Marine Corps hat hooked on the middle finger of his right hand. "You gave one to me, by the way. One of those tracts."

"I remember. Did you read it?"

"God has a wonderful plan for my life."

"He does."

He laughed. "Did He tell you, or did you guess? You say it with such authority."

She looked at the Marine for a moment, at his short-cropped blond hair and dark blue, somewhat glassy eyes that set well into a face that was strong and well-featured. "He made you," she said.

The Marine scoffed. "You don't know the first thing about me."

"I know that God loves you."

"I don't believe it. I don't believe in God either, since you bring up the subject. I don't mean to sound superior."

"You don't. It's your prerogative to believe or not believe anything you like. Some people believe the world is flat." She smiled, reading his name tag. "Your breakfast's getting cold, Lance Corporal Kessler. Perhaps you would like to sit down and we can talk about it."

"We might as well talk about the tooth fairy."

"The offer still holds."

He stared at her for a moment.

"You can invite your friend over too, if you like," she said. "I won't bite."

Kessler glanced over his shoulder. The Marine who came in with him was staring at them from across the room. "Coop? He's okay where he is. He's toilet trained." He set his tray on the table across from her, pulled out a chair and sat down. "Sure, why not? It's Christmas, right? Nathan Kessler," he said, setting his barracks cover on the empty seat between them. "Nate, if you like."

"They call you Teddy Roosevelt too. Never mind," she said, when she saw it went over his head. She reached across the table and shook his hand. "Pleased to meet you, Nathan. I'm Maddie Gallagher. I'm sorry you have to work Christmas."

He shrugged. "I get New Years off. Five whole days of nothing but fun. Nothing in the Bible against fun, is there?" He grinned with an expression that seemed intentionally hard and daring—a look she'd seen in the eyes of so many other servicemen, to mask pain or hurt or loneliness. It was a lost face.

"That depends. What kind of fun?"

"Skiing." He reached for the salt, held the shaker.

"Nothing in the Bible against skiing."

"You sure you don't mind associating with sinners?"

"How do you mean?"

Another grin, the whiskey on his breath cutting through his minty mouthwash.

She watched him sprinkle salt and pepper on his eggs, a sneer curling along his upper lip that made him seem as though he were about to spit. She had seen him at the main gate helping a little boy and his mother, an iconic image in dress blues, like something on a recruiting poster; she had seen him a dribbling drunk, a pathetic caricature. Both images had been upon her lips before God. She wondered who he was now.

He took a mouthful of eggs, looked across the table at her, the sneer working as he chewed. "Gotta think about that one, huh?"

She shook her head. "We're all sinners, Nathan."

"We are, huh? That include kids?"

"Everyone needs the Savior."

His eyes were suddenly cold and deadly. "Think they get what they deserve?" he said quietly. "Kids?"

She frowned. "I don't know what you mean."

"Little kids. Sinners."

"I still don't know what you mean."

He made a noise in the back of his throat. "God has a wonderful plan for my life, huh?" He looked at her hair, her eyes, the line of her chin; his wide-set eyes combing her features with restless energy. "Besides passing out religious tracts, what do you do here, Maddie? Go to school?"

"I've been out of school for a couple of years now," she said, guardedly. She wasn't sure what his motives were in the previous exchange, but she felt something smoldering behind the blue gray eyes. A cold heat.

"Oh?"

She took a sip of coffee, looked up and saw that he was watching her. She felt a little self-conscious. He seemed to be studying her, not in a leering way, but as though she were an unknown commodity that needed

looking over before purchase. It seemed a bit of a game.
She set her cup down. "I'm going to UCSC in the fall."

"UCSC?"

"Santa Cruz."

"Nice town, Santa Cruz. Did some surfing up there
a couple summers ago. Meanwhile, you just kicking
around Naples?"

"Something like that. I live with my family in town.
My father is retired military."

"Oh?" He loaded another forkful of eggs. "What
branch?"

"Navy. He was a Marine in Korea though. He was
an adjutant on Chesty Puller's staff. I'm sure you're
impressed."

"Good old Chesty. What made him switch to the
Navy?"

She smiled. "Turn coat, you mean? I know how it
is between Marines and Navy. He became a chaplain, so
he could minister to Marines."

Nathan poured cream into his coffee, added a
teaspoon of sugar and stirred, leaning forward on his
elbows. "What's he do here…work with the chaplain?"

"He's a missionary. He and my mother operate the
Way Station downtown. It's a place where men can get
a home cooked meal, play games or write letters. Also,
they can study the Bible."

"Sounds like a USO for holy rollers."

"Haven't seen any holy rollers lately," she said. "I've seen plenty of guys having a great time instead of going to the bars, though."

He took a sip of coffee. "Guys like Skip McPherson?"

"Skip comes, yes. But mostly we get men who come in off the Fleet."

"And you're the company drummer?"

She frowned.

He spread jelly on his toast, the sneer making it up into his eyebrows. "You know…a pied piper for losers."

"Losers?" Maddie felt a prickling at the base of her neck. "You think that men searching for God are losers?"

He nodded, pushed out his lower lip in an attitude of mock affirmation. "I don't mean any harm by it." He shrugged, biting toast. "I think they're looking for a crutch, is all."

"You had four crutches helping you out of the bar last night. What are you looking for, Nathan?"

He grinned down at his plate, cut a sausage link with the edge of his fork. "Think I'm going to hell, don't you?"

"I don't know where you're going. But while you live and breathe you have a choice."

"A choice. Sure." He chuckled throatily, his face darkening. "Come to Jesus or burn, baby, burn! O boy, there's a choice for you. What kind of God is that?"

"He's a God of love…"

"God of *love?*" he said quietly, his eyes savage. "God of *love?* I'm sorry, sister, I can't buy what you're peddling. Not a word of it."

She started to say something.

He held up his hand as if stopping traffic. "No." He set his fork down gently on the plate, then immediately picked it up again and jabbed the air between them. "I'll tell you about your God of love."

He glared at her for several long moments, the fork trembling in his hand, then he shook his head. "No I won't tell you."

Maddie watched him stab the sausage with the fork, shove it into his mouth. She sat watching him in silence. It seemed a battle was being waged over his face. "We're not getting off on a good start, are we?"

"Just keep your loving God to yourself, okay? I don't like people shoving Him or it or whatever they think He is down my throat."

"Who's doing that?"

He scoffed, mopped up the last of his eggs with his toast.

Maddie felt her cheeks burn. "I don't recall shoving anything down your throat. I gave you a tract. You can throw it away."

"I already did." Nathan pushed away angrily from the table and stood. He reached into his pocket, tossed a 20 lire coin onto the table. "This ought to cover your cost." He picked up his hat. "Next time you talk to God or Buddha or whoever it is you pray to, tell Him I'm not interested, okay?"

The other Marine came over to the table, grinning. "This looks serious," he said. "Who's your friend, Nate?"

Nathan brushed past him without speaking. The Marine watched him exit the cafeteria, looking back at Maddie. "What was that all about?"

Maddie shook her head, glancing at the entrance of the cafeteria. "I'm not quite sure."

"Nate goes crazy on odd days usually; this is an even day. He must be in love. You were in front of the San Pedro last night."

"Yes, I was." She shook his hand. "I'm Maddie Gallagher."

"Jim Cooper. You should stay away from those places," he smiled. "A lot of bad characters coming out of bars."

"Usually just odd days, huh?"

"Nate? Crazy as a sack of squirrels. Even days are usually safe. You must've done something to him." He grinned, touched his forehead with two fingers and walked away. He looked back and waved. "Merry Christmas."

"Merry Christmas." Maddie shook her head, glanced outside as the Marines in formation ran, boots drumming past her window once again, singing cadence. "That went well, didn't it?"

Chapter Five

NATHAN KESSLER WALKED the eight to twelve shift in the Post Exchange compound, located on the easternmost end of the NSA base in Bolanaro. The post office, commissary, barber shop, and motor vehicles office were also located in the compound. It was a black night, with a big yellow moon rising over the jagged volcanic rim that dominated the skyline to the southeast. A cold breeze was blowing from the bay, five miles away, so only trace amounts of sulfur were lingering in the air, like the bilious scent of the devil's cologne.

He walked a full circuit of the compound, checking locks, windows and doors, shining his flashlight into parked government vehicles. The PX compound abutted the Disbursing compound, which in turn abutted the main gate compound at the westernmost end of the base, in which the Administration building, chapel, library and barracks were located.

Low cinderblock walls separated the three compounds, with wide openings in them, through which vehicles could pass during business hours. After five o'clock, the gates opening onto the street from the PX and Disbursing areas were secured. The Marines assigned to those posts, who now wore starched Marine Corps fatigues and boots instead of blues, went on roving patrol.

Walking past the opening between his post and the Disbursing compound, Nathan saw Gorilla rounding the Disbursing building on his way to the post office, his huge bulk silhouetted in a splash of moonlight. He was twirling his nightstick in a desultory manner, singing, "Louie, Louie, me gotta go…Louie, Louie, oh-oh babee, me gotta go, I say, me gotta go now."

Nathan figured he was going to take a nap inside the post office where it was warm. He waved, but Gorilla didn't see him.

Nathan went to the rear of the PX, stood out of the wind behind one of the thirty-foot high refrigeration units and smoked a cigarette, cupping it with his hand to hide the glow. Marines were not allowed to smoke on post; however, most of the Marines that smoked, smoked on post. Other things were done on post as well. Some of the Marines drank liquor, the stoner crowd smoked dope and a few made arrangements with Luigi to provide female companionship. Luigi was the go-to guy for contraband and pleasant diversions.

Nathan looked over at the apartment building on the other side of the compound wall. Windows were lighted in some of the apartments. Every so often people would move across the windows; sometimes shaded silhouettes, sometimes in full light.

In order to kill time, Nathan thought up stories about their lives. Some stories funny. Some tragic. Walking post was a lonely job with not much else to do, except to think. He could check doors and windows, but he usually accomplished that within the first thirty minutes; afterwards he had three and a half hours to kill which he did by thinking mostly. Walking post provided a stage for the theater of the mind.

Maddie Gallagher stood center stage.

Nathan blew a cloud of smoke at the apartments, watched it swirl in the air before the wind took it. He felt bad the way he had spoken to her. He hadn't intended for the conversation to go the way it did. She was a pretty girl alone at a table—a pleasant conversation over breakfast. The anger had just come up, as if a door had been yanked open, releasing a flock of devils. It had surprised him, but then it shouldn't have. He hated Christians. For good reason he thought.

"She didn't do nothing, Nate."

"I know, Frankie. I know."

"Why'd you beat her up like that then?"

"I have no idea."

"I think you know."

"Yeah. I know."

"You gonna apologize to her?"

Nathan thought about that but had no answer. He looked up at the apartments as a woman passed by a lighted window. A moment later the light went out. No doubt she had been jilted by her boyfriend, and gone into the bathroom to slit her wrists. Nathan shook his head with a chuckle. Let's not be morbid, Brother. Ain't nothing that bad.

He checked his watch and saw that it was 2025 hours. Eight twenty-five p.m.

He took one last pull on his cigarette, flicked it and watched the sparks splash over the tarmac until it died in a puddle. He headed over to the guard booth for his quarter-hour log in, first removing the magazine from his .45 and putting it back into the canvas magazine pouch on his utility belt, in case there was a surprise inspection from the Sergeant of the Guard. Marines were not allowed to carry their pistols loaded. They were issued two magazines, each containing five rounds of .45 caliber ammunition, but the magazines were to remain in their belt pouches unless needed. Heaven help the Marine who was ambushed at night, armed with an empty weapon and a nightstick and ten rounds of useless ammunition in his pouches. It was a stupid regulation, and dangerous. Most of the Marines disobeyed the order.

Nathan stepped into the lighted booth and began writing the time in the logbook, along with the lack of noteworthy events, when a car pulled up outside the gate, a Fiat with a battered door and missing headlight. Luigi was gesturing excitedly with his hand. He came up to the gate and gestured through the bars. "Quick, Marine, come here," he said. "I have a request from Meek. He is at the main gate."

"I know where he is. Doesn't his phone work?"

"He says you are never by phone. He says you are in back watching floor show in apartments."

"What's Mick want?"

"He wishes to know if you will go—what is word? Ah, yes, halfsies on a pizza."

"A pizza?"

"From hotel across street. They make beautiful pizzas." He said this, placing the knuckle of his right forefinger into his cheek and twisting it back and forth.

Nathan could speak fluent Italian, but since Luigi persisted in speaking pigeon English, Nathan obliged him. "What's your cut?" he asked.

Luigi pinched a small space between his forefinger and thumb. "*Solo un po.*"

"That's okay," Nathan said. "I can wait until mid-rats."

"Mid-rats? What is mid-rats when you can have mozzarella and pepperoni and sausage and anchovies?"

"I never cared much for dead minnows," Nathan said. He saw that his joke went over Luigi's head. He thought of trying it in Italian but saw no future in it.

"Tell Mick to go in halfsies with Gorilla," he said. "He's on roving patrol in the post office, inspecting the back of his eyelids." This joke didn't fly too well either.

"*Signore* Meek says Gorilla has no money. He said if he did have money he would eat more than half."

"Tell *Signore* Mick that he's going to have to wait until mid-rats. I'm tapped until Friday."

Luigi's face brightened. "Possibly Luigi could give you a small loan."

"At what markup?"

Luigi shrugged, pushed out his thick lower lip. "Four to one?"

"You black marketer."

Luigi grinned. "I make a good Marine, no? How do you like your new sports car? She is beautiful, no?"

"She is beautiful, yes. I'm looking forward to giving her a spin up to Roccaraso."

"*Roccaraso, ah molto bella.* And the women..." Luigi kissed the tips of his fingers, made a lewd remark about Italian girl skiers as he got back into his cab, and then drove up the street and parked in front of the Hideaway Hotel, opposite the main gate.

Nathan was about to continue his patrol when his phone rang. He picked up the receiver. "Post seven, Lance Corporal Kessler speaking."

"Cut the chin flap," Mick said. "Rock rolls."

"I'll alert AFSOUTH when the coast is clear."

"Roger that, you cheapskate. How come no go on the pizza?"

"No dough, that's why."

Five minutes later Nathan saw the gray 1971 Suburban exit the main gate, then a few moments later drive down the road past his gate, Jim Cooper, driving, Sergeant Rockman—the Rock—in the passenger seat. They hadn't stopped to inspect his post, which was fine with him. He stepped back into the booth and dialed Post 10 at AFSOUTH, told the Marine on duty to alert the other posts there. He'd call the post at Capo.

Chapter Six

CHRISTMAS EVE THE moon shone clear and bright like the star of Bethlehem, its silvery tail shimmering over the black water of the bay. The lights of the city were twinkling in the hard winter night. The Galleria Umberto, with its dome and arcade of convex glass and steel built in the shape of a cross, was lit against the sky with a greenish glow.

Inside the Way Station, crowded with soldiers, sailors, airmen and Marines, the great room was festooned with garlands of plastic holly, blinking lights and shining ornaments. A small group of men was gathered around the tree against the bank of windows, playing guitars and singing "Silent Night" as a sailor set out a porcelain Nativity on one of the side tables that Maddie had purchased from a street vendor in town. Others were going in and out of the bookstore, then plopping down into stuffed chairs to read their purchases in the warm golden glow of the room.

Maddie cleared away the last of the dinner dishes from the table. They'd had honey ham and sweet potatoes, cheese soufflé and tossed green salad. She picked up a cup, paused for a moment holding it thoughtfully.

She could see him across the table in the Admin building from her, looking over her features, his eyes changing colors in the light. She saw the shape of his hands as he ate. Then she imagined him on post, standing duty that night perhaps, and she thought how sad it would be to be alone, thousands of miles away from home on Christmas Eve.

She looked across the room at her father who was sitting, open Bible in hand, with Skip McPherson and a stocky black Marine. Her father's red hair and Irish face glowed in the soft yellow light of the table lamp, as he showed the Marine a passage in the Bible. The Marine, leaning forward with elbows on his knees, rubbed his chin and nodded.

Maddie smiled, looked over the crowd of happy faces. At least not every serviceman would miss celebrating Christmas Eve in a home, with a family that loved and cared for each of them. She carried the dishes into the kitchen and set them next to the sink, where her mother, humming "Silent Night" with those singing by the tree, was elbow-deep in suds.

"Is that the new Marine Skip was talking about?"

Kitty looked through the counter opening into the great room. "That's him. Clarence Pearsall." She rinsed a plate in the tap, set the plate in the rack to dry.

"He seems to be listening intently."

"Yes. I have a feeling the angels will be rejoicing in heaven tonight."

Maddie scraped plate scraps into a paper bag, handed the plate to her mother who dipped it into the sudsy water. "What a wonderful time of year to come to Christ."

Kitty scrubbed the plate, a smile playing over her lips. "Yes, isn't it?"

Maddie took another dirty plate from the stack. "By the way, how did Dad's meeting go with the chaplain the other day? I forgot to ask him."

"The chaplain said he'd talk to Skip. There's not much more he can do though, except pray. He could talk to the CO, but I doubt Skip would want him to raise the issue."

"No, I don't think he would." Maddie was looking over at her dad and Skip talking with Clarence Pearsall, the latter nodding his head thoughtfully. "I need to talk with Skip—encourage him somehow."

"I'm sure he would appreciate that." Kitty took the plate from Maddie and scrubbed it in the soapy water. "Dad tells me you met with Lance Corporal Kessler today. It didn't go well?"

"Not well."

"What happened?"

Maddie shrugged. "We were going along fine, then all of a sudden everything I said only made him angry."

"Oh?"

"Somehow I got on defense. He kept making fun of me. Then the old Gallagher temper took over and everything went south from there."

"I'm sure it wasn't as bad as all that."

"Believe me."

Kitty rinsed the plate and stacked it with the others. "People react in all sorts of ways when the light is turned on them. Anger is one of them. Anger is the fruit of a deeper root."

"He says he's an atheist."

"Oh? I've never met an atheist. I've met people who claimed to be atheists but in reality they were only wrestling with God. They just didn't know it."

Maddie thought about that. "I can't stop thinking about him, Mom."

Kitty looked at her.

Maddie took the last dirty plate and scraped it into the paper bag. "Did God ever bring someone into your life that you couldn't stop praying for?"

"Yes. You. When you were fifteen I lay awake at nights praying that God wouldn't let you wander from him. You had quite a rebellious streak, if you will remember."

"Me?"

"You."

Maddie compressed her lips together in a grim line, shook her head. "I didn't turn out so bad, did I?"

"You turned out just fine." Kitty wiped her hands on a towel and patted Maddie's shoulder. "Let's put away the glum face now, it's Christmas Eve." She went over to the refrigerator and got out the carton of eggnog, carried it over to the counter where there was a tray of glasses. "Time for eggnog and opening gifts."

Chapter Seven

Roccaraso, late December

T HEY WERE SITTING in a padded booth along
the wall of the discothèque in the Italian village of
Roccaraso, high up in the Apennines, nursing their
drinks, when Nathan caught sight of the girl staring at
him from across the room. The booths and dance floor
were crowded with skiers, fresh off the slopes, the dancers
moving in the colored lights to the beat of a bad rendition
of "Ob-La-Di, Ob-La-Da." The music was loud, which
covered the singer's unfamiliarity with the English
language.

"What'd I tell you," Cooper said. "Nobody knows
about this place, except the locals. How is it you speak
Italian, and you've only been stationed here a couple of
months?"

"My grandmother was half Italian," Nathan said, watching the girl. She was with a group of young people, sitting on a stool by the bar, but she was looking at him. "We spoke Italian and English in our home."

"You can be my interpreter," Cooper said, drained his glass, then leered at a girl in a yellow snowsuit grinding past him on the dance floor. "Look at that one. I think I'm gonna book my own room."

"You may have to, Coop."

The girl at the bar stood, then thread her way across the dance floor, never taking her eyes off of Nathan, as though he was the only person in the room. She had dark brown, shoulder length hair, and a great figure that she moved well, in spite of her after ski boots.

She stopped beside Nathan's booth, folded her hands in front of her and, with a smile that could start revolutions, asked, "*Vuoi ballare?*"

"*Certo, mi piacerebbe ballare.*"

Cooper blinked at her, blinked at Nathan. "Did I miss something?"

"She asked me to dance," Nathan said, sliding out of the booth.

"Oh sure."

They danced a couple of fast ones. She was moving to a rhythm not generated by the band, as though she was listening to music that no one else could hear. "You are very tall," she said, moving slowly, curvingly, like a cobra to a flute.

"We stack it high where I come from," he said, watching her swaying her hips. When he saw that the expression didn't translate well, he said, "Sometimes I get altitude sickness."

She looked at him a moment, then laughed. "You are making a joke."

"Not a very good one." In the swirling ovals of colored lights, he could see that she was wearing light blue—perhaps turquoise—bib overalls that showed her figure well, and a hot pink, clingy, turtleneck sweater. "*Come ti chiami?*" he asked.

"Nicoletta. My friends call me Nico."

"Nico. I like that," he said. "*Mi chiamo* Nathan Kessler. *Natanaele.* Nate, if you like."

"I do not like Nate. To me you are Natti."

"Okay, I'm your Natti. Did you ski today?"

"Oh yes. And you?"

"Just got here. How was it?"

"*Non c'e male.* Not too bad. They say it will snow tonight, so tomorrow should be better."

It was the usual small talk that meant nothing. He enjoyed watching her dance. He was intrigued, excited, by her interpretation of the music that seemed to follow her lead. She made the music sound good, though it was played by a second rate Italian band doing their best to look and sound like the Beatles. "May I buy you a drink?" he asked.

"Please."

They sat down in the booth. Cooper gaped at her.

"This is my friend Jim," Nathan said. "*Giacomo.*"

"Ah, *Giacomo.*"

"Close your mouth, Jim, it isn't polite."

Cooper closed his mouth, shook her hand. "Pleased to meet you," he said in pigeon Italian.

"*Piacere di conoscerti,*" she replied.

"James was just leaving," Nathan said in English.

"I was? Right. *Ciaó!*" Cooper slid out of the booth and disappeared into the crowd.

Nico looked at Nathan. "You are American?"

"*Io sono Americano,*" he said.

"I thought you were German. You look German."

"I am German, four generations removed, by way of Morro Bay, California. Mind if I smoke?"

"Are those American cigarettes?"

He offered her a cigarette and lit it.

"I like American cigarettes," she said, blowing smoke away from the table. She studied his face, his eyes, mouth, chin, the width of his shoulders, his hair. "Your hair is very short."

"It's regulation."

"Regulation?"

"I'm a Marine."

"A Marine?"

"You know—Leatherneck, Devil Dog, Mud-sucker. What're you drinking?"

"Chablis. You are a soldier?"

"Marine." Nathan held up a finger at a passing waiter and ordered a glass of Chablis, and a beer. "I'm stationed down in Naples. Bolanaro."

"I know it very well," she said, smoking.

"Smells like rotten eggs," he said. "Literally."

She made a face. "It is the volcanoes."

"So I hear."

"I do not like it there. There are many criminals—I think because there is much military. It is also very dirty."

"That's why I'm here. Very clean. No criminals. No Sixth Fleet. A very beautiful girl."

"Thank you," she said. "And you are very handsome."

"It's dark in here."

"No, but you are handsome. Your face is interesting and not at all like an Italian's." She reached over and put her hand on his face. "Yes, I like your face very much."

"Where are you from?" he asked, rolling the tip of his cigarette in the ashtray. "You're not a local, are you?"

"*Viva a Roma*," she said. "Rome is dirty too, I know, but there is so much more to do there than Naples. There are museums and concerts and, of course, the theater. They have those things in Naples, too, but it is not the same. Do I sound like a snob?"

"Naples has beaches."

"Of course. My family owns a villa on *Isola Ischia*. It is beautiful there."

"That the island near Capri?"

"It is not far. I go there frequently. Have you been there?"

"Not yet. I just got here a couple of months ago."

"I will take you to Ischia," she said.

"Oh?" he said, feeling something move inside him.

"I will show you the beauty of a small island paradise. Do you like sailing?"

"Sure. Haven't done much. Surfed plenty though."

"I will teach you. You will love it."

The drinks came. He held up his glass. "What shall we toast?"

She brightened, showed all of her teeth in a wicked smile. "*Alla nostra salute e avventura.*"

"To our health and adventure."

They touched glasses. Nathan took a sip of beer. "Fine beer."

She was watching him. "Your Italian is very good," she said, sipping her wine. "Where did you learn it?"

"My grandmother was from Florence," Nathan said. "I grew up speaking Italian."

"There is a little accent in your pronunciation, but you could be from Bolzano or Garda. Have you been to Lake Garda?"

"Yes, when I was a boy. I was on holiday with my family."

"Did you water-ski?"

"Yes. The water was very cold—even in summer—so I took off from the pier. Never got wet. It's a beautiful place."

"Yes. There are many blue-eyed, blond Italians in the north. I find them very attractive." She took a sip of her drink, looking at him over the rim of the glass. Her eyes, flickering in the candlelight, were almond-shaped and light-colored—perhaps olive—and very beautiful. "Like you," she said, touching his hand with the tip of her middle finger.

"Would you like to go somewhere less noisy?"

"I know a café."

"Are you with anyone? I saw you with some people by the bar."

"I met them today," she said, sliding out of the booth. "They don't mean anything. Your friend will not miss you?"

Nathan saw Cooper on the floor dancing with the yellow snowsuit. "I wouldn't bet on it."

Then they were out into the sudden quiet and lung-burning cold of the winter night in Roccaraso. The trees along the streets were bare and sharply cut, and the lights strung between the trees twinkled in the clear bright night. People were going by on the sidewalks, some couples, some in small groups, entering and exiting cafés and discothèques.

Nathan and Nico were walking along the lighted storefronts of the hotels and shops that went up and down the steep mountain street, Nathan feeling the altitude but happy to be outside with his arm around a pretty girl, enjoying the clean sharp cold in contrast to the dismal and mustard-smelling foulness of Naples.

They were mindful of their footing, the packed and sometimes slick snow crunching beneath their boots as they paused now and then to admire the latest winter fashions or various foods or pastries on display in the windows.

Nico had put on her ski jacket—turquoise, to match her bib overalls—and scarlet knit cap that framed the oval shape of her face, so that in the bright incandescent window Nathan could see her features.

"Are you here alone, or did you come with someone?" he asked.

"I am here with my family," she said. "We come every Christmas, and stay through the New Year. It is a small resort, but I like it—it is much more intimate. How long will you be here?"

"Through the New Year," he said. "You are very beautiful."

"Thank you," she smiled, and then suddenly, unexpectedly, stepped up onto her toes and kissed him. "I do not really wish to go to a café."

"Where would you like to go?"

"Where are you staying?"

"At the Hotel Veronica. A small place at the edge of the village. It's all we could find without reservations. They have a little bar that shouldn't be too noisy."

"Do they have room service?"

He looked at her.

"I must be back in my hotel before two," she said. "My mother will be waiting up for me."

IT HAD SNOWED during the night. It was still snowing with snow gusts swirling over the street in the wind coming down the mountain. White powder covered the windowsill overlooking the road that led up to the village; snow covered the rooftops and the cars parked along the street with drifts piled against the walls of the buildings. A snowplow was clearing the street, making a white berm along the curbs that merchants shoveled through to make paths to the sidewalks.

Nathan looked back into the room and saw that Cooper's bed had not been slept in, and he wondered what fortune or misfortune had befallen his friend. He went into the bathroom, showered and shaved and donned his winter clothes and down jacket, then he went down to the desk and asked the concierge, "*Vorrei noleggiare degli sci.*"

The concierge said that he could rent skis at any of the larger hotels, or at the lodge. "It will be a good day for skiing with the new snow."

Nathan thanked him, and then went out to his car, a late model Fiat Spider 1600 convertible that he had purchased before the trip, and continued to make payments on, with his extra cigarette, gasoline and liquor rations. Cooper had arranged it through Luigi. Luigi had connections with the underworld. It was illegal, of course, but many of the Marines did it, apparently. It was simply too lucrative not to. Cigarettes and gas paid four-to-one, ten-to-one for liquor. No one used the two hundred liters of gas allotted to him each month, or smoked four cartons of cigarettes or drank ten fifths of liquor. Half those amounts, perhaps; the rest could be sold for cash, or in his case, payments on an automobile.

About five inches of snow blanketed the car. He scraped the windshield with a squeegee and hand-brushed the snow off the rear window, so as not to scratch the plastic.

He started the ignition, pleased to hear the throaty growl of the engine. He waited a minute to let it warm up, watching the white clouds of exhaust in his wing mirror flattening in the wind and then, putting the gear stick into first, released the clutch and, coaxing the accelerator, eased the car out of the snow into the freshly plowed road. He drove slowly up the hill, passing colorful skiers walking toward the lifts with skis on their shoulders, and then he turned into the parking area of the Hotel Primo Abruzzi, with the mountains, freshly snow-covered, rising nobly against the lowering sky.

Walking past the storefront windows of the hotel, and then on past the dining room, the window panes laced with snow-crescents, he saw Nico sitting at a window table, alone, spreading orange marmalade on a piece of brioche. When she saw him, her face brightened and she finger-waved. Seeing her, he felt a sudden jolt of disbelief at his good fortune, and then an aching happiness in his chest. He laughed out loud at the promise of the day.

The hotel was furnished with carved wooden furniture, beautiful stone, wood paneling, and tile work on the walls and floor, with Alpine-themed tapestries, bronze modernist sculptures on the walls and at various focal points. A massive circular stone fireplace with bronze hood and venting, and cushioned seating going round it, dominated the lounge. People were sitting by the fire, drinking coffee and tea and talking. The guests seated at tables and walking through the hotel wore fashionable ski apparel, sported healthy mountain tans, expensive jewelry and coiffures. It was apparent that the hotel catered to the very wealthy.

Nathan entered the dining room and was stopped by a thin, blade-faced maitre 'd, wearing a red waistcoat, white shirt and black bowtie. Nathan could see by the maitre 'd's censuring squint that he didn't like the look of him; Nathan did not exude wealth, did not have a tan, and was clearly an interloper.

"May I help you, sir?" the maitre 'd inquired in a voice that hinted of an emery board filing vowels.

"I'm meeting Nicoletta Consigliore," Nathan said, pointing to her. "The lovely lady by the window. She's a guest." When she turned and waved him to her table, Nathan grinned at the maitre 'd. "See?" He started to leave but stopped. "Oh, you might straighten your tie," he quipped. "Must keep up appearances, mustn't we?" He winked at the man then went into the dining room and sat down in the chair across from her.

She was wearing a yellow turtleneck sweater with the same turquoise bib overalls she'd worn the night before, and she was even more beautiful than he had remembered.

"*Buon giorno*, Nico," he said.

"I have been counting the minutes," she whispered, leaning forward and smiling conspiratorially at him.

"Quite a place."

"We come here every winter," she said. "Don't mind Lorenzo." She indicated the maitre 'd who was discreetly fiddling with his tie. "He's a snob." She bit into the marmalade brioche then licked it off her teeth with her tongue. "Mmmmm. Want some?" she said, offering him the remainder.

"Sure." He took it, popped it in his mouth, tasting the sweetly sour marmalade and warm buttered brioche, and said, "What do you have to do to get some coffee around here?"

She caught the attention of a waiter. "Antonio? *Puoi darci dell'altro caffè, per favore?*"

Antonio the waiter, a thin, pockmark-faced man with sagging gray eyes like an old bull's, nodded admiringly at Nicoletta, then glanced sideways at Nathan as he headed toward the coffee service.

Nathan watched Nico preparing another piece of brioche, first spreading butter with a silver, round-tipped knife, then dabbing a healthy dollop of orange marmalade onto it.

"It is good, no?" she said.

"Very."

Antonio brought the coffee, not looking at Nathan but at Nico.

"*Grazie*," Nathan said. "*Il menu per favore,* Antonio."

Antonio left to get a menu with a wearied sigh, his eyes appearing a little sadder.

"I think he's jealous," Nathan said.

"Of course," she smiled, sipping coffee.

Nathan gazed across the table at Nico. Her thick dark auburn hair, gleaming in the window light with red and yellow and brown highlights, was brushed back from a high and shapely forehead, and held in place by a wide elastic band the same color as her sweater. Then examining her face, seeing it in a light that he could not have seen her in last night, he saw that her eyes were a golden hazel—not olive—with dark brown flecks in them. And with the light coming through the window showing the smooth olive color of her skin and the soft hollows beneath her cheekbones, he felt an ache in his chest, a sudden desperate emptiness that made him feel a little reckless.

"You are observing me?" she said.

"You are very beautiful this morning. Our waiter can't take his eyes off of you. I want to take you into my arms and kiss you."

She pressed a finger against her lips and shushed him. "Here, fill your mouth with this," she said, handing him the remainder of her brioche. "My mother will hear you."

"Your mother?"

"Do not look, but that is her in the green sweater, sitting with the distinguished looking gentleman who is my father. She is inspecting you."

Nathan let his eyes drift furtively over the room, and saw an older couple handsomely dressed in matching green sweaters and chocolate ski pants sitting three tables across from them. The man, graying at the temples and sporting a neat mustache, was drinking coffee and reading a newspaper. The woman, her dark brown, gray-streaked hair brushed back from a high forehead, was glaring imperiously at him. When their eyes met she turned away as though she hadn't been looking.

"She was waiting up for me last night," Nico said.

Nathan frowned at her. "I got you in before two. Did you get in trouble?"

"No."

Nathan glanced back at the mother, who was looking away from him, deliberately, it seemed. "I think your mother hates me."

"I think not," Nico said. "I told her that you were a military officer with a very important position at NATO Headquarters in Naples, and that you were a Roman Catholic. A mother wants to know that a young man has a future, economically speaking, and that he is a good Catholic. Did I lie?"

"Outrageously. As for the 'good' part, I've never met a good anything—Catholic or Protestant. Will she think I'm wonderful?"

"I will convince her. She is very religious. The Pope blessed her rosary a year ago. Also she is very generous."

"How nice for the Pope. What about you?"

"I went to early mass this morning. I made my confession and said my prayers of penance, so that I am without sin. For now." She smiled, took a sip of her coffee.

"God is happy and your mother is happy and you are without sin."

"Of course. You do not go to confession?"

"I don't believe in God."

She set her coffee cup down on the table and smiled at him. "You are joking?"

"I never joke about things I don't believe in."

"But everyone must believe in God. How can you not?"

"I believe in me." He felt a little foolish saying it, perhaps even a little petulant, like a child hoarding a toy at recess—and talking about it now took the edge off the earlier anticipation of promise.

Antonio came to their table, sullen-faced, and handed Nathan a menu. Nathan looked at it. "Did you already order?" he asked her.

"I'm going to have a quiche Lorraine—they are wonderful here."

Nathan told Antonio he'd have the same, but with sausages and plenty of coffee. The waiter left.

"May I have one of your cigarettes? I have been dying for one."

He gave her one, set the pack on the table, and lit her cigarette. "Keep the pack."

"Thank you," she said, smoking. "I do not like to smoke in front of my mother. I am old enough, of course, but she thinks it is a disgusting habit."

He looked across the room and saw that the mother and father had gone.

"They were waiting to see you," Nico said. "They saw you—rather Mother saw you. I told her all about you."

"Not everything, I hope."

"No," she giggled. "That is for you and me."

"And the priest," he said.

She frowned, tapped the cigarette in the ashtray. "You are being silly."

"Yes."

"Anyway…if my mother happens to ask, we were at the discothèque until one-thirty. There is no need to complicate matters."

"Roger that." He had stepped down from his earlier high horse of childish petulance. Now seeing her in profile as she looked out at the snow falling outside in large fluffy flakes, lifting her head to show the classic lines of her chin and throat, her thin, slightly aquiline nose, he felt the sudden happiness once again in his chest.

"You are looking at my nose," she said, blushing, as she slid her eyes back at the table.

"I like your nose."

"I do not like it." She touched her nose. "It is bent."

"Only a little, and it suits your face. It is a nose of great intelligence and beauty. It is the nose of a goddess."

He reached across the table and lifted her chin, angling her face first to the left, then to the right, as though inspecting a work of art. "Michelangelo could not have sculpted it better."

She blew a cloud of smoke over their heads. "You do not believe in God, yet you believe in goddesses?"

"Now you are being silly."

She glanced outside, let out a sigh. "Isn't the snow lovely? I do love it here."

Nathan watched the skiers carrying their skis and poles in the falling snow, their breath trailing. "Should be a great day for skiing."

She reached across the table and took his hand. "We will have a lovely holiday together, won't we?" she smiled. "Look, here come our quiches. The mountain air gives me such an appetite, doesn't it you?"

IT CONTINUED SNOWING heavily off and on for the next two days and nights. By the third day the powder came up to their calves, up to the waist in the drifts, and it was as light as eider down. The fresh powder made the runs new and exciting, so that they felt as though they were the first people ever to ski the mountain. As Nathan skied the trails through the trees alongside Nico, the wind in the pines and the whispering shoosh of their skis the only sounds, he had the unreal sensation that they were flying through clouds.

Nico was a beautiful skier. She would make long languid parallel turns down the runs with seeming effortless grace then, holding her upper body tight to navigate moguls, her legs like springs seemed to work independently from her body.

Nathan attacked the slopes with an abandonment of style, much the same as a hockey player attacking the ice. He was a speed skier. His skiing was goal-driven—get down the mountain as fast as he could. He would race downhill ahead of her, cut deeply into the slope, making a spray of powder to stop and stand, poles poised, grinning against the brightness of the snow as he watched her glide past him like a moving ballerina. He would wave at her and then take off down the mountain as if a gun had released him.

They ate lunch in the lodge that received the major runs. They sat outside on the second level terrace, the racks of skis below, eating ham and cheese croissants and washing them down with glasses of Birra Moretti, the beer cold and cleanly refreshing in the crisp mountain air.

Nathan's thighs and shoulders were heavy with fatigue, but it was a pleasant healthy feeling. They watched skiers coming down the slope, commenting on their ability or lack of ability, and they would observe other couples on the terrace that they'd seen on the mountain and make little jokes about them.

At night they ate dinner in the village restaurants. Nathan, always hungry from the exertion of skiing, ordered antipasto or minestrone soup, followed by spaghetti bolognese and then a heavy course of pot roast and roasted potatoes. Or sometimes he would order beef stew or broiled rack of lamb, and always with the hot fresh baked garlic bread to mop up the sauces.

He would begin with a Birra Moretti or Birra Peroni, a pilsner brewed in Vigevano to the north in Lombardy, and then drink red wine with the meal, particularly enjoying the rich fruity taste of a local wine, grown on the Adriatic slopes of the Abruzzi, but also enjoying the full-bodied wines from Tuscany. He never had a feeling of overeating, or of drinking too much, for there were the demands of the mountain that burned away calories, and to drink too much was to take away from the clarity of happiness of being with one another.

Afterward they went to the discothèques to dance or sit at a table or booth and watch people, but happy to be the two of them, alone, together in their happiness, along with the knowledge that they had a secret no one else could possibly understand.

Nathan would occasionally see Jim Cooper with the yellow snowsuit girl, and it was always like an intrusion into the secret. They would wave at each other across the dance floor or street or lodge, but the two of them never engaged in conversation, because both were content to be on separate holidays.

NEW YEAR'S EVE fell in a thunder of gaiety that rolled down the mountain into the streets of Roccaraso like an avalanche. It began quietly in the late afternoon, as even a carnival begins quietly in the predawn, setting up tents and sideshows, until the word spreads through the town and excitement builds. By early evening it was building a head of steam that was ready to explode. At ten o'clock it exploded with a fireworks display from the roof of the Veronica Hotel. People boiled out of hotels and restaurants and danced in the streets, blowing paper horns and shouting *"Buon Anno! Buon Anno!"*

Roccaraso was one contiguous party, an amorphous organism moving in and out of hotels and restaurants, with pieces of laughter and celebration splintering off the main body to join again at another part of the body. But there was only one body, unified by celebration. When people from one splinter group met people from another splinter group they would embrace and kiss one another, and say, *"Buon Anno!"* and then be absorbed back into the body like an amoeba.

Nathan and Nico started at one end of town and went to the other in roving groups of revelers. At the stroke of midnight they were sitting by the fire in the lobby of the Hotel Reale. The hotel was crowded with revelers. People were laughing and blowing paper horns and pulling string poppers and twirling clackers. People were kissing one another. People were pouring drinks and shouting, *"Buon Anno!"*

"Buon Anno, Nico," Nathan said.

She smiled and kissed him. *"Buon Anno,* Natti."

"Let's drink a toast to my first New Year's in Italy." He poured champagne into her glass. Then he held up his glass at the room of fellow revelers. "To my first New Year's in Italy."

"Buon Anno!" a round-faced man in lederhosen and Tyroler hat shouted.

A woman collapsed in a chair, raised a glass and giggled, "*Buon Anno!*"

Nathan laughed. "I love Italians," he said. "Don't you love Italians?"

"I *am* Italian," Nico said. "Do you love me?"

He kissed her. "*Cara mia, ti voglio bene.*"

"But I am not your sister. It is better to say *ti amo.*"

"*Ti amo, ti amo, ti amo.* I love Italians. *Amo gli Italiani!*" he shouted at the room.

"*Ti amo, ti amo,*" was shouted back. "*Buon Anno!*"

"I think I'm drunk," Nathan said. "I can't feel my face. Can you feel my face?"

She put her hand on his cheek. "It's a beautiful face."

"No, you're the one with the beautiful face. *Come sei bella.* You have the most beautiful face in the world. They should mint coins with your face on them. To my beautiful Nicoletta." Nathan poured more of the champagne. "Let's drink a toast to your face."

"My face is tired of celebrations."

"Yes?"

"My face would like to be alone with your face."

"You have the most intelligent face. It is a face of sound reasoning."

She laughed. "Shut up, you drunkard, and let's go."

"A sound decision from a beautiful face!"

Inside the hotel Nathan saw Jim Cooper passed out on the stairs. He was sprawled on his back, his head pointing upstairs, an empty champagne bottle clutched in his right hand, the yellow snowsuit girl curled at his side like a faithful Labrador retriever. They were both snoring peacefully. People stepped around them, smiling, going up and down the stairs. No one seemed to mind. "Poor Coop," Nathan said. "First casualty of the New Year."

Then it was the day after and the last full day of the holiday. They were sitting at a table on the terrace of the ski lodge with the sun coming up over the peaks, drinking coffee and eating hot buttered brioches with orange and strawberry marmalade, both of them looking up at the skiers essing down the sharp blue shadows of the mountain. There were not many skiers.

Nathan, feeling slightly nauseous and hung-over but aspirined-up and fortified with strong black coffee, could feel his face tight and sunburned. He wore sunglasses to shield his eyes from the alcohol-induced brightness of the snow glare. Only a few people remained on the terrace. The previous night of celebration had gone indoors sometime during the middle of the night and had stayed in bed.

The party was no longer a single moving organism, imbued with a spirit of bonhomie. Now there were only couples or singles or small groups that kept to themselves, sitting quietly, with slightly embarrassed expressions on their faces. The wild camaraderie of the night before was over. New Year's was over.

"I do not want it to end," she said.

Nathan admired Nico. She was hatless, her eyes bright and intelligent with her hair glowing in the early sun. She was lovely. "Nor do I."

"You get a weekend holiday every two weeks?"

"Yes."

"You will come up to see me in Rome?"

"In two weeks."

"Two weeks. *Mi manchi.*"

"But I'm still here, look." He lifted his sunglasses and made a face.

"Yes, but I miss you already. Oh, Natti. I am desperate just thinking about it."

"Then let's not think about it. Let's enjoy the time we have left; that's all there is. We still have the rest of today and tonight, and tomorrow will come when it comes. Would you like to go out on the slopes?"

She smiled at him, reached across the table and took his hand. "This is our last day together, Natti. I have skied enough. Haven't you?"

Chapter Eight

T HE GRAY WET days of January slogged by in a slow-footed cadence over sodden lawns and streets, down narrow bricked and cobbled alleys with shops in the tall buildings looming on either side, wet in fog, and along the Via nuova Marina that curved around the harbor where the ships were moored. Dark, heavy clouds were banked over the bay, and it rained in sets, with days of partial cloudiness between the sets of heavy rain. The trees were dark and bare and ugly in the overcast gloom of January, and the faces of buildings and castles gray in the gloom.

Maddie drove across town to the NSA base, feeling a touch of the blues. It was natural of course to feel that way after the holidays. Many people did. But she felt as though a hole had opened inside her chest that was filling up with a sadness that had only a vague beginning and, seemingly, no end. There were causes to rejoice, of course; several men had come to Christ over the holidays, and were forming Bible studies on the ships. But she felt overwhelmed by a weight of sadness. She had no idea why.

She pulled up to the PX gate, saw Lance Corporal Pearsall standing beside the guard booth, feet apart, hands folded behind his back in a "parade rest" posture. His face seemed to be glowing. When he saw the retired officer's sticker in her windscreen, he clicked his heels and snapped a salute. She put her head out the window. "Morning, Clarence."

He flashed a smile. "Hey, Maddie!"

"Not going to let those rain clouds get you down?"

"No, ma'am. Rain makes the flowers grow."

She had to smile. "Everything going okay in the barracks?"

"Can't complain. The devil's trying to break me down, but that's to be expected. I'm rejoicing in the Lord."

"What's the devil up to now?"

"Oh, some of the guys are making fun—you know. It don't mean nothin'. I did the same at my last duty station. I hate to admit it, but a couple of the guys there had Bible studies, and we'd make fun of them…call them names. Things like that. No good reason for it. Just meanness and ignorance."

"You reading your new Bible?"

"I'm halfway through the gospels," he said. "Skip said I could use his commentaries, but I want to read the Scriptures myself first."

"Good for you."

"It's amazing. Jesus did all those things."

"The Apostle John said that all the books in the world couldn't contain what He did."

"I haven't read John yet, but I'm getting to it. There's so much to learn. I feel like I gotta run to catch up. Did you hear about Jesse Calderon?"

"Jesse Calderon?"

"You've seen him. He's got duty at the main gate later. Little guy…from East L.A. I think."

"Oh yes, I've seen him. What about him?"

"Skip and I cornered him in the head last night. Skip was taking a shower at one end and I was at the other. Jesse was caught in the middle. Didn't have a chance. Skip was givin' him the gospel, and then I'd put my two cents in—not that I know much. I just told him that Jesus loved him and that he needed to quit horsing around with sin."

"Can't get any more eloquent than that."

"Skip picked it up from there and carried it into the end zone. That boy knows his Bible. Jesse said he wanted to hear more about it. I believe he meant it."

"I'll pray for him."

"Get the Hound of Heaven after him—that's what Skip says. If the Hound of Heaven is on your tail, you can run but you can't hide."

"Sound theology." Maddie saw a car pull into her rearview mirror. "Gotta go," she said. "You have a great day, Clarence."

"Can't get any better!"

Again she smiled. She drove into the PX compound, feeling her spirit lifted. New believers did that to her. Their faith was so simple, so childlike, and so full of joy— "lights bursting from darkness." They were infectious— quite the contrast to some older Christians she knew who, though well read in the Scriptures, were sadly lacking that "first love" fervency in their joy.

She parked the Fiat in the PX lot and went into the commissary for a week's supply of groceries.

NATHAN INKED THE last of a series of cartoons he'd drawn for the *Star Spangled Banner*. He wanted to get them into the mail before he left for weekend liberty. The cartoon showed two Marines in 782 gear lounging in a foxhole, one black, the other one Ol' Prive, the latter with his hands clasped behind his head, the heel of one boot resting on the toe of the other. He inked the drawing onto a sheet of Bristol board with a sable brush, then penciled a caption under it:

Black Marine: *Goin' back to the world soon, brother?*

Ol' Prive: *I'm so short I need a stepladder to get off the dime.*

"I've heard that joke before, Nate."

"It's still funny."

"I like that missionary girl better than the Italian one too. She's the real McCoy. You gonna apologize to her?"

"I told you I'd think about it, Frankie."

Cooper walked over to the desk and looked over Nathan's shoulder as he rubbed the drawing with a kneaded eraser. "What're you drawing?"

"A cartoon."

"That one of your 'Ol' Prive's'?"

"Yeah."

"Lemme see." Cooper leaned closer to better see the drawing. "That's pretty funny."

"Thanks."

"Where'd you learn to draw?"

"Here and there."

"Art class?"

"Biology."

"Biology?"

Nathan put the drawing into a large envelope with the others and sealed it. He grinned. "Sure. Biology, history, math and English."

MADDIE EXITED THE commissary, pushing a cart stuffed with brown paper bags with groceries in them, and saw Nathan Kessler coming toward her from the post office. She hadn't seen him in a couple of weeks. He was in uniform, carrying a small bag of purchases, looking in the direction of the hills. She felt a tingle of excitement inside her.

"Hey, it's the carrot top," he said.

"It's me. How was skiing?"

"Skiing? Oh right—my New Year's leave. I had a lot of fun. Plenty of fresh powder and clean air."

"Sounds wonderful," she said, lamely.

"Do you like skiing?"

She shook her head, averting her eyes from his. "I don't know, I've never been."

"You'd like it. Believe me. Roccaraso's not that far away either. It's beautiful."

"Maybe I'll go there sometime."

"You seem an outdoorsy type."

"I enjoy the outdoors." She said it just to say it. She was suddenly nervous, at a loss for words. She'd never been nervous or shy around a guy before; perhaps it was because she'd grown up around so many. They were like brothers to her. Nathan made her nervous. "I've never had an opportunity to ski."

"Really?"

"Really."

They stared at each other. Nathan smiled, peered up at the dark clouds, looked back. Maddie stood holding the cart handle with both hands, her knuckles gleaming white ridges and pink valleys. She glanced up at the sky as a light drizzle began to fall.

"We're getting wet." An airy giggle fluttered in her throat.

"About the other day," he said, ignoring her remark.

"The other day?"

"Before Christmas. In the cafeteria."

"You mean the *other* day."

"That's the one." His expression changed. "I was out of line," he said. "I don't usually blow up like that. I don't know what got into me."

"I was out of line too."

"No you weren't."

"It's my red hair," she said, lifting her eyes to a curl that had fallen over her forehead. "It's true what they say about redheads. Short fuses. My dad calls me the fighter pilot."

"Fighter pilot, huh?"

"Maybe if I cut off the hair I'd be able to hold my tongue."

"Don't do that. You've got great hair." He kept admiring her hair. "Did you know that only two percent of people in the world have red hair?"

She raised an eyebrow.

"I read it somewhere," he said. "An encyclopedia, I think. It's the least common hair color."

"And here I just thought I was rare."

He studied her hair some more, smiled, then let it drift away into a serious stare. "You weren't out of line, either," he said. "You said what you believed. I was an idiot." He stood smiling at her, his eyes darting forays over her features—her eyes, mouth, the bridge of her nose.

She touched it absently, as though to cover the freckles.

"Can we start over?" he asked. "I'd like to be friends."

"I'd like that too." She wiped the edge of one hand over the open palm of the other. "Clean slate. Are you going on duty or coming off?"

"Coming off. I had the four to eight. Worst shift. Your sleep cycle gets thrown all out of whack. Looking forward to the weekend though."

"Going to catch up on your sleep?"

"No, I'm going to Rome."

"Ah, *Bella Roma*. I'll pray that you have a safe trip," she said. "The *autostrada* gets pretty slick when it rains."

He made a face, started to say something, held up his hand as though to stop himself. He smiled. "You really believe that, don't you? Praying and what-not.

"If I didn't, I wouldn't do it."

"And God answers your prayers. Every prayer."

"Yes, He does. Sometimes He answers Yes, other times No. Many of my prayers have yet to be answered. Those are the Wait times."

He made a noise in his throat. "You never doubt?"

"Sometimes I doubt, yes. Does it seem odd to you?"

"That a Christian would admit it, yes."

"You might be surprised how human Christians really are. Sure, I have doubts. Sometimes I wonder why God allows things to happen."

"Like what?"

"I don't know…war, poverty."

"Disease?"

She eyed him curiously. "Yes, disease," she said. "And little black babies with swollen bellies and flies crawling in their eyes. Sometimes it's hard to reconcile these with a loving God. But I always bring my doubts to Him. When I do, an amazing thing happens, I think of Jesus hanging on the cross for my sins and I say, okay, Lord, I may not understand everything right now, but I can wait. God will make it clear. In the meantime I pray. I pray for you, Nathan. Every day."

Nathan was staring down at the sidewalk, shaking his head slowly back and forth.

She went on. "Every one of us has a hole in his life that only God can fill. We try to fill it with people or things or whatever, but only God can fill it. What are you looking for, Nathan?"

He glanced up at her with his eyes, the brim of his hat, now beaded from the light rain, shading them. "God. Jesus. The Christian faith. You hope. You pray." A sardonic grin flicked at the corners of his mouth. "It all seems a cruel joke."

"How do you mean?"

"It doesn't work."

Maddie frowned at him quizzically. There was something in his tone, an edge to his words that opened a fissure in his hard outer wall that gave her a brief glimpse at his soul. The fissure closed as quickly as it had opened, but she had seen him.

"What are you looking at?" he asked, a little defensively.

"You."

"Yeah? And what do you see?"

"A phony. You're no more an atheist than I am."

"No?" His eyebrows pinched together, a red gleam darkened in his eyes, then cooled. He laughed, recovering. "Haven't you heard that even the devils believe and tremble." He grinned, checked his watch. "I gotta get going. Clean slate?"

"Clean slate."

He put out his hand and she shook it, his hand wet in the light rain. He held her hand a little longer than the snap and release allowed by social protocol, peering into her eyes with an intensity that made her blush. She felt another tingle of excitement surging along her arm.

"Maybe I'll see you around sometime, Maddie," he said, releasing her hand.

"That would be nice."

"I mean it."

"So do I."

He smiled, embarrassed. Then he turned and walked away, dropped the little sack he was carrying, picked it up, looked up at the drizzling sky and continued walking across the compound toward the barracks.

Maddie felt as though she might cry.

SHE PUT THE groceries into the back seat of the Fiat 500, and then on her way back to the Station made a side trip up the slope to the summit of Vomero. There was something she very much needed to do there. Driving past 17th Century villas and mansions that were more visible now behind leafless trees, she parked along the curb beside the Castel Sant'Elmo.

The rain had stopped, the skies opening patches of blue over the bay.

She got out of the car and walked down the hill along the wet gravel path curving through groves of olive trees and evergreen shrubs, and past the National Museum and the old monastery, with its beautifully arched cloisters and courtyard. It was a quiet, serene world apart from the hustle and filth of Naples.

There were small ruins situated in vantage points from which to view the famous panorama—the lush hills of the city, stuffed with multicolored houses and villas, like classical dollhouses, curving around the bay, and then Vesuvius, darkly veiled in fog, like some primordial behemoth brooding in predawn mists, with its long hump of back and tail sloping down into the Sorrentine Peninsula.

She found the tree with huge limbs reaching out toward the bay, as if in supplication to the Roman pantheon, and beneath it the marble seat littered with a scattering of wet leaves. She brushed the leaves aside, her mind contemplating the heavens as she sat, gazing out upon the clouded Neapolitan sky. It was her favorite place to think and pray.

She prayed for Skip and for Clarence, asking God to protect them in the barracks, and to increase their faith and give them wisdom. She sensed there was a spiritual opposition building, a counterattack, as it were, by demonic forces against the work of the Holy Spirit who was clearly drawing men to faith in Christ there. The devil didn't like losing souls, whether they were in New York or London, in some tribe along the Amazon or the Marine Barracks or Piazza del Municipio Square in Naples, Italy. He would do everything to keep them in his power. Maddie sensed that there were evil days ahead, a foreboding sense of approaching darkness against which the glory of God would shine through His servants. It both frightened and excited her.

A ferry trailing a silvery wake rounded the Santa Lucia point on its way to Ischia. She prayed that God would draw Jesse Calderon to Christ, and remove any obstacles to saving faith. She had seen him at the main gate on her way out of the base, and had handed him a tract. He had smiled deprecatingly at her, showing a mouthful of white teeth. He told her that he wasn't allowed to have reading materials or any other such contraband on post. But he had put it into his sock and told her that he would read it when he got off post.

Maddie believed him.

Finally she prayed for Nathan Kessler. She didn't know how to pray for him at first, so she prayed in generalities: God save him. God have mercy on him. God draw him to Jesus. Then, honing her thoughts, she prayed that God would remove the sword of anger from his heart, heal the wound caused by whatever act of cruelty or hypocrisy or wickedness that had made him bitter.

"Dear God, help him see you—see your great love for him. Help him to see Jesus."

As she prayed she felt a weight pressing against her chest, as if invisible hands held her heart in their grip and were squeezing it. She thought that she might suffocate beneath the pressure.

"Dear God, dear God, mercy." But there was no relief in her prayers. She felt as though she were wrestling invisible giant toads. The toads were winning. Then she was crying.

"God, I cannot bear this burden," she wept into her hands. "Please take it away from me. Please. Please. Dear God, please."

Chapter Nine

ONCE LIBERTY SOUNDED, Nathan showered

and shaved and put on a pair of blue jeans, a printed shirt
and western boots. As he combed his hair in the mirror
hanging inside his wall locker he could hear Skip
McPherson and some men across the hall, playing guitars
and singing "I Wish We'd All Been Ready." He'd heard
them singing it before. It was a song about the Second
Coming of Christ. There were two sailors as well, playing
guitars and singing, while Skip and the new black Marine
were reading Bibles.

Nathan shut the bedroom door, so that he was alone
in the room. He grabbed his sports bag out of his wall
locker and began packing for the weekend. He had put
another pair of jeans and shirts and sneakers into the bag
when a thought about the missionary girl stopped him
cold.

It wasn't an evil thought. It was a pleasant thought that set him back on his heels. He stared at the wall.

"Whaddya make of that, *amico*?" he said.

He walked over to the window, holding a pair of socks in his hand. A light fog was drifting over the hills, a gray gloom creeping ahead of it. He stared at cars coming into the base and leaving, his mind not on the cars nor on the Marine sentry waving them in. He walked back and sat down on his bed, still holding the socks, and looked across the room at nothing.

"So, what do you make of that?"

He could see her bright, pretty blue eyes that he was sure could root around in the dark nooks and crannies of his soul with fairy insight. He could see the light splash of freckles over an elfin nose that she touched from time to time with an embarrassed smile, see the red and yellow highlights in her impossibly thick hair radiant with dancing flames. Beneath these highlights, hidden in the luxuriant mass of buoyancy around her shoulders, were the dark embers glowing with a deeper flame of mystery.

He shook his head slowly. "No good, Nate. No good."

Maddie Gallagher had him talking to himself.

He'd been with pretty girls that disturbed him momentarily, but it had soon passed. Nico, for instance, possessed a beauty that could crush a man, but her beauty was a thin veneer over an old story that held no surprises. She was a fun read, of course, but Maddie disturbed him profoundly.

She was a beauty set apart, a beauty inside and out that sounded uncharted depths of mystery. The genuine article, a woman without guile, someone who both attracted and repelled him. Attracted him because he'd never met anyone like her before; repelled him for the same reason. Then he thought how a guileless person has a power the world cannot control. Kill, yes. Imprison, yes. Control, never. Perhaps that is what disturbed him.

"I like her, Nate."

"I like her too, Frankie."

"I'm glad you apologized."

"She's got me confused."

"I think you like her a lot. I'm rootin' for her."

Nathan stood, sat down again and peered over at the photo of his family. He took it off the side table and looked at each of them. There were five. His father Karl, tall and lean and serious, a one time architecture professor at Cal Poly. His mother Monica, olive-skinned and good-natured, saw the world as a happy place with good people, despite headlines to the contrary. Through his mother came his Latin heritage. His sister Linda, tall and idealistic, wore a pair of butterfly glasses that framed pale blue eyes. Nathan, a gangly thirteen year old, was standing next to her, his arm draped around her shoulder, a goofy expression on his face. Life was a joke to him then, a cartoon with a variety of punch lines. Finally there was Franklin—little Frankie, dragging his stuffed bear Farley by an arm, the other one hanging by a thread.

Nathan gazed at Frankie's round face; his saucer blue eyes, the laughing mouth. He felt his eyes mist, as they frequently did when he looked at the photo. He couldn't help it. The pain was still fresh, undiminished by time.

"I'm sorry, Frankie."

Frankie said nothing, but even so Nathan could hear him chiding. "Well, you apologized to her didn't you, Nate? She seems like a nice girl."

"She is."

"I think I would like her."

"I think so too, Frankie. I wish you could meet her."

Nathan cleared the emotion from his throat, set the photo back on the side table when he heard Cooper flip-flapping down the hall, singing "Born to be Wild." He frowned at the pair of socks he was still holding, tossed them into his sport bag and stood.

The door opened, stayed open. Cooper flip-flopped into the room, be-toweled and smiling, and opened his wall locker. "What's with the hootenanny? I see McPherson's got the newbie singing Jesus. You meet him yet?"

"Nope."

Cooper began brushing his hair in the door mirror. "Skip figures he's gonna convert the whole barracks. Watch out, Nate."

Nathan said nothing.

Cooper peered around the locker at him. "What's with you? You look dopey."

Nathan zipped up his leather toilet case and dropped it in the bag. "What've you got planned for the weekend, Coop?"

Cooper checked out his image in the mirror. "Gorilla and I are heading up to Pozzuoli. There's a house with Swedish girls."

"The place you went to last week?"

"The same. I hear they got fresh imports. Blonde hair and everything."

"Mick not going?"

"Got some high finance deal cooking in town, he says. Sure you don't wanna come? There's plenty to go around."

"I'm sure."

"Real Swedes, Nate. Straight from Sweden."

"What ever happened to the girl in the yellow snowsuit?"

"Lolie? Didn't I tell you? She got married. I was her last fling before holy matrimony."

"Lucky her."

"Poor husband. He'll never understand why she gets that thousand yard stare in her eyes every New Year's Eve." Cooper threw his head back and howled. "Aarrooooo! Are we gonna have ourselves a time!" He looked back across the hall and grinned. "Hey, Skip? Havin' a prayer meetin'?"

McPherson and the other men looked over at him. "Bible study," McPherson said, guardedly. "Care to join us?"

"Not just now, fellahs. I sincerely thank you for the invite though. No foolin'. But I've got matters of a carnal nature that require my immediate attention. You might pray that I'm successful."

McPherson said seriously, "We won't pray for that but we'll pray for you."

"Say, you guys are okay." Cooper glanced back at Nathan and made a face. "You ever seen a bigger group of morons? Somebody ought to shut 'em up. It's getting so you can't walk down the hall without somebody thumping you with a Bible."

Nathan made no comment. He zipped up his sport bag, lifted it off his bed, smoothed the wrinkles off the top olive drab blanket, and headed to the door. "Take it easy with those Swedish imports," he said.

Cooper grinned, closed his wall locker. "Don't bet on it."

Nathan went out of the room and down the hall, shaking his head, the guitar music following him. He went down three flights of stairs to the Quarterdeck, where Sergeant Halyard, a tall, long-faced black man with a lazy right eye was on duty.

"Big weekend, Kessler?"

"Big weekend."

"Where to?"

"Rome."

"Lucky dog. Don't do anything I wouldn't do."

"That opens the field of possibilities, doesn't it?"

"You bet."

"*Ciaó!*" Nathan went out of the barracks, down the short flight of stairs and walked across the parking lot to his car, popped open the trunk, and stowed his bag. Mick Donovan was pumping toward him from the main gate.

"Hey, Nate, hold on!"

Nathan stood waiting. Mick was hunch-shouldered walking fast. A man stood beside Luigi across the street from the main gate, an Italian in a dark overcoat. He was watching Mick.

Mick came up to Nathan, flushed. He glanced over the Fiat Spider 1600. "She sure is a beauty. Did I ever tell you about my '57 Chevy I got waitin' for me back home?   Candy apple red...chrome moons...glass packs...load levelers. The works."

Nathan shut the trunk. "What's up, Mick?"

Mick put his hand on Nathan's shoulder. "Listen, *amico*, I'm in a bit of a fix. I need twenty bucks, Italian. Can you spot me?"

"Didn't you get paid?"

"Sure, but I need another twenty. I gotta surefire deal cookin' that'll net twenty to one, easy."

Nathan peered across the street. The Italian with Luigi was looking over at them. At this distance Nathan couldn't make out his features or tell what he was thinking. Luigi was smoking a cigarette, nodding his head at the ground. "Twenty bucks is all you need for a surefire deal?" Nathan asked.

"Shoot, no. I already put the touch on some of the fellahs. Thought I had it all, but I'm still short the twenty."

"Luigi couldn't make up the difference?"

"That shark? No way. I'll get it back to you tonight, I promise."

"I won't be here."

"That's right, you're heading to Rome. Rome's great. You'll have a swell time. What do you say—twenty for ol' Mick. It'll be cleaned and pressed on your bed when you get back, with a fiver to keep it company. You got my word on it." Mick jerked a glance over his shoulder at the two men across the street. "Look, if you don't want to loan me just say it."

Nathan could see that Mick was in a hurry to get back to them. "I don't mind," he said, reaching for his wallet.

Mick ran a wet tongue over his thick lower lip, watching Nathan remove twelve thousand lire from his wallet. He snapped the bills out of Nathan's fingers. "You're a pal, *amico.* You won't regret it."

He started to leave, stopped abruptly to rub his palm once more over the smooth finish of the Spider. "You hit pay dirt with this baby," he said, admiring the car but Nathan could see that his mind was across the street. "You'll knock 'em dead in Rome, you got my word on it."

Mick started back across the parking lot with the bills in his fist, walking fast then skipping into a jog. Luigi and the Italian were still talking, the latter with his hands in the pockets of his overcoat.

Nathan shook his head, lowered into the bucket seat, started the ignition, pumped the accelerator a couple times to hear the throaty growl, and then drove to the main gate, where Lance Corporal Jesse Calderon, a short, round-faced Hispanic, waved him through. "Don't take any wooden lire, Kessler," he said, showing a mouthful of teeth.

"Not a chance," Nathan said. Turning left out of the gate, he glanced across the street where Mick and the two Italians seemed in a spirited conversation.

Nathan sped down the road to make the connections to the *autostrada*, first driving past the sellers of cheap statuary on the sidewalk, and then farther down on the right, past the campfire girls, who looked up as he passed. Then he drove onto the onramp. Nathan was happy to be heading north to Rome, happy to be getting away from the stench of Naples. By the time he opened her up on the *autostrada*, Maddie Gallagher no longer troubled his thoughts.

Chapter Ten

NATHAN PARKED THE Spider on a side street

off the Piazza di Spagna, in the heart of Rome, and made his way toward the Spanish Steps, where he and Nico had agreed to meet. The Piazza was wide and paved with smooth gray bricks. Crowds of tourists lined the street, looking into the shop windows beneath buildings of variegated colors of salmon and ochre and yellow. Directly ahead, at the base of the steps, was the fountain by Bernini, a fanciful boat-like sculpture, around which people sat feeding pigeons or throwing coins.

The Spanish Steps ascended the steep slope in wide terraces of travertine to the Piazza del Popolo with buildings on either side, like walls, overlooking the steps.

Couples and small groups of people were sitting at various levels of the steps: artists working, gigolos scouting, and people walking up and down, sometimes stopping to pose for photographs or to take in the scenery of Rome.

Nathan couldn't see Nico for the crowds. Then he saw her sitting midway up on the right side beneath the windows of the house in which Keats died. She was wearing pale yellow bell-bottoms, white blouse, and a blue and yellow beaded bolero jacket, her hair loose and piled on her shoulders. She was smoking, looking away from him. When he called her name, coming up the steps three at a time, she saw him, jumped to her feet and ran down the steps into his arms.

"Natti! Oh, Natti!" They kissed. "I've missed you, Natti."

He held her face tenderly in his hands, gazed into her beautiful eyes. "Nico. Nico."

"My beautiful Natti. Hold me, please hold me. Tighter."

Nathan held her as tight as he could without breaking her, kissing her once more, and then walked down the steps to the fountain. Arm in arm, they stopped again and kissed. "It is really you," she said.

"Yes."

People sat looking at the fountain. A woman wearing a black knit shawl squinted over at Nathan and Nico kissing, then turned her attention back to the fountain.

Nico wrapped her arms around Nathan's neck. "I have never been so happy, Natti. Please, where are you staying?"

"The Hotel Ara Pacis. It's nearby, I think."

"I know where it is."

They drove separately on the Via Condotti, Nico following in a canary yellow Alfa Romeo convertible. They crossed over the Tiber, and were soon parked in front of the hotel. It would have taken five minutes on foot.

Nico parked her car and met Nathan inside at the desk, coming up to him from behind, wrapping her arms around him and laying her head against the back of his neck. "Oh, Natti, I have so been looking forward to this day."

That afternoon they were sitting on the terrace café looking out at the street that encircled the Colosseum. He was drinking a glass of Birra Moretti, admiring the ancient structure, imagining what it might have looked like in its glory days. Those Romans sure had some fine architects, he thought.

He watched the cars and the young men and women on Vespa scooters and mopeds racing past, and then turned his gaze to admire Nico's face in the light that was quickly fading, the earthy colors of the buildings deepening into rich terra cotta hues.

She took a sip of Chardonnay, looked at him and smiled, smoking a cigarette. The wind was in her hair. "My lovely Natti. Did you miss me?"

"You know I did."

"Tell me how much."

"You are my goddess. Apart from you I am nothing."

"It is the same with me. I have no soul but you." She smiled, took another puff of her cigarette and, blowing a cloud of smoke to one side, tapping the ash in a metal ashtray, she glanced sidelong at him along her thick lashes. Her smile faded. "My mother has forbidden me to see you."

He looked at her.

"Because you are an American," she clarified. "It doesn't matter that I told her you were a Roman Catholic."

"She saw me in Roccaraso. Why did she not forbid you to see me then?"

"I told her you were German. But then she saw the return address of your letters."

"She's okay with Germans but not Americans?"

"Her father was killed by American soldiers during the war. He was a Fascist."

"That was thirty years ago."

"She is Italian." She smiled, smoking her cigarette.

"But here we are."

"Yes, I have disobeyed her. She thinks I am with friends. Not to worry. I will confess it to the priest on Sunday, so there is no need for concern." Nico took his hand. "We are here—together. Now. That is all we will ever have."

Nathan sipped his beer. "My grandfather was German, my grandmother was Italian. That should cover me from both ends."

"You wear an American uniform."

"Why didn't you tell me this in your letter?"

"I wanted to see you." She took his hand and squeezed it, her hazel eyes lucent with golden light. "I am crazy about you, Natti. I lay awake at night dreaming about Roccaraso. *Ti penso sempre.* I always think of you."

Nathan felt a sudden hollowness in his chest. "What are we going to do?"

"We have the rest of today and tomorrow and Sunday," she said. "We do not have to think about after. After belongs to no one. Would you like me to give you a tour of the Colosseum, or of Saint Peter's basilica? There are the wonderful Michelangelo frescoes, of course."

"I came to see you. You're all the Rome I want to see. Michelangelo could not imagine such beauty."

"You are very romantic for a Marine."

"When in Rome."

They were walking beneath the bare trees in the park along the Tiber, holding hands; the river, swollen gray and widely smoothing along its banks. "What would you like to do?" she asked.

"Do you have to ask?"

"Yes, and we shall. But let me show you my city."

They came to the Fontana di Trevi, where Neptune, driving a horse drawn shell chariot, was taming the waters with the help of sculpted tritons. There were tourists crowding the fountain, some sitting on the edge bathing their feet, others throwing coins.

Nico sat down on the ledge of the fountain. "You must turn your back to it and throw a coin," she said. "It will bring you back to the city."

"I saw the movie."

"No, but it is true."

"What if I throw two coins?"

"Then you will get married." She crossed the fore- and middle fingers of her right hand in a sign of good luck.

"And three?"

She shook her head, uncrossed her fingers. "Divorced."

"Two it is then." He reached into his pocket and pulled out a handful of change, selected two 20 lire coins, worth a few cents each. "Does it matter how much?"

"No, but you must throw them with your right hand. One at a time."

Nathan turned his back to the fountain and tossed a 20 lire coin over his right shoulder. "That takes care of Rome." He tossed a second one. "That takes care of your mother."

She laughed, dipped her hand in the water and swirled in gently. "Aren't we having a wonderful time?"

"The best."

"And we will spend our weekends together?"

"Every two weeks, like I said."

"I will come down to Naples next time. I do not think your coming to Rome would be wise." She swirled the water some more. "I have a better idea. As I have told you, our family owns a villa in Ischia. It is very lovely. We could spend the weekend there."

"You'd be able to get away?"

"I have done it before. It will take a conspiracy with my friends. Also, you must write a letter, saying that you have found another girl. I will cry for several days and refuse meals. My mother will find the letter that I will hide, so she will not suspect that we are together."

"Sounds very cloak and daggerish."

"Oh, but it is our adventure. Don't you remember?"

"I do. What time do you have to be home tonight?"

"Do not worry about tonight, my love. I am spending the night with my friend Sophia."

"Sophia?"

"It does not matter her name, it is only a fabrication."

"She is one of your co-conspirators?"

"She is my oldest and most trusted co-conspirator."

A dark, good-looking youth, wearing a purple shirt and black vest, glanced over at them. He stopped. "Nico."

"*Ciaó*, Federico."

Federico frowned at Nathan.

"This is my friend, Nathan Kessler," Nico said. "Nathan, this is Federico Cristofani. We are old friends."

Federico looked at her, it seemed with a little embarrassed smile, and shrugged his shoulders.

"Nathan is American," she said. "He is a US Marine."

"An American Marine? What's he doing here? I don't like the looks of him. Is he a tourist?"

"No. He came to see me."

"You? How do you know him?"

"Why don't you ask Nathan?"

"Ask *him*? What do you mean, ask him? Does he…?" Federico looked at Nathan, his face paling. "Do you speak Italian?"

Nathan grinned at him.

Federico shrugged. "I-I thought Americans only spoke English."

"English is just our cover language," Nathan said. "Do you speak English, Federico?"

"No. I speak French and German. And of course Italian."

"You are very brilliant, I'm sure."

Nico laughed. "Go ahead and say something in French, Federico." She pulled at Nathan's arm. "Do not take him seriously, Nathan. He is joking with you. Federico is a big kidder. Federico, tell Nathan that you are joking."

Federico made a noise in his throat.

"Where are you going, Federico?" she asked.

"I am going to the Caffé Greco. Tomasso and Lucia are meeting me there." He glanced at Nathan. "Perhaps you and your American friend would like to join us."

Nico turned to Nathan. "The Antico Caffé Greco is a very famous café."

"I've never heard of it."

"Oh yes, many of the great philosophers and poets and artists would meet there and discuss their ideas and their works. Goethe, Shelley, and Keats. Liszt and Wagner, of course. The list goes on." She whispered something in his ear and giggled.

"Casanova, huh?"

"Oh yes. Also, the coffee is very good. You will find none better…except, perhaps at the Rosati."

"Do they sell beer?"

"Beer? No, it is just for lovers of coffee and literary discussions."

"I'm not feeling very literary. Sorry."

Federico smiled at Nico. "I will tell Tomasso and Lucia that I saw you."

"Please do, Federico. *Ciáo.*"

"*Ciáo.*" Federico walked away through the crowd, his head lowered in thought.

"He didn't like me," Nathan said.

"We were lovers."

Nathan looked at her.

"It is over," she said. "I am sure that you've had lovers, no?"

"None that I care to talk about, or am likely to see when I am with you. Let's get out of here. I think I'm jinxing the fountain."

T HEY WALKED NORTH from the Trevi Fountain into the manicured grounds of the Villa Borghese, with its lakes and trees and sculptures and people walking enjoying the beauty of the park. There were small boys sailing boats in the lake, and old men watching them, and there were families picnicking and couples lying in the grass sunning. It was a beautiful day for a stroll through the park, the late afternoon sun shining, birds in the bare limbs of the trees.

Then they came out onto the Piazza del Popolo, the Obelisk of Pharaoh Ramses II in the center of the wide oval of the piazza, where people and great groupings of pigeons gathered. They sat at a table beneath the awnings on the terrace of the Café Rosatti.

Nathan ordered a beer and a white wine for Nico, and the two of them sat, smoking, watching the people and the traffic going by on the piazza.

"You did not think that I lived in a convent before I met you, did you, Natti?"

"Let's not talk about it."

The waiter brought the beer and the wine, and they were drinking, the sun going down across the piazza, so that the light got under the awning and showed the soft golden contours of her face.

"Natti, my love?" She rested her chin on a folded hand and gazed at him, smiling, her eyes alive in the light. "You are jealous of Federico?"

"No. Not here."

"I like it when you are jealous."

"I'm not jealous."

She stroked his hand with her fingers. "I'm not jealous of your girlfriends. I'm sure there have been many."

"Hundreds. What's with him?"

At the table next to them a longhaired bearded man in black shirt, black stovepipe trousers and sandals was making a passionate speech to two Italian women. The women were young and attractive. One was a dark brunette, wearing a stylish minidress and knee boots. The other, a blonde that was dyed and teased, wore a burgundy pantsuit with large tortoise shell sunglasses, and sat gazing down at the table, fingering a beaded necklace. Each had large shopping bags at their feet with "Dior" written on them.

Nico, whose back was to the trio, leaned forward and whispered in Nathan's ear. "He is talking about the recent elections."

"I take it he's not too happy with the results."

"He says there will be trouble with the Red Brigades, which he welcomes, since he is a communist."

"The Red Brigades?"

"Yes, you've seen them in the streets with their red flags and banners."

"I haven't seen them."

"You might not, in Naples," she said. "They are from around Turin and Milan, but I have seen them here in Rome. They are Marxists. They want Italy to separate from the Western Alliance."

"You mean NATO."

"Of course."

Nathan sipped his beer. He was happy with the change in subject, and felt bad about his childish jealousy over Federico. Who made him morality judge? Who had given him a stone to cast?

The girls at the table were listening politely, sipping wine and trading glances, as the man, leaning forward on his elbows, made enthusiastic gestures to emphasize points of his speech.

The blonde looked over at Nathan and smiled, and Nathan knew that she was embarrassed by the speech.

"I don't think they're buying it," he said.

"No." Nico, leaning forward and cupping her hand beside her mouth, said, "He is trying to convince them it would be better for Italy—if Italy knew what was good for Italy—to distance itself from the Western Alliance. But of course Italy does not know what is good for Italy. She never did. And so there is a need for organizations like the Red Brigades."

"I can hear most of it. He has a thick accent."

"He is from Venice. The Venetians have the accents of pigs." She leaned back in her chair discreetly, smoking, turning her head just enough to blow smoke away from their table without seeming to eavesdrop.

"Now what's he saying?" Nathan asked.

She leaned forward, tapped the ashtray with her cigarette. "He is saying that the Western Alliance is the source of the economic disparity between the working classes of Italy and the wealthy. It is a crime that the wealthy have so much and the poor so little."

"The old drill. What do you think?"

"I think he is a gigolo. In the end he is happy to be at a table with two pretty girls, and would like to redistribute some of their wealth."

"No, I mean about the elections?"

"Me? I'm not political. I think people that are political are angry people. Life is too short to be angry, don't you think?" She took a sip of wine and tapped her cigarette. "We should live to be happy. To me happiness is a virtue."

"Did you learn that at the Café Greco—eat, drink, and be merry, for tomorrow we die?"

"Yes, but today we live." She touched his foot under the table. "That is why you should not be jealous of Federico. What has passed between us has passed."

Nathan felt it rising in him again. "Does Federico share your convictions?"

"I believe so, but he is young."

"Am I young too?"

She raised an eyebrow at him, tapped her cigarette in the ashtray. "You are being silly. You cannot compare yourself with Federico. You are a man and he is a child, and I am crazy about you. There is only you and me now and the happiness we enjoy in each other's arms."

"Are we happy?"

"I could not be happier. Don't tell me that you are sad, my love. I couldn't bear it."

"No more talk about Federico, okay?" he said. "We're here together, and that's all that matters."

She squeezed his hand. "I would sell my soul for your happiness, Natti—you know I would—and let the devil take all."

"Shall we order dinner?"

"After I have kissed you."

Chapter Eleven

MEN AND WOMEN from the Navy and Marine

barracks and hospital, along with Maddie Gallagher, were playing tag football on one of the fields in the crater of an extinct volcano, five miles northwest of the NSA base in Bolanaro. Maddie went long for a pass, running a zigzag pattern deep into defensive territory, when she turned and saw the football spiraling toward her on a flat trajectory. She caught the ball against her stomach, felt the wind leave her lungs, wheeled into Jesse Calderon and bowled him over. The two of them rolled over the grass, limbs intertwining, Maddie holding onto the football as they twisted to a halt.

Phweet! Phweet! Skip McPherson whistled, running over to them. "First down! First down! Great catch, Red."

Maddie was staring at a blade of grass. "What happened?"

"We've got them on the run."

"We do?"

Skip took her arm and helped her to her feet. He cast a censuring eye at Jesse. "Ya big bully. This is supposed to be tag football."

"She ran over *me*."

"Sure. Pass interference. Fifteen yard penalty."

"Aren't you going to help me to my feet?"

Clarence Pearsall came over to him and extended an arm. "Here you go, Jesse. I can see we're up against some ruthless characters."

The two teams made quick loose huddles, then faced each other on the line of scrimmage, four on each side, two men and two women to a side.

Skip called the play. There were only two: run short and run deep. He'd pass to anyone open. Bill Porter, a stout sailor attached to the Naval hospital, snapped the ball at Skip's "Hut, hut," lunged into the incoming legs of Tim Macay, a fellow swabbie who was equally stout, and caught him at shin level.

Tim did a straight-armed and legged somersault over Bill with some artistic embellishments, hit the ground solidly and chewed grass.

Maddie once again went deep, shadowed by Jesse who, running alongside her, waved his arms crazily. Darlene Beaumont, a tall lanky blonde, went short, Nancy Peters covering her. Both women, wearing Navy sweatshirts, blue jeans and sneakers, were lieutenant jg nurses. They sang in the base chapel choir and played a mean game of tag football.

Maddie, running fierce-eyed, faked a move to the right but went left, leaving Jesse chasing air. "Skip! Skip! I'm free!"

Clarence appeared out of nowhere in front of her, his arms extended. "Yeah, throw the ball, Skip!"

"Hey—watch the pass interference," she said, executing a daring flanking move. "Skip! Skip!"

Skip, stepping over Tim's groping hands, shot her a look, eyes wide then narrowing. When he saw that Darlene was clear he launched the ball on a high arcing curve. Darlene, towering over a shorter, plumper Nancy, leapt and caught the ball then ran elbows and knees for the end zone.

"Touchdown!" she shouted, tossing the football into the air.

"Five to four," Skip said, gloating. "That breaks the tie. You guys had enough?"

Clarence picked up the football. "Never."

Darlene looked at her wristwatch. "Oh boy, it's already four-thirty. Nancy and I have to get back to the hospital." She headed over to the picnic table to collect her purse.

"It was a lot of fun," Nancy said. "We'll get you guys next time." She called Darlene, "Could you get my purse, Dar?"

Darlene was walking toward them, loose-limbed, with wide moving hips holding the balance of her spine as though it were a tower of teacups. "Got it," she said. She came up to the group, handed a purse to Nancy and turned to Bill and Tim. "You guys coming back with us, or are you sticking around?"

The corpsmen looked at each other. "Let's head," Bill said. "Don't fancy having to thumb a ride."

Tim agreed.

"We could squeeze you into the *cinque cento*," Maddie offered.

Bill grinned. "Thanks, but I'm not a contortionist. See you later at the Station." The two nurses and corpsmen headed across the field toward the parking lot.

Clarence was spinning the football with his fingers. "Anybody want some more?" He passed the ball to Skip.

Skip, spreading his fingers along the stitching, looked at Maddie. "How 'bout you, Red?"

"I'm bushed," she said. "I'm gonna sit this one out."

Skip threw the ball back to Clarence and walked with Maddie off the field. "Sorry, Clarence. We're going to rest on our laurels."

"Chickens."

They walked over to a wooden picnic table at the edge of the field in Carney Park, where they had eaten a lunch of cold chicken, potato salad and soft drinks. The sky was iron hard and gray as a ship's hull, against which curved the gray green rise of the volcano.

Maddie sat on the bench seat with her back against the edge of the tabletop, sipping her drink thoughtfully as she gazed out over the acres of playing fields and ball diamonds of the park that had been developed by the military for servicemen and their families. People of various military ethnicities were playing softball or soccer or picnicking, enjoying the park on a Sunday afternoon with a regatta of white clouds scudding overhead.

"Great idea coming here, Skip," she said.

Skip was sitting on top of the table beside her, leaning back with his ballplayer hands planted on the tabletop behind him, fingers spread for support, his head lowered into his broad shoulders, with his long athlete's legs crossed at the ankles over the edge of the bench seat. "I've always wanted to come here. I see they've got a golf course."

"A nine-holer. You're a ballplayer, do you play golf?"

Skip shook his head. "Never tried it."

Maddie watched Clarence and Jesse running plays, throwing the ball. "How's it going with Jesse?"

"He's getting close I think."

"I thought he was going to go forward in church this morning. He and Clarence have hit it off."

Skip nodded at the two men playing football. "Clarence is a born evangelist."

A cold wind blew through the bare limbs of the sycamores that grew in sheltering clusters between the picnic tables. Maddie, cooling from the game, felt a chill over her body and put her windbreaker on over her pale yellow sweatshirt. "Brrrrr," she said.

Skip glanced over at the western rim of the volcano. "Sun's going fast."

Maddie sat huddled in her windbreaker, watching a serviceman and his girl walking arm in arm along the edge of the field beneath the trees. The girl stopped abruptly, leaned back against a tree trunk and he kissed her. "Gonna marry that girlfriend of yours when you get out of the Corps, Skip?"

"If she'll have me."

"If she's anything like you describe, she'll have you. Let me see that photo you're always admiring."

Skip got out his wallet and removed a worn and faded color photograph from the window and handed it to her. It was a graduation photo of a pretty brunette smiling to one side of the camera. "Jacqueline," he said. "Jackie."

"She's beautiful. Was she your high school sweetheart?"

"I met her in junior college. We shared a Bunsen burner." He grinned. "I guess you could say we had great chemistry."

Maddie laughed. "And a romance has been heating up ever since?" She handed him back the photo. "Thought about what you want to do when you get out?"

"I'm going back to school…finish my undergraduate work and then go on for a seminary degree."

She looked at him. "You want to be a pastor?"

"That or a missionary. I like what your dad does."

"Ever think of becoming a chaplain?"

"Yes I have," Skip said, returning his wallet to his pocket. "I have a real burden for servicemen."

He gazed out at the field. Clarence and Jesse were talking to some men. "I guess because I know what they're going through. They're all alone, miles away from home. I know what they think about at night on their beds—out on post. They're thinking about their families, their girlfriends—their pals. They're caught between a world that was and their hopes for some kind of a future. In between those worlds is a void they struggle to fill. So the devil comes along with his bag of tricks and dangles the carrot. He doesn't tell them that everything he gives is smoke and mirrors with a hefty price tag. I tell them. I have to."

"So they hate you."

"Some of them do."

Clarence and Jesse had a game going with the men. "How's it going in the barracks?" Maddie asked. "Dad said he talked to Chaplain Simms."

"Things are heating up a bit." Skip sat forward, rested his elbows on his knees and rubbed his hands. "Yesterday we had a surprise room inspection," he said. "I have a picture of Jesus praying in Gethsemane—you know the one by Carl Block. They made me take it down."

"Can they do that?"

"If it's framed and not offensive they let us put up pictures. All the guys have one thing or another on their walls." Skip shrugged. "Apparently Jesus praying is offensive."

"Can't you go to your CO?"

"He was leading the inspection."

She raised her eyebrows. "Hmm."

"I guess some of the men have been complaining about me handing out tracts."

"You did that at your last duty station, didn't you?"

"I did. The CO actually commended me for it—a full bird Colonel. There'd been some racial tension between some of the Marines. A black guy named Wiburne, a white guy named Sugarman. They were the leaders of rival groups in the barracks. I shared the gospel with both of them. They both came to Christ and things quieted down. Wiburne and Sugarman became best friends."

"Imagine that."

"The CO told me I could use the Rec Room for Bible studies if I wanted to. Quite a few of the guys came— black, white, brown. Didn't matter what the color of their skin was." He smiled. "But this is Naples."

"It's a demonic stronghold, Skip. My dad has never sensed it so strongly. I think you've got the devil upset."

"Seems like."

The sun dipped below the rim of the volcano and sent up a corona of golden light that quickly dimmed. Birds flew against the turquoise gloaming, their shapes fleeting and dark. The fields began to thin with families now heading to their cars.

Maddie glanced down at her blue jeans, saw that her knees were grass-stained with mud clots in the seams.

She wiped off what she could, and then with her fingertips traced the multi-colored threads of the *Ixthus* fish she'd embroidered on her jeans. Her mind was once again in the cafeteria of the Admin building. She could see Nathan grinning at her; the hard Marine face that she felt was hiding a story of pain or bitterness—certainly a mask to shield an immortal soul from the light. But she could see him behind the mask, a wounded soul. *Have mercy, God. Have mercy.*

"Earth to Maddie."

She started out of her thoughts.

Skip's hands were cupped around his mouth. "You're a million miles away."

She smiled, glanced away at the tree where the couple had been kissing. They were now walking along the edge of the golf course, his arm around her waist. "What do you know about Nathan Kessler?" she asked.

"Nathan? I don't know him that well. He seems a decent enough sort. He's a squared away Marine, but that's not what you asked."

"God has laid him on my heart."

Skip looked at her. "That'd be something, wouldn't it? I haven't had a chance to talk to him yet."

"I have. He's hard. Real hard."

"So was I at one time."

A laugh jumped impulsively in her throat. "I can't sleep at night praying for him. I've got a weight on my chest that won't leave. It's crushing me."

And then, just as impulsively as she had laughed, she felt her eyes moisten, her throat swell with emotion. "Here it comes again." She wiped her eyes, laughed the emotion out of her throat. "Is this weird, or what?"

"Not so weird."

Maddie stared at him.

"Is there anything more to it, do you think?" he asked.

"I don't know what you mean."

"Is this burden you have for Nathan the same as it was for Clarence…or Jesse? Any of the other men who come to the Station?"

Maddie continued to stare.

Skip shrugged, shook his head and watched the men scrimmaging on the field in the waning light. "He's a good-looking guy."

"What are you saying, Skip?"

"Wouldn't be the first time a Christian fell for an unbeliever."

"For me it would." Maddie stared at him a moment longer, felt a sob swell in her throat. She glanced away at the far rim of the volcano, the volcano dark in a range of purple shadows, her face glowing in the sunless twilight. Then she was crying.

Skip leaned over and put his arm around her. "It's okay, Red. I'm sorry I said anything."

"I don't believe this," she said huskily. She wiped the tears off her cheek with the sides of her thumbs. "This can't be happening."

Chapter Twelve

NATHAN DROVE BACK to the barracks, parked the Spider in the lot beneath a light, and went into the Quarterdeck with his bag. The Quarterdeck was a small ground floor entry room at the top of a short flight of cement steps, tiled with polished terrazzo upon which sat a gray metal desk. To the left of the glass entrance doors was a stairwell that led up to floors housing the administration wing and living quarters for each of the two platoons, as well as down one level to the basement, where supplies were kept.

Sergeant Turpick, a flat top strawberry blond with piercing blue eyes and a chest full of ribbons, had duty. The clock on the wall behind him read 0130 hours. He looked up from the log, his eyes exuding testosterone. "Good time in Rome, Kessler?"

"You bet. Anyone else still out?"

Turpick read the log. "Donovan. Knowing Mick, he probably won't get back much before inspection."

"Doubt it." Nathan checked the guard roster, saw that he had the 12:00 to 4:00, at post #10. "Looks like I've graduated to AFSOUTH."

"What post?"

"Ten."

"Ah, the ghost post."

"Ghost post?"

"What's the matter, Kessler...ghosts spook you?"

Nathan laughed. He walked upstairs to the third level, went through the opened fire door into the hallway. The hallway was deserted and quiet, the terrazzo gleaming in the yellow overhead lights.

He walked as quietly as he could down the length of the hall, past closed doors, one or two showing thin bars of light at their thresholds. His boot heels made soft muted thuds in the echoing stillness. Then at the far end of the hall a sharp wedge of light spilled out of his room into the floor of the hall.

He entered the room and saw Cooper sitting on a towel on the edge of his bed. His hair was wet as if he'd just come out of the shower. He was looking down at himself.

"Hey, Coop," Nathan said, closing the door behind him. He crossed the room and tossed his overnight bag onto his bed. "What's going on? You look lousy."

Cooper turned his head with a hollow-eyed expression. "I think I caught something."

Nathan walked over and looked. "You caught something. Those Swedes gave you a little bonus."

"It can't happen this fast, can it?"

"You were there a couple weeks ago, weren't you? Figure it out."

Cooper stared blankly. "They weren't even Swedes. They were Italians with dyed hair, and talked with fake accents. Can you believe it?"

"*Caveat Emptor.*"

"Huh?"

"Best get up to the dispensary," Nathan said. "A shot of penicillin will take care of it. What about Gorilla?"

"He's got it worse than I do."

"Sounds like a good time was had by all."

Cooper's eyes sank back into a fixed and vacant stare.

"Want me to go to the dispensary with you?" Nathan asked. He nudged Cooper on the shoulder. "Coop?"

Cooper blinked to life, it seemed out of a death coma. "Did you say something, Nate?"

"Want me to take you to the dispensary?"

"Would you?"

"Sure. Where's Gorilla?"

"Gorilla?" Cooper looked over at the closed door. "Last I saw he was in the head, blubbering."

"I'll get him."

POST #10, AFSOUTH, was located in one of four identical U-shaped, brick and glass buildings, used by the Allied Forces Southern Command. The buildings were three stories tall and stood, side-by-side, facing their twins across a manicured square of lawn that was bisected by paved walkways that connected the buildings. At the head of the square, separated by a paved grinder, used for parking and formations, stood NATO military Headquarters for southern Europe, a long, rectangular edifice in which the offices of the flag admiral, his staff and other NATO brass were located. In front stood a rank of white flagpoles, each sporting a flag representing a NATO country snapping proudly in the gray winter breeze.

According to prevailing barracks lore that Nathan had recently gleaned, the building known as Post #10, or the "ghost post," had once been a hospital before the Second World War. He had heard that when the Germans took over the complex, they allegedly slaughtered everyone inside, men, women and children, the ghosts of whom had reportedly haunted the halls and offices ever since. Many of the Marines (as well as *carabinieri*) had cited weird, paranormal happenings: typewriters tapping by themselves, lights coming on after they'd been turned off, radios turning on and off, shadowy figures lurking in dark niches.

One of the more celebrated stories Nathan had heard had supposedly occurred in the early morning hours of a 12:00 to 4:00 shift. Naturally. A Marine and *carabiniere* were standing duty at the front desk beside the glass entry doors. Apparently both men heard footsteps descending the wide tiled stairs that led down into the spacious foyer. This was odd, since the building had been cleared of personnel and secured hours before. The guard and *carabiniere* looked, expecting to see a body accompanying the footsteps, but there was no one, only footsteps. The bodiless footsteps crossed the foyer, passed in front of the desk, one of the doors opened of its own accord, and whatever opened it spirited away, followed by a screaming *carabiniere.* Why the spook didn't just go through the walls was never addressed in the story, but it made for interesting briefing to the barracks newbies.

"Ain't no lie, Natboy," Mick Donovan said in the middle seat of the guard vehicle. "I'm a big believer in spooks."

"Since when?"

"Since I seen one. Honest to Chesty."

Nathan had the window seat on Mick's left, and glanced out at the passing scenery. "What did the spook look like?"

"The spook itself was kind of fuzzy. Like a shadow— but I could feel him. Big as life."

Nathan raised an eyebrow at him. "Feel him, huh?"

"You bet. Seen him too."

"Sure."

"There I was on the second floor, checking offices, going room to room, and all of a sudden it felt like a nail dragging up my back. Goose pimples like a bride. I swung around and there it was, whooshin' across the hall. Gave me the heebie-jeebies to beat all."

"A spook."

"You don't believe me. I don't blame you—I wouldn't either." He jerked his head at Jesse Calderon in the back seat. "You seen 'em, right, Jesse?"

Jesse shook his head. "I never saw a spook."

Mick frowned. "Maybe Mexicans don't see spooks, but I saw it."

Nathan grinned. "Whooshin'."

"You bet whooshin'. One side of the hall to the other. If I'm lyin' I'm dyin'."

Nathan had hoped for some ghost activity on the post; nothing too grandiose or malevolent, a small spook or poltergeist would do, anything supernatural. He listened for the sound of a radio, the light patter of footsteps, a faint whooshing in the halls. He looked expectantly for a light to flicker on, a shadow to shift. Nothing happened, unless the disappearance of the *carabiniere* standing duty with him could be considered paranormal. Once the heavyset, blue-jowled man had arrived and given a spiritless greeting, he yawned, massaged his wide belly with chubby fingers, then took his thermos and dinner bag and scuffed away toward one of the back offices on the first floor. He wasn't seen again for the remainder of the watch.

Without apartment buildings to observe and create humorous scenarios, Nathan filled most of his watch on the ghost post dreaming up scary gags for Ol' Prive cartoons. Once his ideas were exhausted, he gave audience to the theater of the mind; however, it wasn't Nico who occupied center stage, it was Maddie. Again.

She haunted him.

"Nate, DO YOU believe in ghosts?"

"No, Frankie."

"I do."

"Why, have you ever seen one?"

"No, but I get goose pimples to beat all when I watch a scary movie. There have to be ghosts."

"Sure."

"That 'Brides of Dracula' movie we watched tonight was sure scary, wasn't it?"

"It sure was. Just remember there was a film crew filming those vampires. They were just acting."

Frankie seemed relieved. "I love you, Nate."

"I love you too, Frankie. Now go to sleep."

"Can I sleep in your room?"

"No. You're a big boy. No need to be afraid of the dark."

Nathan found him sleeping on the floor by his bed in the morning.

Chapter Thirteen

Maddie got out of bed and did her morning stretching exercises—toe touches, ceiling reaches, windmills—the muscles in her arms and legs sore from playing football. She sat on the floor and pointed her toes, legs together, lowering her face to her knees and holding the soles of her feet. She felt the burn in her hamstrings and lower back, holding the position for a ten-count. Then she varied the exercise, making a V with her legs, locking the backs of her knees and bending toward one foot, holding her ankles for a ten-count, and then stretching toward the other, likewise, until she felt her back and legs limber. Then she hooked her toes under the bed frame and, clasping the back of her head with her hands, proceeded to do fifty sit-ups, touching left elbow to right knee, right elbow to left knee. She hated sit-ups, but suffered through them in order to maintain a flat belly.

Afterwards she stood, cooling, taking in measured breaths through her nose and out through her mouth, rubbing her arms as she looked out the window. The sun was just coming up over the Galleria with golden light glinting on the water in the harbor.

Thoughts of Nathan edged into her mind as stealthily as a cat. She wondered what it would be like to feel his warm embrace, his strong arms holding her close to him. What it would be like to feel his lips against hers.

"No!" she said out loud, shooing the thoughts away. "It can never happen. Not without you, Lord."

She let go a heavy sigh. Then she padded down to the bathroom and showered, enjoyed a modicum of hot water, then came back to her room and shrugged on her light brown corduroys and a powder blue turtleneck sweater. She brushed her hair in the mirror over her dresser, secured it with a broad yellow elastic band, looked at herself, frowned at her freckles, shook her head and left the room, ready to face the day.

Her mother, in robe and curlers, was scrambling eggs in the kitchen. Her father and brother were at the table. "Good morning, Mom," she said.

"Good morning, honey. Coffee's ready."

"Smells delicious." She went over and poured a cup.

"What are your plans today, honey?"

"I don't know. I thought I might take a bus up to Caserta and do a little shopping."

"That sounds like fun. Shoe alley?"

"I need to. The soles on my boots are wearing a little thin. Want to come?"

"I might."

Maddie went around the counter to the table with her coffee and sat down next to her father. He was reading the *Star Spangled Banner* newspaper. Her father was a fine looking man with rugged features and ruddy complexion, with bright blue eyes the color of robin's eggs, and when he wore his reading glasses he always reminded her of a rather large, fierce elf.

Maddie glanced through the opening into the kitchen and watched her mother working at the range, her face an expression of peace and contentment. Of joy. What a beautiful marriage her parents had. Two people who loved God and one another, a love that they showered upon their children and upon so many servicemen and women. How she longed for such a life and love for herself and the man of her dreams. She glanced back at her father.

Flynn must have felt her eyes on him, for he looked up from the newspaper, his eyes twinkling over the half-glasses perched on his nose. "Good morning, fighter pilot."

"Good morning, Dad."

"Sleep well?"

"Fine."

His eyes narrowed. "Is there something on your mind?"

"I was just thinking how blessed you and Mom are."

"Blessed? We are blessed indeed," he smiled. "But you help make it so. Anything else…?"

She shook her head, but she knew that her Dad could probably read her every thought as clearly as the newspaper. "We gonna have a good crowd tonight?" she asked, hoping to change the subject.

"I hope so. The Fleet will be leaving for deep water maneuvers in a couple weeks."

"I didn't hear that."

"Let's hope the Lord brings in a good harvest before they leave."

A slurping sound drew Maddie's gaze across the table. Her little brother was hunched over a bowl of Cocoa Krispies, his left hand holding the box as he looked over the drawing on the back. "Good morning, Sean."

He said nothing. His eyes darted a sideways glance at her left hand, as if it was her hand that had greeted him. Then he extended the fingers of his left hand, peered at them nonchalantly, as if making a comparison, then clasped the box.

"Is there something wrong with my hand, Sean?"

He glanced at her quickly, chocolaty milk dribbling down his chin. "Wha-uddya mean?"

"You keep looking at it, then looking at yours. I've got four fingers and a thumb, just like you." She held up her hand, wiggled the fingers and thumb.

Sean flicked a look at her hand.

"And look at this," she said, touching the tip of her little finger with her thumb. "My thumb is opposable. Contrary to yours." She saw that it went over his head.

He frowned at her. "Yeah? Well, I'm glad," he said, and shot another quick glance at her hand.

"Would you like to take a picture of my hand, Sean? Then you can admire it all day."

"Can I outline it on paper instead?"

Now she frowned.

"It's part of my Science homework," he said, shoveling in another mouthful and talking with his mouth open. "I gu-tta outline ten hands—five boys and five girls." He swallowed. "I already got Mom and Dad's."

Maddie looked at her Dad who, not looking up from the paper, extended his right hand and wiggled his digits, as if to verify Sean's words.

Sean continued, "Miss Hampton said that girls' index fingers are longer than their third fingers. Boys' are shorter."

Maddie frowned at her fingers, noted that her forefinger was indeed longer than her ring finger. She'd never paid attention to it before. "Let me see yours."

"Only if you let me outline your hand. I just need one more girl."

"Fine."

Sean held up an all-boy's hand, complete with stumpy fingers with frayed cuticles and grubby nails that had been chewed down to the nubs. His forefinger was shorter than his third finger by a nail width.

"Hmmm." She glanced over at her father's hand holding the paper.

Flynn held out his hand a second time, still reading, and wiggled the fingers. Maddie compared his with hers.

Flynn lowered the paper, checked his watch. "You about ready, Sean?"

"Sure, Dad." Sean raised his cereal bowl to his mouth and slurped the dregs of chocolaty milk. He wiped his mouth with the back of his sleeve. "After I trace Maddie's hand."

Sean got out a sheet of paper from his binder and came around the table and placed it on the table in front of Maddie. "Lay your hand down. Oh yeah, and spread your fingers."

She laid her hand down on the paper and spread her fingers. "Like this?"

Sean ignored her, chewing his lower lip as he outlined her fingers with a number 2 pencil. He wrote "girl" in the upper right corner. "There. We can go now, Dad."

Flynn folded the newspaper. "First clear your bowl and brush your teeth."

"Aw…" Sean started to protest but it withered under his father's steady gaze. He carried his bowl into the kitchen and disappeared down the hall. A minute later he reappeared with a grin. "All done, Dad."

"Now go back and brush the other half."

Maddie watched the two of them leave and breathed out a wistful sigh. *Family.*

MADDIE SAT IN the quiet void made by her father's and brother's departure. She gazed across the room at the slanting bars of sunlight over the linoleum floor, through which dust moats twinkled like laughing fairies. In some recessed part of her mind morning sounds played quietly like obedient children: dishes clinking softly in the kitchen, the muted drone of city traffic, the hushed ticking of the mantel clock over the fireplace, a voice student on the floor below searching for notes. The fore part of her mind was occupied with thoughts about Nathan Kessler. Troubling thoughts. She would shut him out but always, when she'd let down her guard, he would tiptoe back and whisper her name.

Her mother came over and sat down beside her with a cup of coffee. "You sure you don't want some breakfast, honey?"

"I'm really not hungry, Mom."

"How can you go shopping on an empty stomach? You need fortification."

Maddie turned in her chair. Her mother was smiling at her, her hazel eyes catching glints of morning light. Even in rollers and without makeup, in a robe that had passed its prime years ago, she was a beautiful woman. "Mom, tell me the story of how you met Dad."

"You must know it by heart by now."

"I do, but I love to hear it."

"All right." Kitty thought about what she was going to say, took a sip of coffee, settled back in her chair and began the story that Maddie had heard more than a dozen times since she was a little girl.

"I was working the cosmetics counter at Macy's in San Francisco, and in walks this tall, good looking Marine 2nd Lieutenant with a red crewcut."

"He was a show stopper, wasn't he?"

"I'll say he was. I couldn't take my eyes off of him. He was wandering through the aisles, shopping. I caught him looking in my direction a couple of times, as if undecided about something. I asked him if he needed help. He came over to my counter and said he was having trouble picking out a Christmas present for his girlfriend. He said he was on his way to Korea and wanted to get her something special before he left. That took the wind out of my sails, as you can imagine."

Maddie smiled. "I'm sure."

"Lucky girl," I thought, but in a spirit of magnanimity I suggested a bottle of perfume. Perfume is a sure bet. He thought that it was a little too ordinary. His girlfriend was not at all ordinary. She was beautiful and mysterious. This didn't impress me in the least, but I told him that when she touched a little of his gift behind her ears, it would remind her of him all day."

"He liked that of course," Maddie said. "Dad the romantic."

"He asked if a ring wouldn't be better. I asked if he and his special girl were engaged, and he said not yet, but that he had high hopes. I said a ring is always nice, and that we had a good assortment that were quite reasonable. When he told me his budget I said that perfume was always a winner, and that we had some lovely perfumes in his price range."

Maddie laughed. "Dad the big spender."

"Dad the Irish." Kitty smiled, took a sip of coffee.

"I showed him our samples. He knew nothing about perfumes, of course, so he asked if I had a favorite. I told him that my favorite was much too expensive for a girl on my income. It was outside his budget as well.

He wanted to smell it. So I got out a bottle of Channel #5, and rubbed a little on my wrist. I said if his girl was as beautiful and mysterious as he said then this was the thing. He assured me that she was a goddess. This didn't score any points with me either, but when he leaned over to smell my wrist I thought I was going to die. My heart did flip-flops in my throat! That chiseled face almost touching my skin—let me tell you."

Maddie giggled.

"Then he noticed my bracelet."

"The one Grandma Hammond gave you with the silver cross?"

Kitty nodded. "He asked if it was just decoration, or if it had a spiritual significance. I told him that I was a Christian. He said he was too. That's why he'd asked.

We talked for an hour, in between customers, until the store manager came over and asked if I needed help with this particular customer, since he seemed to be indecisive as to a purchase. He bought the perfume. I gift-wrapped it for him and he left.

Two days later I got a little package in the mail. It was addressed to the beautiful blonde girl at the perfume counter—the one with the cross bracelet."

"What about the girlfriend?"

"There was no girlfriend. He had come to the store to buy a gift for his mother and saw me. The girlfriend was a ruse."

"A lie, you mean."

"A ruse. He really did buy it for his girlfriend. Me."

"I love that story." Maddie sat thinking about it. "And you didn't see him again for over a year."

"Not until he got back from Korea. I prayed for him every day. I kept seeing the news in the papers and worried constantly."

"That must have been difficult."

"I lost ten pounds," Kitty said. "And I didn't have ten pounds to give away. God taught me to trust Him during that time...how to cast all my cares before him."

"When did you first know you were in love with him?"

Kitty tilted her head and frowned. "Have I ever told you this before?"

Maddie shook her head. "I've never asked."

"Really?"

Maddie shook her head.

"Hmmm..." Kitty looked down at the table, smoothed a hand over the clean surface. "When did I first know?"

A smile began to play in the corners of her mouth; her eyes capturing even more light. "We wrote letters. I sent more than I received, but I knew he couldn't always write. I treasured each one. Each letter taught me a little bit more about him. His interests, his dreams for the future. His call to the ministry. He gradually came into focus like a Polaroid."

One morning I woke up, looked over at his picture on my night stand, and realized I couldn't live without him. I couldn't tell you the day or what was so special about that particular morning, but I knew I was in love."

"No bells and whistles?"

"There were bells and whistles, sure. But I can't remember a specific moment when they sounded. He proposed to me the day he got back from Korea. I accepted. We were married six months later."

Maddie felt her eyes water.

Kitty looked at Maddie and smiled. "One day you'll have a story to tell your daughter."

Maddie averted her eyes. In the silence the clock continued to tick, the drone outside became a little louder, the voice student had found some notes and strung them together into a pleasant melody.

"Is there something you would like to talk about, Maddie?"

"No, Mom. Did you keep any of dad's letters?"

"Every one. Would you like to read some?"

"Would it be intruding?"

"Not for you, honey."

Chapter Fourteen

MADDIE CAUGHT A bus to Vomero hill,
walked down to her favorite place and sat on the marble
seat overlooking the Bay of Naples. The skies were
bleakly gray and sodden over the bay, the distant islands
shrouded in a gray gloom. She set the shoebox on the
seat beside her and removed the lid.

Inside were two bundles of letters, one larger than
the other, each bound with a ribbon. The letters covered
the months between August, 1950, through September,
1951. She untied the first bundle, the smaller one. The
envelopes were addressed to Caitlin Hammond, her
address in San Francisco. The return FPO/APO address
showed that they were sent by 2nd Lieutenant Flynn
Gallagher USMC. The ratio of letters was three of hers
to one of his. She set the bundle on the seat beside her.

The second larger bundle had the addresses reversed. She untied it also and set it down beside the first bundle.

She took the first letter on top of the smaller pile, opened it and read. Her father's handwriting was scrawly but legible. The letter asked Caitlin if she had received the perfume and how she liked it. He confessed that there was no girlfriend but that he had said it in order to talk with her. He hoped that she would forgive him for his deception.

He gave censor-proof indications of his situation in Korea. Nothing too revealing or in depth. He was assigned to the staff of Chesty Puller, a colorful Marine. He ended the letter with a cordial close, asking if she wouldn't mind him writing to her.

Maddie set the letter face-down in the shoebox and picked up the first letter in the larger bundle. Her mother's handwriting had not changed over the years. It was neat, legible, and with dramatic embellishments of her capital letters. Her first paragraph thanked Flynn for the unexpected gift of perfume. It had confused her, because he had said it was for his girlfriend. Yes, of course he could write to her; she understood that writing to Stateside pen pals helped servicemen bridge the lonely distances.

Over the next few back and forth letters background information was shared—birthplaces, high schools and colleges attended, interests, hobbies and so forth. Flynn played tennis and collected stamps; Caitlin loved horses and animals. Flynn enjoyed sports; Caitlin dancing. *What kind of dancing?* Caitlin explained. *You danced with Fred Astaire? You look like a dancer.* And so on. Maddie knew most of this. She learned that her father had a pet terrier named Bunko; her mother, a tabby named Ginger (after Ginger Rogers). In one of her letters there was a thumb-smudged, black and white graduation photo of her mother. Long blonde hair, something glorious in her eyes. She was beautiful— "stunning," as her father wrote. Maddie imagined him carrying it in his wallet, gazing at it longingly each night.

It was clear from the tone in each letter that a friendship was evolving, the distance narrowing. They discussed their faith; Flynn was a Baptist, Caitlin (who preferred to be called Kitty), a Presbyterian. Both believed strongly in the inerrancy of the Scriptures, the Person and work of Jesus Christ; the need for world evangelism before his soon return. Both shared a deep love for Christ and a burden for the lost.

Many of the men are receptive here, Flynn wrote. *Wouldn't it be wonderful if there were a place for them to fellowship? Yes, it would. Do they have such places? The base chapel, but it would be nice if there were something more.* Maddie sensed their relationship deepening, a bond forming. Two becoming one in vision.

About six months into their correspondence Maddie noticed a change in her father's letters. His handwriting had become more shaky, strident, suggesting different writing surfaces, tenuous circumstances. Some letters were short—bits of fragmented thoughts scribbled hastily in pencil; others long, in ink, but with run-on sentences. There was a shift in tone.

Maddie felt a longing in his prose, an ache between the lines that revealed a man, living in a war zone, who was lonely, sometimes afraid, often at the brink of despair over the killing and destruction. He lamented the wickedness on both sides, the deaths of lost men. *Why does God allow this?* he wrote with fiery passion. *Why do the nations rage? O God, these men. Have mercy on these men.* His letters frequently ending with the biblical reference "Maranatha, Come, Lord Jesus."

On the other hand her mother's letters were like a balm of oil over a chafed soul. They were filled with Scripture verses, words of encouragement, verses of hymns. Maddie noticed that her mother's letters were worn around the edges, sometimes torn, the folds worn at the creases, as though they had been folded and unfolded several times. There were stains of mud and grease, where her father's fingers had held them. Maddie imagined him reading in his tent, in a foxhole, bumping along a potted road in a jeep; her mother's words bringing comfort to him, instilling hope.

As the year progressed Maddie could almost pick the letter in which her mother gave away her heart. It had been a gradual blossoming—like a Polaroid, as her mother had put it—a bonding of two lives—an ache enjoined, a longing embraced, a vision shared. And then: When will you be returning to the States? Words like "me" and "you" gave way to "us" and "we." The salutations progressed from "Dear" to "My Dearest" and "My Darling." Similarly, the closers moving from "sincerely" to "with deep affection" to "love." I have never met a woman like you, Kitty. I can't imagine my life without you. Nor I you, she responded. God certainly knows what He is doing, doesn't He?

They began talking about the future, about children, his call to the ministry as a Navy chaplain. His final letter gave the date of his return, a hint at something important he would like to ask her. Maddie teared at this because she knew what it was he was going to ask. She guessed her mother did too, for in her final letter she closed with "I am counting the days, my darling. Your loving Kitty."

Smiling down at the letters, Maddie let the tears fall unabated down her cheeks. She retied each bundle, thoughtfully, her heart overflowing with joy. She put the bundles back into the shoebox, replaced the cover, then placed the box on her lap and held it with both hands, as though protecting a great treasure—the collective seed of a family history, a godly nascent legacy. It was a love story between two kids, worlds apart, a love that had since stood the test of two miscarriages, a grueling seminary schedule, the death of Kitty's mother, Flynn's father; numerous relocations, the births of Madeleine and Sean.

As she sat thinking, the joy all too quickly turned to sorrow as disquieting thoughts of Nathan bullied into her mind. Garrulous, troubling thoughts. Tears guttered in her eyes as she looked plaintively to the sky.

"Why God? Why do I have such feelings for him? Is this love? Am I in love? I've never been in love before, so I don't know what it's like. I think about him all the time, but is that love? I think about walking along the beach holding his hand, looking out at the sunset on the bay. I think about his arms around me. I think about kissing him, Father. Is it wrong to think this way? You know all these things, of course, but I have to talk to you about them. I have to know what to do with my feelings. He's not a Christian, as you know. I wish that he were, but he isn't. Did you bring him into my life, Lord? Is there a reason for it that I'm not seeing? I know that you don't make mistakes. Is this a test? Should I stop seeing him? Show me what to do, God. Please give me wisdom. I want a man to love me and hold me. I want a love that you gave to my parents. A love that is genuine. A love where my husband will put you first in everything. I want this man, God. I can't help wanting him but I do."

She listened for a while, as though God might speak audibly or inaudibly to her. She heard nothing but the wind in the leaves above her head. She heard no Yes in her prayers; she heard no No. If only Nathan could see her now, she'd tell him, "This is clearly one of the Wait times."

Just then a thought occurred to her, a very troubling thought. A thought that thundered in her soul. *Maybe I should go back to the States early.* She frowned, thinking it through. "What do you think about that, Father?"

Chapter Fifteen

T HE GUARD CYCLE was over, liberty sounded,
and Nathan and Mick logged out of the barracks with the
Corporal of the Guard. They exited the Quarterdeck and
headed across the parking lot to Nathan's Spider. The
sun was setting, leaving a narrow red band just visible over
the roof of the Admin building. Nathan was wearing a
windbreaker against the chill air, Mick, a brown leather
bomber jacket.

"Looks like it's just you and me, Natboy," Mick said.
"Coop and Gorilla are down with the clap, and it's up to
us to uphold barracks honor."

Nathan started the engine. "Where to?"

"Let's see what's shakin' at the San Pedro."

"Okay by me." Nathan put the car into gear and
headed toward the main gate, where Private Matthews,

one of the stoners in the barracks, had duty. Matthews was standing at a sloppy parade rest, gazing open-mouthed at the sunset as though he'd never seen one before. He was probably tripping.

Mick pointed left. "Go out through the PX," he said, frowning at the taxis parked across the street from the main gate. He ducked low in his seat, but was able to peer out over the window frame of the door with one eye. "I don't want Luigi seeing me."

"Why not?"

"He's been hunting for me."

Nathan turned left into the Dispersing compound, and drove on through the two openings into the PX compound. "That deal of yours not pan out?"

"In a manner of speaking."

"You *do* have bread for tonight, right?"

"I got better than money." Mick sat upright and pulled out two pints of Jack Daniels from his jacket pockets. "These should prime the pump, eh *amico?*"

"It's on me again, huh?"

"*Amico.*"

Mick killed the first pint by the time they got into town, tossed the empty into some shrubs on the side of the road. He was working on the second pint, and the third refrain of "Down on the Corner," by the time Nathan parked the Spider on a street behind the Galleria Umberto.

They made their way down an alley, went through the arcade, past busy cafés and shops, over tiled mosaics, and out onto the clatter of the Via Vittoriano, at the head of the Municipal Square.

The Square was crowded with vehicles and the usual off-duty military and street circus. Mick took a long pull from the flask, offered it to Nathan. "Wanna hit, *amico?* Ain't no good drinkin' alone. You start talking to yourself."

Nathan took the bottle, tipped it up then gave it back to Mick.

Mick drank off another two fingers, threw his head back and crowed like a rooster. "That one had the payload," he shuddered, licking his lips as he palmed the flask into his jacket.

"Looks like you got the pump primed pretty good, Mick."

"That's an affirmative, Marine. Aaaarroooah!" Mick, moving fast, set a course around the Square through the crowds, covering ground with an exaggerated route step. Nathan jogged to catch up.

"You in a race or something, Mick?"

"Life's a race, *amico.* You snooze, you lose."

Three Fleet Marines were leaving the San Pedro; one tall, black and weedy; the other two shorter, white, weedy and pathetic looking. They looked at Mick and Nathan as they came up to the door. "Wouldn't go in there," one of the shorter white ones said.

Mick raised an eyebrow. "And why not—pray tell?"

"You're Marines, right?"

"That's an affirmative."

"There's a bunch of Navy in there. They say it's a closed bar."

"Who said?"

"Fat guy at the bar."

"And you let him chase you girls out? Maybe you should've gotten a note from your mothers."

The Fleet Marines frowned at him. "Go on in if you're so tough."

"Don't mind if we do." Mick yanked open the door, blew into the bar like a hot sirocco.

Inside it was dark, crowded and smoky. The usual dark-haired girls moved through the smoke with trays of drinks. "Bad Moon Rising" was thumping through the jukebox speakers. Heads turned.

Mick stopped, feet wide apart, eyeing the crowd with a daring grin. "As you were, ladies. No need to stand at attention."

Everyone in the bar stared.

Nathan guessed by the hair lengths and longer mustaches and sideburns that most of them were Navy. They looked Navy. There was a fat man at the bar, leaning on a big forearm, holding a glass of beer in a fist. There were other men at the bar, staring at them. "I don't know about this, Mick."

Mick pulled out his flask and drained another two fingers of whiskey, howled, "Aaaarrooohhaa! The Marines have landed!" then headed over to the bar, and stood to the left of the fat man.

The fat man looked at him, then peered down at his beer as he set the glass on the bar. The men on the right side of the fat man glanced around him at Mick, then at Nathan as he came up to the bar on Mick's left.

The fat man said, "This bar don't serve jarheads."

Mick smiled, reaching for his flask. "If we see any jarheads we'll be sure and let them know." He unscrewed the cap, tossed the cap over his shoulder, and aimed the neck at the fat man. "Here's mud in your eye, squid."

He drained the last of the flask, set it down on the bar delicately, his pinkie extended. He slapped the bar with the flat of his hand. "Enrico, buddy, I'm dry. Gimme a whiskey. *Subito!*"

Enrico was watching the fat man.

The fat man waved an arm. "Belay that, Enrico. The jarhead here and his girlfriend were just leaving."

Mick looked him over. "Is that right?"

"That's right." The fat man stepped away from the bar. He stood about five ten, but was thickly built in the arms and girth. He wore a Hawaiian shirt probably to hide his belly. There were palm trees and pineapples on the shirt.

Mick looked him over some more. "You must dress out to what—two-fifty, two-eighty maybe?" He talked over his shoulder to Nathan. "Navy feeds them well, don't it, Natboy?"

Nathan was eyeing the tables of men watching Mick.

Mick slapped the bar twice, sharply. "Enrico, I said gimme a whiskey."

Enrico shook his head. "Not tonight, Meek. You come back some other night."

"You're not going to serve me?"

"I don't want no trouble, Meek. You come back tomorrow."

"I'm here tonight," Mick said, raised an eyebrow at Enrico and smiled. Then his eyes flattened. "I'm going to ask you again, *amico*—real nice. I would like some service. I don't want you looking at Fat Boy here, I want you looking at me. Fat Boy don't matter squat."

The fat man took a step forward with clenched fists.

Mick's eyes were suddenly deadly. "You take another step, Fat Boy, and I swear I'll wipe the floor with you."

Fat Boy stopped. "Who're you calling Fat Boy?"

"You, Fat Boy. Maybe you don't hear so good."

"I hear fine." He glared at Mick. "People don't call me Fat Boy."

"I ain't people. I'm a jarhead, remember?"

Sweat glistened on Fat Boy's upper lip. His eyes flickered. Nathan could see fear in them. He guessed that the man had never been challenged before.

Mick glanced over the crowd. "That goes for the rest of you torpedo jockeys." He cupped his right hand and made a come-and-get-me motion with his fingers. "Anybody want a piece of me, I'm right here. One—ten. It makes no difference. You kill me—fine. I'll take some of you with me. C'mon."

No one moved.

"Let's go, Mick," Nathan said.

"You go now, Meek," Enrico said. "Come back another night." The big Italian with the scar face stood next to him, holding a baseball bat.

Mick looked at him. "You ain't gonna serve me?"

Enrico shook his head. "No whiskey."

"But I'm thirsty."

"No whiskey."

"It ain't worth it, Mick," Nathan said. "Let's go."

Mick chuckled.

"C'mon, Mick, let's go to the Blue Moon."

"Sure. The air in here stinks of squid anyway." He picked up his empty flask, smiled at the label, and then slung it across the bar into Fat Boy's glass, shattering it. Fat Boy jumped back as beer splashed onto his shirt.

Mick gave Enrico a hard look, slapped his palm on the bar once more. "Give the squid another beer, *amico*. He spilled his drink all over his pineapples and palm trees. Now we can go, *amico*."

Mick and Nathan left the bar.

THEY WERE SITTING at a smoky table in the Blue Moon on Carlata San Giuseppe, off the Municipal Square. The bar was a clone of the San Pedro. There were the usual off-duty military and dark-eyed girls working and the usual American hit parade pounding through the jukebox speakers. "Broken Arrow" by Buffalo Springfield was playing.

Mick was glowering into an empty glass, turning it back and forth slowly between his fingers. Nathan was watching him across the table. He lit a cigarette and added smoke to the ceiling cloud.

"That was crazy back there, Mick."

"I know." Mick turned the glass in his fingers, watching the reflection of yellow lights in it. "Enrico had no call to throw us out."

"We might've gotten killed if he hadn't."

"Sure."

"You okay now?"

"I'm okay." Mick shook his head, laughed.

"What's so funny?"

Mick said nothing.

"We could head back to the barracks."

"And do what...play Pinochle?" Mick stared back into his glass, turning it slowly. "Life's a crap game, *amico*, and then you die."

"Cheer up, Mick."

Mick said nothing.

"Come on, Mick. We got the whole night ahead of us. If you don't want to go back to the barracks, there's plenty to do in town. Want to hit the Flamingo?"

Mick said nothing.

"That guy was a blowhard, Mick. You sent him packing. You can't let jerks like that get you down. Mick?"

"I'm seeing it clear, Natboy. Maybe I'm just seeing it."

"Seeing what?"

Mick gazed into his empty glass.

Nathan saw he had it bad. "Want another drink?"

Mick looked up, his eyes sunk deep in their sockets. "Why not?"

Nathan signaled the bar. A girl with teased black hair and dark lewd eyes came over to the table. "You want whiskey or good time?"

Nathan held up two fingers. "*Due* whiskey,"

The girl left.

Mick was staring across the smoky bar at nothing. "I got a feeling my number's up, Natboy."

Nathan tapped an ash onto the floor, ignoring the colored tin ashtray on the table. "What are you talking about?"

"You gotta face facts. The facts've been lining up pretty solid lately. Take a fool to miss 'em." He continued staring at nothing. He chuckled, then he made a noise in the back of his throat. "You believe in God, Nate?"

"What?"

"God. Jesus."

"No."

"I do. I know I don't act like it but I do. I know I'm going to hell but I can't seem to change course. Straight to hell in a slop bucket."

He shook his head slowly from side to side. He had it bad. "I can see it lining up pretty solid, *amico.* Pretty solid."

Nathan said nothing.

Mick turned his head and peered at Nathan from the dark tunnels of his eyes. "You don't believe in God? That ain't American."

Nathan blew smoke through his nostrils. "I got my reasons."

"Oh?"

"None that I'm gonna tell you."

"Okay, tough guy." Mick grinned, pushed away from the table. "I gotta go to the head. Be back in a minute."

Nathan watched him thread through the crowd toward the rear of the bar where he disappeared down a dark hall. The girl came back with the whiskeys. Nathan paid her. She nuzzled her hip against him, tickled her fingers through his hair.

"You no want good time?"

"Not tonight, sugar."

Nathan listened to a James Taylor song, sipping his drink. "Sweet dreams and flying machines in pieces on the ground…" He stubbed out his cigarette, lit another one and thought about what Mick said about believing in God.

"Why don't you believe in God, Nate?"

"I got my reasons, Frankie."

"What reasons?"

"I don't want to talk about it."

"You ain't makin' sense."

"I know."

"Am I the reason, Nate?"

Nathan didn't answer.

Some military came into the bar, followed by two Italians in leather coats. One of these latter was large, with a thick neck and sloping shoulders, the other short with a thin mustache that he clearly spent a good deal of time grooming. They stopped and turned their heads, as though looking for someone, their black, greased-back hair shining in the dim lights. They went over to the bar and said something to the bartender that Nathan couldn't hear. The bartender said something back. Nathan sipped his drink, watching them until a group of servicemen stood up from their table, blocking his view.

Janis Joplin was wailing through "Piece of My Heart" on the jukebox now. Nathan finished his drink, glanced around the crowd. There was no sign of the two Italians. Nathan glanced over at Mick's drink, untouched. He looked toward the rear of the bar. He checked his watch. Fifteen minutes had passed. He stood, dropped his cigarette and stepped on it.

"Natboy!"

Nathan swung around. Mick was coming into the bar from the front door, ranging toward him at a fast clip.

"How'd you get over there?"

"I went out the back." Mick was out of breath, as though he'd been running. "I gotta go."

"Go?"

"I came to tell you." Mick looked toward the rear of the bar, his eyes wide with fear. He had sobered up pretty good. "I gotta go."

"What's wrong?"

"They're after me."

"Who?"

"A coupla guys with artillery. I lost them out back."

"Italians in leather coats?"

"I owe them money. Two grand."

"Two thousand dollars!"

"The deal didn't work out."

"You told me. They want to kill you for two grand?"

"They'd kill you for a buck-fifty."

"Can you get a loan?"

"With what collateral…my shorts?"

"How about your folks?

Mick laughed. "You're breakin' my heart, Natboy. He started for the front door, saw the whiskey on the table and stepped back. He picked up the glass and grinned, "One for the road, eh *amico!*"

He drained it in a gulp, set the glass down then made for the door. Nathan followed him.

As they came out of the bar, the two leather coats were running up onto the street from a side alley, breathing hard. They looked up and down the street, saw Mick and came toward him. The smaller one reached into his coat pocket.

"Later, Natboy!" Mick ran back into the bar.

The Italians came fast. Nathan stood in their path and held up his hands. *"Come sta, amici?"*

The larger Italian shoved Nathan against the wall. Nathan came forward with his fists, but the smaller one showed him an automatic. "You go," the gunman said in pigeon English.

Nathan frowned at the wide black muzzle and backed away.

The two men rushed into the bar with guns drawn. Nathan went in after them. Inside was bedlam. People were jumping out of their chairs, crowding the floor, shouting. Girls screaming.

Nathan pushed through the crowd, saw the heads of the Italians rounding the bar as they disappeared into the darkness of the back rooms. He shoved after them. There was a shot.

"Out of the way! Out of the way!" Nathan shouted.

Then he was free of the crowd. He ran past the bar, down a long hallway lit by a naked bulb on a wire, the bulb swinging, casting harsh shadows, as though someone had hit it, then he ran past the stench of the toilet and out through the back door that opened onto a narrow brick alley. Tall dark buildings crowded the alley on either side.

Nathan swung his head in both directions but saw no one in the darkness of the close buildings. A narrow band of bleached night winking over the broken roofs offered the only light. He strained to hear retreating footsteps, but couldn't make out anything for the noise of the city echoing off the walls.

Nathan chose a direction and jogged, mindful of the uneven bricks and spilled trash cans. He could feel his heart pounding in his chest, pounding in his ears, the thud of his boots striking brick. The alley rose in a steep, broken, winding slope. He came to an intersection where the alley crossed a narrow street, paused to catch his breath. It was a bad neighborhood. The Marines called it "the Gut," or the bowels of hell. A group of hard-looking characters was leering at him from the shadows of a corner bar.

Nathan looked both ways, chose a direction and jogged past bars and bordellos where military didn't go, unless they were looking for male prostitutes or drugs. Names like "Jack's House" and "*I Fratelli*" (The Brothers) winked in hard neon over black windows.

Another shot rang out. He stopped, turning his head to triangulate the sound and ran toward it. He turned into a side alley. There were two shots, one after the other. He ran as fast as he could.

He came out of the dark confines of the alley and headed down toward the lights of the harbor. Then he turned left onto the Via nuova Marina. Crowds of people were moving both ways along the wide sidewalks, horns honking in the crush of traffic. No one seemed concerned about the shots.

Nathan saw four black sailors wearing Afros, bell-bottoms, flowery shirts and platform shoes, standing looking back at something. He ran up to them. "Any of you guys hear shots?"

The sailors eyed him suspiciously.

"Shots. Did you hear shots?"

"Yeah, man," a spidery-legged sailor wearing a wide brim purple hat with silver conches said. "Thought it was a backfire."

"They were gunshots," a heavyset one with a comb angling out of his Afro said. "I know gunshots."

"Did you see anything?" Nathan asked.

The sailors shook their heads. Spider legs said, "Sounded like it came from the Square." He pointed.

Another one asked, "What's going on, man?"

Nathan took off. Behind him he heard, "Hey— what's happening?"

He fast-walked along the busy sidewalk, heading back toward the Square. He was looking forward, glancing back, gazed over at the harbor, thinking Mick might have run toward the ships. But there was no sign of Mick. There was no sign of the two men chasing him. There were no more shots.

A woman with bleached hair and green leather miniskirt angled toward him from a corner. "You looking for good time, Marine?"

Nathan was moving fast, looking past her.

She grabbed his arm. "Twenty dollar, Marine."

"Get lost," Nathan said, yanking free and moving down the street.

Chapter Sixteen

Nathan checked all the bars around the

Square for Mick, but there was no sign of him. He had a
bad feeling about his disappearance, and decided to head
back to the barracks to report what had happened. There
was no point in looking further. Mick could be anywhere.

He walked back to the Galleria Umberto, went
through it past crowds of shoppers and out onto the street
in back where his car was parked beneath a yellow
streetlight. The car was unmolested, but there was a piece
of paper flattened under a windshield wiper, the torn
corner of a newspaper.

Nathan angled it to the light. There were words
written along the margin of the paper with a blunt pencil,
an idiot's scrawl. Mick had written them. The words
read: *Got a lift. Some hoot, huh? Mick.*

Nathan shook his head and cursed. Some hoot all right; it shot the wind out of his liberty. He crumpled the note and tossed it. At least Mick was okay, he thought. He could've been killed. He checked his watch. It was still early, plenty of time to resurrect a good time out of the ashes if he wanted to. He did.

He walked back into the Galleria for a cup of coffee, thinking he might decompress a bit before charging back out onto the Square. People were shopping and milling about, but several of the stores had their shutters pulled part way down to signal that they were closing. The cafés were still in business. He stopped at a magazine rack in the bay of a confectionary store, picked up a travel magazine and thumbed through it. It featured Isola d'Ischia—the Island of Ischia.

He paid the confectioner, went over to a marble-topped table in front of an espresso bar and sat down.

He thought some more about Mick, wondered what kind of deal he had made through Luigi with those characters. They were some bad *hombres*. They were about as bad as he had seen.

A waiter wearing black trousers and a long-sleeved white shirt came out and took Nathan's order. Nathan ordered a *caffé e latte* to wash the taste of whiskey from his mouth. He wished it could remove the stench of the San Pedro and the Blue Moon from his memory. Remove the leather coats with big guns from his mind, and the filth of the streets of Naples. Not to mention the perverts in the Gut who were sizing him up from their dark corners. But that would take some strong coffee.

He thumbed through the magazine, enjoying the glossy photos of the Amalfi coast, the spread on the islands of Capri and Ischia. He stopped when he came to a photographic layout about the village of Sant Angelo. The photos showed the marina and the colorful boats on the spit of beach with fishermen washing their nets, and the rock beyond rising bluntly off the spit that reminded him of the rock in Morro Bay.

"Remember when we went fishin' on the beach in Cayucos, Nate?"

"I sure do, Frankie. I think about it often."

"You showed me how to catch them tiny sand crabs for bait. They'd sure tickle your feet when you walked over them."

Nathan sat thinking about that day. Brothers fishing in their swim trunks, Nate showing Frankie how to cast into the surf, how to set the hook when a fish took the bait.

"We caught a bucket load of sand dabs, didn't we, Frankie?"

"We sure did, Nate. I sure wish we could do that again."

"Me too."

The waiter brought the *caffé e latte.* Nathan paid him and, sipping it, looking at the colorful boats, at the villas cut into the hills overlooking the old world village. He was remembering Nico waving goodbye in front of the hotel with the promise on her lips for the upcoming weekend. There had been no more mention of past boyfriends, or girlfriends, but sitting on the terrace of the

Café Rosatti it had been just the two of them talking and enjoying each other's company, which they did for the remainder of his weekend in Rome.

He flicked open his Zippo and lit a cigarette, frowned at the lighter. He was thinking about the two leather coats again and wondered why men acted so wickedly. Where did men like that come from? Their mothers of course. Their fathers too. Their histories and cultures and religion, of course. He put his money on religion. But what about those two leather coats? They had no religion. They were just evil. And that character at the San Pedro with the palm trees and pineapples; he was evil too, or working mighty hard at it. Where did that come from?

He sat smoking and thinking about religion. What need was there in man to believe in something greater than himself? To believe in something transcendental. Where did that come from? Some ancient chief, no doubt, wanting control over his tribe. If you don't follow my orders the fire god will scorch you, the rain god will drown you, the wind god will destroy your crops. Religion gave one man or group power over another man or group.

Nathan blew a cloud of smoke at the table, watched it flatten and spread then dissipate. What a racket. Religion spawned the haves and the have nots. He made a noise of contempt in his throat. The sanctimonious hypocrites. He hated the lot of them. If there's a hell, they will occupy the deepest, darkest pit.

Nathan glared into his cup. *What does that kind of thinking get you, amico? A trip through the dark and bitter regions of the Netherworld, where hope dies in a lonely bed of tears and the shades know your name. Boy, are you in a black mood, he chuckled. You must've caught it from Mick. Let it go, amico, it'll kill you.*

"Good luck," he said out loud.

He was suddenly tired and soured, so he decided to pack it in. He crushed his cigarette in the marble ashtray. That business at the San Pedro with the Navy had tired him, and then the leather coats at the Blue Moon had whipped him and taken more out of him than he realized. Staring into the muzzle of a .45 will do that to you. Drowning memories in a bottle of hooch or a *caflé e latte* didn't help matters much either. He could always make up for it tomorrow night, followed by a two-day guard cycle, and then Ischia where he would get it all back.

He closed the travel magazine, pushed back from the table when Maddie Gallagher walked into the Galleria and the dark clouds lifted.

She was looking into store windows and didn't see him. Wearing light brown corduroy bell-bottoms, boots and a loose knit poncho over a powder blue sweater, she was lithe and lovely. Her hair, artificially red in the arcade lights, was wildly carefree and bouncing on her shoulders as she walked, long-legged, over the geometric patterns and mosaics of the marble floor.

Seeing her with her face angled to showcase the good line of her profile, Nathan felt something move inside him that he hadn't expected to feel, a tingle of excitement or desire, something indefinable.

When she turned her head in his direction, gazing across the arcade so that their eyes met, she broke stride, appearing to be indecisive as to her next move. Nathan could see the hesitation in her eyes, a decision forming in them.

Maddie frowned. Seeing Nathan staring at her, she felt suddenly unnerved. A tingling of anxiety fingered down her spine like so many spiders. She was not expecting to see Nathan that night, especially on her home turf, and was not prepared emotionally for it. She was confused, not sure how to proceed. But there was no escaping an encounter with him, since he was sitting at a table in direct line with the stairwell to her home.

She took a cleansing breath as she walked over to his table, her thoughts in a whirl.

He smiled broadly at her. "It's the fighter pilot."

"Hello, Nathan."

"We keep bumping into each other." He set the magazine on the table and forgot about it.

"It seems so, but I live here."

"You live *here?*"

"Upstairs." She pointed across the Galleria. "Right through that arch and up three flights. The Way Station's there too, by the way. How was Rome?"

"I had a good time. Have a seat."

"Thank you, but I can't stay. I've got work to do at the Station."

"There's work to do here." He grinned. "You could try and convert me."

"I would if I knew you weren't just mocking."

"You're right," he agreed. "That was dumb. I'm talking stupid because I want you to stay. Just a few minutes, won't you? Five minutes, tops." He leaned over and pushed a chair out for her.

"Five minutes?" She checked her watch. "Okay." She sat on the edge of the chair, as if the rest of the seat were wet. She glanced around Nathan's face, avoiding eye contact. "What would you like to talk about?" There was reticence in her voice. "Did you see all the sights in Rome?"

"Enough."

"I love Rome. The Eternal City."

"Most of the eternal parts are falling down," he said. Looking at her hair that was thick and alive with splashes of red and yellow and brown highlights like a New England Autumn, he had an urge to reach over and run both his hands through it. "You look great."

"You're mocking me again."

"No. Really, you look great."

She glanced away at a woman in a headscarf and shawl pushing a perambulator. She peered down at her hands, her eyes drifting to the colorful tiled mosaic of a cherub beneath her feet. Then she looked back at Nathan's chin, his ear, the tip of his nose. "I really should get going."

"It hasn't been five minutes yet."

She   checked her watch, as though to verify his timekeeping, and smiled a thin, humorless smile at the cover of Nathan's magazine.

"Are you all right?" he asked.

"I'm fine."

"You don't seem your normal affable self. You haven't smiled once since you got here—not a real smile."

She flashed a bigger smile. "How's that?"

"Fake."

"Sorry. I'm a fake person tonight. The real Maddie Gallagher is upstairs helping her mother clean dishes." Her eyes went back to Nathan's magazine. "Have you been to Ischia?"

"I'm going there this weekend—thought I'd read up on it. How about you?"

"I've been there many times. It's beautiful. May I?" she asked, touching the magazine with the tip of her middle finger.

"Sure."

She leafed through it. "I much prefer Ischia to Capri. There aren't the crowds."

The waiter came out onto the floor and asked Maddie if she'd like to order something.

She shook her head, set the magazine down. "I'm not staying."

"Not even for dessert?" Nathan asked. Before she could answer he asked the waiter, "*Quali dolci avete?*"

The waiter recited a list of desserts.

"*Il gelati, per favore…due,*" Nathan said, and held up two fingers. He turned to Maddie. "What's your favorite ice cream flavor? Never mind. *La cioccolata,*" he said to the waiter. The waiter nodded and left. Nathan smiled at Maddie. "Now you have to stay a little longer. I hope you like chocolate."

She frowned at him, made solid eye contact and stared several moments, as if deciding a matter of great importance. Her eyes were a deep blue, a blue that, taking the light, seemed to change depths, like the tides, deepening now as if in flood. With a protracted sigh she set her shoulder bag on the table. "I didn't know you spoke Italian."

Nathan smiled.

Maddie folded her hands on the table. "It just goes to show how little I know about you, Nathan. I would like to know more."

"Not a very interesting subject."

"Tell me about your family. Families reveal so much about who we are. I have a little brother that likes to torment me. What does that tell you?"

"You should be grateful to have a little brother."

She frowned playfully. "If you had a little brother you wouldn't say that."

Nathan said nothing.

They were eating ice cream, Nathan chewing large spoonfuls at a time with his molars, while watching Maddie holding the sides of her dish with her thumb and middle fingers, carving small mounds with her spoon and licking around the edges. "Very good."

"Yes," he said, observing the play of light in her hair that lay thickly over her loose-knitted poncho.

She smiled, continued eating. "You're alone tonight?"

"My buddy headed back to the barracks earlier. Mick. You met him."

"Mick? Right. He's quite a character, isn't he?"

"You could say that."

She smiled, continued eating. "Have you been to any of the museums or theaters in town?"

"Not yet."

"The Opera House is just across the street. They have wonderful…" She looked at him suddenly.

He had been observing the whiteness of her teeth when she smiled, which she did easily and often, and the depth of blue in her inquisitive eyes that sparkled and dimmed and sparkled again, as though torn between laughter and a great suffering. Eyes that veiled a mystery, and because of the mystery he was thinking how much he would like to kiss her, as though kissing her would unlock it.

"What are you thinking?" she asked.

"Nothing."

"I know you are thinking about something. I can hear your thoughts turning."

"I'm thinking how pretty you are. You look like Ann Margret."

"Ann Margret? I haven't heard that one before."

"You're better looking, of course."

She lowered her ice cream, the depth of her eyes flattening to shallow pools. Nathan didn't know if he'd overstepped a line of etiquette, but he did not retreat. "Was that too forward?"

She shook her head slowly, gazing steadily at him across the table. "No. A girl likes to be told that she's pretty."

"You're a pretty girl. When the light hits you a certain way you are beautiful."

She blushed, touched her cheek then lightly rubbed the bridge of her nose as though to hide the sprinkle of freckles. "Thank you."

"You don't believe me."

"I'm not sure." She dipped her spoon into her ice cream, put it into her mouth and withdrew it thoughtfully, smoothing the chocolaty mound with her lips.

"Do you mind sitting here with me?" he asked.

"Not at all. Why?"

"You seem distracted...like something's on your mind."

"I should be helping my mother."

"Right. You said that." He scooped out the last of the ice cream from his dish. "You're really committed to your work, aren't you?"

"I'm committed to people."

"I'll bet you are." He watched her eating.

"Your wheels are turning again," she said, glancing along her eyelashes at him.

"I can't hide anything from you, can I?"

She smiled. Lovely lips, full and moist looking.

"I was thinking that I'd like to take you out some time," he said. "Maybe grab a bite to eat somewhere and talk."

She resumed licking around the edges of her spoon. "We're doing that now."

"You know what I mean. I'm talking about walking along the beach...or along the harbor, or taking a drive down the Amalfi coast."

"You mean a date?"

"Sure."

She studied him a few moments, as if deciding how to respond. There was restraint in her eyes that made Nathan think that behind the dark irises there were smoldering coals of desire that would ignite into flames of passion at the touch of a man's hands, a man's lips. His lips.

"Well?"

"I would like to very much. But..."

He held up a hand. "Don't say it." Nathan peered down into his latte, his expression darkening. "'You shall not be unequally yoked with unbelievers,'" he said. "Saint Paul to the Corinthians."

She studied him inquisitively.

"Just because I don't happen to believe the Bible doesn't mean I haven't read it."

She continued watching him inquisitively.

"Quite an interesting read," he said, bitterness edging into his tone. "All the blood sacrifices, the judges and kings of Israel acting no better than anyone else. The behind the scenes conniving, the holier than thou attitudes. Reminds you of Christians, don't you think?" He grunted. "Do you really think that God is afraid I might corrupt you?"

She set her ice cream down on the table. "You're bitter."

"Am I? Maybe I have reason to be."

Maddie said nothing.

He stared at her for several moments, his mind taking him up one road then down another, searching for possible routes of conversation. "Forget it," he said, and drank off the last of his latte.

"Just like that...forget it? What does that mean?"

"It means forget it."

"You bring your marbles but won't show them to me. All right, forget it." She checked her watch. "I really have to go, Nathan. Thank you for the ice cream."

Nathan felt something dark moving inside him, pushing him down the road he'd been down so many times before. He knew where it would take him but he went anyway. "You haven't asked me about my trip to Rome."

She looked at him guardedly. "All right. How was your trip to Rome?"

"It was great. I saw all the sights."

"I'm glad to hear it. Rome is lovely, isn't it? Did you go with some of your friends? It's always better if you can share it with someone."

"I went by myself."

"Aren't you the adventurer? I guess if you can speak the language. Don't tell me you're going to Ischia by yourself."

"I'm not."

She blushed. "I'm sorry. I didn't mean to suggest anything illicit."

"Illicit?" He chuckled. "I'm going with someone I met in Roccaraso. A girl. She lives in Rome."

"Oh. I see."

"Her name is Nicoletta."

"I'm sure she's lovely."

"Very. Her parents have a place in Ischia and we're going there this weekend. Alone," he added. "I don't know why I'm telling you this."

"Yes you do, Nathan. You know very well why you're telling me this." She stood, hooked her bag over her shoulder. "I trust you'll marry her." She started away.

"I made you angry."

She stopped and looked back. "Whatever gave you that idea?"

"You're angry."

"Do you want me to be angry? I'm sorry but I really haven't the time. It's your life, Nathan. Do what you want with it."

She walked across the Galleria on a straight line, her boot heels clicking angrily as she went through the arch and disappeared up the stairwell.

Nathan glared at the travel magazine on the table, shook his head reproachfully. "Way to go, Tarzan."

Chapter Seventeen

WALKING UP THE stairwell to the Station, the clatter from the Galleria reverberating off the cinder block walls, Maddie felt completely undone. Hot angry tears washed down her cheeks. She had opened herself up for it though. She'd had plenty of warning against it.

The words her father had told her on the night of her sixteenth birthday, years before, struck like a fiery bolt. "You're a beautiful girl, Maddie," he'd said. "Boys will be attracted to you. Christians, hopefully, but there may be non-Christians as well. Just remember, some dreamboat may come along and promise you the moon. As much as you may think he might give it to you, there are no biblical grounds for missionary dating. It displays an attitude of presumption before God, and it's dangerous." He had illustrated this latter point with the familiar adage that you can't change the spots on a leopard. "A leopard is a leopard. Don't be surprised if it bites you."

Once she reached the third floor landing, she paused before entering the Station, reached into her purse, removed a small compact and repaired her face. She peered down the stairs, thought about Nathan sitting alone at the table and felt a pang of regret. A part of her, a very human part of her, wanted to run down the stairs and into his arms; another part, equally human, wanted to slap his face.

"God help me," she prayed. Then, feeling a modicum of composure restored, she opened the door and went into the Station and felt the sudden change of environment she always felt coming home.

She walked down the short hallway and looked into the bookstore on the right. Her father was demonstrating the use of a concordance to three sailors, a pair of half-glasses perched on his nose.

"Hi, Dad."

He looked up from what he was doing and smiled. "Hey, fighter pilot."

The sailors looked over at her, stared round-eyed a few moments, ears and cheeks turning noticeably red, and then looked quickly back at the concordance.

"Busy night?" she asked her father.

"Not bad," he said, and then his bushy red eyebrows came together, making deep grooves across his pale Irish forehead. "Everything all right?"

"I'm okay."

He continued looking at her, his blue eyes probing.

She was convinced her father had telepathic abilities. "I've just gone through a teaching moment with God. I'm okay now."

"Anything we can talk about?"

"We already have."

She continued down the hall into the great room. There was a fairly decent turnout for a weeknight, perhaps as many as twenty servicemen, all branches. Some were playing ping-pong and foosball, others strumming guitars. A few were sitting at the dinner table with their Bibles opened. The room was alive with activity and noise. The noise was different than that down in the Galleria, which was different from the hubbub out on the streets of the Square.

The clamor in the Station was a "happy clatter," as her mother liked to say. But the change Maddie had felt entering the apartment was not one of sound; it was one of darkness to light. The contrast in environments was palpable. It was a cleansing, illuminating, warming change. The atmosphere in the Station glowed with angel song.

Skip, Clarence and Jesse Calderon were sitting in a small circle of chairs in the yellow light of a table lamp in the far corner, away from the happy clatter. Their heads were bowed, their eyes closed. Jesse was praying.

Maddie stopped at a respectful distance and listened as Jesse, in a simple expression of childlike faith, prayed. He used no big words, no eloquent theology, but he acknowledged his sin and his need for the Savior, and she knew that his faith resonated in heaven. It brought tears to her eyes. The others in the room were unmindful of the miracle that was taking place. The ping-pong ball ponged and pinged, the foosball ball clattered and clacked, a guitar strummed vigorously. Even her mother, wiping the kitchen counter, humming "Amazing Grace," seemed unaware that a lost sheep had been found, a sinner saved. But the angels in heaven were rejoicing.

Maddie could almost hear the flutter of wings.

Then the three Marines were standing, laughing and hugging. Skip raised a hand to the room, and said, "Listen up, everybody! Jesse has an announcement."

Jesse was smiling his incredibly wide and guileless smile, his cheeks wet with tears. "I received Jesus Christ as my Lord and Savior. Just now. I'm a Christian!"

The room erupted in applause and cheers.

"Praise the Lord!" Clarence said.

The men added "Amen." Several went over to Jesse and clapped him on the back.

Maddie felt tears leaking down her cheeks. It seemed so simple, so easy, a sinner coming home. Why do some understand and not others? *Why, God?* Then she burst into tears, covered her face with her hands, and quickly crossed the room. She went past the kitchen, past her mother and opened the door into the living quarters.

Kitty glanced over from the counter. "Maddie?"

Maddie, shaking her head, ran down the hall to her room and shut the door. She fell on her bed weeping. "O God, help me. Help me. What am I going to do? I love him, God. I love him. Please take my love for him away. I can't bear it."

Moments later her mother's footsteps padded quietly up the hall and stopped outside her door. The floorboards squeaked. The footsteps went back down the hall. Minutes later a different set of footsteps came down the hall. There was a soft knock. "Honey?"

"I'm all right, Dad. I just need to be alone for a few minutes."

"I'll be back, okay?"

Maddie looked up. "Dad?"

The door squeaked open and her father poked his head inside. "Yes?" he smiled. "Okay to come in?"

Maddie swung her legs around the edge of her bed and sat up. She wiped her eyes with the heels of her palms. "It's safe."

Flynn took the desk chair. He sat leaning forward, hands loosely clasped. He waited a moment, searching her face. "How's my fighter pilot?"

She shook her head. "I'm not a fighter pilot, Dad. I'm a twenty year old woman."

"I know."

He folded and unfolded his hands as if he didn't know what to do with them. He had clearly entered uncharted waters that he wasn't sure how to navigate. He glanced around the room as though there might be a compass bearing written on the walls. He looked back at her. "Jesse Calderon gave his heart to the Lord, did you know?"

"It's wonderful."

"The men are celebrating."

"I can hear."

He folded his hands and intertwined the fingers. "What's going on, honey?"

She laughed through a fresh wave of tears. "Don't you know, Dad?" She wiped her eyes. "I thought you knew everything."

"I don't. Here—" He handed her a tissue from a box atop the desk.

She dabbed her eyes gazing at him. "I want to go home, Dad."

"You are home."

"I mean back to the States. I want to get a job...a real job. I want to get an apartment—maybe a little studio up in Mount Hermon. A place in the redwoods I can call my own."

"This is kind of sudden, isn't it?"

"Me telling you about it, yes. But I've been giving it serious thought for quite a while."

He glanced down at his hands.

"It's not that I don't like it here," she said, "I do. I love seeing what God is doing in the lives of so many men. What just happened out there is a miracle." She twisted the tissue between her fingers, felt more tears leaking down her cheeks. "But I'm tired. I'm just really tired."

"Oh?"

She dabbed her eyes, twisted the tissue some more. "I guess I just want to go somewhere where people aren't looking at me like I'm their kid sister all the time. Or that I've got the plague or something."

"Is someone giving you a hard time?"

"Not in the Station. No."

"Is it something else?"

Maddie said nothing.

"I see." Flynn sat back in his chair, ran thick fingers back and forth through a short crop of red hair, rumpling it. "You couldn't wait to leave until next semester? That was the plan."

"I want to go now."

His kind blue eyes moved over her face, searching. "Is it...?" He started to say something but backed away from it.

She guessed his probing mind knew exactly what was troubling her.

He smiled. "Sweetheart, I know that whatever you decide to do, you will do it because you will have given it a lot of thought, and because you have talked with God about it. Whatever you two work out is fine with me."

He stood to leave.

"Daddy..."

He looked at her.

"Why does God save some and not others?"

"I don't know."

Her eyes misted. "I don't understand Him sometimes."

Flynn rumpled his hair some more. "Neither do I. His ways are not our ways. His thoughts..."

"Are higher than ours. I know." She dabbed her eyes some more. "Sometimes I wish He'd speak just a little clearer."

A warm, fatherly smile spread over his face. "You've grown into a beautiful woman, Maddie. Have I ever told you that?"

She nodded.

"You're not just beautiful on the outside, but on the inside as well. I couldn't be more proud of you." He cupped the side of her face with his hand, leaned over and kissed the top of her head. "I love you, fighter pilot."

"I love you too, Dad."

Chapter Eighteen

N ATHAN WALKED ACROSS the NSA parking

lot in the darkness of the moonless night, feeling the cold of the wind on his face that carried the smell of sulfur from the hills. It added to his black mood. The base was quiet. He kicked a soda can spinning under a car tire with an echoing clatter. The world was an evil place and got whatever it deserved—in spades. He felt dirty living in it.

He looked for something else to kick but he was running out of asphalt. And what about you, *amico*? There's plenty of wickedness in you, too. Don't tell me that business in the Galleria didn't have a little wickedness in it. Just a little. She's about as nice a girl as you'd ever hope to meet and you pull a stunt like that. Where does that come from? You want to smash everything that's good and decent, don't you? Makes you feel superior, doesn't it? Big man, Natboy. Big man.

He went up the stairs of the barracks and stepped over the landing into the incandescent brightness of the Quarterdeck. He squinted. Sergeant Holcomb, a straight-backed, narrow-waisted, four-year man with a slightly boyish face, had duty. He looked at his watch, checked the time against the clock on the wall, and wrote in the log.

"Mick log in yet?" Nathan asked.

"Twenty minutes ago. Him and Dixon."

"Dixon, huh?"

Holcomb finished writing, looked up at Nathan. "You're back early, Kessler. Must've been some good time in town," he said, sarcasm lacing his words.

"A scream."

Nathan looked outside and saw the guard vehicle, falsely yellow under the parking lot lamp, coming in through the main gate with the 4 to 8 shift. "Take it easy," he said, and went upstairs.

Heading down the hall, he saw the light was on in Mick's room. He knocked softly.

A voice said, "Yeah?"

Nathan pushed open the door. Gorilla was in bed reading a Fantastic Four comic.

"Hey, Nate. Back early, huh?"

"Not much happening."

Nathan glanced over at the other bed, at the body sprawled on its back, angled sideways. Mick. His head was tilted a little toward the room, his mouth open. He was still in civvies, his shirttail pulled out, the shirt partially unbuttoned revealing a bare hairy belly. A pant leg stained from crotch to knee hung over the side of the bed, a boot half-pulled off his foot touching the floor. The other leg was draped over the footboard with its foot pointing inward, resting on the seat of the desk chair. "Is it still breathing?"

"I haven't checked lately."

Mick's throat emitted a low gurgling sound, like a sink backing up, followed by a peaceful rattling snore. His lips fluttered when he breathed. The room stank of whiskey and stale cigarettes. It stank of other things that weren't purchased in a bar. "He say anything when he got in?"

Gorilla shook his head. "He just came in and crashed. I thought he was with you."

"He was." Nathan pointed at Gorilla with his chin. "How're you doing?"

"Pretty good, I guess. The doc says I gotta go on light duty."

"Coop too?"

"Yeah."

"Take it easy." Nathan looked once more at Mick, shook his head and closed the door. He went down two doors to Charlie Dixon's room. Dixon, his back to the door, was in his shorts hanging up civvies in his wall locker. There was a poster of Captain Zig Zag taped inside the locker door, a silver chain with a wooden peace symbol dangling from a metal hook. "Hey, Dixon."

"What!" Dixon whirled, as if caught in a crime, slamming shut his wall locker. "Oh, it's you. Don't sneak up on me like that."

"I wasn't sneaking. The door was open."

Dixon narrowed suspicious eyes on the door, as if to verify it, then slid his gaze over to Nathan. His eyes were glassy with dark circles around them, the pupil's dilated. Stoner's eyes. "What do you want?"

"You gave Mick a ride back from town?"

"Mick?"

"Mick Donovan…two doors down?"

"What of it?"

"He tell you anything?"

"What are you driving at?"

"I'm not driving at anything. I asked if Mick said anything to you, that's all."

"If he did it's between him and me."

Nathan saw that Dixon was high. He'd probably given something to Mick as well. He hated stoners. Stoners like Dixon got his sister Linda started on drugs and made a train wreck out of her. He felt a prickling over his scalp as he took a step forward. Dixon backed against his locker, his fists balled. Nathan stopped. Pounding the sand out of the jerk wouldn't change a thing. It would make him feel better for the present but then he would feel bad, and perhaps worse for it. Let evil alone, he thought.

Dixon chuckled.

Nathan turned to leave when he heard the 4 to 8 shift coming up the stairwell, Leon Hackett and Gerald Thomas harmonizing "In The Midnight Hour." Then they were in the hall, combing out their Afros while moving in a rolling, high-low, slide-footed choreography to their singing. It was executed flawlessly.

They stopped in front of the second room on the right, dipping low on a downbeat—"I'm gonna wait till the midnight hour"—snapped their fingers on cue, stood, heels together, spinning on the beat, then went into the room and closed the door, singing. They were good singers.

Karl Matthews had entered the hall behind them. He was holding his barracks cover with one hand, his gun belt draped over his shoulder, as he came up the hall with no rhythm whatsoever. He weighed around one-fifty, with a barely regulation haircut and mustache. He turned into the room where Nathan was standing, without saying a word to him or to Dixon, and tossed his gear onto his bed.

Nathan went down the hall shaking his head. Both of them had fried eggs for brains. They were the go-to guys for dope: hashish, mescaline, LSD, whatever they could arrange through Luigi's connections in the Gut. They were worthless as Marines.

Nathan walked down the hall. Cooper was lying on his bed, hands folded behind his head, staring at the ceiling. "Hey, Coop."

Cooper continued staring.

Nathan tossed his travel magazine onto his bed. "You awake, Coop? Your eyes are open."

"Sure."

"What's on your mind?"

"Nothing."

"Something's on your mind."

Cooper turned his head an inch and gazed at Nathan, as if verifying that it was Nathan who'd come in. Then he stared back at the ceiling; his expression fixed and loony. "You ever think about dying?"

Nathan frowned at the palm of his hand, dragged it over his face wearily, then rubbed the back of his neck. The world was not only wicked, but it had gone crazy too. "What's going on, Coop?"

"Do you?"

"Yeah, I think about dying. Tonight, for instance."

"No, seriously."

"I am serious. Not two hours ago." That sailed around the room and landed nowhere. Nathan went over to the wall locker where he kept his civvies and opened it.

Cooper continued staring at the ceiling. "I've been thinking about it."

"Because you got the clap?"

"We're gonna die, Nate. It's like we're all on death row. Babies...old people. We're all walking dead."

"You think your number's up too?"

Cooper frowned at him. "My number?"

"You and Mick ought to get together for some laughs."

Cooper blinked quizzically a couple of times.

"Forget it." Nathan undressed, slipped a hanger into his shirt and hung it beside the others. "You just figure out that we're all gonna die?"

"I never thought about it."

"Not even in boot camp? Didn't they give you the one-in-ten statistic?"

"Sure. But you never figure you're the one. It's the slob next to you that's gonna get it. There's no getting around this though, we're all in the tank. Don't matter if you live to be a hundred, you're still gonna kick off."

Nathan draped his trousers over a hanger, cuffs to the right, hung it beside his other trousers and shut the locker. He walked back to his bed and fluffed the pillow for reading. "The world is full of spooks tonight."

"Spooks?" Cooper stared back at the ceiling. "I just never thought about it. I guess you think you're going to live forever. Funny."

"A riot." Nathan lay his head back on the pillow and thumbed through the photo spreads in the travel magazine. He made it to the end and started back through from the beginning. He read through an article about the fumaroles on the island but couldn't concentrate. He stared at the ceiling—a lot of inspiration on the ceiling that night.

He could see her image in his mind. Her face, her eyes. The light splash of freckles. Well, you hurt her, didn't you, *amico*? Score one for the home team. You made her angry too, didn't you? Extra points for the anger. Wickedness was going the extra innings tonight, wasn't it?

He reached over and took the framed photo of his family off the side table and held it with both hands. He examined each of their faces; his father's, his mother's, his sister's, his own. His eyes drifted to the round face of his little brother. They always did.

He felt Cooper's eyes on him. "How come you never talk about your family?"

Nathan set the photo back on the table. "They're dead."

Cooper blinked. "Your whole family?"

"My mom and brother. The rest might as well be dead."

"Oh man, Nate, I'm sorry."

"Wasn't your fault."

"What happened? Can I ask?"

"No." He started back through the magazine, trying to think about the upcoming weekend with Nico, but it was no use. Maddie Gallagher was working him over pretty good.

"You shouldn't go to Ischia with that Roman girl, Nate."

"I'm going, Frankie."

"She's no good for you."

"The other one won't have me."

"Yes, she will."

"You have to leave this one to me, Frankie. It's all set."

Frankie said nothing.

Nathan climbed into bed, tossed and turned as if exercising, and eventually fell asleep. In his dream, which he didn't know was a dream, Nico was walking toward him on a curving white beach against the greenness of the island and dark blue of the sea. She was looking at him across the distance, walking barefoot in the sand that was a white brilliance of fairy dust, the sand clinging to the sides of her feet as though made of powdered sugar.

She was wearing a bathing suit with floral patterns in the top and a matching sarong tied at her hip, and bougainvillea flowers in her hair. There were white wooden boats with bands of color beneath their gunwales pulled onto the beach, the fishing nets drying. There were no fishermen, only Nico with thick hair falling over her very tan shoulders, and her arms moving rhythmically with her barefooted beachcomber's gait. Then she was standing before him, touching the spray of freckles over her elfin nose as if to hide them, and then putting her arms around his neck, her menthol blue eyes smiling steadily at him, then tilting her head so that her hair fell in a dark red mass to one side of her face as she kissed him, first tenderly, then with a passion only heightened by the dream. "Isn't God good?" she said.

Nathan groaned. "Nico…Nico…"

She stood back and nudged his shoulder, her breath smelling of kerosene as she said, "I gotta talk to you, Natboy."

"*Io sono qui, mio amoré,*" he said dreamily, then rolled onto his side. "But you smell awful."

"It's me, *amico.* Wake up."

"What's that?" Nathan opened his eyes, his mind still on the beach with Nico, and he realized it wasn't Nico at all that he'd been dreaming about. It was Maddie. Then the brightness of the dream fled with the sudden violence of transition to a dark room, where he was lying in bed with a hulking shape over him that reeked of whiskey. A beefy mitt pawed his shoulder. "Mick?"

"You awake, Natboy?"

"Now I am," Nathan said, feeling the last light of the dream leaving for good. "What's going on? What time is it?" He squinted at the luminescent dial on his watch. "It's two-thirty."

"They're after me, Nate."

"Who's after you? Those two Italians?"

"Spooks. They jumped me when I wasn't looking. Honest to Chesty, Nate. Spooks."

"What spooks?"

"They were all over me…clawin' at my life force. My essence. Know what I mean? My essence. They got inside me with their hooks and nails, clawing at my essence to beat all. They were like to kill me."

"Maybe if you got some sleep."

"That's when they get you. You ain't lookin' for 'em." Mick jerked a look out the window.

Nathan could see his eyes wild in the dim light streaming through the window from the parking lot. "What are you on?" he asked.

"I'm on top of the world, Natboy. Top of the world." Mick jumped back from the window. "I gotta go. You've been a pal, *amico*. You stuck by me."

He took Nathan's hand and shook it vigorously, breathing waves of rank whiskey breath over him. "A real pal. I won't forget it."

"No problem."

"I mean it. Most guys would've cut and run. Not you, *amico*. You stood by me through the thick and nasties." He laughed. "We showed those Navy, didn't we?"

"Sure."

"I owe you, *amico*."

"Let's talk about it in the morning."

"I'd like to but I gotta go." Nathan saw his dark shape fill the doorway, and then only the rectangle of yellow light and the sound of footsteps running down the hall.

Cooper groaned, lifted his head in the darkness. "What's going on? It isn't time for our shift, is it?"

"Go back to sleep, Coop."

Nathan got out of bed and looked out the window. There was nothing in the parking lot but rows of parked cars in shadows and aureoles of pale yellow light. It was like a scene from a horror movie. From where he stood he could see the guard booth lighted at the main gate, the lone silhouette of the Marine inside looking across the street at the blue neon lights of the Hideaway Hotel. It appeared to be Lance Corporal Thompson, but Nathan couldn't be certain from the angle.

He turned and padded across the room in his bare feet. Then he closed the door, came back and climbed into bed. He lay thinking about Mick. He wondered what Dixon had given him. Speed, maybe. Or mescaline. There was plenty of each to be had, or hashish, especially with Luigi's connections in the Gut. He hated guys like Dixon. Pushers.

He thought some more about Maddie, told himself to forget about her, then he rolled over onto his side and faced the wall. He could see her in the Galleria, the light on one side showing the lovely contours of her face, the clean lines of her jaw and throat. Then the startled blush on her cheeks and jump of anger in her eyes, and the bounce of her thick, incredibly alive red hair on her shoulders as she walked away with scissoring steps.

He felt bad the way he had treated her and wished there was some way he could take back the things he had said. There wasn't of course. Later, after he tossed and turned himself to sleep, black-haired ghouls in leather coats chased him through the streets of Naples with automatic weapons with barrels like cannons.

Chapter Nineteen

N ATHAN WOKE IN the morning to a diatribe of

blasphemy. It sounded like Dixon and Matthews out in the hall. They were using profanity, injected with vitriol against God and people who believed in God, and who, because of their beliefs, felt the need to buttonhole everyone within earshot. Christians should be put against the wall; this said with colorful invectives against dubious mothers in general and sons in particular, and colored with layers of sacrilege that bordered comic genius.

Cooper, wearing a towel and flip-flops, flap-footed into the room, holding his toilet bag against his hip with one hand while reading what looked like a religious tract with the other.

"What's going on out there?" Nathan asked.

"Dixon and Matthews don't like being told they're going to hell."

"I can hear. Who's telling them that? Skip?"

"No. Jesse. He's in the showers preaching Jesus. You should hear that boy lay it out. He's a born preacher. He says drug pushers are going to hell and they ought to repent. Fornicators and alcoholics too." He chuckled. "Guess that includes us."

"Jesse Calderon?"

"He became one of those Born Agains last night…telling everybody in ten square blocks about it."

Nathan shook his head.

Cooper put his toilet bag in his wall locker, came around and sat down on the edge of his bed flipping through the religious tract. "He slipped these under everyone's door last night…stirred up a hornet's nest. What do you make of this stuff, Nate?"

"I think it's getting to be a circus around here."

Cooper stopped at a page and read. "We are separated from a holy God because of our sins."

"Bunk."

"You don't believe the Bible?" Cooper frowned at the tract. "My sister believes it. She says she prays for me every night that I'll get my act together." He chuckled, smiled weakly at Nathan. "I guess I'm going to hell."

Nathan looked over at him. "We got calisthenics, you know. What're you doin' taking a shower?"

"I'm still on light duty."

IT WAS A bitter cold morning. The sky was bright and clear with a sulfur breeze blowing. The Marines of 1st Platoon, fifty strong, wearing utility trousers and caps, sweatshirts and boots, were standing at parade rest on the roof of the barracks, blowing breath clouds as they waited to begin morning calisthenics. Sergeant Rockman, the Platoon Sergeant, was standing in front of the formation in masculine virility. His thick hands were planted hostilely on his narrow waist, so that his elbows cut the air at crisp right-angles. His utility trousers were starched, with sharp vertical creases, front and back, and bloused at the top of his spit-shined boots that gleamed like silver moons, the toes of which pointed outward at an angle of forty-five degrees.

"What's the holdup, Sergeant Rockman?" Mick asked, bouncing from foot to foot.

Rockman's pale green eyes swept over to the rooftop door with smoldering contempt, his square-nailed fingers drumming his waist. "The CO wants to address the platoon," he said with a drawling voice that had an edge like a saw blade.

"Don't he know it's freezing up here?"

"Shut up, Donovan."

Mick, still bouncing, turned to Nathan and winked. His eyes, glowing in the early sun, had the tight amphetamine-induced brightness in them, and his breath, undiluted, did not mix well with the sulfur blowing off the hills. Fortunately for Nathan he did not have a hangover. "I got it worked out, Natboy," he said from the corner of his mouth. "Slicker'n snot. Luigi came through."

"Yeah?"

Just then the rooftop door opened and Sergeant Rockman stood at attention. "Platoon, atten…HUH!"

The Marines snapped to attention.

Captain Brickner came out of the stairwell onto the roof in barracks beige and blue, his white barracks hat set square on his chiseled head. He walked stiff-legged with his left hand behind his ramrod back, the right swinging stiff-armed like an upside down metronome, ending with a fist gripping his swagger stick.

The Executive Officer and Sergeant Major followed him across the tarmac like obedient hounds, likewise in barracks beige and blue, their tails neatly and properly tucked with military deference, and stood just behind him in front of the formation.

Captain Brickner stood, feet together, and cast a cold gray eye over the formation, then glared at the Platoon Sergeant.

Sergeant Rockman clicked his boot heels and snapped a salute. "1st Platoon, all present and accounted for…SUH!"

Captain Brickner returned his salute. "Very good, Sergeant. Stand at ease, men."

The Marines stood at ease, shivering.

Captain Brickner, slapping the red stripe on his trousers with the swagger stick, turned from his waist up and glanced over the formation, aiming his proud jaw at the chins of every man in the front rank. A malevolent light flickered in his steel gray eyes when they halted at Skip McPherson.

Brickner made a sound of contempt in his chest. "It has come to my attention that there has been religious proselytizing in the barracks. I want it stopped immediately."

He slapped his leg with the stick to emphasize his point. "If you want to believe in Jesus that's your business. It's a Marine's right to worship the God of his choosing. Pray to him in the base chapel. But do not—I repeat—do not push him down the throats of your fellow Marines. I won't have it. I want him kept behind doors on Sunday mornings where he belongs, is that understood?"

"Yes, sir," the Marines said in unison.

Skip McPherson said, "No, sir."

Captain Brickner stiffened. His neck and cheeks flushed red. His eyes burned. He stepped over to Skip McPherson, leaned forward from his waist so that their faces were inches apart. "Maybe you didn't hear what I said, Marine."

"I heard what you said, sir."

"I don't want you talking to the other Marines about Jesus Christ, is that understood?"

"While on duty, yes sir."

"Whether you are on duty or off, it makes no difference. You are not to proselytize, is that understood?"

"No, sir."

The arteries in Brickner's neck stood out. His lower lip quivered. "That is a direct order, Marine."

"Then I must disobey it, sir. Respectfully, sir. I serve God, country, and Corps, in that order…not the reverse."

Brickner stood back and slapped his leg with the swagger stick. He glared at McPherson with cold hatred. He angled his jaw to the Platoon Sergeant. "Put this man on report. I want to see him in my office at once."

Sergeant Rockman nodded sharply. "Yes, SUH!"

"That is all."

Sergeant Rockman saluted, Captain Brickner returned it, pivoted on his heels and walked back across the roof. The Executive Officer and Sergeant Major followed him.

Sergeant Rockman faced the platoon and growled, "Platoon, atten-HUH!"

The Marines came to attention.

"Lance Corporal McPherson, fall out."

Skip stepped forward out of the front rank and stood at attention.

Sergeant Rockman looked him over, a sneer curling along his upper lip, as though he had a communicable disease. "Report to the CO's office at once, Marine. You better hope there's a God, 'cause you're gonna need Him."

Skip strode across the roof, opened the door and shut it. A cold bitter wind blew over the roof and shivered among the ranks of the formation.

Mick resumed bouncing from foot to foot, grinning. "That mean we can't proselytize Waves or WMs in our rooms, Sergeant Rockman? There's a Wave in Disbursing that could stand some proselytizing."

"Shut up, Donovan, you're at attention."

N ATHAN HEARD IN the showers that Skip was given barracks restriction for one month. He walked down to his room at the end of the hall. He could hear music. Cooper was standing in the hall, looking into Skip's room. Nathan looked past him. Skip, Clarence and Jesse were playing guitars and singing Jesus songs.

Skip seemed undisturbed that he had been given an official reprimand. In fact, he seemed cheerful about it. The other two, likewise, seemed cheery.

Cooper nodded. "Hey, Nate."

"What're you doing?"

"The CO shouldn't have said that. A man ought to be able to believe what he wants."

Nathan glanced into the room at the three Marines, looked back at Cooper. "You getting religion too?"

"I'm just listening. Any harm in that?"

Nathan shook his head dubiously. "Knock yourself out."

He went across the hall into his room, shut the door, opened his locker and changed into his civvies. He had a thought that disturbed him, shook it off and closed his locker. "Forget it," he said.

He started to leave but found himself standing in the middle of his room, staring down absently at the white marble chips in the terrazzo floor. He was thinking about her. He grabbed the back of his neck and gave it a couple of hard pulls. He walked around the room, thinking about her, sat down on his bed, cast a quick look at the framed photo on his side table, stood and walked around the room some more.

Maddie Gallagher had him walking in circles.

"This is nuts." He glanced over at the desk, went over to it and got out the tract with the phone number of the Station stamped on the back. He looked at the number, flapped the tract against his hand as he thought about calling her. He had no idea what he would tell her. He hated talking on telephones. "Phooey," he said, tossed the tract back into the open drawer, shut it and left the room.

Chapter Twenty

Y OUR FATHER SAID you are determined to go
back to the States."

"I think it's best, Mom."

"You've given this a lot of thought and prayer, of
course?"

"Of course."

"I don't understand."

"I don't either."

Maddie looked at her mother, then down at her
plate. They were sitting at the table in the Station eating
a lunch of grilled cheese sandwiches and potato salad.
The sun shone in through the windows of the great room
and lay rectangles of softly glowing light on the floor.
With her father and brother gone to school it was quiet,

except for the muted honk of horns and street traffic outside.

"I just think it best if I go," she repeated, pushing potato salad around with her fork. "I could get a job in Scotts Valley. I went through all this with Dad. He said it was okay."

"Do you really want to go?"

Maddie didn't answer.

"Please tell me, Maddie. Is it because of that Marine? What was his name…Lance Corporal Kessler?"

"Nathan." Maddie lay her fork down, glanced out the windows at the harbor. "I know it's a lame reason, but I have strong feelings for him."

"What kind of feelings?"

"I'm not sure. I think I might be in love."

"You think?"

"I've never been in love before, Mom." Maddie smiled weakly. "Change that. I don't think I love him, I know I do. I'm as sure of it as the morning you woke up and knew you were in love with Dad. The difference is that the man I love is not a Christian."

"What is it about him that you love?"

Maddie thought for a moment. "There's a natural attraction, of course, but there've been a lot of guys I thought were good looking that didn't do a thing for me."

"And Nathan does?"

"Don't ask me why. It's the mystery of the ages. He's hard and brash and arrogant. Sometimes I want to punch him in the nose. I almost did last night. He had to let me know he was seeing some Italian girl this weekend."

"Doesn't that bother you?"

"Of course it bothers me. It makes me want to shout at the moon. It makes me want to kick myself around the block for giving him a nickel's worth of my heart. But when I look into his eyes I see something in them that belongs to me alone."

She gazed down at her plate.

"Maybe it's naiveté or wishful thinking," she continued, "but beneath the hard exterior I see a kind and gentle person. He's built walls around himself a Sherman tank couldn't blast through. Maybe he's been deeply hurt by something or someone in his past, I don't know. I'm just drawn to him."

She looked at her mother. "I think about him all the time. I go to bed thinking about him. I wake up thinking about him. I love him, Mom."

Her mother said nothing.

They were quiet for a few moments. The chimes from the mantel clock struck the quarter hour, its soft golden resonance ringing off into silence.

"Does he share your feelings?" Kitty asked.

Maddie picked up her fork and shoved potato salad around some more. "I don't know."

"You think by leaving you're going to stop loving him?"

"I don't know that either. But I know that if I leave I won't see him, and I know that I won't be tempted to do anything foolish."

"You couldn't just walk away from him and stay here?"

"I wish I could. But I know I would see him eventually at one of the gates, or around base, or in town. We keep running into each other."

"Maybe there's a reason for it."

Maddie frowned at her. "You mean like I'm God's man for the job kind of thing?"

"Woman."

"Why would God bring a non-Christian into my life?"

"For you to be a light to him perhaps. Not to be your mate, of course, but as a friend, maybe."

Maddie shook her head, sighed deeply. "No. I'm not strong enough. I'm afraid of my feelings."

Kitty reached over and patted her hand. "You've never run from anything in your life, honey."

"This is very difficult for me, Mom. Please don't make it more so."

"I'm trying not to. But if you leave—and you're certainly old enough to make that decision—please leave because God wants you to, and not because you're afraid. Never act from fear."

"I'm sorry, Mom. I've got to pack." She pushed away from the table and carried her plate into the kitchen and washed it. As she set the plate on the rack to dry, she glanced over and saw her mother, still sitting at the table, gazing out the windows across the room.

The doorbell rang.

Kitty checked her watch, wondered who it could be at this early hour, stood, then went to the front door and opened it. It was a serviceman, a Marine. He was walking back toward the stairs, as if he had changed his mind about coming to the Station.

"We're home," Kitty said.

The Marine stopped and looked back. It took Kitty a moment to recognize him in civilian clothes, but it was the Marine whom she'd seen at the NSA main gate, two months ago. "You're Lance Corporal Kessler, aren't you?"

He blinked at her, clearly amazed that she knew his name. "Yes, ma'am. Nate—er, Nathan."

"I'm Kitty, Maddie's mother," she said. She extended her hand and he shook it. "Won't you come in?"

Nathan glanced past her into the Station. "That's all right. If you could just tell Maddie that I was here, I'd appreciate it."

"Please wait, Nathan. I'll get her."

He started down the stairs. "That's okay. I'll just catch her later."

"She's leaving for the States in two days."

He stopped and turned. "She's leaving?"

"Sunday morning. Please come in."

Nathan came back and stepped into the hall.

Kitty guided him down the hall into the great room.

"Is she going back for a visit or something?" Nathan asked.

"I'm afraid not. It's quite permanent. Please have a seat," she said, indicating a pair of stuffed chairs by the windows. "We have coffee and soft drinks, if you'd like."

"No thanks." He watched her disappear down a dark hallway to the left of the kitchen. He could see where Maddie got her good looks. Her mother was a beautiful woman. There was something else about her too, something intangible. The woman exuded peace, just like Maddie. He liked that.

He stood in the sudden silence of the room, trying to process the news he'd just heard. He felt a disquieting hollowness in his chest. Maddie was leaving.

He looked around the room at the game tables, at the chairs going along the walls, at the painting of Jesus over the mantel. The sound of a coffeepot percolating drew his eyes past the long dinner table across the room and back to the kitchen. Coffee vapors permeated the air.

He felt uneasy, as if hidden eyes were watching him. He glanced around the room again, looked at the picture of Jesus, and then, feeling a sudden urge to bolt, saw Maddie appear in the entrance of the hallway.

"Hello, Nathan."

She was wearing faded blue jeans and a loose salmon-colored sweater that complimented her red hair that she wore parted down the middle and secured on either side with a cloth barrette. She padded silently toward him in stocking feet, narrow with high insteps, and stood in a square of sunlight coming in through the windows. "We keep bumping into each other," she said, with a guarded tone.

Nathan nodded, his mind drawing a blank on how to respond. "I thought I'd come by," he said lamely.

She indicated an ensemble of stuffed chairs to his right, the same ones her mother had indicated. "Why don't we sit down."

Nathan felt powerless to refuse, and sat in the chair that afforded the best wall protection for his back.

Maddie took the one facing him, brushed her hair back from her shoulders with flicks of her hand, so that Nathan could hear the crackling of static electricity.

She sat, straight-backed, looking at him with her hands gripping her knees, the knuckles showing white. He put his hands on his knees, so that they were like bookends.

He smiled.

She smiled.

"Can I get you something to drink? Soda? Coffee?"

The room was a bit overcharged with politeness and formality. He shook his head. "No thanks." The smile drifted off his face. "Your mom said you're leaving for the States on Sunday."

She nodded.

"I thought you weren't going back until the fall semester."

"My plans have changed. I thought I'd get a head start on a job and a place to live."

"Leaving Sunday, huh?"

"I'm booked on the ten a.m. flight to Rome. Are you sure I can't get you something to drink? There's a fresh pot of coffee."

"I'm fine, really." He glanced around the room, just to be doing something with his eyes. "So this is the Way Station. It's nice. Homey."

"Most of the guys don't get here until late afternoon."

He looked at her. "I came here to see you," he said in a serious tone he hadn't used with her before. "There's something I've got to get off my chest."

Her shoulders stiffened perceptively, the knuckles of her hands whitening even more. "Oh?" She gave him an ironical look. "You mean there's more than last night?"

"I was wrong. I want to apologize."

She sat back in her chair and stared, her eyes measuring his words for leaks. She had been expecting a different answer apparently. "There's no need, Nathan," she said less guardedly. "I told you that your life is your life. I hope I didn't come across as judgmental. I didn't mean to if I did."

Nathan leaned forward, braced his elbows on his knees, let his hands dangle as if they were spare appendages that needed airing. "I wanted to make you angry."

"Why?"

"I had my reasons."

"Would you care to share them with me?"

He shook his head. "I don't know if you'd understand. I don't know if I understand."

"Try me."

He smiled grimly, glanced down at his hands and made a spider-on-a-mirror with them. "I don't like Christians," he said directly. "I don't trust them."

"Why?"

"It doesn't matter why. I just don't trust them. Can we leave it at that?"

She frowned at him steadily for a few moments. "Okay," she said. "Then you don't like or trust me, do you? It would explain some of our conversations."

Nathan looked up from his hands. "No, I *do* like you. I *do* trust you—that's just it. I get around you and I want to be nice. I want to make you laugh. You make me want to believe in the human race. You've got me confused."

"I've got *you* confused?"

"Yes. We talk, things go okay for a bit, and then something comes up in me that just wants to make you angry."

Her eyes were bright, inquisitive, probing. "That *is* confusing."

"I said it was."

"Did something happen in your past that made you bitter towards Christians? Towards God?"

"I'd rather not talk about it."

"Fine. But I think it's important that we do talk about it—if not for my sake then for yours."

He stared at her a couple moments, deciding.

He stood and stepped over to one of the windows and gazed out at the brassy hues of the harbor. A ferry trailing an inverted V of foamy sparkles was rounding the Molo San Vincenzo breakwater for its early afternoon run to one of the islands. He watched the crush of traffic below, people moving about. He glanced over at a pigeon lighting on the slightly green and dirty windows of the Galleria arcade, then sidling over next to one of his buddies.

Nathan massaged the back of his neck, as if that would clear his thoughts. "It'll be lonely around here without you," he said. He peered back to catch her reaction.

"There's your Roman girl. Nicoletta?"

He scoffed, turned back and watched the ferry that he saw now was heading toward Capri. "You may not believe this, but when I'm with her I think about you."

"It sounds complicated."

"I didn't mean it to be." He turned around and faced her, putting his hands in his pockets. "I like you, Maddie. You're a good and decent person," he said. "You're the first real Christian girl I've ever met. I guess one of the reasons I try to make you angry is I want to see if what you believe holds up."

"Interesting."

He shrugged. "I didn't say it made sense."

She sat peering at him, her head down-turned slightly so that her eyes were shaded by her brow. "I'm not especially good, Nathan. It's nice of you to think so, but I can be a jerk just like anyone else."

"No. Not like anyone else. You're the most genuine person I ever met. I mean it. Ever. The rest of them..."

She lifted her head slightly, a lance of sunlight catching the corners of her eyes beneath the long lashes. Her eyes were bright and moist, as if holding back tears. She looked like a little girl. A dream.

A part of him wanted to take her in his arms and hold her tightly, feeling her goodness spread through his body like a healing balm. Another part of him—the old cold deadliness—wanted to smash the china and crystal.

It must have shown on his face, because she said, "Who has hurt you, Nathan? Who has put this sword of anger in your heart?"

He felt a lump in his throat, looked quickly out the window at the wide blue emptiness of the bay. The lump swelled. His vision blurred. Powerful emotions moved through him like breakers—anger, hatred, grief, a host of others—one after the other. He waited several moments for the breakers to subside, cleared the emotion from his throat, and said, "When I was a boy..." He stopped and shook his head. "No."

"Please tell me, Nathan."

"There's nothing to tell."

"When you were a boy–*what*, Nathan? Did someone hurt you?"

His eyes watered again. He bit down hard on his teeth and chuckled, shaking his head. Then he turned to her, made a couple curious sweeps over her face, and glanced at the mantel clock when it struck the quarter hour. "Is that the time?" He checked his watch. "I should be going."

"You're not going to tell me?"

"No."

"Please trust me, Nathan. You don't like Christians. You don't trust them. I want to change your opinion."

"From California?" He grinned ironically.

She glanced down at her hands, looked back at him. "I wish you would trust me."

"Like I said, I do." He walked past her, stopped and waited for her at the mouth of the hallway. She walked him down the hall to the door. They stood facing each other. He smiled. She smiled.

He felt an odd sense of *déjá vu*, as though he had played the scene somewhere before in his past—the red hair, the look in her eyes, the little girl pout on her lips. "Do you mind if I write?"

"I would like that very much."

He extended his hand. "I guess this is it then."

She gazed down at his hand then shook it firmly, as though she meant it. Her hand was cool, her fingers long and smooth.

"It's been nice knowing you, Maddie."

"It's been nice knowing you too, Nathan. Thank you for stopping by." She held his hand for a few moments then let it go. "I'll send you my address when I know what it is."

He shrugged his shoulders, made a helpless palms-out gesture with his hands. "I don't believe this. You're really leaving."

Her eyes misted. "Try not to break too many nice things, Nathan. It's unhealthy."

He stood looking at her, made some more meaningless gestures with his hands, then he took a hesitant step toward her. "Can I give you a hug?"

Her lips trembled. She stepped forward with a lunge, wrapped her arms around his waist and squeezed.

Holding her, feeling her against him, he could smell the clean, strawberry scent of shampoo as her hair brushed the side of his face, felt her hands move up his back, holding tightly, her cheek pressed hard against his shoulder. She felt small. Her shoulders shook lightly. She was crying.

"Maddie…"

She shook her head against him.

"Maddie…"

She stepped back, wiping tears from her eyes. "You'd best go, Nathan."

"I…"

"Please go."

He let his arms fall to his sides, compressed his lips together. "I wish we could've gotten to be better friends."

"I do too, Nathan. Please."

He opened the door and looked back. Her eyes were wide and bright. Tears slid down her cheeks. "Don't stop praying for me," he said.

Her right hand came up to her face, then she whirled and walked away quickly.

He watched her until she disappeared around the corner, heard her padding footsteps fading somewhere in the distance, then listened to the sound of nothing in the empty hall.

He closed the door and went down the stairs.

Nathan walked through the Galleria in a mind fog. A hole had opened up inside him that grew wider and wider. It had opened in a part of him that he didn't know existed, like an untried muscle aching after a new exercise. The hole sucked all light into it, all emotion, like a black hole that shut the light of hope behind an impenetrable iron safe.

He walked out into the Square and headed south toward the harbor in a desultory manner, his feet moving just to be moving. There was no goal in his walking.

He stopped in front of the Castel Nuovo and noticed it for the first time. There had been other buildings along the way that he hadn't noticed but this one was a medieval castle with crenellations surmounting the towers and walls, and it seemed to lunge out into his path. There were children playing on the sloping lawn and people standing around with cameras. He heard the sound of a ship's horn bleating politely in the distance. It would be impressive if he were in a mood to be impressed.

"Well, she's leaving, Nate."

"I tried to stop her, Frankie."

"I think she loves you."

Nathan thought about that. "I think I love her too."

"Then why're you going to Ischia with that Roman girl?"

"It's complicated, Frankie."

"No it ain't."

Nathan ambled east along the harbor, looking out at the ships. The ships meant nothing to him. A liberty boat loaded with eager sailors with fat wallets angled toward the landing.

He checked his watch, saw that he still had an hour to kill before he was to meet Nico at the ferry landing. Thinking of Nico did nothing for him. He headed north along the Square, stopped in front of the San Pedro and peered directly ahead at the Galleria Umberto. He felt loss. He felt the hole widening behind the impenetrable safe in his chest, sucking into it even more light.

Maddie leaving did that.

Chapter Twenty-One

T HE TWO OF them had crossed the bay on the

ferry from the Molo Beverello, to the island of Ischia in the mid-afternoon. They disembarked in the harbor with its multicolored shops and houses and cafés curving against the hills and, because the weather had warmed, Nico drove the coast road in her Alfa Romeo with the top down. It was still the off-season, so there were not many tourists. There were a few Europeans, mostly German, but the majority were local Italians who came over for the day. The road was free of traffic.

Nathan scanned the hills covered in vines. They had been cut back for the winter with new growth just beginning to show on the vines, the parallel rows of stakes following the undulations of the terrain. White plastered houses with tiled roofs stood amid the variety of trees and groves. The island rose on his left, the slopes blue in shadow. As they drove along the curving road, he admired the ruggedness of the volcanic topography and the azure sea, always on his right with sailboats tilting in the wind.

"Isn't it beautiful?" Nico asked.

"Very."

"It is still a secret, but I am sure that it will not last long. Good things do not last long."

Nathan glanced at her. Her hair was blowing wildly in the wind and slapping across her face and shoulders as she drove.

"Am I still your beautiful girl?" she asked, peering ahead at the road.

"You are very beautiful."

"That was not my question. I asked if I were *your* beautiful girl. There is a difference."

"You are *my* beautiful girl. Where's your villa?"

"On the south side of the island. It won't take long."

"We're heading north."

"You must be patient. I know it is not a virtue of men."

Nathan looked back at the hills and said nothing.

They were climbing higher into the dark foothills of Mount Epomeo, the slopes terraced with vineyards and olive groves and fruit trees. They drove through towns and small villages, with churches and campaniles, with the road sometimes cutting into the slope and bougainvillea spilling over stone retaining walls into the narrow road. Locals walking or riding bicycles would stop and stare at the canary yellow sports car winding through the switchbacks with its tires squealing. Some waved. When they did Nico raised a hand into the air.

"You're not afraid to be recognized by your countrymen?" Nathan asked.

"They are my friends. If word is leaked to my mother, she will forbid me to come, but I will find a way, as I always have."

"A nice system you have."

"Isn't it?"

The road swung back on itself, heading south, and once again Nathan could see the blue of the sea with Capri shining in the distance as they drove along the road. And then the car slowed and turned in through the gates of a rather large villa on the leeward side of the slope, while the bay spread out below and beyond the road.

"Do you see?" she said. "It is as I told you."

Later that evening a cool breeze was blowing from the west. It was pleasant and clean and brought with it the smell of wet vegetation up the slopes. There was no smell of sulfur here, even though a volcano had formed the island, but the smell of the sea was immediate and undiluted and cleaned the palate of the senses like a good Chardonnay.

Warbling through the breeze and the smells were the high notes of an Italian tenor bemoaning the tragedies of love.

They were sipping a local white wine on the wide curving terrace of the villa overlooking Sant Angelo and the beach that Nathan had seen in the travel magazine.

Palms planted in earthen pots around the terrace swayed gently in the breeze, their fronds, like long pointed fingers, tickling the stars awake in the darkening sky.

The villa was cut into a slope of vineyards, and even at this height they could hear the surf and the muted cries of seagulls piloting thermal updrafts. Except for the connecting spit, the rock off the point really did remind him of the one in Morro Bay. It was a scene in which to be lost. A scene in which to think and to wonder and hope against hope. But Nathan, thinking it through logically and practically, knew it would never happen now that Maddie was leaving. The hole in his chest grew even larger because of it.

Nico, wearing a saffron silk wrap, crossed her legs at the knees and bounced a bronzed bare foot languidly to a melody apart from the tenor. The light was in her hair with many colors like the late sun on the bay. She was gazing out over the terrace with the last of the sun radiant on her face, highlighting her rich olive complexion, her head turned as if a photographer had posed her especially to capture the soft hollows of her cheekbones in the best light.

Nathan turned away from her and was now watching a freighter heading south, far out in the sea, a burnished glinting silhouette sliding almost imperceptibly across the horizon against a yellow-orange and turquoise sky. But he was not thinking about the ship, or even of Nico, nor was he feeling the cool flagstone tiles beneath the soles of his feet, the tiles smoothly worn and pleasant. Instead, he was thinking about Maddie and he wondered what he had to do to not think about her.

He chuckled inwardly. Nathan Kessler, atheist, falling for a missionary girl. A bright, witty, sincere—oh so sincere—and of course very pretty missionary girl. It seemed a joke, a jest of Fate. But Nathan didn't believe in Fate either. Then he felt the touch of cool fingers on his hand.

Nico was smiling at him in all of her Latin loveliness. "Where are you, my love?"

He frowned at her quizzically. "What do you mean?"

"You are very quiet."

"Am I?"

"Since we left Naples."

"I'm just taking it all in," he lied. "It's beautiful."

"You are thinking about something?" She smiled. "Some*one* perhaps? Is it another girl?"

"No," he lied.

She took a sip of wine, the sun shining through the sparkling amber luminescence as she set the glass back down on the marble-topped table. "I have told you before that it would not matter if there was another girl. I am here and she is not. I am practical about these matters. But please, my love, think about her on her time and not mine."

"What makes you think there's another girl?"

"I am very intuitive. The tilt of your head, the wistful cast in your eye—these speak a language that is clearly heard." She reached for the pack of Salems on the table.

"Now you are jealous."

"I am not jealous." She lit a cigarette and blew smoke into the breeze. "But if I met your girl I would scratch out her eyes."

"You are my girl."

"It is good to lie about her when you are with me. You are a bit clumsy but please continue. And when you go back to her you can lie about me. Is she beautiful? Of course she's beautiful. I hate her."

"What's all this, Nico? There is no other girl, honestly."

"Honestly?" She laughed. "Is there such a word?"

He went to put his arm around her shoulder and she flinched away.

"I am sorry, Natti," she said. "I am your beautiful crazy girl tonight, didn't you know?"

He held her, kissed the back of her neck. "I have two days with you, Nico, and I am crazy about you. There is no one else, I swear."

She laughed throatily. "My dear love, Natti. Forgive me for the fool that I am. I will help you forget your other girl while you are with me."

She took his hand and stood. She kissed him lightly on the side of his mouth. Then she kissed him like she meant it. "Would you like to go swimming?" she asked, tracing his ear with the tip of her finger. "The pool is heated, and there are only the two of us. I'm afraid there is little else here in the way of nightlife."

"Swimming sounds great."

The next morning they had breakfast in a café in the village of Sant Angelo. A heavy fog hung over the marina, making the rock seem very close, and the muted cries of seagulls sounded otherworldly as they swooped to snatch fish from the castoff piles of fishermen.

Nathan sat drinking coffee, watching two fishermen in striped T-shirts haul their boat onto the beach of the spit. They had apparently been out since very early in the morning, or perhaps even all night. One of them was smoking a short pipe as he sorted through the catch, and the other, laughing at something, stood with both hands pressed against his lower back, bowing his chest, as though adjusting his spine. There were more boats coming through the fog into the marina like Stygian shades.

"I like it here," Nathan said, at last feeling free of the mainland. "I could live in a place like this."

"Could you? Americans love their large spaces."

"Where I live is very similar to this, except for the old worldliness of the fishermen."

"Have you told me where you are from?"

"Morro Bay?"

She shook her head.

"It's on the middle coast of California. There is a harbor and a rock, like this one, that the birds use for target practice. Have you ever seen an elephant seal?"

"It sounds like a trick question."

"It isn't. They're huge, with long noses like elephants." He made a nose with his hand and wrist and waved it off his face like an elephant's trunk, raising his head to make a deep-throated coughing bark. "That's a challenge to clear off interloper males," he said.

She laughed. "My lovely Natti has come back to me." She kissed him and lighted a cigarette. "Tell me about Morro Bay. It does not sound very American."

"There's a lot of cattle to the north and of course the beach. The best of both worlds. They've also got a polytechnic university in nearby San Luis Obispo. I would like to go there once I'm out of the Corps and study architecture."

"There is architecture in America?"

"We build a few houses."

"Oh?"

They drove along the coast road past a scattering of houses and buildings, and followed the road down to Maronti Beach. The beach was a long, scalloped bight beginning at the base of the spit of Sant Angelo and terminating at the rocky cliffs at the easternmost end, over a mile away.

There were a few restaurants and hotels along the beach, mostly deserted now in the off-season, except for flocks of birds working the shore and a man far down on the beach fishing the surf. There wasn't the white powder of Nathan's dreams. The sand was coarse and yellow gray in the sun, with a sprinkling of black peppers of volcanic rock, but it was no less beautiful.

They held hands and walked leisurely toward the cliffs in the firm wet sand of the tide reach. The water was too cold for swimming so they removed their shoes, feeling the sand give way beneath their feet as the water rushed and receded with a tumbling of pebbles and broken shells in the foam. They were alone and the cliffs pushing into the sea gave them a feeling of remoteness and of privacy, a world to themselves.

"When the tide is out you can climb up into the rocks and sunbathe," Nico said, pointing. "No one can see you."

"Not even the ships?"

She looked out to sea. "They could see you, of course, if they watched through telescopes."

"I wouldn't put it past sailors."

"Still, it is private. Also there are spas where you can bathe in water heated by fumaroles. They are openings in the base of the volcano."

"I read about them."

"They are therapeutic," she said, glancing toward the hills. "Many tourists come for the mud baths too, which are very healthy for the skin."

"I always got in trouble for taking mud baths. When I was a boy," he added.

She slapped his arm, and then put her arm around his waist. "You are always joking. But don't stop, my love. I like it when you joke. Joking is healthy. I read it somewhere."

"Right now I've worked up a healthy appetite. Is that a restaurant?"

And then they were sitting at a corner table on the covered patio of a restaurant overlooking the beach. The sand came up to the building and beach grass grew along the base of the white clapboard siding. They had come up the wooden steps from the beach, first setting down their shoes on the bottom step then brushing the sand from their feet before stepping onto the patio. They were the only ones there and had their choice of tables.

The waitress was a square-shouldered, red-cheeked woman with blonde braids, and when she came to their table with their drinks she spoke German to Nathan. She thought he was German, since he looked German and there were many German tourists on the island. She was friendly and happy that they were there, and when Nathan spoke to her in Italian she thought he was from up north and could not be convinced that he was American.

"She likes you," Nico said, sipping hot tea when the waitress left with their order. "The way she was holding your face, looking at you."

"I remind her of her son, I'm sure." Nathan sipped his beer, gazing out at the fisherman casting into the surf. "I am the prodigal who has returned at long last."

"Her eyes were not those of a mother."

Nathan, feeling the pleasant smoothness of the tiles beneath his feet and the grit of sand between his toes, peered out at the sea that was blue and bronze and lovely in the sun. He listened to the surf and the cry of shorebirds and gulls and cormorants gathered on the rocks. The fisherman had one on the line and was reeling quickly, the rod bent violently as he stepped forward into the surf.

"You would like to join him?" Nico asked.

"Yes, I would."

"Then we will rent some fishing tools, and I will watch my great fisherman catch our supper."

"We might go hungry."

"We will never go hungry when we are filled with love."

Nathan smiled but said nothing.

The waitress came with their plates. "Tuna salad for the *Signorina*—or should I say *Signora*?"

"We're not married."

"Yes…of course. Well then, I hope you enjoy." The waitress set a plate in front of Nathan. "Here you are, *Signore*…turkey and provolone." The waitress smiled, her cheeks flushed with embarrassment.

Nathan waited until she was out of earshot, leaned forward and said quietly, "That was a little abrupt, don't you think?"

"I did not like the way she was looking at you."

"You're not jealous of a forty year old woman who could probably beat me in an arm wrestle. What's wrong?"

"I have missed two of my monthlies."

Nathan gaped at her numbly, then he sat back in his chair. "Two of your monthlies?"

"I did not want to spoil our weekend together," she said. "It has happened before, so it is not a cause for alarm. I will know for certain in two weeks."

"Aren't you taking the pill or anything?"

"I am Catholic."

Nathan stared down at his uneaten sandwich. Suddenly, as though he were in a dream, he felt as though there was a distance between them; she, sitting at the table, and he, watching her from across the patio.

He heard the cry of seagulls, as though filtered through cotton, the pounding of waves that seemed to move inside him. "I'll marry you," he heard himself say.

"Will you? That is sweet," she said, her voice sounding a great distance away. "But I'll have no martyrs for husbands. Nor one that would marry out of pity." She sipped her tea, looked up at him with her golden hazel eyes. "Besides, what would your other girl think?"

"I said I would marry you."

She laughed, a trilling warble that winged over his head and drifted back an airy flutter. "Natti, you are precious. I am sorry to have mentioned it without knowing for certain. See, you are worried now."

Nathan frowned at her. The dreamlike feeling of sudden distance was gone, as quickly as if he had been awakened by a loud noise. He felt as close in proximity to her now as he could possibly get without actually touching, so that it made him claustrophobic. "It kind of sets you back."

She set her cup down. "You can imagine how I feel."

"I need to think." He pushed back from the table. "We've got to think this through."

An ironic smile played over her lips. "Are our wedding plans annulled so quickly, Natti?"

"I told you I would marry you. I meant it. We'll get married right away."

She chuckled. "Oh Natti." She picked up her teacup and set it back down, gazing across at him. "Surely you must have known there might be consequences."

"I assumed you were protected."

"There is no cause for alarm, as I have said. It was foolish of me to mention it."

She stood and came around behind him, leaned forward against his back with her arms draping around his chest. "Let's not quarrel, Natti. Please, come back to me, my love," she said, kissing his ear. "We have all of today and tomorrow, and there is just the two of us. The other is not certain."

"Sure." But in that moment Nathan felt a chill touch inside of him as though something had died. The death created an empty void in his chest, started there and worked its chilling outward into his arms and down into his legs. He shivered.

"You are cold, my love?"

"No."

She caressed the side of his face with her lips. "There is another solution," she whispered. "It would be scandalous, of course."

"Solution?" Nathan turned in his chair and faced her. "You mean–?"

"Don't look so shocked, Natti. More and more women are doing it."

"Doesn't your religion say something about killing babies?"

"It's a fetus." She raised her hand in front of Nathan's face, holding her forefinger and thumb together so that they were almost touching. "If it exists it is only this big by now. A germ. Nothing more."

"I don't want you to do it."

She laughed.

"I mean it, Nico, don't do it. I said I would marry you."

"Oh Natti, you are so provincial."

Chapter Twenty-Two

Maddie and her mother spent Saturday morning shopping for shoes and clothes in the open markets of nearby Caserta. Many of the clothing items were second hand, but in good shape—perfect for a college girl on a budget. Maddie's taste in clothing ran from Paris and New York chic to street funk. Chic was what you made it: corduroy bell-bottoms with silk blouses, tie-dye T-shirts with knit ponchos, bolero jackets or jeans with holes in the knees, and boots or sandals or bare feet, with or without toenail polish.

The open markets were teaming with shoppers and vendors, some foreign, most Italian, the air rife with excited voices haggling prices. Great deals were to be had for the shrewd and persistent haggler with a good sense of timing.

Maddie bought a pair of beautiful handmade burgundy leather boots with block heels that went well with a skirt in Gallagher tartan she had recently purchased through a mail-order catalog. She haggled the price down to the cuticles. She didn't ask the shrunken old woman with a broken nose and black shawl how she had acquired them, knowing they may have come through the black market. While shopping, her motto was: hear no evil, speak no evil, go for the jugular.

She stared out of the window of the *cinque cento* as her mother made her way out of Caserta on surface streets. Then they got onto the southbound *autostrasse* to Naples, Kitty staying to the right at an impressive one hundred kilometers per hour. Speed boys in Ferraris and Lamborghinis zoomed past her as though she was still in first gear.

"You all packed for tomorrow?" Kitty asked.

"All but the things I bought today."

"Those leather boots are beautiful."

"Uh-huh."

"I think you could've gotten the price down even more."

"Probably."

Kitty glanced over at her, looked back on the road as a low slung Alfa Romeo whooshed by at a cool one-fifty. The little Fiat shuddered. "These drivers," she said. She glanced over at Maddie for a reaction, got none. "You okay, honey?"

"I'm fine."

"Sure?"

"Sure."

They drove in silence for a kilometer.

"Everything go okay with Nathan yesterday?" Kitty asked. "You never said how your conversation went."

"It went fine."

"He seems like a nice man."

"He is."

"He's very polite. And handsome."

"Uh-huh."

"What did he want? We don't have to talk about it."

"There's nothing to talk about. He'd said some rude things to me the night before. He came over to apologize. That was it, really."

Patchwork fields of farmland came up on their left; on their right were industrial, commercial and residential properties that choked the landscape. Maddie closed her eyes, listened to the whine of the tiny motor, the vibration of the little car giving its best. In her mind she could see Nathan at the Station, his back to her as he peered out the window at the harbor. She opened her eyes and he disappeared.

"I think something happened to him when he was a boy," she said.

Kitty looked at her. "Nathan?"

"I don't know what it was. He started to tell me but stopped. I got the feeling that something or someone hurt him. Whatever it was, I think he blames God for it. Christians too."

Kitty shook her head sadly. "No idea, huh?"

"None."

Kitty reached over and patted her hand.

They arrived home in the early afternoon. Sean was home—book satchel on the table, crumbs on the counter, dirty milk glass, the smell of "boy" in the air.

A note from her father was placed on the counter. He had gone back to the base to talk with Chaplain Simms, and would be back before dinner. As they were putting groceries into the refrigerator the doorbell rang.

Kitty was on her tiptoes, putting a bag of flour onto a shelf. "Could you get that, honey?"

"Sure, Mom." Maddie checked her watch on her way to the door. "Who can that be?" she said, knowing the Station didn't officially open for another two hours. She opened the door. It was Clarence and Jesse. They appeared a little sheepish.

"Hi, guys," Maddie said.

"Is it too early?" Clarence asked.

"Not for you. I was hoping I'd see you tonight."

The two Marines followed her down the hallway into the great room. Maddie glanced over her shoulder. "Is Skip coming later?"

Clarence shook his head. "That's what we came to talk to you about."

"Oh?"

They took a seat at the dining table, the Marines on one side, Maddie facing them. They briefed her on recent events.

"The CO gave him a month's restriction to the barracks. He's lucky they didn't court-martial him."

Maddie frowned. "What'd he do?"

"The CO gave him a direct order," Jesse said. "Skip said he wouldn't obey it."

"That doesn't sound like Skip."

"Some of the men have been complaining about us Christians proselytizing in the barracks. The CO told us to cut it out. Skip said as long as he wasn't on duty he had the right to tell others about God."

"He does. It's called the First Amendment."

Clarence shook his head. "The CO doesn't see it that way. He says it's disrupting morale and discipline."

"Morale and discipline?"

Clarence shrugged.

"This happened yesterday morning?"

"At formation, yeah. The CO chewed him out in front of everybody."

Maddie frowned in thought. "Will they let him stand guard?"

Clarence nodded. "He's confined to barracks during liberty. You just won't see him in here for a while."

Maddie shook her head, glared across the room at the windows. "I don't believe this."

The Marines said nothing, turned and watched Kitty as she came over with a tray of tea and homemade cookies and set it on the table. She pulled out a chair and sat down beside Maddie. "What's this about Skip getting office hours?"

The Marines briefed her.

Maddie was staring down at the table, her lower lip clamped between her teeth as she processed the news. Thoughts turned in her mind with the weight and speed of heavy machinery: this cog turning that sprocket, turning this spindle, moving the other wheel. This cause, that effect. It occurred to her just then with supernal clarity, that she was deserting her post, a traitor to the Cause, and in that moment she came to a decision and looked up from the table. "Is Skip allowed visitors?" she asked.

"I think he can have visitors," Jesse said, "but they have to meet down in one of the admin offices. I can check for you Monday morning."

"I'd appreciate that."

Kitty frowned at her. "Aren't you forgetting your flight tomorrow, honey?"

The Marines gaped at her. "What flight?" Clarence asked. "Are you going somewhere?"

Maddie shook her head with resolve. "The flight was canceled."

Kitty shook her head, not understanding. "When did you hear that, Maddie?"

"I just now canceled it."

Chapter Twenty-Three

NATHAN FELT THE change as soon as he stepped onto the Quarterdeck. But it didn't register in his conscious mind at all, rather in his subconscious. It wasn't felt in the cold gray eyes of the Corporal of the Guard looking up at him with a challenge from behind the duty desk; neither was it felt in the driver's lank, lifeless form leaning back against the wall on two legs of the chair with his eyes shut. These were normal. As was the hum of fluorescent overheads, and the smell of the polished wax floor, and the inarticulate droning of night traffic outside. He had no idea what the change was or even *that* it was, but it prompted him to ask, "Anything new?"

"You tell me," Sergeant Turpick said, logging in his name, holding the pencil like he had thumbs for fingers. "You're the one back from liberty. How was it?"

"Fine."

Turpick chortled throatily, finishing the log. He glanced over at Lance Corporal Richey, and offered a lewd speculation out of the side of his mouth.

Nathan ignored the remark, but it prompted a smileless snickering from Lance Corporal Richey, who just then managed the energy to scratch the side of his nose with a long bony finger.

Nathan glanced at the duty roster and noted that he had the twelve to four on the main gate for the next guard cycle. He went upstairs with his bag, walked down the third floor hallway, and felt his scalp tingling for no reason. He jerked an eye quickly over his shoulder, as if someone were sneaking up behind him. There was no one. His boot heels sounded lonely in the empty hall. He glanced from side to side at the doors, some open, most closed.

Lance Corporal Lipton stepped into his doorway, peered down the hall to see who was coming. He was polishing the brass on his belt buckle. Lipton had recently come to the barracks. He wore only a National Defense ribbon—or "fire watch ribbon" as Marines called it—with his dress uniforms. His DD-214 file, according to Corporal Sanchez in administration, revealed that he was a two-year draftee, which made Naples his first, and likely his last duty station.

Nathan didn't believe it. Lipton had the look and presence of a lifer. Further, Nathan didn't like or trust the guy, not because he was a probable lifer but because when he looked at you with his pale, unblinking blue eyes, you got the feeling he was making mental notes that he would later report to the Platoon Sergeant.

The men called him "Teabag" because of his name.

Nathan nodded at him as he approached. "How's it going?"

Lipton nodded noncommittally, looking him over, his pale eyes blinking once like a camera shutter, as though recording details. "It's going. You're Kessler, aren't you?"

"That's right. And you're Teabag."

"I don't like that name. Lance Corporal Lipton, if you don't mind."

"Okay, Lance." It was things like that, "Lance Corporal Lipton, if you don't mind" that gave Nathan the creeps. "Shiny belt buckle you got there."

Lipton held it up to the light, caught a golden gleam, and continued polishing. "Not bad."

Nathan noticed his wristwatch: Marine green plastic body, light face, luminous dials and numerals, green nylon wristband. "That a Staff NCO watch you're wearing? Saw plenty of them at Lejeune."

Lipton glanced quickly at his watch. A shadow crossed his features, disappeared with a casual sneer. "It was a gift," he said and went back into his room, polishing his belt buckle.

Nathan shook his head as he went down the hall.

Then he felt it again—the barracks was different. It had changed over the weekend. Nathan was aware of the change now. It began to register in the back of his mind, like a subterranean aquifer forced by tectonic shifts in granite to surface. He didn't think of it as a change, but as something different in the atmosphere. Something creepy. Maybe it was just his encounter with Lipton.

Nathan glanced over his shoulder again. Perhaps there *was* no change; maybe he was only just becoming aware of something that had been going on around him all the while. Then he heard voices coming from Skip McPherson's room at the end of the hall.

He continued toward the voices, glanced into the open door and saw Marines sitting on chairs and beds. They had Bibles opened. Cooper and Gorilla sat with their backs to the door. Skip was sitting cross-legged on his bed, making a theological point from his Bible—true science does not contradict the Bible. He saw Nathan but kept making his point. Cooper looked back over his shoulder and nodded.

Nathan went into his room and tossed his sports bag onto his bed. The two chairs on either side of the table lamp on the left were missing. He sat on his bed. Vague thoughts fingered through his mind. Nothing of consequence. He checked the time on his watch, made a mental calculation, and wondered if Maddie Gallagher had returned to the States yet. Probably. He wrote her off as an unfinished chapter, but he was used to unfinished chapters. Still, it disturbed him.

He turned to the photo of his family, looked away.

He wasn't in the mood for family reunions tonight. Then he thought about Nico and the possibility of her being pregnant. He thought about her possibly aborting the baby. That would certainly simplify matters, but it troubled him. Killing a baby. His baby. An innocent. It was wrong.

Suddenly, inexplicably, a low voltage prickling, starting from the back of his neck, inched forward over his scalp. He looked up, expecting to see a pair of eyes leering at him from the shadows, but there was no one. He shook it off as the end of the weekend jitters. Then he heard Mick Donovan coming down the hall, singing, "Come on baby light my fire."

Mick slid into the doorway in his socks and skivvies, playing an air guitar. He was wearing a paisley tie around his head for a bandana. "Try to set the world on Fi-aaahhhhh!" He immediately slid into his Jimi Hendrix impersonation, wildly swinging the tie ends: "Doo-doo-dooo…doo-do-do-doooo—purple haze was on my brain!"

Nathan smiled. Good old Mick.

Mick twirled into the room, playing a wild riff on his air guitar with his teeth. Then he collapsed on Cooper's bed, spread-eagled, and stared at the ceiling.

"You're feeling froggy," Nathan said.

"You bet, *amico.*"

"Things looking up for you?"

"That's an affirmative, Marine. The bees are makin' honey. Got a couple small details to work out, but she'll sing."

"Glad to hear it."

Mick lifted his head an inch and peered at Nathan over the length of his body. Then he swung his legs over the bed, sat upright and studied Nathan as though he were a clothier fitting him for a new suit. "We're pals, right?"

"Sure."

"Good pals, right?"

"The best. Whaddya need, Mick?"

Mick narrowed his eyes. "I might need your help, Natboy."

"Sorry, I'm tapped."

"Not your dough." He sat forward, glanced quickly out the door. "Prayer meetin' still going?"

"Whaddya need, Mick?"

Mick planted an elbow on his knee and leaned forward conspiratorially. "Next shift you got the main gate, right?"

"Right."

"Twelve to four, right? I checked."

"Whaddya need, Mick? Why're you whispering?"

Mick pulled on his lower lip, studying Nathan some more. "It's kind of delicate."

"You want me to kill somebody?"

"This is serious, *amico*." He glanced once more out the door at the circle of men in Skip's room. He turned back at Nathan, hunched forward, gestured with his hand. "Closer."

Nathan leaned forward.

Mick whispered hoarsely. "I just need you to keep a lookout for the SOG tomorrow night. That's it. You get wind the SOG's on the roll, you shoot me an SOS on the blower."

"What post you on?"

"Seven."

"What's the gag, Mick?"

"That don't matter. You just keep your grapes peeled—three o'clock-ish of the A.M. I figure the SOG'll be out cold by then—usually is. Just in case, though, you gotta let me know the SOG's on the roll, or it's my head."

"I'll let you know."

"Thanks, *amico*. Oh, and you got to let Luigi into the compound."

Nathan shook his head. "I can't do it."

"You got to. It'll bust otherwise."

"What if those CID spooks over at the Hideaway see it? You forget about them?"

Mick stared blankly. The paisley tie ends hung down the left side of his face like limp seaweed. "You might have something there, *amico*. Let me think on it." He leaned back, pulled on his lip some more and thought about it. "Scratch Luigi. I'll let him in down at the PX. Sure, why not. No one can see him down there."

"What you got going?"

"Don't you mind that, but Ol' Mick'll give you a percentage. You just give me the head's up if the Rock rolls."

"You're going to boost the PX, aren't you?"

Mick's eyes became bull's-eyes. He lunged forward, jammed a finger to his lips. "Shhhhhh!" He darted a look out the door, shoulders hunched as he frowned back at Nathan. "You got a mouth on you, boy. Boost the PX? Where'd you get an idea like that?"

"You gonna boost the barber shop then?"

Mick shooshed him again. "Man, are you crazy or what? Listen, Natboy, you in or out?"

"Out. But I'll keep an eye out for the SOG, just the same."

A magnanimous grin spread over Mick's face. "You're a pal, *amico*. Pals to the end, right?"

"Affirmative. Who's on 5?"

"Skip."

"You won't get any help from him."

"He may be a Bible thumper but he ain't a squealer. That's all that matters." Mick's shoulders dropped, his arms loosened at the joints as he leaned back on the bed on his elbows. He swung his legs onto the bed and crossed them at the ankles. Conference over. He stared at Nathan a while and then grinned. "Say, how's that Roman dish and you getting along?"

"Okay."

"She talking the long walk yet?" Mick chuckled. "You gotta watch them Italian babes, *amico*. They're knockouts until you slap a ring on their left third finger. The gold does something to their body chemistry, honest to Chesty. Turns them into bufferillos."

"I'll keep that in mind."

"You got to trust me on this one, Natboy."

"Roger."

"Bufferillos." Suddenly Mick's eyes became fixed and serious. "Oooo, can you hear it?" His head began to jerk back and forth like a rooster, in rhythm to a melody that only he could hear. "Oh yeah, baby, that's it. We're groovin' now, baby. Yes, we are."

He jumped up onto the bed, struck a dramatic rocker pose and resumed playing his air guitar. "Doo-doo-dooo…doo-do-do-doooo." He leapt onto the floor, not missing a beat as he did the Jimi out into the hall.

He paused momentarily outside Skip's door, listening to him teach. "Preach it, Bro! Preach it! Oh yeah, baby, we're groovin'!" He disappeared in a paisley flash.

Nathan could hear him air guitar-ing down the hall.

COOPER WAS LYING on his bed thumbing through a Bible, frowning, when Nathan came back from his shower. The two missing chairs were back in their place. Cooper looked up. "Hey, Nate. How was Ischia?"

"Okay. That a Bible you're reading?"

"Skip loaned it to me. I never read it before. There's some interesting stuff in here."

Nathan raised his eyebrows.

"It makes a lot of sense, Nate. There really is a God. How else did we get here? Monkeys? There had to be a first cause."

"First cause, huh? You get that from Skip?"

"He says it better than I do. He's a smart guy, Nate. I don't understand it much, but I'm working at it. You should talk to him."

"No thanks." Nathan opened his wall locker and hung up his wet towel. He powdered himself and put on clean skivvies. "What'd you do this weekend?"

"Kicked around the barracks mostly. Went to a John Wayne movie out at AFSOUTH. 'Big Jake'."

Skip came across from his room and stood in the doorway. "Hey, Nathan."

Nathan nodded at him. He shut his wall locker, went around to the desk and got out his drawing pad and a pencil from the top drawer. He went over to his bed and lay down.

Cooper lowered his Bible. "What's up, Skip?"

"If there's anything you don't understand, feel free to ask. Maybe I can help."

Nathan frowned at them from his drawing. "You guys mind not having your Bible study in here. You want to do it across the hall, knock yourselves out. But this is my room."

Cooper glowered at him. "It's my room too, Nate. Can't I have a conversation?"

Skip raised a hand. "Nathan's right, Coop. We can talk in my room. Sorry, Nathan." He started to leave but stopped and looked back. "By the way, Maddie asked about you this morning."

Nathan blinked at him. "Maddie Gallagher?"

"Right."

"But I thought…" He frowned. "That is, I heard she was heading back to the States."

"In the fall, yeah. She was in church this morning. Like I said, she asked about you."

"I thought you were on barracks restriction."

"They let me go to church." Skip went across the hall to his room.

Cooper swung off his bed. "What's eating you, man? Something happen in Ischia?"

"Nothing happened."

Cooper went across the hall into Skip's room.

Nathan grunted. He frowned at his drawing—a Marine standing guard in the rain, getting the business from the SOG. He hadn't yet come up with a gag line that was funny.

He tossed the drawing pad to the foot of his bed. What do you make of that, Natboy? She didn't leave. She stayed. He made a noise in his throat. So what's it to you? That's all changed now, isn't it? You've got yourself into a major complication now, don't you? You sure do, *amico*.

He looked out the window. "Still, she didn't leave," he said out loud. "That's something to think about."

He got up and went over to the desk, opened the top drawer and found the tract she'd given him. He looked for a phone number, and found it on the back. He stared at it a long while, then shook his head. "Forget it," he said. "She doesn't need your kind of grief."

He dropped the card in the drawer and shut it.

Chapter Twenty-Four

NATHAN GOT OUT of the guard vehicle with the rest of the Marines on the twelve to four shift. He was wearing barracks beige and blue with polished leather holster and white gear. As he walked under low-hanging stars that winked between dark rain clouds, he felt the cold air against his face, waking him up. And then it was raining. He went into the cafeteria at AFSOUTH for mid-rats.

Inside, the cafeteria was empty, the tables and linoleum floor and walls dark in shadow, except for a bank of fluorescents over the grill, and the clutch of round tables nearest it. Sounds and voices bounced off cinderblock walls and collided with echoing dissonance.

Behind the grill a short, thickset, rheumy-eyed airman cook with a nest of shiny black curls boiling out from beneath a white paper cap, was tapping scrambled eggs with the edge of a long-bladed spatula.

Nathan, Gorilla and Cooper stood in line to the left of Clarence, Clarence waiting for his order of eggs with a stamped tin tray.

The cook raised his tired eyes to Nathan, who was next in line, wiping a greasy hand on his once-white apron. "What'll you have, buddy?"

Nathan looked over the window glass. "Eight-egg omelet with ham, cheese and chopped onions."

"Will do." The cook broke the eggs into a bowl, tossed the eggshells perfunctorily into a plastic-lined aluminum trash can at his left, beat the eggs with a whisk and poured the yellow goop onto the grill, beside Clarence's order of scrambled eggs. He turned to his previous order. "Yo," he said, folding half of the scrambled eggs on top of the other half.

Clarence put his tray under the counter glass, and the cook spatula'ed the mound of eggs onto it. Clarence thanked him and moved down the counter.

The cook sprinkled handfuls of diced onions, cheddar cheese and ham onto Nathan's omelet, stepped over and added several slices of white bread to the toaster machine, stepped back and looked up at Gorilla with the same weary eyes. "What'll you have, buddy?"

It was a routine he'd apparently done a million times.

Gorilla ordered an omelet with two dozen eggs.

"Will do." Without batting a lash, the cook turned to his right and took the top carton of eggs off a stack of cartons at waist level, thumbed it open, and began breaking eggs into the bowl.

Nathan looked at the eggs, frowned at Gorilla. Gorilla returned his gaze. "What?"

Nathan shook his head. "Nothing."

He slid his tray down the counter, scooped hash browns into one of the corner indents. He caught a couple slices of toast on his tray and, waiting for his omelet, poured a mug of coffee from the aluminum coffee maker.

"Yo."

Nathan came back and slid his tray under the counter window. The cook folded his omelet and then spatula'ed it onto his tray. "Thanks," Nathan said.

"What'll you have, buddy?" the cook said to Cooper.

Nathan grabbed an assortment of butter pads and jam, turned and glanced over the tables. Mick was sitting by himself. Because Mick had roving patrol duty in the PX compound that night, he was wearing Marine Corps fatigues. Nathan went over and sat down across from him. "Hey, Mick."

Mick's eyes shifted furtively to see who might be eavesdropping. No one was. He leaned forward. "We still on, *amico?*"

Nathan buttered and spread jam on his toast. "My grapes are peeled." He raised an eyebrow at the next table as Skip and Clarence bowed their heads and prayed over their meal.

Mick grinned. "Brings a tear to your eye, don't it?"

Panetta, Thompson and Flowers were sitting at the table kitty-corner to theirs, sneering at the Marines at Skip's table. They were snickering. Pfc Panetta, a skinny, slick-haired Brooklynite, made a kissing sound through the circle of his thumb and forefinger.

If Skip and the others heard it they didn't seem to mind.

Gorilla and Cooper came over to Nathan's table with their trays of food. Mick waved them off. "We're havin' a meetin', fellahs. Why don't you join the hallelujah choir next door. I hear they're short a couple of sopranos."

Gorilla and Cooper glanced at each other, turned and went over to Skip's table, grabbed a couple of chairs from another table and sat.

Mick, head lowered between his shoulders, leveled his eyes at Nathan and whispered, "You sure you'll watch for the Rock, *amico*? SOG catches me, I'm tanked."

"I said I would."

"I'm blind without you."

"I told you my grapes are peeled, Mick. Lay off."

Mick leaned forward and clapped him on the shoulder. "I always said you were aces up." He shoveled a forkful of hash-browns into his face, chased it with a gulp of black coffee.

The Marines at Panetta's table were huddled forward on their elbows, their faces close. They were having a conference. One or two of them giggled like girls. All three turned in their seats and leered at Skip's table.

Panetta grinned. "Hey, Gorilla!"

Gorilla, broad-backed and sitting straight in his chair, faced him. "Yeah?"

"You getting religion like them other pansies?" Panetta snickered at the others at his table.

Gorilla started to get up but Skip shook his head.

Panetta hissed through his teeth, said loud enough for Skip's table to hear, "I hear that Bible thumpers are pansies. Is that true?"

Thompson and Flowers nodded their heads, chortling at Skip's table. "That's what I hear," Thompson said.

The Marines at Skip's table continued eating as though they hadn't heard the insult.

"They don't go out with girls. Maybe they like boys," Panetta said. He looked over his shoulder. "You like boys, Gorilla?"

The Marines at Skip's table continued eating, shaking their heads at their plates.

"Hey, Gorilla, do they let fairies in heaven?"

Thompson slapped Panetta's shoulder with the back of his hand. They were clearly enjoying themselves. "They only let angels in heaven, didn't you know that?"

"Oh, that's right," Panetta snickered. "Ain't no fairies in heaven, Gorilla. Didn't Skip tell you that? Guess you boys are out."

The Marines at Panetta's table laughed.

Gorilla chuckled. "Uh-huh, uh-huh-huh, that was funny, Panetta. Excuse me, fellahs," he said, pushing back from the table.

Skip shook his head, but Gorilla went over to Panetta's table and stood beside him. He laid a paw gently on his shoulder. Panetta and the others were still chuckling.

"You got another one, Panetta?" Gorilla asked. "'Cause if you do..." He bent down and said something in his ear, but loud enough for the room to hear. Panetta's grin took a U-turn.

Gorilla patted his shoulder as if he was tenderizing a side of beef. He straightened, leveled his tiny blue eyes at the others at the table. "That goes for the rest of you pinheads, in case you were wondering." He chuckled some more, and then went back to his own table.

Panetta and the others watched him sit.

Mick shrugged his shoulders at Nathan. "Don't look like Gorilla's learned about turning the other cheek, do it?"

"Appears not," Nathan said, polishing off the last of his omelet.

Sergeant Kowalski, the Corporal of the Guard, came over to their table. He was a heavyset, thick-necked, recent promotion that had been made squad leader. "Change in the roster, Kessler. Bingham's in sick bay, so I'm taking you off the main gate and putting you on post 10."

Nathan darted a quick glance at Mick, then back at Sergeant Kowalski. "Who're you putting on the main gate?"

"The supernumerary. Lance Corporal Lipton."

"Teabag? Why don't you put him on 10?"

"Because I'm putting him on the main gate. Any objections?"

"The ghost post gives me the creeps. I get chills thinking about it."

"Tell the chaplain about it." Kowalski went over to the counter and ordered his food.

Mick was pulling on his lower lip. He didn't look well.

"That tears it," Nathan said. "Teabag won't go for it. He'd as soon as report you as look at you."

"I'm thinkin', *amico*. I'm thinkin'."

"Whatever you got going you better call it off."

"Can't."

"He'll see Luigi."

"No he won't. I can work it."

Chapter Twenty-Five

NATHAN STOOD BEHIND the desk in Post 10

reading the log. It was raining outside. He was glad that he wasn't on roving patrol, like Mick and Skip.

He had relieved Dixon, who had relieved Jesse Calderon. Dixon had drawn a peace symbol in the margin of the log book with paisley embellishments. If the SOG saw it he could get office hours. Dixon, a draftee, would probably think that was cool, since he was a short-timer and hated the military. Dixon was what Marines called a "bird." There were other more pejorative names, as well. By all accounts he was looking forward to growing his hair and reentering the counterculture, determined to make up for the two years he'd spent under the boot heel of the industrial war complex.

His eyes had been bloodshot, the pupil's dilated, when he'd handed Nathan the pistol and magazines.

According to his log, nothing noteworthy had happened during the eight-to-twelve shift. Apparently smoking reefers on post did not qualify as noteworthy.

Just then a short round-jowled *carabiniere* with dark, sad eyes, complete with saddlebags, came out from one of the back rooms, adjusting his hat with thick, meaty fingers. His leather belt rode high over his belly, his pistol hung low behind him, as a kind of counterweight. Nathan had never seen him before. "*Buona sera,*" he said. "*Come sta?*"

The carabiniere looked at him with sad watery eyes. They were poet's eyes. The rest of him resembled a New York cabbie. "*Bene grazie, e lei?*"

"*Non c'e male.*"

Nathan introduced himself in Italian. The *carabiniere's* name was Giuseppe Amoretti. He was from Pozzuoli, was married with three small children and wanted to know where Nathan was from and how it was that he spoke Italian. Nathan told him.

"Your grandmother was from Florence?"

"Yes. Her father was Italian, her mother Austrian."

"Then you are *Italiano.*"

"Heinz 57."

Giuseppe did not understand Heinz 57. He thought it might be a country that he hadn't heard of.

Nathan explained the catsup angle, how most Americans are combinations of different nationalities. "My father's family is German and English," he said.

"My mother was one quarter Italian, the rest Irish and Austrian."

"Ah. This is why America is so great…you are made of the strengths of many countries."

"And weaknesses. We have our bad boys too."

"Yes, but America is great. I think that God smiled when he made America."

Nathan raised his eyebrows.

"You do not think so?" Giuseppe asked.

"I don't believe in God."

Giuseppe's luminous watery eyes seemed to swell with emotion, glistening brightly, as though there were tears flowing continuously just beneath the surface, awaiting the slightest provocation to surge and spill over the banks. "How can you not?" he said. "There is evidence of God everywhere. That we are here speaking is evidence. What could explain this? How is there such a thing as man?"

"Man is an accident. A cosmic accident."

"A cosmic accident? I do not understand this term."

"Evolution then."

"Ah, evolution. The accidental creation. But this takes more faith than believing in God, no? I think so."

"How so?"

"Where did it all begin? There must be a beginning."

"A first cause."

"Ah, yes…the first cause. This is only rational. To not believe in God you must believe that the suns and worlds existed from all time."

"It started with the Big Bang."

Giuseppe looked down at the floor and dragged a hand over his blue jowls, making a scratching sound with his thick fingers. "Yes, but where did the *bang* come from?" he asked. "There must be a beginning, don't you see? I think so. The first cause, as you say. Something must have touched off the big bang."

He made a deprecating gesture with his hands. "I am not an educated man. I am sometimes very stupid, but even I can see that there must be a beginning."

"The Big Bang produced the Big Bang. The universe is expanding all the time. In a few billion years it'll contract and there will be another Big Bang. This will keep going and going."

Giuseppe opened his eyes wide in amazement. "Where does one learn such things?"

"Common sense."

Giuseppe shrugged his shoulders. "I do not know. As I have said, to believe this takes great faith, I think. You have explained a possible ending, but you are still left without a beginning."

"Did God have a beginning?"

"Of course not. God has always existed."

"How do you explain *that*?"

"He exists outside of time. He exists in eternity where there is no time. He existed outside of time before he made the worlds. Then he made time and he made the worlds."

"We both are faced with the same dilemma."

Giuseppe pulled on his thick lower lip. "I think so, yes," he nodded. "Both beliefs have no beginning, nor can they. But yours has an impersonal, non-beginning. Mine has a personal one. There is evidence of personality all around us."

He gestured with his hands, wiggling his meaty fingers and gazing upward as though including all of the conceivable universe in a glance. "Yours is a series of accidents in chaos with no personality," he went on, "and yet here we are. We have personality and there is order. To believe as you do, I would fear going to sleep at night, not knowing if it will all change during the night." He smiled a quick, deferential smile.

Nathan asked, "Do you believe then that God is all-powerful?"

"Of course."

"And that he is a loving God?"

"Most certainly."

"Then how do you account for the evil in the world? If God is all-powerful, he could stop it. If he was a God of love, he *would* stop it."

Giuseppe shook his head, poked the air between them with a thick forefinger. "According to you, yes. But you are not God. How can you know such a thing?"

"I know that evil is all around us, and that God—if there is such a being—has permitted it."

"Yes, God has permitted it. But what is evil?"

"War is evil. Killing is evil. Stealing is evil."

Giuseppe opened his hands. "Animals kill and commit horrendous atrocities to each other. They are territorial. They steal. Are animals evil?"

"No. Only man is evil."

"Man is different from animals?"

Nathan thought about that. "No. He is a higher form of evolution, but he is still an animal. He has a more highly developed brain. With it he learns right and wrong."

"This makes no sense. But then I am a simple man, as I have said."

"When animals kill it is survival of the fittest. It is nature's way of thinning the herds."

"*Nature's* way?" Giuseppe's dark eyes twinkled. "Does nature have a mind? A will?"

"It's a figure of speech. I speak of the natural order."

"Order?" A wry smile curled over Giuseppe's thick lips. He made circles in the air with his forefinger. "In chaos there can be no order. How can there be, unless it, too, is accidental? There can be no order in the natural world unless there is One who gives it order."

He removed a thermos from under the desk and unscrewed the plastic top. "But back to your point of evil. How can you say that man is evil then?"

Nathan frowned.

"You said that if God was all powerful He would stop evil," Giuseppe said, his voice small in the large openness of the foyer. "Evil suggests that there are moral choices, such as good and evil, and that men choose to do evil. If man is nothing more than an animal—a cosmic accident—then killing or conquering is only natural and right. It is good that strong people destroy the weak. It is thinning the herd, as you say. We should celebrate men like Hitler and Mussolini. No?"

Nathan scratched the side of his chin.

Giuseppe smiled a small sly smile. "As I have said, evil suggests that there is a moral choice to be made for good but is disobeyed. God gives men the right of choice, to do good or evil. I think men prefer to live as they like, rather than how God would have them live. God does not force us to follow his ways." He shrugged. "As a result, there is evil in the world."

"You're a philosopher."

Giuseppe shrugged, looked up at him with his sad poet's eyes. "No. I am a simple man who—I think—has a little common sense too." He offered Nathan a cup. "Would you like some coffee? I have plenty."

"No thanks. Already had mine."

"I would like to learn American. Perhaps you could teach me." Giuseppe added that he hadn't known any Marine who spoke Italian other than in a broken pigeon form.

"I'd be happy to," Nathan said. "Help pass the time."

"It is difficult to talk when people do not understand each other, so I go into one of the offices and read. It is unfortunate because I would like to learn about America. I would like to go there someday."

"You should go."

"My mother's family is in America. They live in a place called the Bronx. Do you know of this place?"

"It's in New York."

"New York, yes. They own a restaurant. An Italian restaurant. Would you like to see a photograph?"

"Sure."

The photo showed an old man and woman, two younger ones and a little girl standing in front of a table with a red and white checked tablecloth.

"Nice family." Nathan handed him back the photo.

"*Grazie.* This is my mother's sister." Giuseppe pointed to the elderly woman. "This is their daughter, her husband and their little girl. They have lived in America ten years." He put the photo back into his wallet. "You have been to this place, the Bronx?"

"No."

"Do you have a—how is the word? Sweetheart?"

"I've been seeing someone, yes." Nathan got out a wallet-sized photo of Nico and handed it to him. She was sitting on a marble step in an olive green knit skirt and yellow sweater with the wind in her hair.

Giuseppe smiled. "She is very beautiful. *Lei è italiana?* Of course. You are in love with her?"

Nathan raised an eyebrow. "*Love?* I don't know what the word means."

Giuseppe's dark eyes appeared to moisten, as though the undercurrent of tears were surging. "No? This is sad. You are young. You are good looking I think." He looked at the photo of Nico. "This girl she is very beautiful. Is she beautiful in here?" He pointed at his heart.

"Does it matter?"

"Of course. My wife, she is not so very beautiful to look at but she is beautiful in the heart. This is the most important beauty. It outlasts the other. The other will fade away like the flower. Find a woman who is beautiful in the heart and you will learn the meaning of love."

Nathan frowned at him. He took the photo from Giuseppe, put it back into his wallet and stuffed the wallet back in his sock.

Giuseppe shrugged deprecatingly. "I have not been to America," he said. "I would like to go some day."

"You should go." Nathan smiled. Giuseppe smiled.

They had come full circle.

Nathan glanced around the foyer, large and empty in the quiet of the early morning, with the wide curve of stairs to the right that seemed from a different time, only the two of them talking. "Seen any ghosts tonight?" he asked.

Giuseppe looked at him blankly. Then he brightened. "Ah, the ghost post," he said, understanding. "No. I have not seen any ghosts tonight, nor any other night. They are just stories, I think."

"You don't believe in ghosts?"

Giuseppe shook his head. "In ghosts, no. I think that when people die they either go up or down." He pointed with his finger up then down. "I do not think they come back to haunt people still living. This is a fabrication, I think."

"How do you explain the strange things that supposedly happen in this building?"

"I think they are devils."

"Devils?"

"Oh yes. I think they masquerade as people so that people will believe in ghosts. It is a fabrication to deceive. No, I do not believe in ghosts. Devils, yes. There are many devils."

"Have you seen any devils?"

"No. They do not trouble me. Why would they? I am but a simple man."

Nathan grunted. "You are anything but simple," he said, then checked his watch. "I have to inspect the floors."

Giuseppe sipped coffee. "It is a pleasure talking with you. The Marines, they do not speak my language well, and I do not speak theirs. It is good to hear your perspective on the world."

"Likewise."

At twelve forty-five a.m Nathan reported his post secure, then he walked up the wide curving flight of stairs to the second floor. The floor gleamed in polished terrazzo.

"I think he had some good points, don't you, Nate?"

"Maybe."

"I don't believe in ghosts anymore."

"What do you believe, Frankie?"

"I believe in devils. I like what that Italian man said about devils. Devils come at you when you're not looking. I think that Italian man is smarter than he lets on."

"I agree."

The short *carabiniere* had, indeed, made some interesting points; in particular, the non-evil in the animal kingdom. He'd have to think about that. Perhaps there was an evil among animals, but an evil that was commensurate with their stage of evolution. It seemed absurd. Pigs behave like pigs, crocodiles like crocodiles. Who faults a shark for behaving like a shark? They may kill it, but no one would say that the shark had acted evilly when it kills for food. Perhaps a mother seal might think so.

He went into each of the offices, first turning on the lights, and then checking the room. AFSOUTH was the NATO headquarters of the Allied Forces Southern European Command. There were top secret documents in each of the buildings—documents relating to Fleet movements, above water and submarine, troop strengths in the Southern European theater, and so on. Protection of those documents lay in the hands of the Marines.

He checked under desks and in closets. He checked window latches. He went into one office and saw that a desk light had been left on. Dixon hadn't logged it. He probably didn't inspect the floor. He had probably logged in then gone into an office near the front desk where the phone could be heard, smoked a joint and blew fantastical smoke rings. It was easy to do as long as the Marine on the main gate gave a heads up when the SOG was on the roll. Nathan checked the room; everything was okay, then he turned the light off and closed the door behind him.

He walked down the hall to the next office, his footsteps clicking softly. He flicked on the light switch. The office belonged to a major in the British army. Hanging on the wall behind the desk was a portrait of a beautiful dark-haired woman. A painting. The eyes of the woman were dark and mysterious and followed him around the room.

Nathan went over to the desk and looked under it. He felt a vague prickling over his scalp, as though someone was watching him. It was the same prickling feeling he'd had the night before in the barracks.

He looked up but saw no one. Then he checked the adjoining bathroom.

Nathan started to leave when he felt a prickling over his scalp a second time, stronger now. He turned, glanced over the room but again saw no one. He stood listening, his spine tingling as he made quick sweeps with his eyes. Something was in the room; he could feel it. A presence. Something malevolent. Not malevolent in the abstract but a personal evil.

He glanced over the room again and, still, there was no one. Then he saw the painting of the dark-haired woman and his skin crawled. Waves of goosebumps washed over his scalp.

The woman was leering at him with wicked, probing eyes; eyes that seemed to float away from the painting toward him. The woman in the painting was alive. She was smiling evilly at him.

Nathan backed toward the door. He removed a magazine from his canvas pouch, clicked it into his .45 and chambered a round. He could not take his eyes away from the woman in the painting.

He backed into the hall, stopped, still glaring at the woman, leaned forward and felt around on the inside wall of the office with his left hand for the light switch, found it and flicked off the light. Then he quickly closed the door, whirled his back against the wall and stood holding the automatic with both hands.

His pulse pounded in his throat, in his temples. He felt lightheaded, took gulps of air to prevent hyperventilation. "Take it easy, Nate," he told himself. "It's just a painting. There's nothing in there but a lousy painting. Talking to Giuseppe put the spook in your head."

"Are you sure, Nate?"

"I'm sure, Frankie."

"She's like those vampires in the movie."

Nathan said nothing.

MADDIE WAS DREAMING that she was flying over fields of ripened wheat. The sky was clear and bright and the earth rolling with gentle undulations of wheat moving in a golden breeze. She often dreamed she was flying, sometimes flapping her arms like a bird, other times soaring with her arms outstretched like Super Woman. In her dream she lifted away from the wheat fields and flew through an open window into a room on the top floor of a building that was burning. There was someone in the room. A child. She told the child to climb onto her back but the child would not do it. She took the child in her arms and leapt from the window, the child screaming, but then she could no longer fly and she was falling, holding the child.

She sat upright in her bed breathing fast. She stared into the dark, catching her breath, feeling the dream leaving her reluctantly. Goosebumps shivered down her spine. A burden remained heavy upon her as the pieces of the dream dissipated. The luminescent dial of her side table clock showed that it was twelve fifty-five.

She talked to God briefly, believing that the child in the dream was Nathan. There was nothing explicit in the dream to inform her of this but it was what she felt. She could not let him go.

"Father, it is clear that you want me to stay here in Naples to complete your work. Though there may be much pain and heartache ahead of me, give me the strength and grace to endure it. I wish that you would take this trial from me, but as Jesus prayed in Gethsemane the night He was betrayed, let Thy will be done not mine."

Maddie got out of bed and went over to the window and looked down at the street. It had rained and the street was black and shining in the streetlights. The traffic had subsided, but there were still a few pedestrians on the sidewalks with umbrellas. She felt the sudden presence of evil. She turned and faced the room in the darkness. She saw no one, but felt evil coming toward her, a malevolent presence. Since the family had come to Naples she had had many such encounters. Naples was a demonic stronghold, a city of evil palpable in the alleys and back alleys.

Maddie held out a finger and said, "The Lord Jesus rebuke you, devil."

The thing halted as though it had hit an invisible wall of angels. She could almost hear it snarling as it faced her in the darkness. And then it was gone.

Maddie felt an immediate peace envelop her, as palpable as the evil had been, the peace flooding through her and washing her clean. She praised God and then once again she was thinking of Nathan and began to pray. The longer she prayed the more intense she felt the burden for him. The burden would not leave her.

She lay down on the floor, face down, her arms outstretched. "God have mercy on him," she prayed. "Have mercy. Draw him to you by your Spirit. Open his eyes to your goodness."

She prayed that God would give Nathan courage to tell her what had happened in his youth. Something had put a sword of anger in his heart, a faith killer. "Please, God."

Then she prayed for Skip and for Clarence and Jesse that God would protect them against the evil one. She sensed there was a wicked front moving through the barracks and that the Christians there were targets. She prayed for the men in the barracks, for Jim Cooper and for Gorilla, for the CO and the staff, that God would draw these men to Himself.

An hour passed and the burden lifted. She fell asleep on the floor.

Chapter Twenty-Six

NATHAN WAS HALFWAY down the wide, curving stairs of Post 10 when he saw Giuseppe heading toward the doors with the keys. He noticed the guard vehicle parked outside, Cooper's head leaning back on the seat behind the wheel, his eyes closed, the SOG heading up the outside steps, and Giuseppe unlocking the doors.

Nathan hurried back up the stairs out of view and removed the magazine from his .45, since it wasn't regulation to carry it in the pistol. He ejected the round from the chamber and inserted the round back into the magazine. He holstered his weapon, returned the magazine to its pouch and headed back down the stairs.

Sergeant Rockman was waiting at the desk. Giuseppe was putting the keys on the peg behind it. They watched Nathan come down the stairs and cross the foyer to the desk.

Rockman put his hands on his waist. "Well?"

Nathan reported his post secure. He didn't mention that Dixon hadn't logged the missed light upstairs.

Rockman inspected Nathan's uniform, told him to shine his brass before coming back on duty. Nathan told him that he would. "Let me see your weapon."

Nathan removed the .45 from its holster, locked open the breech and handed it to him, butt first. Rockman looked it over, handed it back. Nathan released the slide home, clicked the trigger, and holstered the weapon.

Rockman went around the desk and checked the shelf for contraband: cigarettes, magazines, liquor. "Any contraband to report, Kessler?"

"I'm clean."

"What's this?" Rockman asked, holding up a thermos.

Giuseppe stepped forward and took it from his hand and put it back on the shelf. He seemed a little miffed. Rockman appeared disappointed. "You're not supposed to keep stuff here," he said gruffly.

Giuseppe shrugged, said, "*Non capisco,*" then walked away toward the back offices looking up at the walls with his hands folded behind his back.

Rockman watched him disappear around the corner. "Lousy Italians."

He checked the shelves, under the lamp stand, in the drawer where a telephone directory was kept. He put a thick hand on his chin, pulled at the folds of his cheek as he glanced over the foyer, his tiny black eyes probing. He really did remind Nathan of a pit bull, and he thought of a cartoon.

"What're you looking for, Sergeant Rockman?"

"Contraband."

"Any contraband in particular?"

"Bibles."

"*Bibles?*"

"One of them Jesus freaks has been leaving them on post. You wouldn't know anything about that?"

Nathan shook his head. "I've never seen one."

"Those little black ones."

"I know the kind you mean. I've never seen one on post. I've found *Playboys* and *Penthouses* left behind, but no Bibles."

"We're looking for Bibles."

Nathan grinned. "You starting a mission, Sergeant Rockman?"

"Shut up, Kessler." Rockman looked over Nathan's uniform some more. "You find a Bible, you log it, you hear?"

"Aye, aye."

"Don't forget to shine your brass."

"Will do."

He followed the SOG to the glass doors and locked them. Cooper nodded at him from the driver's seat, as he pulled the gearshift lever on the steering column. Nathan raised a couple of fingers. The guard vehicle pulled away from the curb and headed towards the Headquarters building.

Nathan went quickly back to the desk and called Gorilla and told him that the SOG was outside his building and coming up. Nathan asked if he got a heads up from NSA. Gorilla said no. Nathan phoned Clarence on post 12 and got the same answer; no one had given him the heads up either. "Want me to call Capo?"

"No, I'll call," Nathan said.

He hung up the phone and looked across the foyer, thinking. The SOG had not stopped to inspect the NSA compound, apparently, but went straight on through the main gate and on to AFSOUTH. Mick or Skip would have called otherwise. Since they were both on roving patrol they must not have seen him. But Lipton would have seen him. There was no way off the base except through the main gate. Lipton had to wave them through. Lipton was a jerk. He probably liked it when guys got busted on post.

Nathan logged the SOG's inspection. He looked up the flight of stairs, thought about making another round, but all he did was think about it. He got out a sheet of paper from under the desk and made a quick sketch of Ol' Prive, reclining against a fence post on perimeter guard. The sergeant of the guard was standing over him, his scowling face bearing a remarkable resemblance to a pit bull.

SOG: *Sleeping on post is a court martial offense, Private!*

Ol' Prive: *Uh..I wasn't sleeping, Sarge, I was reading the UCMJ on the back of my eyelids.*

Nathan chuckled. He'd draw it out proper back at the barracks, maybe think up a funnier tag. He folded the drawing and put it inside his left sock. From his right sock he removed a pack of cigarettes, tapped one out and lit it. He thought about the SOG's inspection. It was a witch hunt, of course. They were hunting Christians.

He glanced around the desk, saw nothing. He poked around in the trash can. Hidden by some trash was a small black book. Sergeant Rockman hadn't seen it.

Nathan fished it out. It was a Gideon's New Testament. There was writing inside the front cover. *"Thy Word is a lamp unto my feet, and a light unto my path." Psalm 119:105*

Nathan thought about that. Dixon had relieved Jesse Calderon. He checked the log and compared handwriting. Jesse had left the Bible, Dixon had obviously tossed it into the trash, too stoned perhaps to log it. A good thing for Jesse the SOG had missed it, and that Dixon hadn't logged it. Jesse was bucking for a court-martial. He shook his head and stuffed the Bible in his other sock.

THE SKIES OVER Naples were black and packed with low-hanging stars when Nathan was relieved of duty. It had stopped raining. The streets were shiny wet and puddled, the smell of wet asphalt permeating the air. Early morning traffic was light, with municipal vehicles and bakery trucks and commuters. A cold breeze sifted through the streets and alleys, lifting bits of debris over the sidewalks. Birds were still asleep in their nests, frogs were still lounging in their mud holes, but elsewhere in the city, at the NSA compound, at Headquarters AFSOUTH, at the airfield at Capodichino, tired Marines were being relieved of their posts by tired Marines, recently stirred out of too-little slumber, to stand guard against the enemies of the free world.

Nathan was holding a tray of eggs, pancakes, coffee and orange juice as he sat down at Mick's table in the AFSOUTH cafeteria. He glanced over the tables.

There were men sitting in groups of twos and threes, some talking and smoking, their voices echoing in the large, nearly empty cafeteria that seemed even emptier because of the hour, and because of the darkness outside the windows that made eating breakfast seem strange. Skip and Clarence were sitting at a table by themselves, eating quietly. The men were all tired.

Mick was hunched over a plate of scrambled eggs and sausages, his elbows planted on the table.

"How'd it go, Mick?"

Mick took a quick slurp of coffee and raised his eyes. "How'd what go, *amico?*"

"You know..."

Mick shrugged, reached for the salt shaker.

"Okay, play it stupid," Nathan said as he poured maple syrup over his stack. "You never saw the SOG leave the compound?"

Mick shook his head and resumed eating. "Sorry, *amico.* Teabag should've given you a heads up."

Nathan glanced over and saw Lipton sitting at a table in the shadows. He was by himself. Lipton didn't have any friends that Nathan knew of. "He didn't say a thing," he said.

"You know I'd've let you know if I saw him."

"Yes, but you were otherwise occupied, right?"

Mick slurped his coffee. "You're talkin' trash, Marine."

"You think? Okay then, is Luigi happy?"

"Luigi's always happy. He's Italian. What're you driving at, Natboy?"

"Nothing, Mick. Have it your way."

Mick finished his coffee and frowned at him. "What you don't know won't hurt you, *amico*." He got up from the table and went over to the coffee machine.

Nathan watched Mick refilling his mug—tall, broad-shouldered and loose-limbed, his head tilted a little to one side watching the coffee stream into his cup. Nathan shook his head, cut a wedge of pancakes, put it into his mouth and chewed.

He looked back over his shoulder and caught a pair of pale blue eyes staring at him from the shadows, like twin moons. "Thanks for the heads up, Teabag," he said. "I'll remember it the next time I'm on the main gate."

Lipton checked his watch. It was a different watch, Nathan noticed, one with a wide leather band and brass loops. He shook his head slightly from side to side, turned back and cut another wedge of pancakes.

Mick came back to the table and sat down, picked up the cream dispenser and tipped a little cream into his coffee. He stirred in a couple cubes of sugar and took a sip. He tasted it thoughtfully, licking his lips, set the mug down and held it with both hands, as if warming them. "You got an old man, *amico*?"

"Everybody's got an old man."

"You know what I mean."

"Sure I got an old man. I haven't seen him in six years. Why?"

"You don't get along?"

"We got along fine. We just don't talk anymore. Why?"

"I don't know. I was thinking about my old man. Just now, gettin' my coffee. I haven't thought about him in years, and then I'm thinkin' about him."

Nathan frowned at him. Mick had gone away one man and come back another. He brought back with him a somber mood that hung low over the table like a fog.

Mick gazed at a shadowy niche across the cafeteria. "My old man was sent up when I was two," he said reflectively, then chuckled. "Armed robbery. Held up a gas station." He grunted. "A lousy gas station. Made off with fifteen bucks—least that's what the newspapers said. He killed the attendant. Shot him with a sawed-off pump."

Nathan said nothing. He figured Mick needed to talk about it, so he let him.

Mick sipped coffee and glanced across the cafeteria, holding the cup in his hands. "They gave him the chair."

"Man!"

Mick shrugged. "Ain't no biggie. I never knew what happened to him 'till I was eighteen. My mom kept it hid from me pretty good. We moved around a lot, so I never got razzed in school." He lifted his coffee cup and took a sip.

"How'd you find out about it?"

"Your sins will find you out, *amico*. That's in the Bible I think." He set the cup down.

Nathan nodded.

"I was going through the attic, rootin' around for my baseball card collection to pawn, when I come across an old packing box. The whole story was in it—newspaper clippings, news photos of my old man between a couple hard boy detectives, one of his eyes swollen. Looked like that one of Oswald. They beat him up pretty good."

He chuckled at his hands holding the cup. "The gas station attendant was sixteen years old," he said, glancing at Nathan for a reaction. "He just shot him."

Nathan said nothing.

"My mom broke down and gave me the rest of it when I showed her the stuff in the box. She showed me their wedding photo. They were just kids. Smilin' at the camera like they knew somethin' no one else did. Just a coupla kids."

Mick stared into the shadows. "They had no money. Me coming along didn't help much. I guess he got desperate. I guess we all get a little desperate sometimes."

Nathan thought about that. "What'd you do after you found out?"

"What'd I do? I joined the Corps the next day, that's what I did. I figured I'd go to Vietnam and get killed or something. You know—a life for a life. Got a Silver Star instead."

Nathan stared blankly. "I didn't know you had the Silver Star. How come you never wear it? It's regulation."

Mick stared into his coffee cup.

"Why're you telling me all this, Mick?"

"Beats me." Mick laughed, took a sip of coffee. "I ain't never told that story to anybody but you, *amico*. Don't ask me why I told *you*. I guess maybe you're the best friend I ever had."

Nathan blinked at him.

Mick turned his head away with a grin. "Somebody better pass me a shovel. It's piling up pretty deep in here."

Chapter Twenty-Seven

MADDIE FOLLOWED CORPORAL Sanchez up the stairwell to the second floor administration wing of the Marine barracks. Corporal Sanchez, a short round-faced Hispanic with pleasant manners and wide friendly eyes, guided her through a door off the second floor landing into a large open bullpen, where a handful of Marines in beige shirt sleeves and olive trousers, sat behind gray metal desks, ticking at electric typewriters.

The ticking stopped abruptly as Maddie entered the room. Curious eyes swept over her loose-knit poncho and embroidered jeans and curvy figure, back up to her face, her hair, her mouth.

She smiled, uncomfortable with the unabashed scrutiny, then looked away at a row of offices to the left of the bullpen. Name plates beside the doors indicated that the offices were occupied by officers and high ranking NCOs. To the right of the bullpen were more offices.

Corporal Sanchez guided her that way and stopped beside an open door. "Lance Corporal McPherson is in the briefing room," he said, gesturing politely with a small brown hand. "Let me know when you want to leave, and I'll escort you out."

"Thank you," she said and went into the room, leaving the door open.

The ticking of typewriters resumed behind her.

The briefing room was long and narrow, with metal-framed windows filling the left wall. The windows opened onto the west end of the base compound, the cinder block wall bathed in late-morning sun, filtered through a gray overcast. Most of the polished terrazzo floor space in the room was occupied by two rows of six foot long folding tables and chairs, five tables to a row, front to back, with an aisle between the rows like in a classroom. A projection screen was pulled down over a blackboard on the right-hand wall.

Skip was sitting at one of the tables in his guard uniform: blue trousers and beige shirt. He stood as Maddie entered.

"Hey, Red. Thanks for coming." He indicated a chair across from him. "Have a seat. Can I get you anything? Coffee? Water?"

"No thanks. I brought a book for you," she said, removing a thick paperback from her handbag. "It just arrived at the Station. Thought you might like it." The cover photo showed the earth from space with dramatic titling over it. It was a book on End Time prophecy.

"Wow!" Skip glanced over the book, front and back covers. "I was going to order this. How much do I owe you?"

"It's a gift."

He frowned at her. "What? No, let me pay for it."

"It's a *gift*," she repeated. "Thought it might help with your restriction."

Skip thumbed through the book. "Thank you, Red. I really appreciate it."

Maddie watched him read the back cover. In the brief silence the muted ticking of typewriters, men's voices, and the ringing of a telephone drifted into the room.

"Have you read this yet?" he asked.

"I glanced through it. We're living in exciting times."

Skip set the book down on the table, left his hand on it, palm down, and looked across at her. "Sorry we have to meet this way."

"Don't be. How are you doing?"

He patted the book. "Great, now that I have some new reading material."

Maddie felt a little awkward. She'd never been in the barracks before. "Jesse and Clarence have been coming to the Station," she said. "They seem like they're doing okay."

"They are." He darted a look out the door, glanced back at her. "They can't get enough of the Bible," he said, lowering his voice.

Maddie, taking the cue, lowered her voice. "The men giving them a hard time?"

"The usual. Jesse gets a little hot under the collar." He grinned. "That hot Spanish blood of his."

Maddie smiled, glanced out the door as a thin, pale-faced Pfc peered into the room as he walked past the door holding a folder.

Skip asked, "How are things at the Station?"

She told him that many of the men from the Fleet were coming to Christ. It seemed that God was moving powerfully in the world, and especially in Naples. Naples, of all places.

Skip agreed. Naples was a city of darkness, a modern day Babylon that even appalled Italians. Skip had often said that *Bella Napoli* was a demonic stronghold, a haunt for some real bad boys. The Italians attributed it to the presence of NATO, and to the influx of military forces that opened the doors to prostitution and drugs, and every kind of evil under the sun. But in truth evil had existed in the city for millennia, ever since there was a port. But now, Naples has seen a great light. The light was spreading through the Way Station, through the barracks, through the Naval hospital, the ships, through one-on-one encounters on street corners. But as the light spread, the darkness became more resistant.

Skip said that he sensed the darkness moving in the barracks, becoming more intense and apparent in the lives of some of the Marines. The barracks was polarizing over spiritual matters; some more tolerant and willing to listen, others more openly hostile.

"Marines are no different than any other men," he said. "You shine the light on them, and they'll either run toward it or from it. Keep praying for Jim Cooper and Gorilla."

"I will. What about Nathan?"

Skip shook his head. "I don't get a read on him, except that he doesn't like to talk about Christ. That doesn't mean anything, of course. But he plays his cards pretty close to the vest. He said something about you leaving for the States?"

"That was a bit of miscommunication between God and me. God communicated, I missed it. I'm staying."

"That's a relief."

"Nathan said you were supposed to leave yesterday. I told him that you must have an identical twin, then, because you were coming over to see me today."

"Oh? How'd he react?"

"He just raised an eyebrow at me and walked away. Like I said, it's hard to get a read on him."

Maddie thought about that, glanced once again out the door at the room full of Marines. She looked at Skip. "Anything I can pray about, Skip?"

"Pray for boldness. Pray that God will articulate His word through me, so that men can understand it better."

"I will. Can I pray for you before I go?"

"Sure."

Maddie bowed her head and prayed quietly that God would accomplish His good will and purpose in the barracks. She prayed for Skip, for the other Marines. As she prayed she once again felt a burden gripping her heart, squeezing. A sob caught in her throat.

"It feels different praying in here," she said, wiping a tear from her eye.

Skip smiled. "You're behind the lines."

Maddie frowned. "I never thought of it that way. But it's true, isn't it? We're in a stronghold."

"We are." His eyes glistened. He looked away and cleared the emotion from his throat. "I love these guys, Red," he said. "I hate seeing how the enemy keeps them from coming to the truth."

"I know." She was silent for a few moments, thinking of things to add to that, but she was at a loss for words. "Have you written to Jacqueline?"

"Sure. No response yet, of course, but I know what she'll say." He laughed. "She'll tell me that she's got her women's group praying for me and to keep my chin up."

Maddie smiled. "Watch out for those women prayer warriors." She peered out the door, then back at Skip. "Well, I guess I should get going."

"Thanks for coming." He picked up the book. "And thanks again for the reading material."

Maddie shouldered her handbag and they stood.

Skip walked her out into the bullpen and over to Corporal Sanchez' desk. Sanchez looked up from his typewriter. "All done?"

Skip nodded. "All done."

Corporal Sanchez led Maddie out of the bullpen through a gauntlet of curious eyes, then down the stairwell to the Quarterdeck. The sergeant behind the desk logged her out, then she left the barracks and headed across the tarmac toward the Admin building for a hamburger.

She lifted her eyes to the gray gloom of the overcast sky, still feeling the weight of the burden upon her heart.

She went up the stairs and into the building, stopped just inside the cafeteria and scanned the room. A sizable crowd of people were talking and laughing. "Aqualung," by Jethro Tull, was playing on the jukebox.

Maddie saw Nathan, wearing beige and blue, sitting at a far table by the windows. His back was to her. It looked like he was writing a letter, but she couldn't tell from where she stood. She knew this would happen; she would see him from time to time on the base. She also knew that when she saw him it would stir a host of emotions inside her that would war against each other and only leave her confused or angry.

A little boy was standing beside him, his elbows on the table, watching Nathan working his pencil. It was the same boy she'd seen with his mother talking to Nathan at the main gate, weeks before. He was about eight years old with a blond crewcut. The boy seemed very curious about what Nathan was doing, which seemed odd to Maddie if he was writing a letter. Nathan indicated something to the boy with his pencil. The boy angled his head to see, laughed suddenly, which seemed even more odd to Maddie.

She watched as Nathan handed the paper to the boy. The boy gaped at it as though he was holding a great treasure, a big smile curving over his face. From Maddie's perspective it appeared to be a drawing of some kind.

Then the boy's mother came over to them from one of the tables, glanced at the paper Nathan had given the boy and smiled. The woman appeared to be in her late-twenties. She said something to Nathan, and then she escorted the boy out of the cafeteria, the boy waving back at him.

Nathan returned the boy's wave, eyed them leaving the cafeteria, and then went back to whatever he was doing. He was alone.

Maddie felt a sudden pang of anxiety, turned and walked away. The hamburger could wait. She got as far as the front entrance of the building and stopped. She looked down at her feet and frowned. Coward.

She walked back into the cafeteria, went over and stood a little to one side of Nathan's left shoulder and saw that he was drawing a cartoon. He seemed intent on what he was doing and hadn't heard her approach, apparently.

He was making exaggerated expressions with his eyes as he drew, arching his eyebrows, pursing his lips, as though he was modeling for his cartoon character.

She observed him drawing for a while, not certain what to say, or how to begin, or if she should sneak away and not disturb him. Then she knew she had waited too long and, should he suddenly turn, was at risk of being found staring at him. "I didn't know you were an artist, Nathan."

He whirled, his eyes and body tensing.

"I'm sorry," she said. "I didn't mean to startle you."

When he saw that it was Maddie his shoulders relaxed, and then the rest of him relaxed, and he smiled. He had a great smile. "You shouldn't sneak up on people."

"I couldn't have made more noise if I were three elephants in tap shoes." She angled her head to better see what he had made. "What are you drawing?"

"It's just a cartoon."

"Showing the little boy how to draw?"

"Something like that. I drew a caricature of him wearing a helmet."

"Did you give him a cartoon at the main gate the other day?"

He frowned. Then he brightened with a short laugh. "Oh…right… Yes, I drew a quick cartoon of a bulldog for him. Marine Corps mascot, you know. His dad's a Naval JAG officer but he likes Marines."

"He likes you, you mean. You have a way with kids."

He said nothing to that.

She indicated the drawing pad. "May I?"

"Sure." He handed her the pad.

The drawing showed two Marines wearing fatigues and utility belts with pistols—barracks guards on roving patrol. One was driving a forklift, the other standing at attention on the tines before a befuddled sergeant with a COG band on his arm. "What are the Marines doing with a forklift?"

"Reporting their posts all secure to the corporal of the guard. It actually happened here at the barracks. The Marine guarding the PX hot-wired a forklift and picked up the guard on Post 5—the Dispersing compound—and hauled him over to the Quarterdeck to report their posts. They were busted, of course."

She shook her head in amazement at the drawing. "This is really good, Nathan. I'm not just saying it."

He said nothing.

She smiled at him, not sure how to proceed in the conversation.

"I heard you hadn't gone back," he said.

"I've decided to stay." She indicated the drawing. "What's the cartoon for?"

"The *Star Spangled Banner*. They just picked up the series. You should start seeing them in a week or so."

"The *Star Spangled Banner*? I'm impressed." She was smiling at the drawing. "Ol' Prive. It reminds me of the old *Willy and Joe* cartoons."

"You know about Willy and Joe?"

"Dad has a book at home with a collection of Bill Mauldin drawings."

"Bill Mauldin was the best. He was the cartoonist's Ernie Pyle."

"I can't get over this," she said. "The *Star Spangled Banner*. Aren't you excited?"

Nathan said nothing. He was staring at her mouth.

She felt her cheeks flush, and turned her attention to the drawing. She suddenly heard people's voices at tables around them; a Diana Ross and the Supremes song piping through the jukebox, the squeak of a chair.

"How come you didn't leave?" he asked.

Her eyes were fixed on the drawing. The drawing was safe. "I've still got a lot of work to do here," she said. "With the Fleet in town, I thought it best to stay."

"Is that the only reason you didn't go back?"

She set the drawing pad down on the table in front of him. "You're really very good, Nathan. How long have you been drawing?"

"Since I was old enough to hold a pencil." He sketched some lines on the pad. "You didn't answer my question."

She scanned his face without making eye contact. In a swift glance she noticed the shape of his head and jawline, the ears close to the shaved sides of his head, the tan line of his hat across his forehead, the way the sunlight showed the red and brown and yellow hairs in the neat taper of bristles. She felt strong emotions stirring inside her breast. She knew she loved him and there was no doubt about it, even though it solidified her feelings of confusion and desperation. "When I heard about Skip I canceled my flight."

"Skip, huh?"

She looked at him steadily now. "No. That's not the only reason. I'd be lying if I said it was."

"And Christians don't lie, do they?" Nathan pulled out the chair next to him. "Have a seat. Why didn't you go back?"

"For the reasons that I told you." She sat down, set her bag on the floor beside her feet, and took a deep breath. "But also because of you."

"What about me?"

"I have feelings for you."

"*Feelings?*" He frowned. "What does that mean? I have feelings for a cheeseburger. It sounds wimpy."

"I'm afraid I *have* been wimpy lately."

"That's out of character for you, isn't it? You're the fighter pilot."

She said nothing.

He set his pencil on top of the drawing pad, pushed the pad away about a foot. He gazed at her, as if measuring what he was about to say. "When you told me you were leaving for the States it felt like something died inside of me," he said. "A big part of me just suddenly stopped breathing. I walked around in a daze. You had me talking to myself. No one's ever done that to me before, Maddie."

"Not even your Italian girl?"

"I don't love her. She's beautiful—yes. But I don't love her. I love you."

Maddie stared. Her ears burned. The cafeteria sounds muted, receded far into the background. Vague drumbeats pulsed through the silence, or maybe it was her own pulse she heard.

"I love you too, Nathan," she heard her voice say. "I've loved you since that day when I first saw you with the little boy at the main gate. I've loved you since that night when your friends carried you out of the San Pedro bar."

It was his turn to stare.

She looked down at her thumbnail and rubbed the other thumb over it. "I have been wrestling with it ever since."

"Then why can't we just love each other, Maddie?"

She frowned at him. "We can love each other, Nathan; it just can't go anywhere."

"Because I'm not a Christian? We're back to that?"

"Yes. And we will always come back to that. I love you and I don't trust my feelings. I'm afraid of what I might do. That's why I wanted to return to the States."

He sat back in his chair, staring at her, raised his hands in a spiritless gesture that aborted mid-flight. He let them fall back into his lap. "I don't get it. You love me so you want to get as far away from me as possible?"

Maddie worked her thumbnail some more, flexed her fingers to release tension.

"Does that make sense to you, Maddie?"

She raised her eyebrows. "About as much sense as your spending the weekend in Ischia with another woman and saying that you love me."

He said nothing to that.

They sat in silence for several moments; he in his world, she in hers. The worlds turned on their axes, their orbits widening.

"This was a mistake," she said quietly.

"Yes," he said, his voice sounding suddenly tired. "I've gotta get ready for guard." He collected his drawing materials and stood gazing down at her. "We're on a merry-go-round, Maddie. Round and round and round we go."

"How do we get off?"

He shook his head, put on his barracks cover, took a few steps and looked back. "Do us both a favor, Maddie, and go back to the States. I'm no good for you. You're no good for my head." He chuckled at the floor.

"What's so funny?"

He raised his eyes. "A missionary and a Marine falling for each other. There's a cartoon in there somewhere, only I can't see the humor in it."

He turned and walked away.

Maddie didn't watch him leave. Instead, she listened to the sound of retreating footsteps over the hard floor. She didn't know if she should get up and leave or just sit there and wait until the scenery changed. Then she only heard the noise of the cafeteria, and the music playing through it.

Chapter Twenty-Eight

THAT NIGHT NATHAN went back up to the second floor of the Post 10 building and inspected the offices. He stood outside the office of the British major and fed a magazine into his .45. He pushed open the door, flicked on the lights and glared at the painting of the beautiful woman. She was staring at him.

He walked across the room. She was still following him with her eyes, but it was just a painting. He inspected under the desk, in the closet and the adjoining bathroom. They were just rooms. There were no devils. No spooks. He looked at the painting once more.

"Did you ever love someone, lady? The devil? He's left you for another. You were unequally yoked, didn't you know?"

The painting said nothing.

"I don't believe it either, sister. The only thing unequally yoked is love with no love. St. Nate to the Unrequited."

He removed the magazine from his .45 and put it back into the pouch on his utility belt. He holstered the automatic. He made a deprecating noise, left the room and closed the door behind him.

He finished inspecting the floors and went down to the desk. Giuseppe was pouring coffee into his thermos cup. He glanced up and smiled at Nathan and watched him with black soulful eyes as he logged the inspection.

"You're a wise one tonight, *amico*," Nathan said to himself as he wrote in the log.

He closed the logbook and held the ball-point pen. He walked over to the plate-glass doors and stared out at the quiet grass square of the NATO complex, soft yellow cones of light glowing here and there over the tarmac. He tapped the end of the pen against his palm. He shook his head. "You've got the old wisdom flowing tonight, *amico*, that's for sure. Trouble is, nobody's listening."

Giuseppe sighed deeply. "There is something troubling you, my friend," he said, walking from behind the desk. "You are talking to yourself."

Nathan continued staring out at the square. "It's a habit I'm trying to kick, old friend."

"You have been on—*come si dice in Ingles*? On the knife?"

"On edge?"

"That is it. On the edge. Forgive me for intruding––it is none of my business, but you have had a fight with your beautiful Italian girl?"

Nathan was thinking of something else and glanced back at him. "Who?"

Giuseppe smiled a deprecating smile and shrugged. "It is nothing. Italian women have much passion. They yell loudly and throw plates. They break things. But they are also great lovers. You must take the good with the bad."

"Tell it to the lady—it doesn't matter which one. I just got off the merry-go-round."

Giuseppe's eyebrows came together. "*Come?*"

"It's an American expression. Don't ask me what it means."

Nathan checked his watch. It was half-past the hour. He walked back to the desk, set the pen on top of the logbook, picked up the phone and called the Corporal of the Guard and reported his post secure.

The COG said, "You're not walking off with the Admiral's silver over there, are you, Kessler?" There was an edge to his tone.

"Whaddya mean?"

The receiver went dead. Nathan glared at the instrument in his hand. He set it down in the cradle, frowned at the desktop.

"You...are...good Marine," Giuseppe said in broken English.

Nathan was thinking about what the COG said.

"The Marine...before you..."

Nathan looked at Giuseppe, his mind still thinking about what the COG said—the way he'd said it. "What's that?"

"The Marine...Dixon. Did I say it well?" he asked in Italian. "I have been practicing."

"You said it great. What about Dixon?"

"He goes into an office and sleeps. He asks me to wake him if the phone rings. Sometimes I smell strange smoke. It is drugs I think." He touched his head. "Drugs make you *stupido nella testa*."

"That's an affirmative." Nathan kept thinking about what the COG had said to him, the way he'd said it. Something was screwy. He called Mick to see if he'd heard anything strange, but got no reply. He called Skip. Skip picked up on the sixth ring. "Post 5, Lance Corporal McPherson speaking."

"It's Nate. Anything going on over there?"

"Sorry, Nate, I can't talk." The receiver went dead.

Nathan glared at the phone. He dialed Mick's number again. Lance Corporal Peters picked up on the third ring. Peters was a Marine in the 2nd Platoon. "Where's Mick?" Nathan asked.

"He's with CID. Place is crawling with 'em."

Nathan felt the blood drain from his face. "CID? What's going on?"

"No idea. I got hauled off liberty to stand in for him. Gotta go." The receiver went dead.

Nathan hung up the phone. He stared numbly across the foyer.

THEY WERE HOLDING Mick in a cell in the Navy barracks. The prevailing scuttlebutt, with creative permutations added as the story spread, was that he had boosted several large boxes of cigarette cartons from the PX and loaded them into Luigi's cab. Luigi had been under surveillance by CID agents who had been observing him from an upper room in the Hideaway Hotel, overlooking the main gate. The next night they were laying in wait.

Luigi had apparently sniffed the trap and escaped. Mick was not so fortunate. As he came in through the second story window of the PX for a second helping, agents nabbed him, at which time Mick reportedly remarked: "Hey *amici*, what's shakin'?"

Nathan was told to report to Captain Brickner at 0700. He arrived promptly.

Brickner was standing beside his desk, which stood against the window overlooking the parking lot. The furnishings in the office were spartan, every bit as no nonsense as Captain Brickner himself. His nameplate was carved in black marble and stood center-desk in a pen set with American and Marine Corps flags on either side. A low slung, straight-armed sofa, matching chairs and coffee table ensemble crowded one corner beside a healthy potted palm. Adorning the gray walls were photographs of the President, Flag Admiral, and Marine Corps Commandant. Beneath these were framed photos of Brickner's various promotions and commendations, his pretty blonde wife looking on proudly in each one. An officer's Mameluke sword, angled through a mahogany plaque with a brass globe and anchor surmounting it, gleamed in a muted shaft of sunlight on the wall adjacent to the desk.

Brickner didn't look happy. To one side of him Nathan saw there were two men. One was a man he'd never seen before, a short, square-cut Navy lieutenant junior grade. The other was Lance Corporal Lipton. Teabag.

"This is Lieutenant Garvey," Brickner said. "The other is—" He turned to Garvey. "I take it the cat's out of the bag, Lieutenant?"

Garvey nodded. Brickner jerked his chin. "The other is Staff Sergeant Lipton. These men are with the Criminal Investigation Division. They have a few questions."

"Yes, sir," Nathan said, narrowing his eyes at Lipton, who was holding a leather valise in his left hand. He saw that he was also wearing the watch with the green nylon strap. "I like your watch," he said, so that only Lipton was aware of the sarcasm.

Lipton scoffed, making no effort this time to conceal the watch.

Lieutenant Garvey opened a small notebook with a spiral going along the top. "You know Private Donovan, Lance Corporal Kessler?"

Nathan glanced at the notebook. "Yes, sir."

Garvey wrote something. "Would you consider him your friend?"

"He's a friend of mine, yes sir."

"You go into town together on liberty?" Lipton asked.

Nathan didn't look at him. "You've seen us go out on liberty."

Garvey wrote something. "What kind of things do you talk about?"

"Things? We talk about all kinds of things." Nathan turned to the CO. "May I ask what this is about, sir?"

Brickner growled, "Just answer the questions, Kessler. And don't get smart with Staff Sergeant Lipton."

Nathan looked back at Garvey.

"What kind of things do you talk about?" Garvey repeated.

Nathan watched him writing in the notebook. "The usual…girls. Booze. Girls. The weather."

The CID men didn't think it was funny. Garvey wrote something in the notebook. "Do you and Private Donovan ever talk about the black market?"

Nathan shook his head. "No, sir. Can't say that we ever have."

"Did you know he was heavily involved with the black market?"

"Mick? I don't believe it."

"There was an incident in town the other night involving two Italians and your friend Private Donovan. There was shooting. They tried to kill him."

"Yes, sir, I was there."

"We know," Lipton said. "What do you make of that, Kessler?"

"Naples is a rough town." Nathan wouldn't look at him.

Lieutenant Garvey glared at him with dead eyes, flipped back several pages in the notebook, and read what was written there. "We've been monitoring the activities of Luigi Fonticelli."

Nathan pushed out his lower lip, shook his head. "Never heard of him, sir."

"He parks his cab in front of the main gate."

"You mean Luigi the cabbie? Yes, sir. I didn't know him by his last name. What about him?"

Garvey was writing in the notebook. "Did he ever try to buy anything from you—cigarettes? Gasoline? Liquor?"

Nathan felt a cold drop of sweat trickling down his right side. He wondered how much they knew. "No, sir."

"You're sure."

"I think I'd remember something like that, sir. Wait a minute, he tried to sell me a pizza once. I told him I was tapped until payday."

Garvey eyed him some more. Nathan suspected he knew he was lying. "Your friend Private Donovan stole several hundred dollars worth of cigarettes from the PX.

He was working with Luigi Fonticelli. You wouldn't know anything about that, Marine?"

"Now I do, sir. It's hard to believe."

"I saw you talking to him the other night at mid-rats," Lipton interjected.

Nathan narrowed his eyes at him. "I talk to a lot of the guys when I eat mid-rats. It helps the digestion."

"Don't get smart, Kessler," Captain Brickner barked. "Just answer the question."

"Yes, sir." He turned to Lieutenant Garvey. "What was the question again, sir? I must've missed it."

"What were you and Private Donovan talking about at mid-rats?"

Nathan glanced at a corner in the ceiling. He was certain, now, that Lipton had been eavesdropping; had probably heard most—if not all—of what they said. He tried to remember the conversation.

"We talked a little about his folks," he said. "We talked about why he joined the Marine Corps. Oh—" He frowned at Lipton. "We also talked about the Silver Star he was awarded in Vietnam. Did you know that, under fire, and at great bodily risk to himself, he carried three wounded Marines to safety?"

Lipton said nothing.

"Private Donovan's war record is not being discussed here," Garvey said, "He didn't tell you he was going to rob the PX with Luigi Fonticelli?"

"No, sir."

"Are you sure?"

"That's not something I would forget, sir."

"You're lying," Lipton said.

Nathan turned to Captain Brickner. "I'm not lying, sir. Mick never told me he was going to rob the PX with Luigi."

Brickner frowned at Lipton. "Do you have any proof of your accusation, Staff Sergeant Lipton?"

"Show him the photograph," Garvey said.

Nathan looked quickly at the valise that Lipton was holding, felt another drop of sweat trickling down his side.

Lipton removed an 8-by-10 black and white glossy photograph from the valise and handed it to Nathan. "Who do you see?"

It was a grainy print, taken at night, beneath the light at the main gate. Mick and Nathan were in civvies, Luigi in a dark windbreaker, a sports cap on his head. The photo was taken from an elevated position. Nathan had just given Luigi the month's car payment with his gas and cigarette rations; however the photograph just showed the three of them under the light.

"It looks like Luigi talking to Mick and me, sir," he said. "But it's hard to tell, it isn't a very good photo, is it?" He handed back the photo. "You must've been in one of the rooms above the Hideaway Hotel."

Lipton took the photo, said nothing.

"We'd like to know what the three of you were discussing," Garvey said.

"Discussing? Could I see that photo again?" Lipton handed it back to him. "I don't have a clue, sir," Nathan said, inspecting it, wondering if there was a microphone hidden somewhere on the post. "We might have been asking Luigi for directions. Got any others?"

"Just look at the photo, Kessler."

Nathan examined it again, knowing now that they had nothing on him. "Yes, sir, I think that's what we were doing, it's coming to me now. This was taken a couple weeks ago, wasn't it, Sergeant?"

Lipton stared at him with cold unblinking eyes.

Captain Brickner glared at Lipton. "Well?"

Lipton nodded, not taking his eyes off Nathan. "Yes, sir. Two weeks ago."

"That's it then," Nathan said. "There's a bakery in town we wanted to check out. They have killer pastries. We were asking Luigi for directions." He handed back the photo, smiled a short one at Lipton, then turned to Captain Brickner.

Brickner addressed the CID men. "Any more questions?"

Lieutenant Garvey shook his head. "None right now."

Brickner turned to Nathan. "That's all, Kessler. Don't talk to any of the other men about this."

"I won't, sir." He winked at Lipton on his way out.

SEVERAL OF THE Marines were brought in for questioning over the next several days, men who had been friends with Mick. Mick had a lot of friends. No one knew anything.

An attractive JAG staffer, who had been particularly ingratiating to a few of the Marines in the barracks, leaked that a General Courts-Martial was in the offing, and that if convicted Mick could get twenty hard ones in Leavenworth with a dishonorable kicker. The prosecution would downgrade to a Special Court if he laid out the particulars of the operation: his contacts, where they met, and so on. Of particular interest was the whereabouts of Luigi Fonticelli, since he had apparently blown town with a sizable cut of Uncle Sam's booze and cigarettes.

"I don't think he'll sing," Gorilla told Nathan and Cooper in their room. "Not Mick. Nossir."

Cooper shook his head. "I don't know, Gorilla. Twenty years versus maybe six months. That's a lot of water to carry for some Italian hoods you'll never see again. What do you think, Nate?"

Nathan was lying on top of his bed, staring at the back of his wall locker. It was late afternoon. Half of the room was in shadow, the other half sucking light through the window. "I think they better guard him well."

"Why do you say that?" Gorilla asked.

"Those shooters we tangled with the other night probably don't know a whole lot about one court over another. They're pretty efficient at back alley law though."

"They ought to know he wouldn't sing."

"He owes them money. More than what Luigi skipped off with."

Gorilla frowned at Cooper, turned back to Nathan. "Think they'll allow visitors?"

"Nope. Already asked."

Cooper stood. "We best be heading into town, Gorilla. It's getting late. Want to come with us, Nate?"

Nathan frowned at him. "Where to?"

"We thought we'd go over to the Way Station."

"Clarence and Jesse say they got great chow," Gorilla added, picking at a shaving scab on his cheek.

"Great chow, huh?"

Gorilla nodded. His cheek was bleeding. "That's what Jesse said. Didn't he, Coop?"

"That's what he said. You wanna come, Nate?"

"Nope."

"There's that girl—what's her name?"

Nathan shook his head. "Ancient history."

"Oh yeah? What're you gonna do?"

"I'm spending the evening with a friend."

After Cooper and Gorilla left, Nathan got a pint of bourbon out of his locker and lay in bed sipping at the bottle. He had seen plenty of CID and JAG boys going in and out of the Navy barracks all afternoon. They were coming out of the woodwork like wet earwigs. They had to be giving Mick the business. Mick would spill it. The Criminal Investigation boys wanted to cut the head off the local black market snake, and they had a solid lead with Mick. He'd sing. He had to.

Nathan took a longer pull, turned the bottle in his hands and read the label. Twelve year old Tennessee hooch. "Good stuff, Nate. Good stuff. Luigi don't get this one." He took another pull to prove it.

His thoughts moved around a circuit—the old merry-go-round. Then he was tired of thinking. He drank some more.

After a while, lying there, holding the bottle in his fist, staring vaguely at the back of his wall locker, he felt the sun sinking outside. He had seen the sunset many times from the main gate on the 4 to 8 shift. He'd seen the sunrise on the same shift, twelve hours later. The 4 to 8 had some great sunrises and sunsets.

He watched shadows driving a triangle of light up the wall, herding it into a corner on the ceiling. The room glowed softly, seeming to shiver in the light. He imagined the sun hanging on to the rim of the volcano crater, just the top of it showing, holding as if it were doing a chin-up, then sinking, sending one last flare of golden light into the sky before dropping out of sight.

The room darkened quickly. Nathan didn't turn on the light. There was nothing to see but the back of his wall locker, the bare walls, an empty ceiling.

By now he was feeling no pain.

"Ain't good to drink alone, *amico*," he said, remembering Mick's advice. "You'll end up talking to yourself." He took another slug of bourbon. "Thanks for the heads up, Mick. See where it got you."

He glanced over at his family on the side table. The frame was a dark rectangle against the outside parking lights. He couldn't see their faces, but he didn't need to see them. Their images were burned into his retinas. "Ain't alone, Mick. Ain't never alone. I got a family of lepers to keep me company."

He raised the bottle. "Here's to the lepers," he said, and drained a couple fingers, letting some excess dribble down his chin and throat. He wiped his mouth with the back of his hand.

"What'd you think of them apples, Maddie? You don't know about that kettle of fish, do you?" He chuckled, sipping at the bottle. "She's got you talking cliches now, don't she?"

He started to think about Maddie and then shook his head. "No. Ain't going down there tonight. That's a well you can't climb out of." He took another pull of whiskey, chuckling. "Well, well, well—that's a deep subject. Ain't going down that well. Nope, sir."

He lay with his head propped against the headboard on a pillow, his chin dug into his chest, the half-empty pint of bourbon held in a fist on his hip. He thought about Mick some more. He'd sing. He had to.

"Sure you will, Mick. You'll sing every stanza of the song that'll cut nineteen-plus years off your hitch. You'll sing it in triplicate. You ain't no dummy, Mick. Sing, brother."

He took a big swallow, felt his head swell, the ceiling swirl. "That one had the payload, Mick. The merry-go-round's in fine shape tonight, brother. You better sing, boy. Sing!"

Chapter Twenty-Nine

MICK SANG. HE was tried in a Special Court and given six months imprisonment at hard labor, six months reduction of pay, and a dishonorable discharge— the old six, six and a kick. They were holding him in the cell off the quarterdeck of the Navy barracks until his paperwork was ready, at which time they would send him Stateside. No Rota, Spain, country club. He was allowed visitors.

Nathan went over to visit him.

Mick was sitting on the edge of his bed looking gloomy, his elbows planted on his knees as he stared through the bars of the cell at Nathan.

Nathan sat on a metal chair outside the cell. A Navy guard wearing duty whites with white leggings and white web belt with three stripes on his sleeve was sitting back in his chair looking at them from the quarterdeck. He was biting his nails. A black billy club that looked like it might have seen some action in the previous war lay on the desk in front of him. The guard had round pink cheeks like a baby's behind, only fuzzier, his white sailor cap pushed forward over his right eye to give him a tough look. He looked like he could whip his weight in caterpillars.

"How're you holding up, Mick?" Nathan asked.

Mick grinned. "Not too bad, *amico.* Three squares. Free smokes. Cushy digs. I could go for a bottle of hooch."

"I'll see what I can do."

"You're a pal, Natboy."

"Pals to the end."

"You bet. You look like you just woke up, by the way. You hungover?"

"Semper Fi."

Mick grinned. "That's the old Nate." The grin faded. He stared through the bars, vague bar shadows playing over his face and up the gray cinder block wall behind him. "This is gonna be hard on my mom. She wanted me to make good."

"You can still make good."

"With a DD chasing me? Sure."

"Lots of businesses'll hire you. Nowadays they'd probably put you in charge of a division or something." Nathan felt bad saying it.

"Sure. They'll put me in charge of the goldbrick division."

Nathan chuckled.

"I know she's praying for me."

Nathan looked at him. "Your mom?"

"She's pretty religious. I never told you? Sure. She speaks in tongues and everything. You bet. She's gonna take this hard."

He lit a cigarette, held a tin ashtray in his hand and tapped the edge with the ash. "Apple don't fall far from the tree, Natboy."

"You're not your dad. You didn't kill anyone."

"No?" Mick made a noise in his throat. "Don't kid yourself, *amico*." He looked out through the bars smoking. "Six months ain't so bad."

"You can do it standing on your head."

"Piece'a cake." He tapped an ash into the tin. "What do you know about Portsmouth?"

"It ain't Leavenworth."

Mick was shaking his head looking out through the bars. "I can do 'er." He turned to Nathan. "Would you do me a big favor, *amico*?"

"Name it."

"Would you write my mom and tell her what happened? I don't want her hearing it from one of them Remington Raiders in Admin."

"Sure. But why don't you write her? I'm sure she'd appreciate it more from you."

"I'm not much good at letter writing. I dropped out of school before I learned much."

"You can write, can't you?"

"You ever read my logs?" He laughed. "Ain't likely to win any Pulitzers."

"I'd be happy to write your mom, Mick."

Mick gazed at him long and hard. He started to say something, nodded instead, then said, "I told you, you were a pal."

"'Till the end, Mick."

They sat in silence; Mick smoking, Nathan thinking what to say. There was nothing to say. Mick was going to do six months of hard time. He'd leave the service in disgrace, his Silver Star tarnished. Maybe it wouldn't matter anymore. Maybe they *would* promote him. After all, they spit at men in uniform nowadays, don't they?

"I saw the CO heading over here this morning," he said.

Mick rolled the tip of his cigarette in the ashtray. "He told me that my testimony helped nab a couple of bad boys in town. They're still looking for Luigi."

"Good luck."

Mick chuckled, blew a cloud of smoke through his nostrils and crushed his cigarette. "Guess I left old Luigi kinda short, didn't I?"

"He'll get over it."

The guard with the baby's-butt-for-cheeks stepped over to them with a set of keys. "Time to take you to chow, Donovan." He unlocked the cell.

"See what I mean, Natboy? Service. Got my own limousine and chauffeur." He turned to the baby-faced sailor. "Where to today, my good man? The Ritz or the Biltmore?"

"Very funny." The guard's voice squeaked, as if it hadn't changed yet.

Mick stood, shrugged out of the cell and looked him over. "Navy guards look like real world-beaters, don't they, Natboy? You go through pooberty yet, admiral?"

"Let's go," the guard said, lowering his voice.

Nathan smiled.

Mick shook his head in disgust. "You iron that uniform with a waffle skillet? Got no pride in your appearance. Look at them shoes. Looks like you shined them with Brillo pads."

"Don't you worry about my shoes, Marine."

Mick leveled his eyes at him. "You bet, 'Marine'. I could lick a dozen of you torpedo jockeys without breakin' a nail."

The guard rested his palm on the billy club. "Want me to put the cuffs on you, tough guy?"

Mick chuckled, winked at Nathan.

Nathan followed the guard and Mick outside the barracks where a gray Suburban was parked and idling. There was a sailor behind the wheel.

Mick glanced up at the sky, took a deep breath. "Smell that air, Natboy. *Bella Napoli.* Ain't it enough to turn your stomach? I sure won't miss that."

The guard started Mick down the steps when two men in black leather coats stepped out from behind a parked car with automatics pointed at Mick and loosed off a fusillade.

Mick went down, the guard went over the stair wall. Nathan hit the deck.

A dark sedan roared through the parking lot and skidded to a halt beside the Suburban, the rear door swinging open. The two shooters jumped in, slammed the door and the sedan sped away in a squeal of tires and smoke toward the main gate. It happened in a few seconds.

Nathan jumped to his feet. The Marine at the main gate was Lance Corporal Spinoza. Nathan saw him draw his weapon and level it at the sedan as it roared past him but nothing happened. His two .45 magazines were probably neatly stowed in their canvas pouches, according to regulation.

The sedan disappeared down the road.

Nathan looked down at Mick. Mick was lying sideways at the bottom of the steps. Blood oozed from dark holes in his chest and torso.

The Navy guard poked his head over the stair wall. "Is he all right?"

"Call an ambulance!" Nathan shouted.

The guard hiked over the wall and ran back into the quarterdeck.

Nathan got down on one knee, lifted and held Mick's head. Mick was groaning. "Mick, can you hear me? Mick?"

Mick's eyes rolled open, searching for him. "That you, Natboy?"

"It's me, Mick. Take it easy, the cavalry's on the way."

"What happened? Am I hit?"

"Don't talk, Mick. You're going to be okay."

"That the same two shooters?"

"Looked like it."

"Italians can't take a joke." Mick started to laugh, coughed blood and gritted his teeth against a stab of pain. Blood showed on his teeth and lips. "Don't look like I'll be needing the hooch, *amico*."

Nathan counted at least five places where Mick had been hit, two of them in his chest. "Don't talk, Mick."

Mick was gazing at the sky. "Wasn't supposed to go this way."

Marines and sailors spilled out of their respective barracks and crowded around Nathan and Mick. Bill Porter from the Navy barracks held out his arms, waving the men away.

"Stand back," he shouted. "Give him air."

The men stepped back.

Captain Brickner pushed through the crowd and knelt beside Nathan. He glanced over the wounds. "Take it easy, Donovan. You're going to be fine." "I called the hospital," Bill Porter told the Captain. "The ambulance will be here in a minute."

"You hear that, Donovan?" Brickner said to Mick. "Help is on the way."

Mick was laboring to breathe, blood bubbling on his lips. "Yes…yes, sir."

"Hang tough, Marine. That's an order."

"Yes, sir." Mick grinned, holding himself against the pain. "Don't look like I'll be doing brig time, sir."

"Yes you will…all six months. You're a good Marine."

"Semper Fi." Mick smiled.

Nathan saw everything change on his face; the change in his eyes.

"Nate? Nate?"

"Right here, Mick." He heard sirens.

"Hang in there, Marine," Brickner growled. "The ambulance is here. Don't you quit on me, Marine."

"No…no sir…" Mick stiffened, his eyes ranging for a focal point. "You there, Nate…?"

"Right here…"

"They're comin' for me, Natboy. I can feel 'em." Mick was sucking and blowing his cheeks, the lips and cheeks fluttering. "I don't wanna go to hell, Mama," he cried. "Please don't let me go to hell. Tell me about Jesus, Nate. Tell me…"

"Tell you?" Nathan looked around at the faces in the crowd. "Where's Skip?"

Bill Porter started to say something, but Mick grabbed Nathan's shirt and pulled him close. "You tell it, *amico*. Tell me…"

"I don't know how, Mick. Jesus loves you. He loves you, Mick…"

Mick's eyes rolled toward him. "My mama thinks so…" he said calmly. He shuddered as a spasm of pain wracked his body, his cheeks fluttering. "…h-help me, Jesus…I'm a sinner…"

"He died for your sins, Mick."

"Yes…yes…He did…Jesus, save me. Mercy. Jes…" The name finished as a gasp. Mick grew still, his face settled, at peace, his eyes fixed.

"Don't quit!" Nathan shouted. "Mick! Mick! Don't leave me, Mick!"

He felt a hand on his shoulder. It was Captain Brickner.

"He's gone, Kessler."

"No!"

"Let's go, Marine."

Chapter Thirty

THAT AFTERNOON NATHAN used another of his liquor rations and bought a pint of Jack Daniels at the liquor outlet on base. It was Mick's favorite brand. Nathan was partial to it as well. Then he got into his Fiat Spider, opened the bottle and pointed the neck at the windshield.

"Here's to you, Mick," he said, and drained three fingers.

"Don't do it, Nate."

"Stay out of it, Frankie. You don't understand."

"You're gonna get hurt, Nate. Please don't do it. I love you."

"I love you too, Frankie. Leave me alone now."

Nathan lounged idly in the bucket seat drinking whiskey, and listening to songs on the Armed Forces station. The sky was darkly clouded over the rim of the crater, streaked with a riot of crimson and maroon and blood reds, and there were thunderheads over the bay threatening rain.

He took another long pull from the bottle and felt it solidly. Then he started the engine, put in the clutch, but let it out too quickly. The Spider lurched forward and stalled. He started the engine, revved her a few times, got her going smoothly and went out through the PX gate, nodding at the sentry, then knocking back a hefty pull as he swung out onto the road.

By the time he got into town he was drunk. He parked the car behind the Galleria Umberto, drained another two fingers and got out of the car.

He leaned back against the door, his feet spread wide, lifted the bottle and drained the last of it. He looked at the bottle, held it up to the light and frowned. He tipped it upside down and jerked it a couple times, peered at it again.

"Another dead soldier." He chuckled sardonically. "Marine, *amico*. Dead Marine."

Holding the bottle by the neck, he ranged down to the Square with a belligerent swinging of his arms, an overcompensation in his stride. Crowds of people came toward him and swerved out of his way. He wheeled into a man with his shoulder, intentionally, causing him to stumble. The man cursed. Nathan laughed.

A woman with bleached hair, green miniskirt and knee boots stood on the corner outside the San Pedro bar. It was the same woman he saw the other day.

She smiled at Nathan. "Twenty dollar?"

"Not tonight, sister," he snarled, and pushed into the bar.

The bar was filled with the usual crowd of military, dark-eyed girls and smoke. "Fortunate Son" thumped through the jukebox. Nathan stood in the middle of the floor, eyed the crowd with open contempt and raised the empty bottle in a fist. "To Mick Donovan," he shouted.

Heads turned.

"Best Marine there ever was." The bottle fell out of his hand and smashed against the floor.

The man at the nearest table sneered. It was the fat Navy with the palm trees and pineapple shirt, only now he was wearing outrigger canoes and volcanoes. He liked Hawaiian shirts apparently. "Lousy jarhead can't hold his liquor."

The men around him laughed.

"Where's your idiot boyfriend?" Fat Boy jeered. He turned away, laughing.

Nathan went over the table and grabbed the fat man by the neck and tore the collar away from his shirt. Fat Boy came out of his chair and Nathan hit him back hard against the table, spilling glasses and bottles.

People jumped back from the table. Nathan felt hands on his shoulders from behind; he whirled and hit the nearest face. More hands grabbed him. He turned, lowering his shoulder to swing, when light exploded behind his eyes and he felt the hard jolt of the floor. He sank into darkness.

He didn't move but heard feet shuffling around his head. He blinked open an eye, saw fluid dripping down his face onto the floor. It was red but smelled like whiskey. Then he felt hands pulling at him and the sensation of weightlessness and movement, a blur of light and color and voices yelling, and then a rush of cold air as he fetched the hard impact of concrete against his face and shoulder.

He was outside on the sidewalk. The cement was wet. There was a heavy mist crawling over the ground. He lay groaning with the side of his face on the hard, cold, wet surface.

Feet moved past him in both directions. Voices loud, then going away. People laughing in a welter of traffic noise. A face lowered in front of him, the face contorted. "Whaddya know, a drunk Marine." The face went away, trailing laughter.

Nathan tried to crawl up onto his knees, but felt a stab of pain in his right shoulder. He groaned and lay back. A pair of black boots appeared in front of his face. Women's boots, with stiletto heels. A woman's voice said, "Want help, Marine?"

Nathan felt hands on him—gentle hands—saw the ground moving away. Shapes swirled around him: faces, lights. "Wait a second," he said. He fell onto his knees. Blood dripped onto the cement.

The boots appeared beside him again. He felt a hand on his shoulder, rubbing it softly. He spat blood and bile from his mouth and groaned.

"Need help?" the voice said.

Nathan got up onto one knee. "Wait a sec'." He climbed onto his feet, uncertain of his footing, pain shooting through his head as he stood. He winced, staggered a few dizzy steps toward the street.

Vague car shapes rushed past in the mist, sucking wind. Horns blared. Thunder rumbled over the Square.

A hand took his arm and pulled him in a different direction. "You come," the woman's voice said in pidgin English.

Nathan swung his head past a face, looked back and saw it was the bleached blonde with the green miniskirt. "Can walk?"

"Speak Italian," he said. "I'm okay. Give us a moment."

"Your head is bleeding," she said in Italian.

Nathan felt the back of his head. It was sticky wet. His hand came back covered with blood. He was soaked in whiskey. "Somebody cracked a bottle over me."

The woman guided him along the sidewalk. People walked past looking at him. They were featureless faces. "You come to my place," she said. "I'll put something on that."

"No, that's okay." He started to pull away but almost fell over. "Wait a sec'…wait a sec'."

The mist was heavier now, and then there was drizzling rain. "You come with me," she said. "The weather is turning bad."

"Okay."

They went up an alley that was dark and paved with uneven bricks. He tripped and almost went down but the woman steadied him. The noise of the Square muting behind them, then dying, and then it was quiet in a light rain. Lightning flickered off the walls of the buildings and thunder crashed over their heads. Big drops of rain spattered against the bricks and against the lids of trash cans. Then it was raining.

They turned onto a narrow street, a dull streetlamp lighting the corner of the building and street in pale yellow light. The rain was fine and bright against the light, and Nathan knew they were in a bad neighborhood. They were in the Gut.

There weren't any bad characters that he could see, but he was past caring. They went down another alley, turned and went up a narrow flight of steps of broken tile. They stopped at a tiled landing, in front of a painted door that was worn and peeling.

Nathan's head throbbed. He felt dizzy and nauseous standing in the rain.

The woman opened the door and Nathan stumbled into a dark room. She came in behind him and flicked on a bare overhead light, the light throwing harsh shadows over the floor and walls.

The apartment was a small living area with a stuffed chair and reading lamp in the inside left corner, a made bed with red pillows against the right wall, a kitchen area straight ahead, separated by a wooden counter, and a hall leading away from it to the left. Colored glass beads hung over the opening. There was pale light coming through the beads from down the hall. Nathan felt it coming up.

"Where's the head?" he asked. "*La toilette?*"

She pointed at the beads.

He got there just in time to hit the toilet. He flushed, spitting. He stared down into the filthy water, listened to the tank filling with water, smelling foul and his clothes wet from the rain. He groaned. Then he spat and flushed again, felt the earth whirling, waited until he could move without his stomach twisting knots.

"Wonderful," he said, spitting.

After he had finished, he climbed to his feet, steadied himself against the sink and flicked on the light. He looked at himself in the mirror over the sink, the mirror smoky with age. His hair was matted over his forehead. His right eye was swelling. The right side of his head was a scab. Blood had dribbled down his neck into his shirt and his shoulders were wet.

He turned on the cold water, let the water run clear of brown sediments, and splashed some on his face. He splashed on more water, washed the blood off the side of his face as best he could.

The woman came in behind him holding a bowl of water. She set the bowl down in the sink, took a towel off a metal rack and dipped it in the bowl. The room was too small for both of them. She stood very close to him as she touched the side of his face lightly with the wet towel. Her perfume was strong, and Nathan thought he might lose it again. For the next several minutes she cleaned his head and face. The water on the towel was warm and soothing.

Her face was inches from his. "I am sorry, but I do not have a dry shirt for you to wear," she said.

"The moisture won't kill me."

Nathan watched what she was doing in the mirror to avoid eye contact. He noticed her blouse was wet. Then he looked down at her face as she worked on the side of his head, lifting the warm wet towel from the bowl to his cheekbone, the fingers of her other hand touching his face gently to guide and steady his head. She picked pieces of broken glass from his blood-matted hair and shirt collar, and set them on the edge of the sink. She was very gentle.

She had cocoa brown eyes, with dark flecks in them, with heavy liner on top and bottom, the eyes concentrated on the side of his face. The platinum hair showed about an inch of dark roots. Her lips were red and glossy. She was probably in her late twenties and might be pretty under the makeup, but there were already signs of age showing around her eyes and thin upper lip.

"Could you sit down on the toilet seat," she said, lowering the seat for him. "I can't see the top of your head."

Nathan sat down and she worked on him some more. "The San Pedro is a rough bar," she said.

"You bet."

"I would stay away from there if I were you."

"Sound advice."

She moved around him, her body brushing against him in the tight space as she touched his face. She opened the mirror and removed something from the cabinet behind it. "This will hurt," she said and dabbed fluid from a small bottle onto the back of his head.

Nathan winced. "Ouch!"

"It is only iodine." She leaned back and looked at his head, at his face, angling it to the light with her warm wet fingers. She dabbed iodine on the cut beneath his right eye. "This is all I can do for you," she said. "You should go to the hospital."

"Thank you." Nathan stood, felt woozy and braced himself against the sink. "You would make a good nurse."

She smiled. From her expression he might as well have said she could fly without wings.

"What do I owe you?" he asked.

"Nothing. Twenty dollars if you would like the other."

"Not tonight."

"I did not think so."

He followed her out of the bathroom, stopped in the hall to look into a small, dimly lighted room opposite. An older woman was sitting on a straight-backed chair. She was holding an infant in her arms, bouncing it and singing softly. She looked up at Nathan without interest, gazed back at the infant, singing.

Nathan went out through the beads into the living area.

The platinum-haired woman was washing out the bowl and towel in the kitchen sink. She turned and looked at him as he came into the room. "I have seen you before in the Square. You are permanent personnel?"

"Yes. The kid yours?"

She looked automatically at the curtain of beads. "Yes."

The baby was crying.

She wiped a strand of hair from her eyes. "It is time for feeding," she said. She told Nathan to wait a moment and went back through the beads down the hall, unbuttoning the top buttons of her blouse.

Nathan listened to her talking to the older woman. He guessed she was her mother. He looked at the small crucifix gleaming dully on the wall over a cheap radio that was set on a milk crate. A faded print of the Virgin and Child hung beside it. He frowned at the beads, listened to the baby crying then settling.

"Nuts," he said, reached into his wallet, grabbed a handful of bills and laid them on the counter. He crossed the room, opened the door and stepped out into the rain.

Chapter Thirty-One

IT WAS RAINING hard. Rain lashed the streets and

sidewalks and ran in the gutters. By the time Nathan got back to the base from town he was sober, sick and wet to the skin. The back of his head hurt, his right eye was swollen nearly shut, his mouth tasted like vinegar and paste, the palms of his hands were skinned, the knees of his jeans ripped, his knees skinned and bloody. His empty stomach was doing flip-flops. He stank of whiskey and vomit. He felt like slugging someone.

The Corporal of the Guard and the driver were talking about Mick when he stepped onto the quarterdeck out of the driving rain. He shook the rain off his shirt. They both looked at him. It was Sergeant Hastert and Corporal Spinoza.

Nathan knew from their expressions that he had been the subject of their conversation, along with Mick.

Sergeant Hastert logged him in, looking at him. "What happened to your eye, Kessler?"

Nathan touched it. "I had a disagreement in town."

"What'd the other guy look like?"

"Don't have a clue."

"Too bad about Mick," Hastert said. "You were there, huh?"

"I was there."

"You want to tell us about it?"

"No." Nathan went up the stairwell.

"What's with him?" he heard Spinoza say.

A knot of Marines was in the hall feeding the scuttlebutt mill. Nathan knew they were talking about Mick's death. They stopped talking and looked at him as he approached. He ignored them.

"What happened to you?" Washington said, running a pick through his Afro.

Nathan said nothing.

Thompson grabbed his arm. "Hey, Kessler, tell us what happened."

Nathan flinched away. "Lay off," he growled, and continued on down to the end of the hall. He heard the men talking behind him, but paid them no more mind than he would flies on the ceiling. He turned to go into his room, but wheeled when he heard Skip's voice.

"Nathan?"

The door to Skip's room was open. Skip was lying on his bed holding a copy of *Field & Stream*. Nathan stared at him from his doorway.

Skip tossed the magazine onto his bed, swung his legs over and stood. "You okay? You look terrible."

"I was holding a wake for Mick. It got a little lively. Did you want something?"

Skip shook his head. "I just wanted to say that I'm sorry about Mick."

"You didn't kill him."

"I know he was your friend."

"He was."

Nathan turned to enter his room but stopped and looked back at Skip steadily, feeling the old cold deadliness moving inside him. Then it burned in his chest. He walked across the hall into Skip's room. "Got any pearls of wisdom for me, Skip? Any verses of Scripture to help the wounded soul? Got any verses for my eye, Skip?"

Skip shook his head. "No."

"What about an eye for an eye? Or plucking the speck out of your brother's eye? I know a lot about that one. It's deadly. Got any more?"

"No, Nathan."

"No verses telling how Mick probably got what he deserved? How he was walking in the path of the wicked."

Skip said nothing.

Nathan jabbed the air with a forefinger. "You're not gonna tell me there's a reason for it? Doesn't God want me to see His goodness in it, and if I don't it's because I don't have faith? Isn't that what Christians believe?"

Skip took a step toward Nathan. "I don't understand why it happened anymore than you do."

"I'm sick of you people." Nathan put his hands on Skip's chest and shoved. Skip fell back against the side of his bed, rolled sideways into the side table and knocked his head against the leg, hard enough to joggle the lamp.

Skip groaned, sat up feeling the back of his head. He lowered his hand and inspected it for blood. There wasn't any. He looked up at Nathan. "Why'd you do that?" he asked quietly.

Nathan glared down at him, his fists doubled. He felt like a heel. "Sorry."

"It's okay," Skip said. He picked himself off the floor and stood facing Nathan, his arms hanging loosely at his sides. The hair on one side of his head was tufted where he'd hit the table. He said nothing.

Nathan put his hand on the doorjamb and looked back. He started to say something, compressing his lips together. Skip wasn't hurt too bad, probably just a bump on the head. A bump for the Cause. He'd probably write a song about it. Nathan patted the doorjamb, then he went into his room and shut the door.

Nathan took a shower, changed into clean skivvies, turned off the lights and then lay in his bed in the dark looking up at the ceiling. The rain beat against the window with a soft drumming. He was thinking about Mick. He remembered talking to him in the Navy barracks that morning, Mick alive and well, thinking about his future, and now he was lying in the morgue at the hospital, dead. One minute alive and the next minute no more tomorrows. Taken out by a bus, a bullet or a bug. Death is no respecter of persons. It comes with its scales; to some, tipping its hat with a deprecating smile; to others with a fist. You fight against it, you take pills against it, you pray your guts against it—boy do you pray against it, but it comes grinning with the vultures to pick through with their ready clichés. There's plenty of those vultures, aren't there, Natboy?

Then he felt the old bitterness smoothing over him, starting in the center of his chest, seeing their pious faces, their mouths working, their words cutting, then the bitterness working into his limbs with a shiver. He rubbed his arms, listening to the rain.

He felt a pang of remorse for shoving Skip. Skip meant well. Like Maddie he seemed genuine; he was just there. A symbol. He shook his head. Beating up the world won't bring them back, Nathan. None of them.

"Isn't that right, Frankie?"

Frankie said nothing.

"No 'I told you sos?'"

Frankie said nothing.

Just then the door opened, admitting a wedge of light from the hall. A figure stood briefly in the doorway, silhouetted against the light. It was Jim Cooper. He edged into the room, closing the door. Leather soles crept over the tiles.

Nathan could hear him undressing, laying his clothes over a chair. He could see his dark shape climb into bed and settle. Cooper muttered something under his breath. Nathan couldn't hear what he said. Then:

"You awake, Nate?"

"I'm awake."

"I didn't wake you, did I? Skip said you'd be awake."

"I was awake."

Cooper sat up in bed. "I just heard about Mick. I can't believe it."

"Believe it."

"Two guys shot him?"

"Same two guys as the other night. You just now heard about it? You been on the moon?"

"I was at the Way Station with some of the guys. No one knew about it. Skip said you were with him when he died."

"I was with him."

"Man, I'm sorry, Nate." Nathan could see him sitting up on his bed, vague, watery light from outside in the parking lot silhouetting his shape. "Old Mick."

"Old Mick." Nathan didn't want to talk about it anymore. He'd been through it all day and didn't feel like nursing someone else through it. Talking about it just made him feel lousy. "Did Skip say anything else?"

"About what?"

"Nothing. You were down at the Station?"

"Me and the guys, yeah."

"You're spending a lot of time down there."

Cooper peered at him a few moments, glanced out the window, light glinting on his eyes. "Boy is it raining."

"Coop?"

Cooper looked back at Nathan. "I became a Christian tonight."

Nathan closed his eyes. "Perfect."

"Me and Gorilla. It all just came together. I could see it. Funny, it was there all along but tonight I could see it."

Nathan rolled his head slowly back and forth. "I don't want to hear it, Coop. Not tonight."

"Okay."

Nathan rolled over onto his side and faced the wall. He hadn't heard Cooper lay back down, so he guessed he was probably still sitting on his bed, staring across at him. Rain splashed against the window.

Nathan blinked at the dark wall. He felt empty and sick and he just wanted peace, but there was no peace.

"Maddie's dad was teaching from the Bible," Cooper said, "and it was like God was speaking directly to me. I could feel it burning. I never felt that way before. Then I heard that Jesus loved me and I believed it."

Nathan closed his eyes.

"I feel clean, Nate. Nothing tingly or weird or anything but I feel clean. Inside clean. It's hard to explain."

Nathan said nothing.

"Gorilla too," Cooper chuckled. "The big kid. He couldn't stop laughing. He laughed all the way back to the barracks. Maddie and her dad prayed with us. She asked about you."

Nathan opened his eyes and stared at the wall. Lightning flickered against the wall. Moments later, thunder rumbled in the distance. Rain drummed against the window.

"I still can't believe it about Mick," Cooper said. "Skip said he asked about Jesus and you told him. Is that true? Nate?"

"Please don't talk about it, Coop," Nathan said. "What does it matter what I said? Mick's dead."

"It matters a lot, Nate."

"Shut up, Coop. Please."

"Sure." Cooper said nothing for a solid minute. "They gonna have an honor guard for him? Mick was decorated."

Nathan made a noise in his throat. "I don't think he cares much about it one way or another."

"They should give him an honor guard."

THERE WAS NO honor guard. Mick's body was flown back to the States in the hold of a 747, along with the other luggage. The CO addressed the men during morning inspection, remarking on Mick's service in Vietnam, his Silver Star, and then warned the men not to have dealings with Italians connected to the black market.

He said if anyone knew of anyone connected with the black market, Italians or otherwise, they should turn in the names of said black marketers to the platoon leader. CID would hunt them down.

Nathan knew for a fact that the platoon leader sold some of his rations to Luigi; he'd seen him doing it. He'd seen plenty of other guys doing it too. There'd be plenty of names on that list, his own included. Then he wondered how Luigi planned on collecting now that he'd disappeared into the scenery. He'd turn up. Luigi would turn up.

After inspection Nathan wrote to Mick's mother and told her that he was his friend and that he was with him the day he died. Mick had spoken about her in his last moments, he had wanted to know about Jesus, and that he had told him. Nathan felt funny writing about it, but thought that it might bring her a little comfort. He hoped it would.

The cartoon that week showed Ol' Prive standing over the helmeted graves of his fellow Marines with the single word caption:

Why?

Chapter Thirty-Two

IT WAS THURSDAY afternoon field day and the

Marines in 1st Platoon moved in and out of their rooms, cleaning windows and sills, dusting hard surfaces, spit-shining leather gear, polishing brass, and scrubbing and polishing the toilets and shower stalls in the head. The men arranged uniforms and civvies in lockers, the dress blouses and shirts facing uniformly, chevrons showing, and trousers lined according to Marine Corps regulation.

The men clowned around, running up and down the hall snapping towels, but every man did the work assigned to him by the platoon sergeant. Then they buffed the waxed floor in their rooms, and afterward Nathan moved the buffer down the hall, guiding it lightly, the pad whirling from side to side, shimmying, humming, buffing half-moon scallops into the high luster of the terrazzo surface. He allowed a grim smile. There was nothing cleaner in the universe than the floor in a Marine Barracks after a field day.

Friday morning, at 0700, Captain Brickner came down the hall with the inspection team—the XO, Sergeant Major and Sergeant Rockman, the latter holding a clipboard. They started at the stairwell, inspected the first room on the right, then went across the hall and inspected the first room on the left, and so on, working back and forth toward the far end of the hall.

Inside the rooms the Marines stood at attention beside their beds, dressed in barracks blue and beige, their white and leather gear laid out in Marine Corps fashion on their beds, their wall lockers opened showing uniforms in the first two, civvies in the third.

The inspection team spent more time in some rooms than in others; one room given a cursory look-see, another given the white glove treatment. As a room passed inspection the Marine or Marines occupying the room were given weekend liberty.

Nathan could hear them coming down the hall. He knew whose room was being inspected by the sound of the voices in the room; the CO making comments, a Marine answering. They took a long time in Jesse's and Gorilla's room, which was halfway down the hall on the left. Nathan glanced over at Cooper standing at parade rest at the foot of his bed.

"They're putting the screws to Gorilla and Jesse," Nathan said.

Cooper glanced over at him then back at the open door, a benign smile playing over his lips. He said nothing.

Nathan stared at his bunkmate a moment longer. He was a different man. He was the same Jim Cooper on the outside but something was different. Regardless of what Nathan thought about Christians, Coop seemed more at peace with himself and the world around him. Nathan glanced out the door when he heard the inspection team approaching, saw them go across the hall into Skip's and Clarence's room.

"Atten-huh!" Skip said.

"As you were," Brickner replied.

Nathan could hear the CO making comments about Skip's leather gear and Clarence's white gear. Next he made comments about their personal items and about something on the wall, his voice edged with obvious contempt.

The XO and Sergeant Major's comments were likewise edged with contempt. The inspection took longer than normal. Skip and Clarence failed. They would not be given liberty until their room was squared away.

The inspection team came across the hall into Nathan's room, Captain Brickner in front holding his swagger stick.

"Atten-huh!" Nathan said, and he and Cooper snapped to attention.

"As you were," Brickner replied, stepping over to inspect Nathan's wall lockers. The XO and Sergeant

Major stood just behind him, looking on, the Platoon Sergeant with pen and clipboard. "Looks squared away, Kessler," Brickner said. "Outstanding. Log it, Sergeant Rockman."

Rockman logged it.

Brickner crossed over to Cooper's locker. The inspection team followed and stood behind him.

From where Nathan stood at the foot of his bed he could see them huddled around the lockers. They were looking at something on one of the doors. Voices murmured. Angry voices.

Cooper tensed.

Nathan felt an immediate change in the atmosphere. There had been the air of sudden authority in the room when the team had entered, but there was something else now. He had felt it that night at the ghost post. There was an unseen vibration in the room, an unholy presence that had come in with the entourage, and the thought of it caused a vague prickling over his scalp.

"Come here, Cooper," Brickner growled.

Cooper went over to him and stood at attention. "Yes, sir?"

Brickner pointed at the door of the wall locker with his swagger stick. "What are these orange stickers, Cooper?"

"'Try Jesus' stickers, sir."

"They're on government property. Get rid of them."

"Yes, sir." Cooper stood looking at him.

"Now."

"Yes, sir." Cooper stepped forward and began picking at a sticker with his fingernail, tearing thin strips away and putting them in his hand. "I'll need to use a razor blade, sir."

"I don't care what you use, just get rid of them. I'll have no proselytizing in this barracks." Brickner turned to Sergeant Rockman. "Log it."

Rockman wrote on his clipboard.

Brickner tucked the swagger stick under his arm and riffled through the uniforms with his hands. He pulled out a utility shirt, the XO and Sergeant Major looking at it over his shoulder. "Irish pennants," he said, indicating a loose thread at a buttonhole. He tossed the shirt to the floor.

Cooper stooped to pick it up.

"Leave it there."

"Yes, sir."

Brickner looked down at Cooper's feet. "Let me see your shoes."

Cooper looked down at his shoes. "My shoes, sir?"

"Take them off."

"Yes, sir." Cooper took off his shoes and handed them to the CO.

Brickner looked at the toes and heels. They were like mirrors. He showed the shoes to the XO and Sergeant Major, they nodded their disapproval. "You can do better than this, Cooper."

"Yes, sir."

Brickner dropped the shoes on the floor, and kicked them out of his way.

Cooper glanced down at them and continued picking at the sticker in his wall locker.

Brickner stepped around him and came over to Nathan's bed and inspected the hospital corners, the tautness of the green wool blanket, then he inspected the gear laid out over it. He nodded approvingly, then he picked up the barracks cover and admired his reflection in the visor. "Outstanding, Kessler. Outstanding. Make a note of it, Sergeant Rockman."

Rockman made a note of it.

Brickner gave Nathan the once-over. "What happened to your eye, Kessler?"

"It's nothing, sir."

"You didn't answer my question, Marine."

"I got into a dispute with some Navy downtown, sir."

"Oh?"

"They insulted Mick, sir. Mick Donovan."

"I see. They look any worse than you?"

"I got some licks in, sir."

"Outstanding." Brickner turned. The XO and Sergeant Major followed.

Nathan was given weekend liberty; Cooper was not. Nathan could see no difference between the shine on his shoes and Cooper's, but he passed inspection and Cooper failed. Each of the Christians had failed.

The rest of 1ˢᵗ Platoon, except for Dixon and Matthews, passed and were given liberty. Dixon was not given liberty because he was missing a pair of military trousers in his locker. Matthews' white gear looked as if he'd used it to scrub the toilets.

The CO hadn't cited the personal items of other Marines left out on night-stands: books, magazines, even a package of Zig-Zag cigarette papers. Unframed posters on walls—one, a vulgar rendering of the 23rd Psalm—had apparently escaped notice. A peace symbol sticker on Washington's locker had either been missed, or ignored.

It had been a hunting expedition.

Cooper picked up his dress shoes and compressed his lips together.

Nathan watched him. "Want me to help with your shoes?"

"That's okay, thanks." Cooper got shoe polish out of his locker and went over to the chair with his shoes. "Skip said it was coming."

"What do you mean?"

Cooper shook his head. "Nothing. I don't think you'd understand."

Chapter Thirty-Three

T HE FOUR MARINES were sitting around the

table in the downtown Way Station, hunched over bowls of beef stew. It was late. Outside it was dark and clear with stars showing above the greenish glow from the arcade of the Galleria Umberto. The sound of traffic was still strong in the Square. The servicemen who had been there earlier had gone back to their bases or ships, and it was just the Marines from the barracks there now.

Maddie watched them, the men bent over their bowls eating quickly and silently. Earlier, she had heard news that appalled her, but she wanted to wait until they had made a dent in their meals before asking about it.

Clarence glanced up from his stew and smiled at Kitty. "Thank you for opening up for us, ma'am. They just gave us liberty."

"You're welcome, any time," Kitty said.

"Any time," Flynn added, smiling.

Gorilla and Cooper glanced up from their stew, smiled with embarrassment at Flynn, then resumed eating. The men were hungry. Spoons clinked against bowls. A timer buzzed in the kitchen.

Kitty stood. "There're the rolls."

Maddie watched her mother leave the room, then turned to Cooper. "We heard that a Marine was killed in front of the Navy barracks. Someone shot him?"

Cooper nodded, eating. "Mick Donovan."

"Mick? Was he the one I saw with you and Gorilla outside the San Pedro a few months ago?"

"That's him. They shot him right outside the Navy barracks. Two Italians."

Maddie tried to remember Mick's face, but couldn't. All she could muster was a vague impression of a toothy grin and the smell of whiskey. "Why'd they do it?"

Cooper shrugged. "I think Mick was pretty involved with the black market. Nate could tell you more about it—he was there." He continued eating.

"Nate was there? I hadn't heard that."

Jesse was looking at Maddie. "Tell her what he did, Coop."

Cooper reached for his glass of raspberry punch. "Nate shared the gospel with him."

"Mick asked him to," Jesse added. "Bill said he knows the Bible pretty good. There was a big crowd, but Nate shared the gospel with him anyway. Bill was there and saw everything."

"Bill Porter?"

Jesse nodded. "He said Mick prayed the sinner's prayer then died in Nate's arms."

Maddie stared.

Clarence looked across the table at Flynn. "Do you think Mick's in heaven, Mr. Gallagher?"

Flynn nodded thoughtfully. "If what you say about Mick is true then, yes, I would say he was in heaven. God has given faith to many in their final moments. You remember the thief on the cross?"

Clarence and Cooper nodded. Everyone sat around the table gazing in different directions.

Maddie was staring across the room at the mantel clock over the fireplace, grieved by the violence that had touched so close to home. She was mystified by the thought of what Nathan had done. She imagined the scene in front of the Navy barracks; Mick lying on the pavement dying, his features still vague; Nathan holding him in his arms and telling him about Jesus. It was a scene of grace, of mercy, of a tenderness demonstrated in and through the lives of two Marines, to a huddle of astonished spectators.

"Wow," Jesse said, breaking the silence. "Mick's in heaven."

Maddie cleared the emotion from her throat, before turning to Cooper. "How's Nathan taking it, Coop? You're his roommate."

"It's hard to say," he said. "Nate doesn't open up much. He's wound pretty tight. He's been drinking more

I know. Maybe that's his way of numbing it. You okay, Maddie?"

"I'm fine," she said, palming tears from her cheeks. "It's upsetting."

"I can tell Nate you asked about him."

"That's not necessary."

"It's no trouble. I'll tell him."

The sound of a toilet flushing jolted into the great room like a discordant note.

Sean padded out of the hallway from the living quarters. He was barefooted and wearing pajamas. His hair was messed up and it looked as if he'd been sleeping. He stood at one end of the table, looking at the four Marines. His arms hung limp at his sides, his pajama top was mis-buttoned and was hiked up and riding a little to one side. "Who got shot?"

Flynn gazed across the length of the table at him. "You should be in bed, Sean."

Sean dug a finger in his ear. "I had to go to the bathroom and I heard someone got shot by two Italians."

"This is not the bathroom."

Sean frowned. "How come I can't hear? I never get to hear anything." He turned and went back into the hall frowning down at his feet. "I'll find out about it tomorrow at school."

Kitty came in from the kitchen with a basket of hot rolls. "These ought to do the trick."

"We didn't expect you to feed us, Mrs Gallagher," Clarence said.

"It's my pleasure." Kitty smiled. "There was plenty left over."

"It sure is good," Jesse said, reaching for a roll. "You don't get cooking like this at the base."

Gorilla took two rolls from the basket. "You bet."

"There's more stew, Henry," Kitty said, offering the bowl.

Gorilla looked at her. "Uh, sure, ma'am," he said, reaching a long arm in front of Cooper's face. "Everyone just calls me Gorilla, though. No one calls me Henry."

Kitty frowned. "Not even your mother?"

"She calls me Cricket...uh-huh-huh-huh," he laughed softly.

The Marines stopped what they were doing and stared at him blankly.

Gorilla chuckled. "That's because I was a cute baby."

Jesse shook his head. "You were a baby?"

Gorilla, ladling stew into his bowl, frowned indignantly. "Sure I was a baby." To Kitty: "You can call me Henry if you want to, ma'am."

The bowl was passed around and the eating resumed. Flynn poured cream into his tea. "How's Skip?" he asked, stirring in a teaspoon of sugar. "His barracks restriction is over soon, isn't it?"

"This weekend—right, Clarence?" Maddie asked.

Clarence nodded, buttering his roll. "Unless they find something else to throw at him."

"They were searching pretty hard today," Cooper said.

Clarence described how Gorilla's and Cooper's recent conversions had caused a stir in the barracks, and how the field day inspection and the darkness they had each felt had been like a counter-offensive by the enemy. "Brickner's on the warpath."

Jesse nodded. "Tell them what they did, Clarence. About Skip's picture."

"Skip has a picture of Jesus hanging on his wall...the one of Him praying in Gethsemane."

"You're allowed to put up framed pictures if they're not offensive," Jesse put in.

"That's right. Skip had one of those 'Try Jesus' stickers on it and they tore it off, ripping a hole in the picture. Apparently Jesus praying is offensive."

Kitty frowned. "Can they do that?"

Clarence shrugged. "They said Skip was proselytizing."

"You should see what some of the other guys have on their walls," Jesse said.

Maddie was watching her father, the deep grooves of his face coming together as he peered around the table at each of the men.

He sipped his tea. "Jesus said that no matter how men treat you, you are to love them. You are to pray for them."

The men lowered their heads. Clarence looked up. "It's hard, isn't it?"

"Jesus told us to take up our cross and follow Him," Flynn said. "Unto death if need be. It's not something you can do with your own strength. You need God's grace."

The four Marines were staring at him.

Flynn raised a finger, the lines in his face deepening. "We're in a battle for the souls of men. There are invisible forces that will do everything in their power to shut you up, or marginalize your witness. Remember, we wrestle not against flesh and blood, but against the spiritual forces of evil in the heavenly realms."

The men glanced at one another solemnly.

"It's hard to think of invisible forces when someone's calling you names that I can't repeat here," Cooper said. "It makes you want to punch somebody."

"Don't do that," Flynn smiled. "The men are watching you. They're testing to see if what you profess is genuine. They'll try to make you stumble. If you strike back it validates their unbelief. Just remember that all of mankind is bound under the power of Satan, the god of this world. Each of you were, too, until very recently."

"It still makes you want to punch someone," Cooper said.

The Marines frowned at him.

Cooper shrugged. "What did you expect me to say? I'm new at this."

Maddie smiled. She let the smile drift as she glanced again at the mantel clock, once again feeling a burden for these men. There was indeed a war being waged in the barracks for the souls of men. Invisible battle lines were being drawn, with forces massing along the lines, pushing salients into enemy territory, or pouring into breaches or along weak points.

She could see it clearly. It was as though she were standing on a hill, watching the battle form in the valley below; the armies massing, standards snapping, the sound of bugles. Mick Donovan was the first casualty. She wondered who would be next.

LATER, AFTER THE men had gone back to the barracks, Maddie put on her robe and padded barefoot out into the great room and stood in a spill of moonlight. She looked out the windows at the harbor, at a ship heading out past the Molo San Vincenzo.

The room was quiet and still except for the steady ticking of the clock over the mantel. There was still a feeling of the presence of the men around the table and of them eating and talking about Mick, and the discussion about spiritual forces, and her father teaching them, and warning them, and encouraging them as a commander before combat.

The burden she felt was stronger now than before. She had seen it in the eyes of her father. He knew. He had been in war and he walked close with God, and she felt it stronger now.

She prayed for the men, naming each one, and she prayed for Nathan. Nathan was a weak point in the enemy lines, if not a breach. She was convinced of it. What he had done for Mick made that clear. She sensed the enemy would double its efforts to shore up the breach, or to remove him from battle.

There are many ways to remove a man from battle; you can wound him, or you can fill him with fear, or cut him off from his lines. One way is always successful.

Kill him.

Chapter Thirty-Four

EARLIER THAT DAY, Nathan drove downtown

to the ferry landing at the Molo Beverello and parked. It was a beautiful sunset with low dark stripes of clouds over the turquoise and yellow and orange sky. A gentle breeze was blowing in from the bay.

Nico was standing beside her yellow Alfa Romeo, looking out at a ferry coming into the harbor high against the darkening sky. She was wearing white pedal-pushers, espadrilles, and a blue and white striped fisherman's shirt.

Nathan locked his car and started toward her, carrying his sports bag.

She turned, her olive skin beautiful in the bright glow of the early evening, her eyes brightening when she saw him. "My love, my love," she cooed, running into his arms. "I do not think I will be able to endure these separations." She kissed his mouth, kissed the sides of his mouth, saying, "My lovely, lovely Natti."

"I'm sorry I'm late," he said, dropping his bag and holding her away from him with both hands to better see her. "I had a cartoon deadline to make."

She scrunched her nose.

"My cartoon strip," he clarified. "I told you about it."

"Never mind that." She slipped between his arms and held him tightly. "You are here in my arms at last. I could squeeze you to death."

"You're doing a pretty good job of it."

"My love." She kissed him again and gazed up at him adoringly. She frowned. "What happened to your eye?"

"It's nothing. You should've seen it a week ago."

"You were in a fight?"

"Of sorts."

"My poor Natti." She kissed the tips of her fingers and touched around his hurt eye lovingly. "Here, and here, and here," she kissed with her fingertips. "I hope he looks worse. The brute."

"Let's talk about us." He looked down at her stomach. "So, what's the score? Did the rabbit die?"

"The rabbit?"

"Did you have your monthly?"

"Ah, the rabbit. Yes, I will have my monthlies from now on."

"Then you're not pregnant?"

"Do not think of it. It is past."

She laid her head against his chest and squeezed him. "My Natti. We have the whole weekend to play and forget the world. Now that the weather is fair I will take you sailing. And we can lie on the beach and go to our secret place in the rocks where no one can see us."

"Is that a yes or a no?"

She frowned at him. "I am no longer pregnant," she said seriously. "It has been taken care of." She took his arm. "Now we must hurry if we are going to catch the ferry."

Nathan felt his chest suddenly grow cold. "Then you *were* pregnant."

"Yes. But what does it matter? I am no longer. Come, let us hurry."

They were walking toward her car.

"So you killed the baby?"

"I had an abortion, yes. But do not worry, the doctor said I am perfectly fine. He was very gentle."

Nathan stopped. "But the baby is dead."

"I had it aborted, yes. I already told you. There were no complications."

"Except the baby."

She looked at him. "Natti…?"

"It was mine too, Nico."

She flushed. "Yes, but it was in my body. What does it matter? We talked about this, don't you remember?"

She clutched his arm, smiling, stepped forward on her tiptoes and kissed his mouth. "Enough of this gloominess, we're free now. The doctor gave me pills, so we don't have to worry about anything. Isn't it wonderful?"

Nathan glanced over at the ferry loading cars.

She stepped around in front of him. "Natti?"

He shook his head. "I gotta think about this, Nico. It's a blow."

He picked up his sports bag and walked over to the sea wall and sat down. He watched the seagulls on the rocks of the breakwater, small waves lapping against the rocks. The clouds were darker now that the yellows in the sky reddened.

She came over to him. "It was the size of a tiny frog. A frog. Can't you be reasonable about this?"

He looked at her. "A frog?"

"It wasn't like it was alive or anything."

"No?"

She shrugged her shoulders. "Not really."

"It was a baby, Nico…our baby. A boy or a girl. Doesn't that mean anything to you? He would have had your eyes and mouth and maybe my ears and nose. She would have laughed on her birthdays and cried when she skinned her knees. The child would have been ours, Nico. It's dead now."

"We can talk about it later, my love. We'll miss the ferry." She took his arm.

He pulled free. "You take the ferry."

"Natti…?"

"No. You go on ahead. I gotta think. Go ahead, I'll join you later." Nathan stood and looked away from her.

She put her hand on his face and turned it to face her. "You don't want to come with me, Natti?"

He turned away. He couldn't look at her. "I said I'd come later."

"But you won't, will you? You have no intention of coming. You're not coming ever."

Nathan said nothing.

"Because of the baby?"

He frowned at her. "Because of you. Because of me. We're death for each other, Nico. Don't you see it? We make babies and kill them."

"Perhaps you would have liked me fat and ugly."

"People have babies all the time. They get fat and have babies and raise families that are happy. I would have married you, Nico."

"How gallant of you. You are the saint. They should name a monastery after you."

"Somebody could've adopted him or something. People have babies they don't want and give them to people that can't have them. Couldn't we have done that?"

"We?" She laughed. "I'm the one who would have to carry it inside me for months, waddling around big as a house." She made a sound of contempt. "You can afford to make fine speeches now that you're free."

Nathan watched the ferry loading cars.

"Oh Natti," she said dismissively. "We're just having a lovers' quarrel. Don't you see? A little spat. By tonight we will have forgotten it." She took his hand, nuzzled against him smiling. "I will make you forget it."

He pulled away. "You're going to miss the ferry."

Her face changed. Red lights flickered in her eyes. Red spots rose on her cheeks. "This isn't about the baby at all, is it? It's another woman." She laughed. "Of course it is. It's your other girl."

"There isn't another girl."

"You are not a very good liar, Nathan. Is she a virgin? Do you worship her? Does she absolve your sins?" She was crying. "You have your way with me and then leave the bill on the nightstand and go on to your next conquest. You are quite a hero. Oh yes."

"All I said was I need to think about this."

"So think, moralist," she said bitterly. "Take your high ground. You think you are above it. You think that you walk with the angels, but your soul is just as black as mine, Nathan. You're just as guilty before God as I am."

He was sick of the discussion. He was sick of Nico. "I'll tell a priest about it," he said. "That ought to clear me for the day, don't you think?"

She slapped his face hard and told him to go to hell.

He glared at her, felt the slap warm on his cheek. He chuckled sardonically. "If there's a hell, I'm sure I'll have plenty of company."

He grabbed his bag and walked away toward his car.

She didn't follow.

NATHAN WENT INTO the Blue Moon, walked over to the bar and ordered a whiskey neat. The bartender stopped wiping the counter, got out a bottle and poured the drink. He pushed it across the counter and held out a meaty palm. Nathan tossed a bill into it. The bartender looked at the bill, a twenty thousand lire note.

"Let it ride," Nathan said, and threw the drink back in a gulp. "*Un Altro ancora whisky.*"

The bartender filled his glass. A dark-eyed girl sidled up against his hip. "Not interested," Nathan said, lighting a cigarette. The girl flirted with him some more until he stared at her with deadly eyes. "Beat it."

The girl went away blowing her lower lip.

The music was loud. People were laughing and carrying on behind him, girls working the floor hard. It was a lively bar. Plenty of army and air force.

Nathan stood at the bar drinking and smoking, not listening to the music pounding the air or paying attention to the crowd. He looked at himself in the mirror behind the bar. Well, Natboy, what do you make of that? She killed the baby. First Mick and now the baby. There's a little evil for you. That's the right word for it, all right. He threw back his drink.

"*Un'altro ancora whisky,*" he said, pushing the glass at the bartender. The bartender filled it.

"Purple Haze" hammered through the jukebox speakers. Nathan thought he heard Mick's voice and turned, and just for an instant expected to see him ranging toward him playing his air guitar. But it wasn't Mick, it was an army or airman howling, and Nathan knew that Mick was dead. He cursed into his drink.

Evil's been coming at you high and inside lately, Natboy. Those two shooters were some evil. They were evil in spades. How do you account for *that* evil? What would old Giuseppe say about those moral choices?

And then he thought about a few of the Marines in the barracks. They disturbed him as well, but for reasons that angered him. Why did they mock and antagonize? What evil made them do it? Or for that matter, why did *he* mock and antagonize? Why did he want to smash the good in Maddie? If there were no God then where did such evil come from? Why such evil? He figured that Giuseppe had it right on that one. Evil is a man thing. Animals are not evil, man is evil. Giuseppe had it right about the ghosts on Post #10, too. They were likely demons with nothing better to do than to kick up trouble like incorrigible children.

He sipped his drink. And what about that business at inspection yesterday? You felt it pretty solidly then too, didn't you? Like before at the ghost post. Where does that kind of evil come from? Some dark page from your childhood? You know there was some evil there. Some ecclesiastical evil. What did you say, Giuseppe? Devils? Red suits and pitchforks? Whatever, it sure has Skip and the boys in its sights, doesn't it?

He looked across at his reflection in the mirror, elbows planted, hunched over his drink with both hands. It was his face all right; the same dead eyes gazing out of dark holes, the same grim mouth, but he was looking at someone else. Something dark had come up from the emptiness in his belly. There it was watching him. He didn't like what he saw.

He sipped his drink, swirled it around in the bottom of the glass.

And then there's the baby. Killing a baby. Account for that moral choice, why don't you, Giuseppe. That one came over the inside corner of the plate just above the knees. You didn't see that one coming, but you swung at it. That's strike three, isn't it? But that last was your doing, wasn't it? You had a part in that evil. You were pitching some curve-balls yourself, *amico*. All that adoption business. He threw back his drink. She certainly doesn't have a corner on evil. No sir. That old evil is the great pretender, isn't it?

Nathan lit a cigarette, clamped it in his teeth and, shoving through the press of bar patrons, left the bar trailing smoke.

There were crowds of people out on the street moving, like two rivers flowing simultaneously in the same channel, one up, the other down the wide walks of the city. There was what sounded like a continuous growling of animals.

Nathan made his way down through the boil to his car, unlocked the door and climbed into the bucket seat. He pulled a pint bottle out of the glove box and opened it. "You've got it good tonight, *amico*. That old evil's working double-shifts tonight, brother."

He drained a couple of fingers and roared away from the curb into the traffic, shaking his head.

Chapter Thirty-Five

MEANWHILE, SKIP WAS given liberty. A group of men and women from the church, and from the Marine and Navy barracks, met at Carney Park for a day of picnic and fun. It had been a beautiful clear day. Low white clouds scudded silently over the rim of the crater like barges of cotton.

Now, as dusk fell, they built a bonfire in one of the pits and everyone gathered around it and roasted marshmallows. Skip and Bill Porter were playing guitars and singing Christian songs. The singing was a magnet. People came over from every quarter of the park, and soon there was quite a large crowd gathered.

Some came in close to the singers and sat on picnic tables or on the grass, swaying to the music with the glow from the bonfire flickering on their faces. Others stood back along the periphery of the firelight, remaining at a distance but curious.

Maddie was sitting on the top of a picnic table between Darlene Beaumont and Jesse Calderon, with some of the others from the church.

Darlene was looking at something to her right. "Well, what do you know?"

"What is it?" Maddie asked.

Darlene pointed with her chin. "Jim Cooper's talking to Sally Jenkins."

Cooper was sitting at the rear of the circle, beside an attractive brunette with his Bible opened. "Someone you know?"

"She's a nurse in Radiology. I've tried talking to her many times about the Lord, but she wouldn't give me the time of day."

"You were the wrong sex."

MOST OF THE crowd had gone back to barracks or ships or quarters. Darlene and Nancy had gone back to the hospital with the other nurses, except for Sally Jenkins, who had gone off somewhere with Jim Cooper. Those that remained were separated into small groups around the bonfire that had died down to black and red glowing embers.

The night huddled close around the glow, except when someone would toss a log onto the fire and send a geyser of sparks into the air, and then the night would leap back, as if startled. Skip was playing the guitar, his face lit with deep shades of yellow and red, people sitting closer to him, singing along.

Jesse and Maddie were still sitting on top of the picnic table, listening to the music. "You mustn't let them get the best of you, Jesse. They make fun of you because you are no longer walking in darkness."

"I have a temper. It's my Latin blood."

"I have a temper too. It's my Irish blood. You must put it to death."

Jesse shook his head. "You don't know what a temper is. My temper doesn't die so easily. I think it is dead, but it is only hiding." He looked at her. "I can't believe that you are ever angry."

"My temper is legendary," she said. "You just haven't seen it. It's my red hair."

Jesse nudged her arm. "Over there," he said, nodding at the far side of the gathering.

Standing just outside the light, in the umbrage separating the fire glow from the hard darkness of the night, was Nathan Kessler holding a pint of whiskey. He seemed to be having difficulty standing. He was shifting his weight from foot to foot as though trying to keep from falling.

"He's drunk," Jesse said.

Nathan's eyes ranged over the group, stopping when they found Maddie's. He stepped back to catch his balance, then lunged forward. He staggered sideways, fell backward and landed on his backside, holding the bottle up with his fist. He laughed.

People gaped over their shoulders at him.

"I'm gonna help him," Jesse said.

"I'm coming with you."

Nathan was lying on his back, holding the neck of a bottle of Jim Beam with a tight fist. His knees were drawn upward, his feet flat on the ground. He was staring at the stars, an idiot grin on his face.

Maddie stooped down beside him, opposite Jesse.

Nathan turned his head, his eyes ranging and glassy. "Maddie! There you are."

"Give us a hand, Jess," Maddie said, and she and Jesse took hold of Nathan's arms and pulled.

Nathan growled, "Hey, don't spill my hooch."

They got him into a sitting position. "You've had enough," Maddie said.

"Enough?" Nathan leered at her. "I haven't had enough." He tilted the bottle back and Maddie watched bubbles gurgling in the bottle. "Never enough, Maddie. I'm drinking for two. Mick and the baby."

He set the bottle on the ground gingerly. "Stay boy. Stay," he said pointing at the bottle as if disciplining a dog. "Good boy."

Still woozy, he stood.

Maddie steadied him.

"You're okay, Maddie," Nathan chuckled stupidly. "You too, Jess." He was hugging Jesse by the neck.

He hunted around for the bottle. "Hey—where'd you go, boy?" It was behind him. It was about three-fourths empty. "There you are," he said brightening. "Good boy."

He bent down, grabbed the bottle by the neck and straightened. He started to go over backward again but Maddie caught him, and with Jesse's help got him steady.

"You guys are okay," he said, grinning sloppily.

"Come on, Nathan," Maddie said, and put her head under his right arm to support him. Jesse got under his left.

They started toward the nearest picnic table.

Nathan reeked of whiskey and cigarettes and stumbled between them. He peered at Maddie. "Hey, you really are a fine looking missionary girl, you know that?" He shook his head. "That other girl—Nicoletta."

"It's a beautiful name," Maddie said, straining under his weight.

"She's gonna have a baby. But not no more. She don't like babies. Nope. I like babies but she don't. I was a dad for a coupla months. Not even a real dad, either—just a dud dad."

"I'm sorry to hear that, Nathan."

He glared woozily at her. "Why're you sorry? You didn't kill it." He almost went down but Maddie and Jesse kept him moving forward.

Nathan shook his head. "Don't mean nuthin'. Nosssir. Don't mean a thing. Say—you like babies?"

They were walking, supporting Nathan. "I love babies."

"You do? Hey, where'd you go?" He swung his head. "What're you doin' in my armpit?"

"Keeping you from falling on your butt."

"See what I mean? You're the one, Maddie. Nico never meant a thing."

"That's nice."

"I mean it. You're a nice Chrish-ian girl."

He tried to drink from the bottle but couldn't get to it around Maddie's face. He swung his head at Jesse. "But she don't love me," he groaned, "she loves Jesus. Did you know that, Jess? There's no hope for me 'cause we're unequally yoked. St. Paul to the Romans."

"Corinthians," Jesse puffed.

Nathan frowned. "I said Corinth-ans." He swung his head back at Maddie. "Didn't know I knew the Bible, did you? I read it plenty."

"I'm glad to hear it," Maddie said.

"It's the truth."

They got him over to the picnic table and sat him down, just outside the glow from the bonfire. "Thanks, Jesse," Maddie said. "I think we'll be okay now."

Jesse was breathing hard. "I'll stay here with you."

Nathan squinted at him. "Go on, beat it. I ain't gonna wet my pants."

Jesse glanced at Maddie, who nodded to him, then he went over to the group singing around the bonfire. He peered back at Maddie and Nathan.

Deep golden light flickered over Nathan's face as he listened to Skip singing. "He sings pretty good, don't he?" His eyes watered. It appeared as though there were tears in them.

"Yes, he does," Maddie agreed. She wasn't sure if the tears were from alcohol or because of an obvious burden he was carrying. "I'm really sorry about Mick, Nathan," she said.

"Water under the bridge."

"He was your friend. I heard what you said to him. I get emotional just thinking about it."

"He was dying. I'd've recited the Constitution if he asked me to."

"But he didn't."

Nathan grunted. He fell silent for several minutes, dark shadows playing over his eyes.

She didn't press it. Instead, she leaned back just behind his peripheral vision and watched him out of the corners of her eyes. He was clearly brooding over a dark pool deep inside him.

His eyes moved and flickered, as if watching things moving in that pool—dark oily serpents hidden beneath the surface that only he could see. Things that caused anger; caused a hatred for God. She didn't think it was solely because of Mick, or because of the loss of his baby——as horrible as those losses were. No. The anger and rage in Nathan predated Mick's death. There were demons driving him to self-destruction long before Naples. She was certain of that. Naples was just another battlefield.

As he stared at the dying flames of the bonfire, the hood of his brow hiding his eyes in shadow, a tear rolled down his cheek, caught a glint of light, then dropped. "Yes sir, that's nice music," he said, his voice gravelly.

He raised his chin an inch and dark red light gleamed pinpoints in his eyes. He glanced at Maddie. "Did I ever tell you about my little brother? Frankie? His name was Franklin but I called him Frankie."

Maddie watched him. "I didn't know you had a brother."

"I don't. He's dead." He took a drink from the bottle that he held loosely between his knees. "Frankie was the best of the bunch."

Maddie let him talk, prayed silently that he would continue.

"Leukemia," he said. "Died'a leukemia." He laughed low and guttural. "You bet. We were churchgoers. Did I ever tell you that?"

She shook her head. "No, you didn't."

"The whole family. My dad, mom, my sister Linda, me and Frankie. The whole tribe."

Nathan stared at the bonfire, a dark expression sweeping the light off his face. "We went to church every Sunday," he said in an articulate voice, seemingly devoid of alcohol. "I won awards for Bible memory in Sunday school. We went to church on Wednesdays, too, but we didn't have enough faith."

He glanced at her, looked back at the bonfire.

"When Frankie got sick, a bunch of them came over and prayed. The pastor, some elders and deacons. A couple old ladies too. Real prayer warriors."

He shook his head, a laughing groan rattling deep in his chest. "They said we could move mountains if we only had faith. What was leukemia next to a mountain? Nothing, I said. But what did I know? I was only fifteen. I prayed my guts out. God, heal my little brother. You can do it, God, I know you can. I believe. I have faith, plenty of it. What's leukemia next to a mountain?"

He picked up the bottle and jiggled its contents.

"Frankie shriveled down to skin and bones. He couldn't lift his hand, he was so weak. I held his hand and prayed for him. I read the Bible to him. I told him God would heal him. 'Trust me, Frankie, I gotcha covered.' Know what Frankie said? 'It's okay, Nate. I'm not scared. Jesus is watching over me.'"

Nathan choked, as if strangled, cleared his throat and took a quick pull on the bottle.

"Old Frankie. Shriveled to nubs. Then one day— phhsstt!" He snapped his fingers. "Gone. His spirit flown. I can see him lyin' peaceful on his bed, a kind of smile on his face. The face of an angel."

Nathan slanted his eyes at Maddie, fleering his teeth in a sardonic grin. "Know what the pastor said at the funeral?"

Maddie was afraid of the answer.

"God needed Frankie in heaven." Nathan laughed. He set the bottle down between his feet, clawed a cigarette out of a pack in his shirt pocket and lit it one-handed with a Zippo. The flame served to uplight his nose and eyes and cheekbones in hard flaring shadows.

"Imagine that," he said, blowing smoke through his nostrils. "God needed Frankie. What do you make of that?"

Maddie shook her head.

He flicked the silver lid down on the lighter and squirreled it back into his jeans pocket. "After the funeral a couple of those dear prayer warrior hens came up to my folks. Get this… They said it's too bad we didn't have enough faith. The Lord had told them. Yessir. A word from on high."

He tapped the ash, grabbed the cigarette with his teeth and inhaled deeply. "If we only had faith Frankie wouldn't've died."

He flicked the cigarette, watched it skip over the dirt. Then his expression darkened. Red lights burned in his eyes. "We didn't have faith. My mom crying out to God every night, but no faith."

He made a snarling growl of contempt. And then he lowered his head, grabbed his face with both hands. His shoulders began to shake as sobs jumped into his throat, one after the other. And then he was weeping solidly with deep-chested violence, as though the fountains of the deep had broken forth.

Maddie cried with him.

Nathan made a fist and pounded his thigh. Raising his head quickly, he cleared his throat with a hard rasp, grabbed up the bottle and took a long hard pull from it, letting the spillage dribble down his chin.

"Can you believe it?" he laughed. "No faith. It was our fault. Mom bawling her eyes out, Dad staring wide-eyed at the floor like a crazy man, and they said that God would've healed Frankie if we really wanted Him to."

He grabbed his face once more and shook his head, weeping bitterly. "I'm sorry, Frankie. I'm sorry. I failed you, Frankie."

Maddie put her arm around him and drew him close. "Dear God, have mercy on him," she prayed silently.

He held his face, shaking his head.

"I'm so sorry, Nathan," Maddie said. "I can't believe anyone would say such a thing."

"*No?*" He yanked away from her with a savage expression. "You don't be-*leeve?* O, ye of little faith," he laughed gruffly.

"That's not what I…"

He held up a hand and growled, "My mom went insane with grief. No one came around to see her. Not that lousy pastor, not one of those long-nosed church biddies came around to comfort her. Not one."

He squinted at Maddie with one eye, held up the bottle and pointed the neck deliberately. "She had no faith, you see. She was an unbeliever. And you mustn't, mustn't, mustn't go near the unbeliever. Unbelievers are lepers, you see. Filthy lepers."

He started to drink from the bottle, lowered it and held it on his knee. He stared out into the darkness. "I found her in bed, staring at the ceiling. Her heart just gave out. Dead. No faith. Them old hens probably kicked their heels over it."

He shook his head.

"My dad just took off. I haven't seen him in six years. My sister? Last I heard she was livin' on a beach in Kauai, selling drugs and whatever else."

He held the bottle against the firelight, eyed it judiciously. "Lepers all," he said, then he drained its contents and flung it to the ground. "Old Nate joined the USMC when I came of age. Yessir. Uncle Sam's Misguided Children."

He looked at her, his eyes red and hollow and lost. "I'm done with all of it," he said.

Nathan got up from the picnic table, sat back down hard, then stood again. He bobbled a moment then walked away unsteadily on an oblique, side-stepping gait that made it appear as though there was broken glass in his path.

Maddie went after him. "Where are you going, Nathan?"

He glanced back and grinned rakishly. "To hell, didn't you know?"

She stopped.

He laughed, almost fell. "Gotta get me another bottle."

"You're going to kill yourself."

"I hope so." He looked up at the stars. "It's a beautiful night, don'tcha think?"

Jesse came over, picked up the empty whiskey bottle, and carried it to Maddie. The two of them watched Nathan walk a little sideways into the darkness.

Chapter Thirty-Six

A BRIGHT YELLOW BAR of sunlight probed over Nathan's closed eyes. He rolled open an eyelid, shut it against the angry glare of the sun and groaned. His eye hurt. His head hurt. The hair on his head hurt. He imagined he was in his bed with three kinds of hangover but that didn't feel right; the position was wrong. He was vertical. Sort of. He had no idea where he was.

He cupped his left hand over his eyes and tried it again slowly, squinting at the glare, shutting them, then trying again.

Before him he saw through a flickering gauze a steering wheel, a burl dashboard, a leather key fob with a Fiat logo glinting dully on it. His car. He was sitting in the driver's bucket seat, his legs straddling the gearshift console with both his feet in the passenger leg well. How he got there, in that position, was a mystery. Why he was still there was a skull-buster.

There was a bottle of Jack Daniels in his right fist. He held it up to the windshield and saw there were about two fingers left in the bottom. He drank them off, shuddered, felt the warming effect spread through him as he dropped the bottle onto the passenger seat. His tongue tasted as though the 1st Marine Division had bivouacked on it.

He drew up his knees, navigated the console and gear shift with his feet, caught his cuff on the knob, uncaught it and, one at a time, lowered his feet into his own leg well. It took a lot of effort. He was sweating.

He opened the car door, swung a leg out onto the pavement. It felt dead. He swung out the other leg. It was no more alive than the first one. He heard seagulls. He heard people's voices. He looked around, winced at a sharp pain in his neck, and saw that he was at the ferry landing in a parking space by the entrance to the parking lot. He had been there all night apparently.

There was a small crowd by the landing watching a ferry heading away from the dock and making for the Molo San Vincenzo.

He stood, wavering, feeling sick and dizzy, his head aching and listing thirty degrees to starboard from sleeping wrong on it. He turned around slowly to hold himself against the roof of the car for support.

He remembered leaving the park now, opening the second bottle on the way back to the city. The recollection was still a fog. He remembered driving to the landing, but didn't remember his reasons for doing so. None that made sense. Perhaps last night they did.

Another ferry was entering the harbor, crossing the foamy wake of the one that had just left. He pinched a cigarette out of the pack in his shirt pocket, but it was broken in half. He tossed it. So were the next two. The pack was crushed. He hooked around and found one that was merely bent, straightened it as best he could and lit it. It smoked okay.

He stood leaning against the roof of his car smoking and watching the ferry coming in straight then slowing to dock. According to Nathan's wristwatch, it was 12:05 in the afternoon. The ferry was coming from Ischia. There were people on the foredeck waving at the people on the landing.

The ferry docked. A ramp rolled into place. People walked over the ramp and got into waiting cars and drove away. Soon cars on the ferry began rolling over the ramp onto the landing, then heading into the city. There were quite a few cars. None of them was a yellow Alfa Romeo.

Nathan dropped his cigarette and stepped on it. "Well, what'd you expect, *amico*? That's all dead, isn't it? That died with the baby, or maybe even before the baby. Maybe it was always dead.

He got into his car, started the engine, and headed back to the base.

MADDIE LEFT THE base chapel with a mixed group of sailors, Marines and nurses. They were heading toward the Admin building to have lunch in the cafeteria, the group spread out in small clutches of conversation. Maddie was walking with Jim Cooper, Darlene Beaumont and Sally Jenkins. Sally was looking down at her new Bible as though it was made of beaten gold.

Cooper eyed her proudly.

Maddie smiled. As they reached the base of the Admin building stairs, she heard the sound of a sports car behind her and turned. It was Nathan Kessler.

"He lives," Cooper said.

Maddie watched as Nathan drove by in his Spider with a low throaty growl. He looked over at her. Even at this distance she could see that he'd had a rough night. She waved, but he kept going, giving no indication that he had seen her.

The group headed up the stairs, but Maddie stood watching Nathan's car slowing, then it turned into a space near the Marine barracks and stopped.

Darlene looked back from the top of the stairs. "You coming, Maddie?"

"I'll be with you in a minute." Maddie started toward the barracks.

N ATHAN GOT OUT of the Fiat and shut the door.

"Nathan!"

He turned. She was walking toward him in a yellow print dress, blue pumps and thin blue belt that matched her shoes and hair band. Her hair bounced jauntily over her shoulders as she came toward him in long-legged loveliness.

"Good morning, Nathan." She stopped, smiling, the sun showing a million shades of red in her hair, the downy texture of her skin. Her irises, pulling vibrant colors of blue from the morning light, deepened in hue to a rich cobalt.

He made a weak attempt at a smile. "I would've stopped," he said, then glanced down at himself, "but I'm kind of a mess. I need a shower."

"I was worried about you. Last night…"

"Last night never happened. It's buried in a fog in my brain and will never see the light of day unless you took pictures. Did I say anything stupid?"

"Nothing stupid." She regarded him for several moments, as if deciding what to say next. "You talked about your brother. Frankie."

His head bobbled, as if he'd been lashed internally. He started to walk away.

She caught up to him. "I just wanted to tell you how sorry I am, Nathan."

He stopped and turned, a cruel expression twisting his features. "You're always apologizing for things you didn't do. Why is that, Maddie?"

"I can't imagine what it would be like to lose my little brother. Or to lose my mom. It would tear a hole in me. On top of that you've lost a friend and your baby. I think I'd be…" She searched for a word.

"Crazy? Go on, say it."

"I was going to say distraught beyond measure."

"Then you know why I hate Christians."

"Christians are people, Nathan. They fail. In your case they failed miserably. I'm not excusing what those people did to you and your family. The church is full of wolves in sheep's clothing. Jesus said to watch out for them."

Nathan started to walk away.

She caught his arm. "Nathan, please let me be your friend."

He laughed. "Who are you kidding? Look at me. I'm working off a drunk. I smell like six kinds of paint thinner. My eyes hurt. My neck's stiff from sleeping in a car all night. I'm a wreck, Maddie."

"I still want to be your friend."

He shook his head. "I'm poison, Maddie. Stay away from me."

"No." Tears streamed down her face as she stepped toward him with open arms.

Nathan took a step backward. "What are you doing?"

She put her arms around him, lay her head against his chest and held him tightly. "I'm holding you. You're not a leper—*see?* I'm holding you, and I'm not letting go."

He tried pushing her away but she clung to him. "You're not a leper, Nathan."

"I'm sick."

"I'm holding you."

"No," he said. "Maddie, please. Don't. Please don't, Maddie. NO!" He pushed away from her. "It's no good."

"Nathan…"

He ran up the steps to the quarterdeck, turned just outside the doorway and glanced back. Maddie was standing in the parking lot beside his car, her hands hanging limp at her sides. She looked small.

He shook his head and went inside the barracks.

Chapter Thirty-Seven

SEVERAL DAYS PASSED and Maddie did not see

Nathan. Then there were weeks between them. Her only contact with him—if it could be called contact—was through his weekly comic strip in the *Star Spangled Banner*.

As she sat at the table in the Way Station, the sun bright and slanting through the windows facing the bay, her father and brother gone to school, her mother out shopping in town for the evening meal, she thought of him. It felt good to be alone in the quiet of the Station where she would clip out the week's cartoon and paste it in a scrapbook. In this way she would spend time with Nathan.

Each night before turning out the light in her bedroom, she'd sit at the tiny desk by the window overlooking the Galleria and once again look at the cartoon. She would ponder it, hoping to gain a little insight into the man. Oftentimes, she did. That he was a sensitive man with a fairly good handle on the human condition was apparent in each drawing, each humorous tag.

"Ol' Prive" was a mirror in which the world could view its foibles, its feet of clay, its pain, and yet somehow manage to laugh or smile. She saw herself in the mirror, too. The longing of the Ol' Prive character for justice and companionship, though it always eluded his grasp, resonated in her soul.

During that time, in the lovely weather of the spring, she and the group from the Station spent Saturdays at the beach in Ischia, or driving down to the ruins in Pompeii, or tooling along the Amalfi coast, shopping in the little towns, or picnicking at Carney Park. They were good days.

Jim Cooper and Sally Jenkins were seeing quite a lot of each other. They looked good together and were growing in their faith. It was inevitable that one day they would be married.

On the downside there were no more conversions in the barracks.

THE POLARIZATION THAT Skip had mentioned was now all the more apparent. Those who were hostile to the faith were more open in their hostility, baiting arguments, looking for opportunities to belittle and mock. Those who had been indifferent to the gospel now seemed colder and more hardened to it. Barracks inspections seemed staged to punish, rather than to maintain military discipline. The men took this in stride, even rejoicing in their trying circumstances.

And then an eerie calm crept into the barracks, haunted the hallways, as though battle lines were being drawn during an unspoken detente. A felt hostility pervaded the barracks. Marines eyed one another with suspicion and distrust. Gone was *esprit de corps.*

Matters came to a head one morning on the Quarterdeck, before the 8 to 12 shift. Four Marines were waiting to be posted to AFSOUTH when the guard vehicle returned after posting Marines to the main gate, Disbursing and PX compounds—Lance Corporals Cooper, Gorilla, Thompson and Washington. There was a dispute between the driver, Corporal Spinoza, and Gorilla. Sergeant Hastert had the duty as Corporal of the Guard.

"Christians are peaceniks," Spinoza taunted Gorilla. "How can you be a Marine and a peacenik at the same time? Are you a conscientious objector?"

Thompson and Washington, standing to one side, snickered.

"I'm not a conscientious objector," Gorilla said. "I will fight if I have to fight."

"Really?" Spinoza chuckled at the others, looking back at Gorilla. "Didn't Jesus say to turn the other cheek? How can you turn the other cheek and be a Marine? You so-called Christians are hypocrites."

Gorilla frowned. He looked over at Cooper.

Cooper was quiet. He was scowling at Sergeant Hastert behind the desk, as though imploring him to halt a potential fight. The sergeant was writing something in the log book.

Gorilla looked back at Spinoza. "I am a Christian and I am a Marine too."

"You can't be," Spinoza hissed. "Didn't Jesus say to pick up your *cross* and follow him? He didn't say to pick up your gun belt."

Gorilla frowned in thought. "If taking off my gun belt would prove to you that my faith is genuine I would do it."

"No you wouldn't. You're a hypocrite."

"I told you I would do it."

Spinoza laughed. "No you wouldn't."

Cooper saw a decision forming in Gorilla's eyes.

Gorilla started unfastening his gun belt. "If I can't be a Christian and a Marine at the same time," he said, "then I'll be a Christian." He laid his belt on the desk of the Corporal of the Guard. "I quit."

Sergeant Hastert peered up at Gorilla as though he had suddenly sprouted a third eye. "What do you mean 'Quit?' You can't quit."

"I just did," Gorilla growled. "I'm going upstairs to see the CO."

"Come back here, Lundgren!" Hastert shouted.

Spinoza watched Gorilla with a mixture of fear and incredulity in his eyes.

Cooper was stunned. He stood gaping at the empty stairwell as a resolution formed in his own mind. He was proud to be a Marine. His father was a career Marine, who had served in the Second World War, Korea and Vietnam, for which Cooper was proud. He had grown up on Marine bases, ran the obstacle course at Parris Island when his father was a battalion commander there, sang the Marine Corps hymn in military school assemblies. He knew the Marine Corps, inside and out. When he decided to enlist rather than wait to be drafted there was really only one choice in his mind. Marine Corps. But something was different about the situation here in the barracks. It wasn't the regulations or strict discipline; he thrived on them. Spit and polish, weapons training and *esprit de corps*, were what made Marines a cut above the others. But when he felt his religious freedoms were under fire in ways he had never witnessed before in the Corps, he was determined to take a stand, right or wrong.

He unfastened his gun belt and laid it on the desk. "I quit too," he said and headed out the doors of the barracks.

"Where are you going!" Sergeant Hastert shouted.

Cooper ran to the main gate. Skip McPherson stepped out of the booth. "What's going on, Coop?"

Cooper told him. The gray suburban suddenly screeched to a halt at the gate. Spinoza shouted at Cooper to get back in the vehicle. Skip told Spinoza that they'd better get the supernumerary to relieve him because he was quitting too. It was like dominoes.

Five Christian Marines put down their gun belts that morning and stood before a befuddled Captain Brickner. This had never happened before. He offered each of the men admin assignments or easier duties as drivers, anything to salve a volatile situation, but the men wanted nothing to do with it.

"This isn't about the duty, sir," Skip said. "We are proud to be Marines."

"You don't see a way to resolve this?" Brickner offered.

"No, sir. If we can't be Marines and Christians, sir, then we will be Christians."

"No one has said that you couldn't be Christians. I have only said that I will not have you proselytizing in the barracks. It is disruptive to the morale of the men." Captain Brickner studied each of their faces. "I have tried to be fair. I will ask you once more, will you go back on duty?"

The Marines said nothing.

"Very well. Dismissed."

The men were confined to their rooms. They sang songs and prayed. A few hard case Marines came into Skip's room and listened to him sing. They asked him why they had done it. "They're trying to burn you with a General Court," Thompson said.

Panetta nodded. "You could get life."

Skip and the others were resolute. "That's in God's hands."

And then came the trial.

The prosecuting attorney tried for a General Court, on the grounds that the Marines had staged a premeditated mutiny. He grilled each of the Marines to admit a confession of premeditation. But there was no evidence of mutiny, as hard as the prosecution worked to conjure it, so after protracted deliberations it was decided that the five Marines be tried under a Special Court.

Since Gorilla and Cooper had refused to go on post they were given four months hard labor at the Navy brig in Rota, Spain. McPherson had just been posted to the main gate and then asked to be relieved, so he was given three months. Calderon and Pearsall who had served their watches but refused to go back on post each got two months.

While awaiting extradition, the *Star Spangled Banner* ran an article entitled, "Bible-totin' Marines Sentenced to Brig." It was a big wind, its case and circumstances thundering around the globe.

Nathan stopped outside Skip's room and looked in. Skip and the other four Marines were reading Bibles. He didn't hate them. He just didn't understand.

Skip looked up and saw him in the doorway. "You're welcome to join us, Nate."

The others agreed, and waved him to come in. "Come on in, Nate," Cooper said.

Nathan stared for a moment longer, then he turned and went across the hall into his room and shut the door.

Chapter Thirty-Eight

NATHAN SAT ALONE in the cafeteria of the Admin building, drinking a cup of coffee. He had just gotten off post. His elbows were braced on the table, a pencil and drawing pad to his right as he thought about the court martial of the five Marines and an Ol' Prive cartoon to illustrate it. Nothing came to mind. He couldn't see the humor in it. It made him angry. It made him a little despondent too. Why did the wicked prosper, and the good seem to fade away like whispers on the wind?

He opened the letter he'd received earlier in Mail Call. The letter was from Mick's mother. The envelope was powder blue and smelled like an older woman's perfume. Inside were two carefully handwritten pages in dark blue ink and a slightly overexposed 3-by-4 color photo of Mick standing next to his '57 Chevy Nomad.

The car was candy apple red with chrome moons. Mick was wearing a white T-shirt with a pack of cigarettes rolled up in the left sleeve, rolled up blue jeans, and he was wearing black Converse All Star high-tops. He had a longish pompadour, complete with a curl in front and slicked sides, and he looked like he was in high school. He was grinning at the camera like he owned the world.

Nathan, feeling his eyes watering, smiled at the photo. He laid the photo on the table, took a sip of coffee, and read the letter from Mick's mom.

The photo was the only one she had of his car. She knew how much Mick had liked it, and thought that Nathan would like something to remind him of his friend.

He picked up the photo again and gazed at it. He set it back down and continued reading. Nathan's letter had brought her much comfort during a very difficult time.

Mick was her only child. From the time that he was a small boy she had prayed daily for his soul. He was a wild boy without a father to guide him, but she loved him as only a mother could. When Mick joined the Marines she was afraid he would be killed in Vietnam. What troubled her even more was that he would die without Christ, lost for eternity in hell. She prayed that God would send one of His servants to share the gospel with him—someone special. Someone who would model a godly Christian character. She was grateful to God for sending Nathan. She was certain he was a fine Christian.

Nathan stared grimly at those last words. A fine Christian. He looked out the window at the rows of vineyards on the hillsides beyond the compound wall. He pictured Mick's mother writing to him, folding the photo with the letter into an envelope, then addressing and placing a stamp on it. It took an effort.

He shook his head, folded the letter and laid it on the table. He picked up the photo once more and studied it for a long while. "Ol' Mick."

ONCE LIBERTY SOUNDED Nathan drove into town, parked near the Castel Nuovo, and walked along the seawall in the late afternoon sun. He walked idly along the sidewalk watching people photograph the harbor and the ships in the deepening hues of the day. He had no destination in mind. The San Pedro and Blue Moon bars were anathema. He would not go in them. There was nowhere he wished to go. It didn't feel like a liberty.

He stopped and watched a liberty boat unloading sailors and a few Marines onto the dock. It was the last night before the Fleet left Naples for deep water exercises in the Mediterranean and the men scrambled quickly into town. He wondered how many of them would return to the ships that night with money left in their wallets, or without little bonuses from the street walkers and campfire girls, a tradition, he was sure, dating back through countless sailors to ancient times.

Glancing out at the ships, he decided to get a beer someplace quiet, maybe even a pizza. He knew a little waterfront trattoria that he had gone to a few times that was neat and quiet and the food good. There were outside tables along the marina terrace with good views of the harbor, and in the afternoons the tree limbs cast shade patterns over the walls. It was a pleasant place to eat.

He started walking toward it when he looked down at his feet and saw a discarded pamphlet on the sidewalk. A religious tract. He picked it up, recognized the cover art, and glanced quickly over at the San Pedro bar across the Square. That was her territory, wasn't it? The Square. He saw the usual military and civilians prowling, but there was no sign of the girl with red hair.

He went over to the trattoria and sat outside at one of the tables under a green canvas awning and ordered a Birra Peroni and pizza from the girl whose family owned the restaurant. He enjoyed talking with her father, a thickset balding man who had fought in the war against the Fascists, and who welcomed the NATO presence in the city. The girl was friendly and young, maybe fourteen, and he caught her peeking out at him through the windows. He pretended not to see her. He sat back in his chair, sipping beer in the shade of the awning, and looking out at the harbor and the people walking by on the terrace as he waited for the pizza.

He thumbed through the religious tract. He didn't think much of the cartoons. The message was simplistic but he read through it anyway. *God has a wonderful plan for my life.*

He chuckled lamely. "So far, my plans have been a roaring success, haven't they?"

He wondered if God's plan for the five Marines included them going to the brig. If it did, it seemed a strange plan. But then His plan included Jesus dying on the cross for the sin of the world, didn't it? He remembered a verse of Scripture, "For my thoughts are not your thoughts, neither are your ways my ways, saith the Lord."

Nathan thought about that, as he sipped his beer. He was about to toss the tract, but looked again at the stamped address on the back page.

"She gave one of those to you too, Nate."

"I know, Frankie."

"She might be on the Square right now passing them out."

"I know, Frankie."

In his mind's eye he could see her handing a tract to some sailor or Marine or airman, her lovely lips framing a mouth full of beautiful white teeth as she said, "Jesus loves you."

"You could buy her an ice cream in the Galleria."

"It won't work, Frankie."

He sighed roughly. The girl with the red hair was working him over pretty good. Even when she wasn't with him she was with him, trying to convince him of a better way. She was the first Christian that he'd known who was genuine. She endured ridicule from wicked men—himself included—and yet she continued to demonstrate Christian character. He didn't understand but he admired her for it, despite his ridicule.

Maddie disturbed him profoundly: her natural beauty, her guilelessness, her indefinable something that clawed mercilessly at his core like a caged rodent. He had no defenses against her.

He also admired the five Marines who had put their personal comforts aside and were court-martialed because of their convictions. He thought about each of them.

Skip was probably born with a Bible in his hands, clutching it like Jacob grabbing his brother's heel. Skip was the kind of guy that didn't tilt at windmills, he was much more rational than that, but he wasn't afraid to take on adversaries larger and more powerful than himself, without regard for his personal safety or reputation. Why? A man like that not only disturbed Nathan, he frightened him. Such men were banished, or put in cages or put against a wall. Perhaps they were simply crucified.

And Jim Cooper was a changed man; there was no denying it. What turned your head, Jim? he wondered. Is it true then that a leopard can change its spots? What made you change yours? You were my friend, my comrade in liberty. My boon companion through thick and thin. Did I leave you or did you leave me? Perhaps we never met.

Gorilla was changed as well; no longer did he go to the bars and bordellos on liberty. He went to the Way Station. He didn't know Clarence or Jesse very well, but he could see the glow on their faces. They had something genuine, didn't they?

He remembered his little brother Frankie's words: "It's okay, Nate. I'm not scared. Jesus is watching over me." Frankie had it too. He had something that Nathan didn't have, an inarticulate something inside him, an inchoate gleam of light that Nathan yearned for. Of joy.

"What do you make of that, Frankie?"

Frankie said nothing.

"Everything is changing so quickly, Frankie. It's unsettling."

Frankie was uncharacteristically quiet.

Nathan glanced out at the harbor. Somehow it seemed different to him, a bit out of focus. He watched a gull swoop low then, wing-brake and alight on a dock pile. He watched the colors on the bay change, the reds and purples deepening as the sun set. It would seem beautiful were it not eclipsed by a vague, disconsolate gloom that had crept upon him like a morning fog, giving him a feeling of uncertainty and melancholy.

He looked once more at the tract in his hands, slapped it against his palm, and put it into his shirt pocket. And then the girl brought him the pizza and he ordered a second beer.

Chapter Thirty-Nine

T HE FLEET WAS gone. Maddie stared glumly
over the seawall at the empty harbor. Sometime during
the night the ships had slipped away in the fog, one after
the other, like so many lovers tiptoeing away from
midnight trysts.

Maddie always felt glum when the Fleet left town,
glum from the sudden emptiness of it, and from the
emptiness and quiet that would follow in the Station, but
she was glum for other reasons.

She had just returned from the airfield in
Capodichino, where the five Marines had taken off for
Rota. Sally Jenkins was already there waving to Jim
Cooper, while touching beneath her eyes with a tissue.
Maddie had arrived too late to talk to the men because of
traffic, and they were already on the tarmac with their
seabags, standing at the base of the steps, ready to board

the Navy DC-3. They were giving their names to a flight officer with a clipboard and then ascending the steps in the fog. She could just see the faded places on their sleeves where their ranks had been. There was a Marine sergeant behind them with a web belt and billy club, an MP armband on his left arm.

She'd called out to them from the gate and waved, the men turning and waving, each of them smiling. They seemed cheery. She said that she would be praying for them. Skip said that he would write. The sergeant gestured them forward, and then they were gone. As she and Sally watched the plane disappear into the clouds Maddie felt a great hole open in her chest.

A ferry was making its turn around the Molo San Vincenzo, sounding its horn as it made for the landing.

Maddie broke from her thoughts, took a deep breath and checked her wristwatch. It was three-thirty in the afternoon. They were probably in Sardinia by now, refueling.

She glanced once more at the empty harbor then, shouldering her purse, she headed across the road to the Municipal Square.

The foot traffic was lighter now and less boisterous. Italians mostly—businessmen, women shoppers, school children returning from school. A few American servicemen were out and about, too, but they were permanent personnel, and there was less hunger in their eyes.

The city that had been one thing the day before was now another. The Castel Nuovo was still standing guard over the bay, proud and old and tired. Vesuvius still lay motionless against the pale Neapolitan sky like a sick dragon down on its knees. Traffic still swelled and churned and raced around the Square, as commuters rushed home from their jobs. The late afternoon sun still shone bright and pale, and the smell of sulfur coming off the hills had the same noxious odor it had the day before. She was still *Bella Napoli*, as she had been for centuries, but the city had changed. Perhaps she had only just exhaled.

She wondered if she would run into Nathan Kessler. Probably not. Their lives were moving on parallel planes, seemingly miles apart with little hope of converging. She felt a pang of sadness. It had been weeks with no word. She knew that she loved him terribly but that it was to remain unrequited. She felt a groan in her spirit. She missed him.

Standing on the northeast corner of the Square, in front of the San Pedro bar, a woman in a green miniskirt, stiletto heels and bleached hair, the hair teased and parted in the middle, was leaning against a corner lamppost, rocking a hip as though she'd been rocking it a thousand years.

Maddie had seen her every day on the same corner. The woman was gazing down at the harbor, a wistful intensity glinting in her dark Latin eyes, but as Maddie drew nearer she saw that it was probably desperation.

She felt a prompting to stop. She reached into her purse for a gospel tract written in Italian and handed it to her. "*Gesù vi ama*," she said, using one of the few Italian phrases that she knew. Jesus loves you.

The woman stopped rocking her hip, looked at Maddie and then looked down at the tract. The writing on the cover said, "*Dio ti ama.*"

As she flipped through the tract Maddie saw wrinkles at the corners of the woman's eyes that she had done her best to cover. The mascara was too thick, the lipstick too bright, an inch of dark roots showing along the part of her platinum hair. She shook her head slowly.

"*Non è possibile*," she said, and started to hand the tract back to Maddie. "*Sono una prostituta*," she said.

"*Si, è possibile,*" Maddie said, opening the tract and pointing at the writing on the first page. "*Gesù vi ama. Gesù ama le prostituta.*"

The woman shook her head. "*Non è possibile*," *she repeated.*

"*Si, Gesù vi ama*," Maddie said, giving her the tract.

The woman smiled a small deprecating smile. "*Grazie*," she said, her eyes a little downcast.

Maddie put her hand on the woman's shoulder and squeezed it affectionately. "*Prego*," she smiled and walked away.

Reaching the curb, she looked back. The woman was gazing down at the tract, thumbing through it. Then she put it in her purse and continued looking out at the harbor. "Just one soul, Lord," Maddie prayed. "Please, just one soul."

She crossed the Via Vittoriano, walked along the sidewalk until she came to the Galleria Umberto, and turned into it. The arcade was empty except for a few shoppers, and a couple of old men in gray suits smoking and drinking coffee at one of the tables. Pigeons flew high against the arched glass dome of the Galleria, alighting on stone ledges and windowsills, cooing plaintively. A man in a blue vest and shirtsleeves with a tape measure draped over his neck, stood in the doorway of a clothing store and watched her as she passed. She smiled, he nodded, then looked away at the empty gloom of the arcade.

The Fleet was gone.

Chapter Forty

NATHAN SAT AT the desk in his room, inking a cartoon of a Navy chaplain conducting a service to a group of Marines in 782 field gear, their helmets and backpacks camouflaged, as they were about to go out on patrol. Nathan penciled the caption beneath it.

Ol' Prive: *I sure hope the Padre don't preach about sin. I got weekend liberty comin' up.*

Nathan erased the pencil lines on the drawing with a kneaded eraser and slid the finished drawing into a manila envelope with the others. He put away his drawing tools in the desk drawer and sat in the chair looking out the window at the Navy barracks across the courtyard. He couldn't look at the steps below where Mick had died.

Nathan had died a thousand deaths with Mick's passing. Mick was a true hero, an antihero, perhaps, but a hero nonetheless. He was the kind of Marine to charge machine guns, someone who ate nails for breakfast and spat bullets. He was Nathan's friend, and now he was gone.

Nathan pushed back in his chair and looked over at Cooper's empty bed to his left. The bed was stripped of its linen and bare in the room that was now quiet. The third floor of the barracks was also quiet with the five Marines gone to the brig, and everyone else from 1st Platoon out on weekend liberty. Nathan was the only one left on the floor.

He wondered who would replace Cooper, or who would replace Skip and Gorilla and the others. Corporal Sanchez in Admin said their replacements would be arriving in a couple of days.

Sitting alone in the room, Nathan was suddenly very tired. He could feel the quiet. He could also feel a gloom in the emptiness of the barracks, like a living thing that had come at him in whispering footsteps. He knew he needed to get away. Something else was in the room too, an inarticulate presence of something malignant that now and then raised the hair on the back of his neck. It was oppressive. He wasn't sure where he would go, but he knew he needed to get away from the gloom of the barracks.

He looked out the window again and shook his head. He missed Mick Donovan.

"Why don't you go and see the girl, Nate?"

"What girl?"

"You know the one. The pretty girl with the red hair."

"No, Frankie."

"Why not?"

"I was mighty cruel to her that day. She doesn't want to see me."

"I think she does, Nate. I bet she would love to see you. You could see her at the Way Station."

"I've got to go, Frankie. I can't stay here."

He put some overnight things into his sports bag and left the room, closing the door behind him. With his friends now in the brig, and with Mick gone, and with no one in the barracks that he would have cared to weekend with, he headed into town by himself.

He stowed his sports bag in the trunk of the Spider, climbed into the bucket seat and drove out of the base. He decided to take the car ferry to Ischia and stay at a beach hotel on the north end of the island to get away from Naples, hoping that the fresh sea air would drive away the gloom. Maybe he'd rent a rod and reel from one of the hotels, catch some sand crabs and do some sea fishing. Nico's family villa was on the south side of the island near Sant Angelo, so he was fairly certain they wouldn't run into each other.

He felt lousy. The oppression he had felt earlier in his room had come with him in the Fiat. He had brought it with him. It had crept up onto his shoulders and sat hunched like a gargoyle grinning in his ear.

He needed a quiet place to escape, a refuge in which to battle the oppression if he could; maybe find shelter from it, or build a fortification against it. But he could feel the thing weighing on his shoulders, sending waves of goose pimples down his spine, and he didn't think he could get away from it. Perhaps he could escape it in Ischia.

He parked the Spider in the parking lot of the Molo Beverello landing. He had a half-hour to kill before the ferry, so he walked along the seawall gazing out at the near-empty harbor. It was quiet with the Fleet gone, only the sound of gulls punctuating the silence. The sibilant whispers of the wind in the trees were occasionally drowned out by the bawling of a ship's horn.

As he walked through the Molosiglio Gardens near the marina, the trees and shrubs bursting with new leaves, flowers spilling from sidewalk grottos and planters, he saw a woman sitting alone on one of the iron park benches. She was silhouetted against a yellow oval of dappled light caught between a parenthesis of dark green shrubs and bowery. It was the prostitute who had helped him.

She was wearing a brown miniskirt now with ankle boots and a cotton shirt, and her bleached hair was no longer teased in the back, but parted in the middle with the ends flipping forward along her jawline. For just a moment, with her head bowed over something she was reading, she was beautiful.

She glanced up at him as he approached and smiled. The sunlight dappled her face, catching glints of light in her dark eyes, and showing the hard lines of her jaw, and all of that beauty changed. "It is the Marine from the San Pedro bar," she said.

"*Sono io,*" he replied.

"I see that your face is much improved."

"Thanks to you," he said.

She shook her head. "I did nothing. Anyone else would have done the same."

"It was you who helped me," he said. "How is your baby?"

She smiled appreciatively. "He is a good baby. My mother is with him. He will sleep for two hours."

Nathan glanced out through the trees at the boats in the marina and the breakwater against the harbor beyond. "Things will be quieter now with the Fleet gone."

"Yes. But I hope to find work."

"*Bella Napoli.*"

She nodded reflectively. "*Bella Napoli.*"

He checked his watch and turned to leave, but when he saw she was holding a small pamphlet in her hand he stopped. The cover was written in Italian. "I see that you are holding one of those religious tracts," he said.

"I was reading it."

"May I see it?"

She looked at the tract, handed it to him. "*Certa.* There are parts I don't understand."

"God has a wonderful plan for your life," he read. "I have one just like it in English." He checked the back cover and saw the address stamped on it. "Did a woman with red hair give this to you?"

"Yes. She was very kind. And very pretty," she added. "She put her hand on my shoulder and told me that Jesus loves me." Her face clouded momentarily. "How can this be? I don't understand…"

He said nothing. He felt a vague prickling over his scalp, sensed the gargoyle on his shoulders with its weighty darkness clawing into him.

A rush of color spread over the woman's face. "I am a prostitute," she said. "How can God love me? How can He…? I have done wicked things."

"We have all done wicked things," he said. "You took care of me when no one else did."

She shook her head, watched a bee working some flowers in one of the beds. "When the nuns pass by me on the street corner they will not look at me," she said quietly, "but I can feel their eyes. I am going to hell, they think. I am sure of it. They talk to each other when they pass and I think they are discussing my sins."

Nathan resisted the urge to put his hand on her shoulder as Maggie had done. "Jesus loves sinners and prostitutes," he said, feeling compelled to say it. "Don't think about those nuns. They're hypocrites."

She frowned at him. "But how can you say this? They have been blessed by the Pope. They have taken vows to live holy. "

"They are no holier than you or me. Jesus loved sinners and prostitutes. I am sure He loves you."

Her eyes watered. "How do you know this?"

"Because…" He could not answer because of the invisible weight on his shoulders.

She leaned forward, looked down at her hands and then back at him, her expression a little desperate in the speckled light.   "I have a baby to feed," she said quietly. "It is the only thing I know how to do to earn money. Is this what God has planned for me?"

Nathan thought about that. "I don't think so. But you should ask the girl with the red hair. Her name is Maddie."

"I am asking you," she said solemnly. "You are here."

Nathan stared blankly.   Suddenly the dark thing shifted its weight from his shoulders to his throat, forcing him to cough. And then he trembled as something like the movement of unseen tumblers clicked deep in his chest—*left one…right two*—locking mechanisms that were slowly turning, each click of the dial a pricking thorn.

He glanced out at the harbor and said nothing for a long while. In the silence he saw Mick's face looking up at him in pain, his eyes bright with expectancy. "You tell it, *amico*. Tell me about Jesus. You tell it, *amico*. *You tell it.*"

"You are very quiet," the woman said, breaking into his thoughts.

He turned to her and shook his head. "I am not the one to answer you," he said quietly. "I, too, am a sinner. A great sinner."

"Oh no, but I think you are close to God," she objected. "You cannot hide this. I see it in your eyes. I feel His presence so close to you. There is much good in you."

"You are mistaken," he said. "God and I have a long-standing argument."

She touched his arm with her fingertips. "But this is a silliness," she said, her eyes a shining intensity. "You cannot hope to win this argument."

"I'm not sure I believe in God anymore," he said, more to himself than to the woman.

She gaped at him open-mouthed. "Then how can you have this argument with him?"

He frowned. Once again he felt the dark thing shifting its oppressive weight, digging its claws deeper into his flesh, followed by the movement of tumblers deep in his chest—*left three...right four.* He saw Skip and Cooper and the other Marines singing and reading their Bibles, their faces full of life and joy, and he felt a great sadness welling up inside him.

He took hold of the back of his neck and tried to squeeze the image away. "I used to be close to God," he said, clearing emotion from his throat. "I loved Him. I trusted Him. But everything changed."

"I do not understand," she said earnestly. "What has changed? Has God changed?"

He could not hold her gaze. "You must talk to the girl with red hair," he said. "She lives at the address on the back of this tract."

He showed the address to her. "You know the place."

"Yes, I have seen her coming from the Galleria many times. I have watched her passing out these little pamphlets to the servicemen and to others like me. They laugh at her but there is such joy in her eyes. I think she must be a saint."

"If anyone is a saint, she is," he agreed.

Nathan saw the Ischia ferry was making its way to the landing, people forming a queue alongside the dock. He felt a prompting to leave now and catch it.

"Do not think about the nuns," he said, handing her back the tract. "Not everyone who says they are Christian are Christians. Jesus ate with prostitutes. He would eat with you. Ask the girl with the red hair," he said. "She would tell you this I'm sure."

"She does not speak Italian very well. But your Italian is very good. Would you go with me?"

"Go...?" Nathan made a face.

The tumblers turned—*left five...right six*—and he saw Maddie sitting across from him in the cafeteria. Beautiful guileless Maddie. He saw her in the Galleria eating ice cream, and again outside in the NSA compound, each time her words piercing his mocking defenses.

He glanced once more at the ferry, checked his watch and he knew that he would not catch it.

He sat down beside the woman. "What is your name?" he asked.

"My name is Caterina," she said and blushed to her roots. She glanced up at him. "My mother named me after Caterina of Siena."

"The patron saint of Italy."

"Yes. My mother wanted me to be a nun. Strange, isn't it?"

"Not so strange."

"I would like to be holy like the nuns," Caterina said. "If I could start over I think I would become a nun. I would not sell myself to men."

"You can start over," he said. "It says so in that little pamphlet." He showed her the place.

Her eyes watered as she read the passage. "I would like this to be true. Would you please take me to the girl with the red hair?"

He glanced once more out at the harbor as the last of the tumblers fell into place, clicking solidly—*left seven*—until he felt something give way deep inside him. At that moment he understood. A door of golden light slowly opened in his soul, and peering through the door he saw the great mystery unfolding.

In that moment Nathan sensed the heavy weight of darkness lift from his shoulders, its leathery wings flapping bitterly as it carried with it the gloom and oppression that had tormented him for years. And through the door that had opened he heard a song that he had long ago forgotten.

It was the song of the Shepherd.

A groaning rush of emotion leaped into his throat as he saw it clearly. Everything in focus. Tears flowed freely down his cheeks. "I'll take you to see the girl with the red hair," he said, wiping his cheeks with the heel of his palms.

"Yes?"

He took hold of Caterina's hands, and gazed into her tear-streaked eyes. "But first I will explain to you what the little pamphlet teaches if you will allow me."

She blinked at him. "*Certamente.*"

He turned to the first page in the tract, pointed to a verse of Scripture. "The Bible teaches that we all have sinned and fallen short of the glory of God…"

Chapter Forty-One

M ADDIE TURNED INTO the opening of her apartment building and started up the three flights in the stairwell. At the second floor level she heard a girl's voice trying very hard to hit a note that she would never hit in this life. She continued on up to the third floor, opened the door into the landing and went into the Station. It was quiet, the landing filled with peace. She walked past the bookstore, glanced inside but no one was there. Then she heard voices ahead. Italian voices. Curious, she continued along the hall and into the great room, where sunlight streamed in through the bank of windows on her right.

"Mr and Mrs Russo," Maddie said, seeing the couple next to her parents. The Russos were missionaries to Naples.

"Hello, Maddie," Mr Russo said. He was a tall, dark-haired American of Italian ancestry.

His wife was sitting at the table beside a bleached blonde Italian woman. It was the woman Maddie had given a gospel tract to. The prostitute. She was daubing her eyes with a handkerchief. Sitting beside her was a Marine in civvies. She almost didn't recognize him at first.

"Nathan."

Nathan stood as Maddie came into the room and he smiled.

"Sit down, please, Nathan," she said, feeling a strange fluttering in her chest. He remained standing. She frowned at each of her parents. "What's going on?"

Kitty winked at Maddie. "Nathan has been telling us a very interesting story."

Maddie turned to him. "I love stories."

There was something different in his face, his eyes. They shone. "This is Caterina," he said, indicating the woman. "She came here to ask some questions. Your dad called the Russos and they came right over. Thought maybe they could help her."

Maddie glanced from the Russos, to the woman—Caterina—and then to her parents.

"She has received Christ as her Savior," Flynn said. He smiled at Nathan. "It was Nathan's doing."

Helen Russo, a matronly brunette in her early forties, translated the conversation to Caterina.

Caterina brightened, beamed at Maddie, as she continued drying her eyes. "*Sì. Sono un Cristiano! Sono nato di nuovo! Nathan mi ha mostrato la via per Gesù. Sono pulito!*"

Helen Russo smiled. "She said that Nathan has shown her the way to Jesus. She is born again and clean."

"She is?" Maddie didn't know how to respond. She shook her head, confused. She blinked at Nathan. "Did I miss something?"

"Nathan speaks the gospel fluently," Flynn said. "He led Caterina to Christ."

"And with impeccable Italian," Mr Russo put in.

Maddie stared at Nathan, emotion collecting in her throat. "Is this true, Nathan? I'm not dreaming?"

Nathan walked over to Maddie and stood looking at her. He was tall and handsome and the light of inner joy clearly glowed in his eyes. "You opened the door, Maddie. I merely led her through it."

Maddie felt her eyes brimming with tears.

Kitty patted Flynn's hand and looked over at the Russos. "What do you say we take Caterina into the kitchen and have some tea?"

Helen Russo nodded. "Good idea." To Caterina: "*Vuoi del té, Caterina?*"

Caterina stood. "*Sì. Grazie mille!*" She joined the Russos and Maddie's parents as they went into the kitchen.

Nathan and Maddie were alone in the room.

"Is this true, Nathan?"

"Yes."

"How…how did it happen?"

"You made it happen, Maddie. You changed me. Skip and the guys changed me. Mick changed me. God used Caterina to bring it home. A prostitute. She told me that arguing with God was silly. I had no ready answers."

Tears trickled down Maddie's cheeks.

"I got tired of fighting," Nathan said, his own eyes welling with tears.

She glanced at the door that her parents had gone through. She turned back to Nathan, saw the joy in his eyes, his smile. Then she felt her face going to pieces and burst into tears. "Oh Nathan!"

She rushed into his arms, put her arms around Nathan's neck and squeezed as the two of them wept.

Nathan laughed, emotion rising from his throat. "Look at us, Maddie, blubbering like babies."

Overwhelmed with joy, Maddie laughed through a fresh wash of tears. "Oh Jesus, thank you."

THAT NIGHT NATHAN penciled an Ol' Prive cartoon onto Bristol board. It was nighttime in the drawing and Ol' Prive was sitting on a rock grinning up at the stars. Two of his buddies were dressed in civvies, each of them hefting armloads of whiskey bottles.

1st Marine: Ain't you comin' with us on liberty?

Ol' Prive: You fellas go without me. I got plenty of liberty right here.

Chapter Forty-Two

Isola Ischia - Summer 1972

THEY HAD COME over on the ferry with the others from the Navy hospital and barracks. The group had chosen an area near the bluffs at Maronti Beach, away from the early-summer crowds that were mostly gathered in front of the hotels above the beach, their blankets spread out in the sun in the lee of the bluffs. The surf was better there for bodyboarding. At low tide, pools gathered around the rocks at the foot of the bluffs for snorkeling, with scuttling crabs, sponges, yellow anemones moving in the currents, and tiny fish caught in the pools. Everyone was swimming and throwing frisbees in the surf.

Maddie and Nathan headed down the curving beach by themselves, with the Sant Angelo rock rising out of the sea about a mile ahead. As they walked barefoot in the cool firmness of the shore break, feeling the sand giving way beneath their footfalls in the lapping pulse of the surf, it felt as though the earth were disappearing under their feet.

Maddie giggled. "Isn't this fun?"

"The best," he said, as he picked up a stick of driftwood, bleached white in the sun, and flung it into the surf. He watched tiny crabs beetling into the sand in the backwash of the surf, and it reminded him of catching them for bait on the beach at Cayucos with Frankie.

"Do you remember, Nate?"

"Sure I do, Frankie."

"That was fun, wasn't it?"

"You bet it was. We caught some big ones, didn't we?"

"You can say that again. Eatin' them was fun, too. Remember how we cooked them?"

"With a little olive oil and lemon pepper. Sometimes with egg batter and breadcrumbs."

"Those were the ones I liked best. I can still taste 'em."

He smiled, thinking about his little brother, knowing for certain now that one day he would see him again. He looked up at the gulls tracing lazy sine waves in the offshore wind, crying their siren calls, and it was like seeing the world brand new. He saw the fingerprints of God in everything, and he saw his greatness and goodness evidenced in the ecosystem of the world with all of its complexities and simple beauties.

Nathan glanced ahead at the multicolored umbrellas dotting the beach in a haphazard array like giant windblown flowers, with families of sunbathers from the hotels spread beneath them and children building sandcastles against the tide.

He watched Maddie from the corner of his eyes.

She was wearing a floral-patterned sarong over her two-piece, as he had seen her in his dreams. She walked with a dancer's elegance, her long shapely legs tanned and glistening down to her freshly pinked toenails and, with the offshore breeze tossing her hair about her face and shoulders and the sun in her eyes—eyes the color of a Mediterranean sky—he could not believe how beautiful she was.

"This is lovely, isn't it?" she said, holding the hair back from her face as she gazed leisurely out to sea at sailboats tilting in the wind and a large freighter moving against the horizon.

"Yes," he said, but watching her.

"Isn't it wonderful about Caterina?"

"Yes, it is."

Through her father's connections with the Italian missionaries and the base chaplain, Chaplain Simms was able to find her a job working in the PX, as well as helping the Russos with the Italian ministry in town. Caterina spent much of her free time handing out gospel tracts to campfire girls and to others of their profession, sharing her new faith with them. The joy of Christ shone all over her.

Maddie mentioned the letters she'd just received from Skip and the other Marines in Rota, and the joy she had hearing of prisoners coming to Christ in the brig, and the revival that was sweeping the nation. She glanced back at the men and women splashing in the waves. "Sally Jenkins is really growing in her faith," she said. "I think she and Cooper will tie the knot when he gets out of the Corps."

Nathan smiled thoughtfully.

When they were halfway down the beach he looked up at the hotel where he and Nico ate lunch that day when she had told him about the possibility of a baby. It brought back a painful memory and the sudden jolt of it was like an armed intruder breaking into the sanctity of his home.

"You are very quiet," she said. "You're thinking about her, aren't you?"

"This is where we came."

"It's a lovely hotel."

He said nothing.

They walked in silence.

"Will there be ghosts between us?" she asked.

"I don't believe in ghosts," he said. "I never have. That part of my life is dead and buried."

"I have no ill feelings toward her."

He glanced at her but said nothing.

Walking close together, the beach ahead clear of sunbathers, she turned to him.

He could feel her eyes probing. "What are you thinking?" he asked.

"I'm thinking how nice it would be if you put your arm around me."

"Oh?"

"That's what I was thinking."

He put his arm around her waist, their hips touching as they continued down the beach, and he could feel the soft warm curve of her waist and the gentle rise and fall of her hips as she walked.

Thoughts of Nico were gone. "Everything is so new to me," he said. "This is nice."

"Yes."

It felt good, as it was meant to be felt, he presumed, though he was still unsure of the theology of his feelings. There was nothing immoral in them, he knew; there was only the innocence and joy of walking beside a beautiful woman that he knew, now, he loved very much, and with whom, he was certain, he would like to spend the rest of his life.

"Nathan...?"

"Yes?"

"Do you ever think about kissing me?"

He stopped.

She turned in front of him and, extending her arms in a languid reach to either side of his head, clasped her fingers lazily behind his neck, and looked up at him through her lashes. She smiled at him in a way that made him feel a little lightheaded.

He felt his throat thicken with emotion so that he didn't trust himself to speak. "Yes," he said, almost choking the word.

"Then kiss me, Nathan," she said, gazing at his mouth. "I won't bite."

She stepped into his arms and he pressed his lips against hers. He felt a tingling sensation shiver down the length of his body. Her lips were warm and moist and responsive, tasting of cherry lipstick, and he felt as though it was the first time he'd ever kissed a girl.

"I keep wanting to pinch myself but I'm afraid I'll wake up," he said.

"You're quite awake," she smiled. "Nathan, you told me once before that you loved me. Is it true?"

"I'm afraid, Maddie. I keep having a dream. I don't remember the details, but it's like *déjá vu* where I can see everything before it happens, and I know I'm going to wake up and find I'm sitting in the San Pedro bar staring into an empty glass of whiskey."

"Was that a yes or a no?"

He pulled her close to him.

"Maddie, I love you more than I ever thought it possible to love a woman. I can hardly breathe. If there were a better word than love to describe how I think and feel I would use it. But I'm afraid of losing you. I've lost everyone I've ever loved or cared about."

She gently pressed the sides of his face with her fingertips and kissed the side of his mouth. "Does this feel real?" she said and then kissed the other side of his mouth. "How about this?"

Then she kissed his mouth fully.   Afterwards, she buried her head in his chest, with the thick mass of her hair falling over his arms.   "I'm not going anywhere, Nathan."

"There's room in my heart for only one woman, Maddie," he said, holding her against him.   "Do you believe me?"

She nodded her head against his chest.

"There'll be no ghosts between us."

She shook her head.

Nathan touched the bottom of her chin and lifted her face.   "Maybe it's too early to ask," he said, "but I have to ask."   He cleared his throat, cupped her face in his hands.   "Wait a minute!" he said, breaking away from her.   "I have to do this properly."

He started to kneel, stumbled against the unfamiliar exercise of bone and muscle, and nearly went over, but he managed to plant a knee in the sand.   He looked up at her.   "Will you marry me, Maddie?"

A sob caught in her throat and she laughed, pulling him to his feet.   "You silly, come here," she said and kissed him again.   "I love you, I love you, I love you," she said, kissing him each time.

"Was that a yes or a no?"

"I have prayed for this moment, Nathan. Yes, I will marry you! A thousand times yes!"   There were tears in her eyes.   "Hold me."

He held her against his chest, his arms wrapped around her in a loving embrace. "I don't have a ring just yet."

"Your arms are my ring."

He could feel her firm and feminine in his arms, and it made him feel he was her protector, and that he would never harm her in any way. He couldn't believe the happiness he felt. And then he could feel her shoulders trembling, and he knew she was crying.

"What's wrong?" he asked.

"Nothing's wrong. I'm just so very happy."

And coming to a wall of whitened cliffs cutting into the beach, with the rock of Sant Angelo showing ahead to their left, they stood alone in the wash of the sea against a retaining wall of large boulders with bougainvillea, lush with flowers, growing wild and spilling over the wall onto the sand.

He picked a garland of flowers and arranged it in her hair like a crown. She gazed up into his eyes from beneath her thick lashes, her elfin blue eyes hinting at an ancient mystery. Then she wrapped her arms around his neck and, stepping up on her toes, kissed him long and lovingly. She giggled, "What do you think, Nathan, does God have a wonderful plan for our lives?"

Nathan laughed heartily. "Yes, Maddie. I believe He does." And kissing her again, he knew it wasn't a dream.

The End